ALSO BY TILLIE COLE

A Thousand Boy Kisses

a
thousand
boy

Kisses

a novel

Tillie Cole

bloombooks.com

Bloom *books*

young adult

Published by Bloom Books, an imprint of Sourcebooks
P.O. Box 4410, Naperville, Illinois 60567-4410
(630) 961-3900
sourcebooks.com

Originally self-published in 2016 by Tillie Cole.

Cataloging-in-Publication data is on file with the Library of Congress.

Printed and bound in the United States of America.
WOZ 10 9 8 7 6 5 4

For believers in true, epic, soul-shattering love.
This one's for you.

Prologue

Rune

THERE WERE EXACTLY FOUR MOMENTS THAT DEFINED MY LIFE.
This was the first.

———————

Blossom Grove, Georgia
United States of America
Twelve Years Ago
Aged Five

"Jeg vil dra! Nå! Jeg vil reise hjem igjen!" *I shouted as loud as I could, telling my mamma that I wanted to leave, now! I wanted to go back home!*

"We're not going back home, Rune. And we are not *leaving. This is our home now,"* she replied in English. *She crouched down and looked me straight in the eye.* "Rune," *she said softly,* "I know you didn't want to leave Oslo, but your pappa got a new job here in Georgia." *Her hand ran up and down my arm, but it didn't make me feel any better. I didn't want to be in this place, in America.*

I wanted to go back home.

"Slutt å snakke engelsk!" *I snapped. I hated speaking English. Since we'd set off for America from Norway, Mamma and Pappa would only speak to me in English. They said I had to practice.*

I didn't want to!

My mamma stood up and lifted a box off the ground. "We're in America, Rune. They speak English here. You've been speaking English for as long as you've been speaking Norwegian. It's time to use it."

I stood my ground, glaring at my mamma as she walked around me into the house. I looked around the small street where we now lived. There were eight houses. They were all big, but they all looked different. Ours was painted red, with white windows and a huge porch. My room was big, and it was on the bottom floor. I did think that was kind of cool. Sort of, anyway. I'd never slept downstairs before; in Oslo my room was upstairs.

I looked at the houses. All of them were painted bright colors: light blues, yellows, pinks... Then I looked at the house next door. Right next door—we shared a patch of grass. Both houses were big, and our yards were too, but there was no fence or wall between them. If I wanted to, I could run into their yard and there'd be nothing to stop me.

The house was bright white, with a porch wrapped right around it. They had rocking chairs and a big chair swing on the front. Their window frames were painted black, and there was a window opposite my bedroom window. Right opposite! I didn't like that. I didn't like that I could see into their bedroom and they could see into mine.

There was a stone on the ground. I kicked it with my foot, watching it roll down the street. I turned to follow my mamma, but then I heard a noise. It was coming from the house next to ours. I looked at their front door, but nobody came out. I was climbing the steps to my porch when I saw some movement from the side of the house—from next door's bedroom window, the one opposite my own.

My hand froze on the rail and I watched as a girl, dressed in a bright blue dress, climbed through the window. She jumped down onto the grass and dusted off her hands on her thighs. I frowned, my eyebrows pulling down, as I waited for her to lift her head. She had brown hair, which was piled up on her head like a bird's nest. She wore a big white bow on the side of it.

When she looked up, she looked right at me. Then she smiled. She smiled at me so big. She waved, fast, then ran forward and stopped in front of me.

She pushed out her hand. "Hi, my name is Poppy Litchfield. I'm five years old, and I live right next door."

I stared at the girl. She had a funny accent. It made the English words sound different from the way I had learned them back in Norway. The girl—Poppy—had a smudge of mud on her face and bright yellow rain boots on her feet. They had a big red balloon on the side.

She looked weird.

I looked up from her feet and fixed my eyes on her hand. She was still holding it out. I didn't know what to do. I didn't know what she wanted.

Poppy sighed. Shaking her head, she reached for my hand and forced it into hers. She shook them up and down twice and said, "A handshake. My mamaw says it's only right to shake the hand of new people that you meet." She pointed at our hands. "That was a handshake. And that was polite, because I don't know you."

I didn't say anything; for some reason my voice wouldn't work. When I looked down, I realized it was because our hands were still joined.

She had mud on her hands too. In fact, she had mud everywhere.

"What's your name?" Poppy asked. Her head was tipped to the side. A small twig was stuck in her hair.

"Hey," she said, tugging on our hands, "I asked for your name."

I cleared my throat. "My name is Rune, Rune Erik Kristiansen."

Poppy scrunched her face up, her big pink lips sticking out all funny. "You sound weird," she blurted.

I snatched my hand away.

"Nei det gjør jeg ikke!" I snapped. Her face screwed up even more.

"What did you just say?" Poppy asked as I turned to walk into my house. I didn't want to speak to her anymore.

Feeling angry, I spun back around. "I said, 'No, I don't!' I was speaking Norwegian!" I said, in English this time. Poppy's green eyes grew huge.

She stepped closer, and closer again, and asked, "Norwegian? Like the Vikings? My mamaw read me a book about the Vikings. It said they were from Norway." Her eyes got even bigger. "Rune, are you a Viking?" Her voice had gone all squeaky.

It made me feel good. I stuck out my chest. My pappa always said I was a Viking, like all the men in my family. We were big, strong Vikings. "Ja," I said. "We are real Vikings, from Norway."

A big smile spread across Poppy's face, and a loud girly giggle burst from her mouth. She lifted her hand and pulled on my hair. "That's why you have long blond hair and crystal-blue eyes. Because you're a Viking. At first I thought you looked like a girl—"

"I'm not a girl!" I butted in, but Poppy didn't seem to care. I ran my hand through my long hair. It came down to my shoulders. All the boys in Oslo had their hair like this.

"—but now I see it's because you're a real-life Viking. Like Thor. He had long blond hair and blue eyes too! You're just like Thor!"

"Ja," I agreed. "Thor does. And he's the strongest god of them all."

Poppy nodded her head, then put her hands on my shoulders. Her face had gone all serious and her voice dropped to a whisper. "Rune, I don't tell everyone this, but I go on adventures."

I screwed up my face. I didn't understand. Poppy stepped closer and looked up into my eyes. She squeezed my arms. She tilted her head to the side. She looked all around us, then leaned in to speak. "I don't normally bring people with me on my journeys, but you're a Viking, and we all know that Vikings grow big and strong, and they are really, really good with adventures and exploring, and long walks and capturing baddies and…all kindsa things!"

I was still confused, but then Poppy stepped back and held out her hand again.

"Rune," she said, her voice serious and strong, "you live right next door, you're a Viking, and I just love Vikings. I think we should be best friends."

"Best friends?" I asked.

Poppy nodded her head and pushed her hand farther toward me. Slowly reaching out my own hand, I gripped hold of hers and gave it two shakes, like she'd shown me.

A handshake.

"So now we are best friends?" I asked, as Poppy pulled her hand back.

"Yes!" she said excitedly. "Poppy and Rune." She brought her finger to her chin and looked up. Her lips stuck out again, like she was thinking very hard. "It sounds good, don't you think? 'Poppy and Rune, best friends for infinity!'"

I nodded because it did sound good. Poppy put her hand in mine. "Show me your bedroom! I want to tell you about what adventure we can go on next." She began to pull me forward, and we ran into the house.

When we pushed through my bedroom door, Poppy rushed straight to my window. "This is the room exactly opposite mine!"

I nodded my head, and she squealed, running toward me to take my hand in hers again. "Rune!" she said excitedly, "we can talk at night, and make walkie-talkies with cans and string. We can whisper our secrets to each other when everyone else is asleep, and we can plan, and play, and..."

Poppy kept talking, but I didn't mind. I liked the sound of her voice. I liked her laugh, and I liked the big white bow in her hair.

Maybe Georgia won't be so bad after all, *I thought,* not if I have Poppy Litchfield as my very best friend.

And that was Poppy and me from that day on.

Poppy and Rune.

Best friends for infinity.

Or so I thought.

Funny how things change.

Broken Hearts and Boy Kiss Jars

Poppy
Nine Years Ago
Aged Eight

"WHERE ARE WE GOING, DADDY?" I ASKED AS HE HELD MY HAND GENTLY, guiding me to the car. I glanced back at my school, wondering why I was being taken out of class early. It was only lunch break. I wasn't supposed to leave yet.

My daddy didn't say anything to me as we walked; he just squeezed my hand. I searched along the school fence, a strange feeling pulling in my stomach. I loved school, I loved to learn, and we had history next. It was my absolute favorite subject. I didn't want to miss it.

"Poppy!" Rune, my very best friend, was standing at the fence, watching me go. His hands were holding real tight to the metal bars. "Where are you going?" he shouted. I sat next to Rune in class. We were always together. School was no fun when the other wasn't there.

I turned my head toward my daddy's face for answers, but he didn't look back at me. He stayed silent. Looking back at Rune, I shouted, "I don't know!"

Rune watched me all the way to our car. I climbed in the back and sat on my booster seat, my daddy buckling me in.

I heard the whistle blow in the schoolyard, signaling the end of lunch. I glanced out the window and watched all of the kids running back inside, but not Rune. Rune stayed at the fence watching me. His long blond hair was blowing in the wind as he mouthed, *"Are you okay?"* But my daddy got in the car and started driving away before I could answer.

Rune ran along the fence, following our car, until Mrs. Davis came and made him go inside.

When the school was out of sight, my daddy said, "Poppy?"

"Yes, Daddy?" I replied.

"You know Mamaw has been living with us for a while now?"

I nodded my head. My mamaw had moved into the room opposite mine awhile back. My mama had said it was because she needed help. My pawpaw had died when I was only a baby. My mamaw had lived on her own for years, until she came to live with us.

"Do you remember what your mama and I told you about why? Why Mamaw could no longer live by herself?"

I breathed in through my nose and whispered, "Yes. Because she needed our help. Because she's sick." My stomach flipped over as I spoke. My mamaw was my very best friend. Well, she and Rune were tied at the absolute top. My mamaw said I was just like her.

Before she was sick we would go on lots of adventures. She read to me every night about the great explorers of the world. She would tell me all about history—about Alexander the Great, the Romans, and my favorite, the samurai from Japan. They were Mamaw's favorite too.

I knew my mamaw was sick, but she never acted sick. She always smiled; she gave tight hugs and made me laugh. She always said she had moonbeams in her heart and sunshine in her smile. Mamaw told me that meant she was happy.

She made me happy too.

But over the last few weeks Mamaw had slept a lot. She'd been too tired to do much of anything else. In fact, most nights I would now read to her as she stroked my hair and smiled at me. And that was okay, because Mamaw's smiles were the best kind of smiles to get.

"That's right, pumpkin, she is sick. In fact, she's very, very sick. Do you understand?"

I frowned but nodded my head and said, "Yes."

"That's why we're going home early," he explained. "She's waiting for you. She wants to see you. Wants to see her little buddy."

I didn't understand why my daddy had to bring me home early to visit my mamaw, when the first thing I did every night after school was go into her room and talk to her while she lay in bed. She liked to hear all about my day.

We turned into our street and parked in our driveway. My daddy didn't move for a few seconds, but then he turned to me and said, "I know you're only eight, pumpkin, but you have to be a big brave girl today, okay?"

I nodded my head. My daddy smiled a sad smile at me. "That's my girl."

He got out of the car and walked around to my seat in the back. Taking my hand, my daddy guided me out of the car and toward the house. I could see there were more cars here than usual. I had just opened my mouth to ask whose they all were when Mrs. Kristiansen, Rune's mamma, came walking across the yard between our houses with a big dish of food in her hands.

"James!" she called out, and my daddy turned to greet her.

"Adelis, hey," he called back. Rune's mamma stopped in front of us. Her long blond hair was down today. It was the same color as Rune's. Mrs. Kristiansen was real pretty. I loved her. She was kind and called me the daughter she never had.

"I made you this. Please tell Ivy I'm thinking of you all."

My daddy released my hand to take the dish.

Mrs. Kristiansen crouched down and pressed a kiss on my cheek. "You be a good girl, Poppy, okay?"

"Yes, ma'am," I replied and watched her cross the grass to go back into her house.

My daddy sighed, then tipped his head for me to follow him inside. As soon as we were through the front door, I saw my aunts and uncles sitting on the couches and my cousins sitting on the floor of the living room, playing with their toys. My aunt Silvia was sitting with my sisters, Savannah and Ida. They were younger than me, only four and two years old. They waved at me when they saw me, but Aunt Silvia kept them sitting on her lap.

Nobody was speaking, but lots of them were wiping their eyes; most of them were crying.

I was so confused.

I leaned into my daddy's leg, clutching on tightly. Someone stood in the doorway to the kitchen—my aunt Della, DeeDee as I always called her. She was my absolute favorite aunt. She was young and fun and always made me laugh. Even though my mama was older than her sister, they looked like each other. Both had long brown hair and green eyes like me. But DeeDee was extra pretty. I wanted to look just like her one day.

"Hey, Pops," she said, but I could see that her eyes were red, and her voice sounded funny. DeeDee looked at my daddy. She took the dish of food from his hand and said, "You go on back with Poppy, James. It's almost time."

I started to go with my daddy but looked back when DeeDee didn't follow. I opened my mouth to call her name, but she suddenly turned around, put the dish of food on the counter, and rested her head in her hands. She was crying, crying so hard that loud noises came from her mouth.

"Daddy?" I whispered, feeling a strange feeling in my stomach. My daddy wrapped his arm around my shoulders and guided me away. "It's okay, pumpkin. DeeDee just needs a minute alone."

We walked to Mamaw's room. Just before daddy opened the door, he said, "Mama's in there, pumpkin, and Betty; Mamaw's nurse is in there too."

I frowned. "Why is there a nurse?"

Daddy pushed open the door to Mamaw's room, and my mama got up from the chair beside Mamaw's bed. Her eyes were red and her hair was all messy. Mama's hair was never messy.

I saw the nurse at the back of the room. She was writing something on a clipboard. She smiled and waved at me when I came in. Then I looked to the bed. Mamaw was lying down. My stomach flipped when I saw a needle sticking in her arm, with a clear tube leading to a bag hanging off a metal hook at her side.

I stood still, suddenly frightened. Then my mama moved toward me, and my mamaw looked my way. She looked different from how she looked last night. Her skin was paler, and her eyes weren't as bright.

"Where's my little buddy?" Mamaw's voice was quiet and sounded funny, but the smile she gave me made me feel warm.

Giggling at my mamaw, I rushed to the side of the bed. "I'm here! I came home early from school to see you!"

Mamaw lifted her finger and tapped the end of my nose. "That's my girl!"

I smiled real big in response.

"I just wanted you to visit a little while. I always feel better when the light of my life sits beside me and talks to me some."

I smiled again. Because *I* was the "light of her life," "the apple of her eye." She always called me those things. Mamaw secretly told me it meant I was her favorite. But she'd told me I had to keep it to myself so it didn't upset my cousins and little sisters. It was our secret.

Hands suddenly gripped my waist, and my daddy lifted me to sit beside Mamaw on her bed. Mamaw took hold of my hand. She squeezed my fingers, but all I could notice was how cold her hands were. Mamaw breathed in deep, but it sounded funny, like something was crackling in her chest.

"Mamaw, are you okay?" I asked and leaned forward to press a soft kiss on her cheek. She normally smelled of tobacco from all the cigarettes she smoked. But I couldn't smell the smoke on her today.

Mamaw smiled. "I'm tired, girlie. And I'm…" Mamaw sucked in another breath, and her eyes briefly squeezed shut. When they opened again, she shifted on the bed and said, "…and I'm gonna be going away awhile."

I frowned. "Where are you going, Mamaw? Can I come too?" We *always* went on adventures together.

Mamaw smiled but shook her head. "No, girlie. Where I'm going, you can't follow. Not yet. But some day, many years from now, you'll see me again."

My mama let out a sob from behind me, but I just stared at my mamaw, confused. "But where are you going, Mamaw? I don't understand."

"*Home,* sweetie," my mamaw said. "I'm going *home.*"

"But you are home," I countered.

"No"—Mamaw shook her head—"this isn't our true home, girlie. This life…well, it's just a great big adventure while we have it. An adventure to enjoy and love with all of our heart before we go on to the greatest adventure of all."

My eyes widened with excitement; then I felt sad. *Really* sad. My bottom lip began to tremble. "But we're best buddies, Mamaw. We always go on our adventures together. You can't go on one without me."

Tears had begun falling from my eyes down to my cheeks. My mamaw lifted her free hand to brush them away. That hand was just as cold as the one I was holding. "We do always go on adventures together, girlie, but not this time."

"Aren't you afraid to go by yourself?" I asked, but my mamaw just sighed.

"No, girlie, there's no fear to feel. I'm not scared at all."

"But I don't want you to go," I pleaded, my throat starting to ache.

Mamaw's hand stayed on my cheek. "You'll still see me in your dreams. This isn't a goodbye."

I blinked, then blinked again. "Like you see Pawpaw? You always say he visits you in your dreams. He talks to you and kisses your hand."

"Exactly like that," she said. I wiped my tears away. Mamaw squeezed my hand and looked at my mama behind me. When she looked back to me, she said, "While I'm gone, I've got a new adventure for you."

I stilled. "You do?"

The sound of glass being placed on a table came from behind me. It made me want to look around, but before I could, Mamaw asked, "Poppy, what is it that I always say was my favorite memory from my life? The thing that always made me smile?"

"Pawpaw's kisses. His sweet boy-kisses. All the memories of all the boy-kisses you ever got from him. You told me they're the most favorite memories you have. Not money, not things, but the kisses you got from Pawpaw—because they were all special and made you smile, made you feel loved, because he was your soulmate. Your forever always."

"That's right, girlie," she replied. "So, for your adventure…" Mamaw looked to my mama again. This time, when I did look around, I saw she was holding a big mason jar filled to the top with lots and lots of pink paper hearts.

"Wow! What's that?" I asked, feeling excited.

Mama placed it in my hands, and my mamaw tapped the lid. "It's a thousand boy-kisses. Or at least, it will be, when you've filled them all out."

My eyes widened as I tried to count all the hearts. But I couldn't. A thousand was a lot!

"Poppy," my mamaw said, as I looked up to see her green eyes shining, "*this* is your adventure. How I want you to remember me while I'm gone."

I looked down at the jar again. "But I don't understand."

Mamaw reached out to her nightstand and picked up a pen. She passed it to me and said, "I've been sick for a while now, girlie, but the memories that make me feel better are the ones where your pawpaw kissed me. Not just every-day kisses, but the special ones, the ones where my heart almost burst from my chest. The ones that Pawpaw made sure I would never forget. The kisses in the rain, the kisses at sunset, the kiss we shared at our prom…the ones where he held me close and whispered in my ear that I was the prettiest girl in the room."

I listened and listened, my heart feeling full. Mamaw pointed to all the hearts in the jar. "This jar is for you to record your boy-kisses, Poppy. All the kisses that make your heart almost burst, the ones that are the most special, the ones you want to remember when you're old and gray like me. The ones that will make you smile when you remember them in your mind."

Tapping the pen, she continued. "When you find the boy that will be your forever always, every time you get an extra-special kiss from him, take out a heart. Write down where you were when you were kissed. Then when you're a mamaw too, your grandbaby—your best buddy—can hear all about them, just like I've told you all about mine. You'll have a treasure jar of all the precious kisses that made your heart soar."

I stared at the jar and breathed out. "A thousand is a lot. That's a lot of kisses, Mamaw!"

Mamaw laughed. "It's not as many as you think, girlie. Especially when you find your soulmate. You have a lot of years ahead of you."

Mamaw sucked in a breath, and her face screwed up like she was in pain. "Mamaw," I called, suddenly feeling very scared. Her hand squeezed mine. Mamaw opened her eyes, and this time a teardrop fell down her pale cheek. "Mamaw?" I said, quieter this time.

"I'm tired, girlie. I'm tired, and it's nearly time for me to go. I just wanted to see you one last time, to give you this jar. To kiss you so I can remember you every day in heaven until I see you again."

My bottom lip began to tremble again. My mamaw shook her head. "No tears, girlie. This isn't the end. It's just a little pause in our lives. And I'll be watching over you, every single day. I'll be in your heart. I'll be in the blossom grove that we love so much, in the sun and the wind."

Mamaw's eyes flinched, and my mama's hands came down on my shoulders. "Poppy, give Mamaw a big kiss. She's tired now. She needs to rest."

Drawing in a deep breath, I leaned forward and pressed a kiss on my mamaw's cheek. "I love you, Mamaw," I whispered. Mamaw stroked my hair.

"I love you too, girlie. You're the light of my life. Never forget that I loved you as much as a mamaw ever could love her baby granddaughter."

I held on to her hand and didn't want to let go, but my daddy lifted me off the bed and my hand eventually broke away. I clutched onto my jar super tight, my tears dropping onto the floor. My daddy put me down and, as I turned to go, Mamaw called my name. "Poppy?"

I looked back, and my mamaw was smiling. "Remember, *moonbeam hearts and sunshine smiles...*"

"I'll always remember," I said, but I didn't feel happy. All I felt was sad. I heard my mama crying behind me. DeeDee passed us in the hallway. She squeezed my shoulder. Her face was so sad too.

I didn't want to be in here. I didn't want to be in this house anymore. Turning, I looked up to my daddy. "Daddy, can I go to the blossom grove?"

Daddy sighed. "Yes, baby. I'll come and check on you later. Just be careful." I saw my daddy take out his phone and call someone. He asked them to check in on me while I was at the grove, but I ran before I could find out who. I headed for the front door, clutching my jar of a thousand empty boy-kisses to my chest. I ran out of the house, then off the porch. I ran and ran and never stopped.

Tears fell down my face. I heard my name being called.

"Poppy! Poppy, wait!"

I glanced back and saw Rune watching me. He was on his porch, but immediately started to chase me over the grass. But I never stopped, not even for Rune. I had to get to the cherry blossom trees. It was my mamaw's favorite place. I wanted to be in her favorite place. Because I was sad that she was going away. Going to heaven.

Her real home.

"Poppy, wait! Slow down!" Rune shouted as I turned the corner to the grove in the park. I ran through the entrance; the large blossom trees, which were in full bloom, made a tunnel above my head. The grass was green beneath my feet, and the blue sky was above. Petals in bright pinks and whites covered the trees. Then, at the far end of the grove, was the biggest tree of all. Its branches hung low. Its trunk was the thickest in the whole grove.

It was mine and Rune's absolute favorite.

It was Mamaw's too.

I was out of breath. When I got below Mamaw's favorite tree, I sank to the ground, clutching my jar as tears fell down my cheeks. I heard Rune stop beside me, but I didn't look up.

"*Poppymin*?" Rune said. That's what he called me. It meant "my Poppy" in Norwegian. I loved him speaking Norwegian to me.

"*Poppymin*, don't cry," he whispered.

But I couldn't help it. I didn't want my mamaw to leave me, even though I knew she had to. I knew when I returned home, Mamaw wouldn't be there—not now, not ever.

Rune dropped down to sit beside me and pulled me in for a hug. I snuggled into his chest and cried. I loved Rune's hugs; he always held me so tight. "My mamaw, Rune, she's sick and she's leaving."

"I know; my mamma told me when I got back from school."

I nodded against his chest. When I couldn't cry anymore, I sat up, wiping my cheeks. I looked at Rune, who was watching me. I tried to smile. When I did, he took hold of my hand and brought it to his chest.

"I'm sorry you're sad," Rune said and squeezed my hand. His T-shirt was warm from the sun. "I never *ever* want you to be sad. You're *Poppymin*; you always smile. You're always happy."

I sniffed and leaned my head on his shoulder. "I know. But Mamaw is my best friend, Rune, and I won't have her anymore."

Rune didn't say anything at first, then said, "I'm your best friend too. And I'm not going anywhere. I promise. Forever always."

My chest, which had been hurting so bad, suddenly didn't hurt as much. I nodded my head. "Poppy and Rune for infinity," I said.

"For infinity," he repeated.

We stayed quiet for a while, until Rune asked, "What's that jar for? What's inside?"

Pulling back my hand, I took hold of the jar and lifted it in the air. "My mamaw has given me a new adventure. One that will last all my life."

Rune's eyebrows drew down and his long blond hair fell over his eyes. I pushed it back, and he smiled his half-smile as I did. All the girls at school wanted him to smile like that at them—they told me. But he only ever smiled at me. I told them none of them could have him anyway; he was my best friend, and I didn't want to share.

Rune waved at the jar. "I don't understand."

"Do you remember what my mamaw's favorite ever memories are? I've told you before."

I could see Rune thinking hard, and then he suddenly said, "Kisses from your pawpaw?"

I nodded my head and pulled down a pale-pink cherry blossom petal from the branch hanging down by my side. I stared at the petal. They were my mamaw's favorite. She liked them because they didn't stay for long. She told me that the best and prettiest things never stay around for long. She said that a cherry blossom was too beautiful to last all year. It was more special because its life was short. Like the samurai—extreme beauty, quick death. I still wasn't real sure what it all meant, but she said I would understand more the older I got.

I think she was right, though. Because my mamaw wasn't that old, and she was going away young—at least that's what Daddy said. Maybe that's why she liked the cherry blossom so much. Because she was exactly the same.

"*Poppymin?*"

Rune's voice made me look up.

"Am I right? Was kissing your pawpaw your mamaw's favorite of memories?"

"Yes," I answered, dropping the petal, "*all* of the kisses she got that made her heart almost burst. Mamaw said that his kisses were the bestest thing in the world. Because they meant he loved her so. That he cared for her. And he liked her for *exactly* who she was."

Rune glared down at the jar and huffed. "I still don't understand, *Poppymin.*"

I laughed as his lips stuck out and his face screwed up. He had pretty lips;

they were really thick with a perfect cupid's bow. I opened the jar and pulled out a blank pink paper heart. I held it up in the air between me and Rune. "This is an empty kiss." I pointed to the jar. "Mamaw gave me a thousand to collect in my life." I put the heart back in the jar and took his hand. "A new adventure, Rune. To collect a thousand boy-kisses before I die, from my soulmate."

"I...what...Poppy? I'm confused!" he said, but I could hear the anger in his voice. Rune could be real moody when he wanted to be.

I lifted my pen from my pocket. "When the boy I love kisses me, when it feels so special that my heart might almost burst—*only* the *extra*-special kisses—I'm to write the details down on one of these hearts. It's for when I'm gray and old, and I want to tell my grandbabies all about the really special kisses in my life. And the sweet boy that gave them to me."

I jumped to my feet, excitement running through me. "It's what Mamaw wanted from me, Rune. So I have to start soon! I want to do this for her."

Rune jumped to his feet too. Just then a gust of wind blew cherry blossom petals right past where we stood, and I smiled. But Rune wasn't smiling. In fact, he looked downright mad.

"You're going to kiss a boy, for your jar? A special one? One that you love?" he asked.

I nodded. "A thousand kisses, Rune! A *thousand!*"

Rune shook his head and his lips pursed again. "NO!" he roared. The smile fell from my face.

"What?" I asked.

Rune took a step closer, shaking his head harder. "No! I don't want you kissing a boy for your jar! I won't let it happen!"

"But—" I tried to speak, but Rune took hold of my hand.

"You're *my* best friend," he said and puffed out his chest, pulling on my hand. "I don't want you to kiss boys!"

"But I have to," I explained, pointing to the jar. "I have to for my adventure. A thousand kisses is a lot, Rune. A lot! You'd still be my best friend. No one will ever mean more to me than you, silly thing."

He stared hard at me, then at the jar. My chest hurt again; I could see he wasn't happy by the look on his face. He'd gone all moody again.

I stepped closer to my best friend, and Rune's eyes fixed on mine.

"*Poppymin*," he said, his voice deeper—hard and strong. "*Poppymin*! It means *my Poppy*. For infinity, forever and always. You're *my* Poppy!"

I opened my mouth to shout back at him, to tell him this was an adventure I just *had* to start. But as I did, Rune leaned forward and suddenly pressed his lips to mine.

I froze. I couldn't move a muscle as I felt his lips against my lips. They were warm. He tasted like cinnamon. The wind blew his long hair over my cheeks. It started to tickle my nose.

Rune pulled back, but his face stayed near mine. I tried to breathe, but my chest felt funny, kind of light and fluffy. And my heart was beating so fast. So fast that I pressed my hand over my chest to feel it racing underneath.

"Rune," I whispered. I lifted my hand to press my fingers against my lips. Rune blinked and blinked again as he watched me. I pushed my hand out and pressed my fingers against his lips.

"You kissed me," I whispered, stunned. Rune lifted his hand to hold mine. He lowered our joined hands by his side.

"*I'll* give you a thousand kisses, *Poppymin*. All of them. No one will kiss you *ever*, but *me*."

My eyes widened, but my heart didn't slow down. "That would be forever, Rune. To *never* be kissed by anyone else means we'll be together forever, and ever and ever!"

Rune nodded his head; then he smiled. Rune didn't smile a lot. He normally half-smiled or smirked. But he should smile. He was real handsome when he did. "I know. Because we're forever always. For infinity, remember?"

I nodded my head slowly, then tipped it to the side. "You'll give me all my kisses? Enough to fill this *whole* jar?" I asked.

Rune gave me another small smile. "All of them. We'll fill up the whole jar, and more. We'll collect way more than a thousand."

I gasped. I suddenly remembered the jar. I pulled back my hand so I could get my pen and open the jar lid. I snatched out a blank heart and sat down to write. Rune kneeled before me and placed his hand over mine, stopping me from writing.

I looked up, confused. He swallowed, tucked his long hair behind his ear,

18

and asked, "Did…when I…kissed you…did…did your heart almost burst? Was it extra special? You said only extra-special kisses make it into the jar." His cheeks turned bright red and he lowered his eyes.

Without thinking, I leaned forward and wrapped my arms around my best friend's neck. I pressed my cheek to his chest and I listened to his heart.

It was beating just as fast as mine.

"It did, Rune. It was as special as special can be."

I felt Rune smile against my head, and then I pulled back. I crossed my legs and placed the paper heart on the jar lid. Rune sat cross-legged too.

"What will you write?" he asked. I tapped the pen to my lip as I thought hard. I sat up straight and leaned forward, pressing the pen to the paper:

Kiss 1
> *With my Rune.*
> *In the blossom grove.*
> *My heart almost burst.*

When I finished writing, I put the heart in the jar and closed the lid tight. I looked up at Rune, who'd been watching me all along, and proudly announced, "There. My very first boy-kiss!"

Rune nodded his head, but his eyes dropped to my lips. "*Poppymin?*"

"Yes?" I whispered. Rune reached for my hand. He started tracing patterns on the back with his fingertip.

"Can I…can I kiss you again?"

I swallowed, feeling butterflies in my stomach. "You want to kiss me again…already?"

Rune nodded his head. "I've wanted to kiss you for a while now. And well, you're mine and I liked it. I liked kissing you. You tasted like sugar."

"I ate a cookie at lunch. Butter pecan. Mamaw's favorite," I explained.

Rune took a deep breath and leaned toward me. His hair blew forward. "I want to do it again."

"Okay."

And Rune kissed me.

He kissed me and kissed me and kissed me.

By the end of the day I had four more boy-kisses in my jar.

When I got home, Mama told me that my mamaw had gone to heaven. I ran to my bedroom as quickly as I could. I hurried to fall asleep. Like she promised, Mamaw was there in my dreams. So I told her all about the five boy-kisses from my Rune.

My mamaw smiled big and kissed me on my cheek.

I knew this would be the best adventure of my life.

2

Musical Notes and Bonfire Flames

Rune
Two Years Ago
Aged Fifteen

SILENCE FELL AS SHE SETTLED HERSELF ON THE STAGE. WELL, NOT EVERY-thing was silent—the thunder of blood rushing through me roared in my ears as my Poppy carefully sat down. She looked beautiful in her sleeve-less black dress, with her long brown hair pulled back in a bun, white bow positioned on top.

Lifting the camera that was always around my neck, I brought the lens to my eye just as she put her bow against the string of her cello. I always loved to capture her at this moment. The moment she closed her big green eyes. The moment the most perfect expression drifted over her face—the look she wore just before the music began. The look of pure passion for the sounds that were to follow.

I snapped the picture at the perfect time, and then the melody began. Lowering my camera, I focused simply on her. I couldn't take pictures while she played. I couldn't bring myself to miss any part of how she looked up on that stage.

My lip hooked up in a small smile as her body began to sway to the music. She loved this piece, had been playing it for as long as I could remember. She needed no sheet music for this; "Greensleeves" poured from her soul through her bow.

I couldn't stop staring, my heart beating like a damn drum as Poppy's lips twitched. Her deep dimples popped out when she concentrated on the difficult passages. Her eyes remained closed, but you could tell which parts of the music she adored. Her head would tilt to the side, and a huge smile would spread on her face.

People didn't understand that after all this time she was still mine. We were only fifteen, but since the day I'd kissed her in the blossom grove, aged eight, there had never been anyone else. I had blinders on to any other girl. I only saw Poppy. In my world, only *she* existed.

And she was different from any other girl in our class. Poppy was quirky, not cool. She wasn't concerned with what people thought of her—she never had been. She played the cello because she loved it. She read books, she studied for fun, she woke at dawn just to watch the sunrise.

It was why she was my everything. My forever always. Because she was unique. Unique in a town full of carbon-copy bimbos. She didn't want to cheer, or bitch, or chase boys. She knew she had me, just as much as I had her.

We were all we needed.

I shuffled on my seat as the sound of her cello became softer, Poppy bringing the piece to an end. Lifting my camera again, I snapped a final shot as Poppy raised her bow off the string, a contented expression gracing her pretty face.

The sound of applause made me lower the camera. Poppy pushed the instrument off her chest and got to her feet. She gave a small bow, then scanned the auditorium. Her eyes met mine. She smiled.

I thought my heart might smash through my chest.

I smirked in return, pushing my long blond hair back off my face with my fingers. A blush coated Poppy's cheeks, and then she exited stage left, the house lights flooding the auditorium with light. Poppy had been the last to perform. She always closed the show. She was the best musician in the district for our age group. In my opinion, she outshone anyone in the three age groups above.

I once asked her how she was able to play like she did. She simply told me that the melodies poured from her bow as easily as she breathed. I couldn't imagine having that kind of talent. But that was Poppy, the most amazing girl in the world.

When the applause faded out, people began to leave the auditorium. A hand pressed on my arm. Mrs. Litchfield was wiping away a tear. She always cried when Poppy performed.

"Rune, sweetie, we need to get these two home. Are you okay to meet Poppy?"

"Yes, ma'am," I replied and quietly laughed at Ida and Savannah, Poppy's nine- and eleven-year-old sisters, sleeping on their seats. They didn't much care for music, not like Poppy.

Mr. Litchfield rolled his eyes and threw me a small wave, then turned to wake the girls to get them home. Mrs. Litchfield kissed me on my head, and then the four of them left.

As I made my way out of the aisle, I heard whispers and giggling coming from my right. Glancing over the seats, I spotted a group of freshman girls all looking my way. I ducked my head, ignoring their stares.

It happened a lot. I had no idea why so many of them paid me so much attention. I'd been with Poppy for as long as they'd known me. I didn't want anyone else. I wished they'd stop trying to get me away from my girl— nothing would ever do that.

I pushed through the exit and made my way to the backstage door. The air was thick and humid, causing my black T-shirt to stick to my chest. My black jeans and black boots were probably too warm for this spring heat, but I wore this style of clothing every day, whatever the weather.

Seeing the performers begin to pile out the door, I leaned against the wall of the auditorium, resting my foot against the white painted brick. I crossed my arms over my chest, only unfolding them to rake my hair from my eyes.

I watched the performers getting hugs from their families, then, catching the same girls from before staring at me, lowered my eyes to the ground. I didn't want them to come over. I had nothing to say to them.

My eyes were still cast down when I heard footsteps coming my way. I looked up just as Poppy threw herself onto my chest, her arms wrapping around my back, squeezing me tightly.

I huffed a short laugh and held her right back. I was already six feet tall, so I towered over Poppy's five feet. I liked it though, how she fit perfectly against me.

Inhaling deeply, I took in the sugary-sweet scent of her perfume and pressed my cheek against her head. After one last squeeze, Poppy pulled back and smiled up at me. Her green eyes looked huge under her mascara and light makeup, her lips pink and lush from her cherry lip balm.

I skirted my hands up her sides, stopping when they cupped her soft cheeks. Poppy's lashes fluttered, making her look all kinds of sweet.

Unable to resist feeling her lips on mine, I slowly leaned forward, almost smiling as I heard that same hitch of breath Poppy expelled every single time I kissed her, in that moment just before our lips touched.

As our lips met, I exhaled through my nose. Poppy always tasted like this, of cherry, the taste from her lip balm flooding my mouth. And Poppy kissed me right back, her small hands gripping tightly to the sides of my black shirt.

I worked my mouth against hers, slowly and softly, until I finally pulled back, laying three short, feather-light kisses on her swollen mouth. I took in a breath and watched Poppy's eyes flutter open.

Her pupils were dilated. She licked along her bottom lip before casting me a bright smile.

"Kiss three hundred and fifty-two. With my Rune against the auditorium wall." I held my breath, waiting for the next line. The glint in Poppy's eyes told me that the words I hoped for next would spill from her lips. Leaning in closer, balancing on her tiptoes, she whispered, "And my heart almost burst." She only ever recorded the extra-special kisses. Only the ones that made her feel her heart was full. Every time we kissed, I waited for those words.

When they came, she almost blew me away with her smile.

Poppy laughed. I couldn't help but smile widely at the sound of the happiness in her voice. I pressed another quick kiss to her lips and stepped back to drape my arm over her shoulders. I pulled her close and rested my cheek against her head. Poppy's arms wrapped around my back and stomach, and I led her away from the wall. As I did, I felt Poppy freeze.

I lifted my head to see the freshman girls pointing at Poppy and whispering to each other. Their eyes were focused on Poppy in my arms. My jaw clenched. I hated that they treated her this way—out of jealousy. Most of the girls never gave Poppy a chance because they wanted what she had. Poppy said she didn't care, but I could tell that she did. The fact that she stiffened in my arms told me just how much.

Shifting in front of Poppy, I waited for her to lift her head. As soon as she did, I ordered, "Ignore them."

My stomach dropped as I watched her force a smile. "I am, Rune. They don't bother me."

I tipped my head to the side and raised my brows. Poppy shook her head. "They don't. I promise," she said, trying to lie. Poppy glanced over my shoulder and shrugged. When she met my eyes with her own, she said, "But I get it. I mean, look at you, Rune. You're gorgeous. Tall, mysterious, exotic… Norwegian!" She laughed and pressed her palm over my chest. "You have that whole bad-boy, indie-style thing going for you. The girls can't help but want you. You're you. You're perfect."

I shifted closer and watched her green eyes widen. "And *yours*," I added. The tension leaked from her shoulders.

I slipped my hand into the hand still on my chest. "And I'm not mysterious, *Poppymin*. You know all there is to know about me: no secrets, no mystery."

"To me," she argued, meeting my eyes once more. "You're not a mystery to me, but you are to all the girls in our school. They all want you."

I sighed, beginning to feel pissed. "And all I want is you." Poppy watched me, like she was trying to find something in my expression. It just pissed me off more. I linked our fingers and whispered, "For infinity."

With this, a genuine smile tugged on Poppy's lips. "Forever always," she eventually whispered in reply.

I dropped my forehead to rest against hers. My hands cupped her cheeks, and I assured her, "I want you and only you. I have done since I was five years old and you shook my hand. No other girl will change that."

"Yeah?" Poppy asked, but I could hear the humor back in her sweet voice.

"*Ja*," I replied in Norwegian, hearing the sweet sound of her giggle wash into my ears. She loved it when I spoke to her in my native language. I kissed her forehead, then stepped back to take hold of her hands. "Your mama and daddy took the girls home; they told me to tell you."

She nodded her head, then looked up at me, nervously. "What did you think of tonight?"

I rolled my eyes and crinkled my nose. "Terrible, as always," I said dryly.

Poppy laughed and hit my arm. "Rune Kristiansen! Don't be so mean!" she scolded.

"Fine," I said, pretending to be annoyed. I slammed her into my chest, wrapping my arms around her back, trapping her against me. She squealed when I began kissing up and down her cheek, keeping her arms locked by her side. I dropped my lips to her neck and caught her breath hitch, all laughter forgotten.

I moved my mouth up until I tugged on her earlobe with my teeth. "You were amazing," I whispered softly. "As always. You were perfect up there. You owned that stage. You owned everyone in that room."

"Rune," she murmured. I heard the happy tone in her voice.

I pulled back, still not unlocking her arms. "I'm never more proud of you than when I see you up on that stage," I confessed.

Poppy blushed. "Rune," she said shyly, but I ducked my head to keep eye contact when she tried to pull away. "Carnegie Hall, remember. One day I'll be watching you perform at Carnegie Hall."

Poppy managed to free one of her hands and softly swatted my arm. "You flatter me."

I shook my head. "Never. I only ever say the truth."

Poppy pressed her lips to mine, and I felt her kiss all the way to my toes. When she drew back, I released her and threaded our fingers together.

"We heading out to the field?" Poppy asked as I began leading her away across the parking lot, holding her just that little bit closer as we passed the group of freshman girls.

"I'd prefer to be alone with you," I said.

"Jorie asked if we'd go. Everyone is there." Poppy looked up at me. By the twitch of her lips, I knew I was scowling. "It's Friday night, Rune. We're fifteen, and you've just spent most of the night watching me play the cello. We have ninety minutes left until curfew; we should actually see our friends like normal teenagers."

"Fine," I submitted and wrapped my arm around her shoulders. Leaning down, I placed my mouth at her ear and said, "But I get you to myself tomorrow."

Poppy put her arm around my waist and gripped me tightly. "I promise."

We heard the girls behind us mention my name. I sighed in frustration when Poppy briefly tensed.

"It's because you're different, Rune," Poppy said, without looking up. "You're artsy, into photography. You wear dark clothes." She laughed and shook her head. I pushed my hair back from my face, and Poppy pointed up. "But mainly it's because of that."

I frowned. "Because of what?"

She reached up and pulled on a strand of my long hair. "When you do that. When you push your hair back like you do." I raised an eyebrow, bemused. Poppy shrugged. "It's kinda irresistible."

"*Ja?*" I asked, before stopping to stand in front of Poppy, raking my hair back in exaggeration until she laughed. "Irresistible, huh? To you too?"

Poppy giggled and pulled my hand from my hair to wrap around hers. As we followed the pathway to the field—a patch of the park where the kids from our school hung out at night—Poppy said, "It doesn't really bother me that other girls look at you, Rune. I know how you feel about me, because it's the exact way I feel about you." Poppy sucked in her bottom lip. I knew it meant she was nervous, but I didn't know why, until she said, "The only girl that bothers me is Avery. Because she's wanted you for so long and I'm pretty sure she'd do anything to make you hers."

I shook my head. I didn't even like Avery, but because she was in our group of friends, she was always around. All my friends liked her; they all thought she was the prettiest thing around. But I never saw it, and I hated how she was toward me. Hated how she made Poppy feel.

"She's nothing, *Poppymin*," I reassured her. "*Nothing.*"

Poppy curled into my chest and we turned right, toward our friends. I held Poppy tighter the closer we got. Avery sat up as we approached.

Turning my head toward Poppy, I repeated, "*Nothing.*"

Poppy's hand gripped my shirt, telling me she'd heard. Her best friend, Jorie, jumped to her feet.

"Poppy!" Jorie called excitedly, coming over to pull Poppy into her arms. I liked Jorie. She was ditzy, rarely thought before she spoke, but she loved Poppy and Poppy loved her. She was one of the only people in this small town who found Poppy's quirkiness endearing and not just weird.

"How are you, sweets?" Jorie asked and stepped back. She looked at Poppy's black performance dress. "You look beautiful! So damn cute!"

Poppy bowed her head in thanks. I took hold of her hand again. I guided us around the small fire that they'd lit in the fire pit and sat down. I leaned back against a log bench, pulling Poppy down to sit between my legs. She flashed me a smile as she sat down with me, pressing her back against my chest and tucking her head against my neck.

"So, Pops, how'd it go?" Judson, my best friend, asked from across the fire. My other close friend, Deacon, was sitting beside him. He tipped his chin in greeting, his girlfriend, Ruby, throwing us a small wave too.

Poppy shrugged. "Fine, I guess."

As I wrapped my arm across her chest, holding her tight, I looked at my dark-haired friend and added, "The star of the show. As always."

"It's only the cello, Rune. Nothing too special," Poppy argued softly.

I shook my head in protest. "She brought the place down."

I caught Jorie smiling at me. I also caught Avery rolling her eyes dismissively. Poppy ignored Avery and began talking to Jorie about class.

"Come on, Pops. I swear Mr. Millen is a damn evil alien. Or a demon. Hell, he's from somewhere outside of what we know. Brought by the principal to torture us weak young earthlings with too-hard algebra. It's how he gets his life force; I'm convinced of it. And I think he's onto me too. You know, the fact I *know* he's an extraterrestrial, because, *Lord!* That man keeps failing my ass and giving me the stink eye!"

"Jorie!" Poppy laughed so hard that her whole body shook. I smiled at her happiness, and then I zoned out. I leaned further back against the log as our friends talked. I lazily traced patterns on Poppy's arm, wanting nothing more than to leave. I didn't mind sitting with our friends, but I preferred to be alone with her. It was her company I craved; the only place I ever wanted to be was with her.

Poppy giggled at something else Jorie said. Her laugh was so hard she knocked the camera hanging around my neck to the side. Poppy flashed me an apologetic smile. I leaned down, tilted her chin toward me with my finger, and kissed her on the lips. I only meant for it to be swift and soft, but when Poppy's hand threaded into my hair, pulling me closer, it became more. As Poppy opened her lips, I pushed my tongue to meet hers, losing my breath as I did.

Poppy's fingers tightened in my hair. I cupped her cheek to keep her in this kiss as long as possible. If I didn't have to breathe, I imagine I would never have stopped kissing her.

Too lost in the kiss, we only broke apart when someone cleared their throat from across the fire. I lifted my head to find Judson smirking. When I glanced down at Poppy, her cheeks were blazing. Our friends hid their laughter, and I squeezed Poppy tighter. I wouldn't be embarrassed for kissing my girl.

Conversation picked back up again, and I lifted my camera to check it was okay. My mamma and pappa bought it for me for my thirteenth birthday, when they could see that photography was becoming my passion. It was a 1960s vintage Canon. I took it with me everywhere, snapping thousands of pictures. I didn't know why, but capturing moments fascinated me. Maybe it was because sometimes all we get are moments. There are no do-overs; whatever happens in a moment defines life—perhaps it *is* life. But capturing a moment on film keeps that moment alive, forever. To me, photography was magic.

I mentally scrolled through the camera roll. Pictures of wildlife and close-ups of cherry blossoms from the grove would occupy most of the film. Then there'd be photos of Poppy tonight. Her pretty face as the music took its hold. I'd only ever seen that look on her face one other time—when she looked at me. To Poppy, I was as special to her as her music was.

In both cases, it was a bond that no one could break.

Reaching for my cell, I lifted it out in front of us, the camera lens facing our direction. Poppy was no longer taking part in the conversation around us. She was silently running her fingertips along my arm. Catching her off guard, I snapped the picture, just as she looked up at me. I let out a single laugh when her eyes narrowed in annoyance. I knew she wasn't angry though, despite her effort to look so. Poppy loved any picture of us I took, even if it was taken when she least expected it.

When I focused on my cell, my heart immediately started slamming against my chest. In the picture, as Poppy stared up at me, she looked beautiful. But it was the expression on her face that floored me. The look in her green eyes.

In this moment, this single captured moment, there was *that* expression. The one she gave to me as readily as she gave to her music. The one that told me I had her just as much as she had me. The one that ensured we had stayed together all these years. The one that said even though we were young, we knew we'd found our soulmate in the other.

"Let me see?"

Poppy's quiet voice pulled my attention from the screen. She smiled at me and I lowered the phone to let her see.

I watched Poppy, not the picture, as her gaze fell upon the screen. I watched as her eyes softened and a whisper of a smile ghosted on her lips. "Rune," she whispered as she reached down to take hold of my free hand.

I squeezed her hand and she said, "I want a copy of that one. It's perfect." I nodded and kissed her head.

And this is why I love photography, I thought. It could pull out emotion, raw emotion, from a split second in time.

Turning off my phone's camera, I saw the time displayed on the screen. "*Poppymin*," I said quietly, "we have to head home. It's getting late."

Poppy nodded. I got to my feet and pulled her upright.

"You heading out?" Judson asked.

I nodded. "Yeah. I'll catch you Monday."

I threw them all a wave and took hold of Poppy's hand. We didn't say much as we made our way home. When we stopped at Poppy's door, I took her in my arms and pulled her to my chest. I placed my hand on the side of her neck. Poppy looked up. "I'm so proud of you, *Poppymin*. There's no doubt that you'll get into Julliard. Your dream of playing at Carnegie Hall will come true."

Poppy smiled brightly and tugged on the camera strap around my neck. "And you'll be at Tisch School of the Arts at NYU. We'll be in New York together, like it was always meant to be. Like we've always planned."

I nodded my head and brushed my lips along her cheek. "Then there would be no more curfew," I muttered teasingly. Poppy laughed. Moving to her mouth, I pressed a soft kiss to her lips and backed away.

As I let go of her hands, Mr. Litchfield opened the door. He saw me moving away from his daughter and shook his head, laughing. He knew exactly what we'd been doing.

"Night, Rune," he said dryly.

"Night, Mr. Litchfield," I replied, seeing Poppy blush as her daddy gestured for her to go inside.

I walked across the grass to my house. I opened the door, walked through to the living room, and found my parents sitting on the couch. They were both sitting forward in their seats, and they seemed tense.

"*Hei*," I said, and my mamma's head snapped up.

"*Hei*, baby," she said.

I frowned. "What's wrong?" I asked. My mamma shot a glance at my pappa.

She shook her head. "Nothing, baby. Did Poppy play well? Sorry we couldn't make it."

I stared at my parents. They were hiding something, I could tell. When they didn't continue, I slowly nodded my head, answering their question. "She was perfect, as always."

I thought I glimpsed tears in my mamma's eyes, but she quickly blinked them away. Needing to escape the awkwardness, I held up my camera. "I'm going to develop these then go to bed."

As I turned to walk away, my pappa said, "We're going out as a family tomorrow, Rune."

I stopped dead. "I can't come. I've planned to spend the day with Poppy."

My pappa shook his head. "Not tomorrow, Rune."

"But—" I went to argue, but my pappa cut me off, his voice stern.

"I said no. You're coming—that's final. Poppy can see you when we get back. We won't be gone all day."

"What's really going on?"

My pappa walked to stand before me. He put a hand on my shoulder. "Nothing, Rune. I just never see you anymore because of work. I want to change that, so we're having a day out at the beach."

"Well then, can Poppy come with us? She loves the beach. It's her second-favorite place to go."

"Not tomorrow, son."

I stayed silent, getting pissed, but I could see he wasn't going to budge. Pappa sighed. "Go develop your pictures, Rune, and stop worrying."

Doing as he said, I walked down to the basement and into the small side room my pappa had converted into a darkroom for me. I still developed film in the old style instead of using a digital camera. I thought it made for a better result.

After twenty minutes, I stepped back from the line of new pictures. I had also printed the photo from my phone, of Poppy and me at the field. I picked it up and carried it to my bedroom. I stuck my head into Alton's room as I passed, checking that my two-year-old brother was sleeping. He was, curled up tight to his brown stuffed bear, his messy blond hair spread out over his pillow.

I pushed through my door and turned on my lamp. I looked at the clock, registering it was near midnight. Running my hand through my hair, I made my way to the window and smiled when I saw the Litchfield house in darkness, save for the dim light from Poppy's nightlight—Poppy's sign that the coast was clear for me to sneak in.

I locked my bedroom door and switched off the lamp. The room was plunged into darkness. I quickly changed into my sleep pants and shirt. Silently, I lifted the window and climbed out. I sprinted across the grass between our two houses and crawled inside Poppy's room, closing the window as quietly as I could.

Poppy was in bed, tucked under the covers. Her eyes were closed and her breathing was soft and even. Smiling at how cute she looked with her cheek resting in her hand, I padded over, placed her present on the nightstand, and climbed in beside her.

I lay beside her, my head dropping to share her pillow.

We'd done this for years. The first night I stayed over was a mistake; I climbed into her room, at age twelve, to talk, but I fell asleep. Fortunately, I woke early enough the next morning to sneak back into my own bedroom unnoticed. But then the next night, I stayed on purpose, then the night after that, and almost every night since. Luckily we'd never been found out. I wasn't too sure Mr. Litchfield would like me the same if he knew I slept in his daughter's bed.

But staying beside Poppy in bed was becoming more and more difficult. Now I was fifteen, I felt differently around her. I saw her differently. And I knew she did me. We kissed more and more. The kisses were getting deeper, our hands starting to explore places they shouldn't. It was getting harder and harder to stop. I wanted more. I wanted my girl in every possible way.

But we were young. I knew that.

It didn't make it any less difficult though.

Poppy stirred beside me. "I wondered if you were coming tonight. I waited for you but you weren't in your room," she said sleepily as she pushed my hair from my face.

Capturing her hand, I kissed her palm. "I had to develop my film, and my parents were acting weird."

"Weird? How?" she asked, shuffling closer and kissing my cheek.

I shook my head. "Just...weird. I think something's going on, but they told me not to worry."

Even in the dim light I could see Poppy's eyebrows were pulled together in concern. I squeezed her hand in reassurance.

Remembering the present I'd brought her, I reached behind me and took the picture from the nightstand. I'd put it in a simple silver frame. I tapped the flashlight icon on my phone and held it up so Poppy could see better.

She gave a small sigh, and I watched as a smile lit up her entire face. She took hold of the frame and stroked her finger across the glass. "I love this picture, Rune," she whispered, then placed it on her nightstand. She gazed at it for a few moments, then turned back my way.

Poppy lifted the covers and held them high so I could shuffle underneath. I laid my arm over Poppy's waist and moved closer to her face, peppering soft kisses over her cheeks and neck.

When I kissed the spot just below her ear, Poppy began to giggle and pulled away. "Rune!" she whispered, "that tickles!"

I drew back and threaded my hand through hers.

"So," Poppy asked, lifting her other hand to play with a long strand of my hair, "what are we doing tomorrow?"

Rolling my eyes, I replied, "We're not. My pappa is making us go out as a family for the day. To the beach."

Poppy sat up excitedly. "Really? I love the beach!"

My stomach dropped. "He said we have to go alone, *Poppymin*. Just the family."

"Oh," Poppy said, sounding disappointed. She lay back down on the bed. "Have I done something wrong? Your pappa always invites me along with y'all."

"No," I assured her. "It's what I was saying before. They're acting strange. He said he wants us to spend the day as a family, but I think there's something else."

"Okay," Poppy said, but I could hear the sad tone in her voice.

I cupped her head in my hand and promised, "I'll be back for dinner. We'll spend tomorrow night together."

She took hold of my wrist. "Good."

Poppy stared at me, her green eyes wide in the dull light. I stroked my hand along her hair. "You're so beautiful, *Poppymin*."

I didn't need the light to see the blush coating her cheeks. I closed the small space between us and crushed my lips against hers. Poppy sighed as I pushed my tongue into her mouth, her hands moving to grip onto my hair.

It felt too good, Poppy's mouth growing hotter and hotter the more we kissed, my hands dropping to run down her bare arms and down over her waist.

Poppy shifted onto her back as my hand slipped down to touch her leg. I followed and moved above her, Poppy snapping her mouth from mine with a gasp. But I didn't stop kissing her. I dragged my lips over her jaw to kiss along her neck, my hand moving beneath her nightdress to stroke the soft skin of her waist.

Poppy's fingers pulled at my hair, and her leg lifted to wrap around the back of my thigh. I groaned against her throat, moving back up to take her mouth with mine. As my tongue slid against hers, I traced my fingers further up her body. Poppy broke from the kiss.

"Rune…"

I dropped my head to the crook between her neck and shoulder, breathing deeply. I wanted her so much it was almost too much to take.

I breathed in and out as Poppy dropped her hand to stroke up and down my back. I focused on the rhythm of her fingers, forcing myself to calm down.

Minutes and minutes passed, but I didn't move. I was content lying over Poppy, breathing in her delicate scent, my hand pressing against her soft stomach.

"Rune?" Poppy whispered. I lifted my head.

Poppy's hand was immediately on my cheek. "Baby?" she whispered, and I could hear the worry in her voice.

"I'm okay," I whispered back, keeping my voice as quiet as possible so as not to disturb her parents. I looked deep into her eyes. "I just want you so damn much." I dropped my forehead to hers and added, "When we're like this, when we let it get this far, I kind of lose my mind."

Poppy's fingers threaded through my hair and I closed my eyes, loving her touch. "I'm sorry, I—"

"No," I said forcefully, a little louder than intended. I shifted back. Poppy's eyes were huge. "Don't. Don't ever apologize for this, for stopping me. It's never something you have to be sorry for."

Poppy parted her kiss-swollen lips and let out a long sigh. "Thank you," she whispered. I moved my hand and lowered my fingers to link them through hers.

Shifting to the side, I opened my arm and flicked my head for her to come to me. She laid her head on my chest. I closed my eyes and just worked on breathing.

Eventually, sleep began to take me. Poppy's finger traced up and down my stomach. I had almost drifted off when Poppy whispered, "You're my everything, Rune Kristiansen. I hope you know that."

My eyes snapped open at her words, my chest feeling full. Placing my finger under her chin, I tipped her head upward. Her mouth was waiting for my kiss.

I kissed her gently, softly, and slowly withdrew. Poppy's eyes remained closed as she smiled. Feeling like my chest would explode at the contented look on her face, I whispered, "For infinity."

Poppy snuggled back into my chest and whispered back, "Forever always."

And we both fell asleep.

Sand Dunes and Salty Tears

Rune

"RUNE, WE NEED TO TALK TO YOU," MY PAPPA SAID AS WE ATE OUR LUNCH in the restaurant overlooking the beach.

"Are you getting divorced?"

Pappa's face paled. "God, no, Rune," he assured me quickly and took hold of my mamma's hand for emphasis. My mamma smiled at me, but I could see the tears building in her eyes.

"Then what?" I asked. My pappa slowly leaned back in his chair.

"Your mamma has been upset with my job, Rune, not with me." I was completely confused, until he said, "They're transferring me back to Oslo, Rune. The company has hit a glitch there, and I'm being sent back to fix it."

"How long for?" I asked. "When will you be back?"

My pappa ran his hand through his thick, short blond hair, just the way I did. "Here's the thing, Rune," he said cautiously. "It could be years. It could be months." He sighed. "Realistically, anything from one to three years."

My eyes widened. "You're leaving us here in Georgia for that long?"

My mamma reached out her hand and covered mine with hers. I stared blankly at it. Then the true consequences of what Pappa was saying began seeping into my brain. "No," I said under my breath, knowing he wouldn't do this to me. *Couldn't* do this to me.

I looked up. I saw guilt wash all over his face.

I knew it was true.

I understood now. Why we came to the beach. Why he wanted us to be alone. Why he refused Poppy's company.

My heart was sprinting as my hands fidgeted on the table. My mind spun in circles…they wouldn't…he wouldn't…*I wouldn't!*

"No," I spat out, louder, drawing stares from nearby tables. "I'm not going. I'm not leaving her."

I turned to my mamma for help, but she lowered her head. I snatched back my hand from under hers. "Mamma?" I pleaded, but she slowly shook her head.

"We're a family, Rune. We're not being split up for that long. We have to go. We're a *family*."

"No!" I shouted this time, pushing my chair back from the table. I got to my feet, my fists clenched at my sides. "I won't leave her! You can't make me! This is our home. *Here!* I don't want to go back to Oslo!"

"Rune," my pappa said, placatingly, standing up from the table and holding out his hands. But I couldn't be in this closed space, with him. Turning on my heel, I ran out of the restaurant as fast as I could and headed down onto the beach. The sun had disappeared behind thick clouds, causing a cold wind to whip up the sand. I kept running, heading for the dunes, the coarse grains hitting my face.

As I ran, I tried to fight against the anger ripping through me. *How can they do this to me? They know how much I need Poppy.*

I was shaking with anger as I climbed the tallest dune and dropped down to sit on its peak. I lay back, staring at the graying sky, and pictured a life back in Norway without her. I felt sick. Sick at just the thought of not having her by my side, holding my hand, kissing my lips…

I could barely breathe.

My mind raced, searching for ideas of how I could stay. I thought and I thought of every possibility, but I knew my pappa. When he decided on something, nothing would change his mind. I was going; the look on his face had told me clearly that there was no way out. They were taking me from my girl, my soul. And I couldn't do a damn thing about it.

I heard someone climbing the dune behind me and I knew it was my pappa. He sat down beside me. I looked away, staring out over the sea. I didn't want to acknowledge his presence.

We were silent, until I eventually cracked and asked, "When do we leave?"

I felt my pappa stiffen beside me, causing me to glance his way. He was already watching my face, sympathy in his expression. My stomach sank further. "When?" I pressed.

Pappa dropped his head. "Tomorrow."

Everything stilled.

"What?" I whispered in shock. "How is that possible?"

"Your mamma and I have known for about a month now. We decided not to tell you until the last minute because we knew how you would feel. They need me in the office by Monday, Rune. We've organized everything with your school, transferred your transcripts. Your uncle is preparing our house in Oslo for our return. My company has hired movers to empty our house in Blossom Grove and ship our belongings to Norway. They arrive tomorrow shortly after we leave."

I glared at my pappa. For the first time in my life, I hated him. I gritted my teeth and looked away. I felt sick with the amount of anger coursing through my veins.

"Rune," my pappa said softly, putting his hand on my shoulder.

I shrugged off his hand. "Don't," I hissed. "Don't ever touch me or speak to me again." I snapped my head around. "I'll *never* forgive you," I promised. "I'll never forgive you for taking her from me."

"Rune, I understand—" he tried to say, but I cut him off.

"You don't. You have *no* idea how I feel, what Poppy means to me. No damn idea. Because if you did, you wouldn't be taking me away from her. You'd tell your company that you *wouldn't* move. That we have to stay."

Pappa sighed. "I'm the Technical Officer, Rune, I have to go where I'm needed, and right now that's Oslo."

I said nothing. I didn't care that he was the damn technical officer of some failing company. I was pissed he was only telling me now. I was pissed we were going, period.

When I didn't speak, my pappa said, "I'm getting our things together, son. Be at the car in five minutes. I want you to have tonight with Poppy. I want you to at least give you that much."

Hot tears built in my eyes. I turned my head so he wouldn't see me. I was angry, so angry that I couldn't stop the damn tears. I never cried when I was sad, only when I was angry. And right now, I was so pissed I could barely draw breath.

"It won't be forever, Rune. A few years at most, and then we'll be back. I promise. My job, our life, is here in Georgia. But I have to go where the company needs me," Pappa said. "Oslo won't be so bad; it's where we're from. I know your mamma will be happy to be near family again. I thought you might be, too."

I didn't reply. Because a few years without Poppy was a lifetime. I didn't care about my family.

I was lost, watching the rhythm of the waves, and I waited for as long as I could before I got to my feet. I wanted to get to Poppy, but at the same time, I didn't know how to tell her I was leaving. I couldn't stand the thought of breaking her heart.

The horn sounded, and I ran to the car, where my family was waiting. My mamma tried to smile at me, but I ignored her and slid into the back seat. As we pulled away from the coast, I glared out the window.

Feeling a hand on my arm, I turned to see Alton clutching on to the sleeve of my shirt. His head was tilted to the side.

I ruffled his messy blond hair. Alton laughed, but his smile faded, and he kept glancing my way the whole journey home. I found it ironic how my baby brother seemed to get how much pain I was in, way more than my parents did.

The drive felt like an eternity. When we pulled into the driveway, I practically dived out of the car and sprinted to the Litchfield house.

I knocked on the front door. Mrs. Litchfield answered after only a few seconds. The minute she took in my face, I saw her eyes fill with sympathy. She glanced across the yard at my mamma and pappa, who were unpacking the car. She gave them a small wave.

She knew too.

"Is Poppy here?" I managed to ask, pushing the words through my thick throat.

Mrs. Litchfield pulled me into a hug. "She's in the blossom grove, sweetie. She's been there all afternoon, reading." Mrs. Litchfield kissed my head. "I'm so sorry, Rune. That daughter of mine will be heartbroken when you leave. You're her whole life."

She's my whole life too, I wanted to add, but I couldn't bring myself to speak a single word.

Mrs. Litchfield released me and I backed away, jumping off the porch, sprinting all the way to the grove.

I got there in minutes, immediately spotting Poppy under our favorite cherry blossom tree. I stopped, keeping well out of sight as I watched her reading her book, her purple headphones over her head. Branches filled with pink cherry blossom petals fell around her like a protective shield, sheltering her from the bright sun. She was wearing a short white sleeveless dress, a big white bow pinned at the side of her long brown hair. I felt like I'd walked into a dream.

My heart clenched. I'd seen Poppy every day since I was five. Slept beside her almost every night since I was twelve. Kissed her every day since I was eight, and loved her with everything I had for so many days I'd stopped keeping track.

I had no idea how to live a day without her next to me. How to breathe without her by my side.

As if she sensed I was there, she looked up from the page of her book. When I stepped out onto the grass, she flashed me her biggest smile. It was the smile she had only for me.

I tried to smile back, but I couldn't.

I trudged over the fallen cherry blossoms, the path so littered with fallen petals that it looked like a stream of pink and white beneath my feet. I watched Poppy's smile fade the closer I got. I couldn't keep anything from her. She knew me as well as I knew myself. She could see that I was upset.

I'd told her before, there was no mystery with me. Not with her. She was the only person who knew me completely.

Poppy stilled, only moving to pull the headphones off her head. She placed her book beside her on the ground, wrapped her arms around her bent legs, and just waited.

Swallowing, I dropped to my knees before her, and my head fell forward in defeat. I fought against the tightness in my chest. Eventually I raised my head. Apprehension was clear in Poppy's eyes, like she knew whatever was going to come from my mouth would change everything.

Change us.

Change our entire lives.

End our world.

"We're leaving," I finally managed to choke out.

I watched her face pale.

Glancing away, I managed to drag in another short breath, and add, "Tomorrow, *Poppymin*. Back to Oslo. Pappa is taking me away from you. He's not even trying to stay."

"No," she whispered in response. She leaned forward. "There must be something we can do?" Poppy's breathing sped up. "Maybe you could stay with us? Move in with us? We can work something out. We can—"

"No," I interrupted. "You know my pappa wouldn't allow it. They've known for weeks; they've already transferred my schools. They just didn't tell me because they knew how I'd react. I have to go, *Poppymin*. I have no other choice. I have to go."

I stared at a single blossom petal as it broke from a low-hanging branch. It drifted like a feather to the ground. I knew that, from now on, whenever I saw a cherry blossom I'd think of Poppy. She spent all of her time here in this grove, with me beside her. It was the place she loved the most.

I squeezed my eyes shut as I imagined her in this grove all alone after tomorrow—no one to go on adventures with her, no one to listen to her laugh…no one to give her heart-bursting boy-kisses for her jar.

Feeling a sharp pain strike my chest, I turned back to Poppy, and my heart tore in two. She was still frozen to her spot against the tree, but her pretty face was flooded with streams and streams of silent tears, her small hands balled into fists that were shaking at her knees.

"*Poppymin*," I rasped, finally letting all my hurt free. I rushed to her side and cradled her in my arms. Poppy melted into me, crying into my chest. I closed my eyes, feeling every bit of her pain.

This pain was also mine.

We stayed that way for some time, until finally, Poppy raised her head and pressed her shaking palm to my cheek. "Rune," she said, her voice cracking, "what will…what will I do without you?"

I shook my head, silently telling her that I didn't know. I couldn't speak; my words were trapped behind my clogged throat. Poppy lay back against my chest, her arms like a vise around my waist.

We didn't speak as the hours ticked by. The sun faded to leave behind a burnt-orange sky. Before long, the stars appeared, and the moon too, bright and full.

A cool breeze whipped around the grove, forcing the petals to dance around us. When I felt Poppy begin to shiver in my arms, I knew it was time to leave.

Lifting my hands, I ran my fingers through Poppy's thick hair and whispered, "*Poppymin*, we have to go."

She only gripped me tighter in response.

"Poppy?" I tried again.

"I don't want to go," she said almost inaudibly, her sweet voice now hoarse. I glanced down as her green eyes looked up and fixed on mine. "If we leave this grove, it means that it's almost time for you to leave *me* too."

I ran the back of my hand down her red cheeks. They were freezing to the touch. "No goodbyes, remember?" I reminded her. "You always say that there's no such thing as goodbye. Because we'll always see each other in our dreams. Like with your mamaw." Tears spilled from Poppy's eyes; I wiped the droplets away with the pad of my thumb.

"And you're cold," I said softly. "It's really late, and I need to get you home so you don't get into trouble for missing curfew."

Poppy forced a weak smile onto her lips. "I thought real-life Vikings didn't play by the rules?"

I laughed a single laugh and pressed my forehead to hers. I placed two soft kisses on the corner of her mouth and replied, "I'm walking you to your door, and once your parents are asleep, I'm climbing into your bedroom for one last night. How's that for rule-breaking? Viking enough?"

Poppy giggled. "Yes," she answered, pushing my long hair from in front of my eyes. "You're all the Viking I'll ever need."

Taking hold of her hands, I kissed the tip of each finger and made myself stand. I helped Poppy get to her feet and pulled her into my chest. I wrapped my arms around her, keeping her close. Her sweet scent drifted into my nose. I vowed to remember exactly how she felt in this moment.

The wind grew stronger. I broke our embrace and took hold of Poppy's hand. In silence, we began walking down the petal-strewn path. Poppy rested her head on my arm, tipping her head back to take in the night sky. I kissed the top of her head and heard her sigh deeply.

"Have you ever noticed how dark the sky is above this grove? Like it's darker than anywhere else in town. It looks jet-black, but for the bright moon and twinkling stars. Against the pink of the cherry blossom trees, it looks like something from a dream." I tipped my head back to see the sky, and a smirk tugged at the corner of my mouth. She was right. It looked almost surreal.

"Only you would notice something like that," I said as I lowered my head back down. "You always see the world differently from everyone else. It's one of the things I love about you. It's the adventurer I met when I was five."

Poppy tightened her grip on my hand. "My mamaw always said that heaven looks however you want it to look, you know." The sadness in her voice made my breath hitch in my throat.

She sighed. "Mamaw's favorite place was under our cherry blossom. When I sit there and look out along the rows and rows of trees, then up at that jet-black sky, I sometimes wonder if she's sitting at that exact tree up in heaven, looking out along the cherry blossom trees just as we do, staring at the black sky above just as I'm doing now."

"I'm sure she is, *Poppymin*. And she'll be smiling down at you, like she promised she would."

Poppy reached out and captured a bright-pink cherry blossom in her hand. She held it out in front of her, staring at the petals in her palm.

"Mamaw also said that the best things in life die quickly, like the cherry blossom. Because something so beautiful can never last forever, *shouldn't* last forever. It stays for a brief moment in time to remind us how precious life is, before fading away just as quickly as it came. She said that it teaches you more in its short life than anything that is forever by your side."

My throat began to close at the pain in her voice. She looked up at me.

43

"Because nothing so perfect can last an eternity, can it? Like shooting stars. We see the usual stars above us every single night. Most people take them for granted, even forget they are there. But if a person sees a shooting star, they remember that moment forever; they even make a wish at its presence."

She took in a deep breath. "It shoots by so quickly that people savor the short time they have with it."

I felt a teardrop fall on our joined hands. I was confused, unsure why she was talking about such sad things.

"Because something so completely perfect and special is destined to fade. Eventually, it has to blow away into the wind." Poppy held up the cherry blossom that was still in her hand. "Like this flower." She threw it into the air, just as a gust of wind came. The strong bluster carried the petals into the sky and away above the trees.

It disappeared from our sight.

"Poppy—" I went to speak, but she cut me off.

"Maybe we're like the cherry blossom, Rune. Like shooting stars. Maybe we loved too much too young and burned so bright that we had to fade out." She pointed behind us, to the blossom grove. "Extreme beauty, quick death. We had this love long enough to teach us a lesson. To show us how capable of love we truly are."

My heart fell to my stomach. I swung Poppy around to face me. The devastated look on her beautiful face cut me where I stood. "Listen to me," I said, feeling panicked. Placing my hands on either side of Poppy's face, I promised, "I'll come back for you. This move to Oslo, it won't be forever. We'll talk every day, we'll write. We'll still be Poppy and Rune. Nothing can break that, *Poppymin*. You'll always be mine; you'll always own half of my soul. This isn't the end."

Poppy sniffed and blinked away her tears. My pulse raced with fear at the thought of her giving up on us. Because that had never even entered my head. We weren't ending anything.

I stepped closer. "We're not done," I said forcefully. "For infinity, *Poppymin*. Forever always. *Never* done. You can't think like that. Not with us."

Poppy lifted onto her tiptoes and mirrored my stance, placing her hands on my face. "Do you promise me, Rune? Because I still have hundreds of boy-kisses that I need you to give me." Her voice was timid and shy…it was racked with fear.

I laughed, feeling the dread seep from my bones, relief taking its place. "Always. And I'll give you more than a thousand. I'll give you two, or three, or even four."

Poppy's joyful smile soothed me. I kissed her slow and soft, holding her as close as I possibly could. When we broke apart, Poppy's eyes fluttered open, and she announced, "Kiss number three hundred and fifty-four. With my Rune, in the blossom grove…and my heart almost burst."

Then Poppy promised, "My kisses are all yours, Rune. No one else will ever have these lips but you."

I brushed my lips against hers one more time and echoed her words. "My kisses are all yours. No one will ever have these lips but you."

I took her hand and we headed back toward our houses. All the lights in my house were still on. When we reached Poppy's doorway, I leaned in and kissed the tip of her nose. Shifting my mouth to her ear, I whispered, "Give me an hour and I'll come to you."

"Okay," Poppy whispered back. Then I jumped as her palm landed gently on my chest. Poppy stepped closer to me. The serious expression on her face made me suddenly nervous. She stared at her hand, then ran her fingers slowly over my chest and down over my stomach.

"*Poppymin?*" I asked, unsure what was happening.

Without saying a word, she pulled her hand away and moved toward her door. I waited for her to turn around and explain, but she didn't. She walked through the open door, leaving me glued to the spot on her driveway. I could still feel the heat from her hand on my chest.

When the light in the Litchfields' kitchen came on, I made myself walk back to my own house. As soon as I walked in the door, I spotted a mountain of boxes in the hallway.

They must have been packed and stored away to keep them from my sight.

Pounding past them, I saw my mamma and pappa in the living room. My pappa called my name but I didn't stop. I entered my bedroom just as he came in behind me.

I moved to my nightstand and began gathering everything I wanted with me, especially the framed picture of Poppy and me that I had taken the previous night. As my eyes scanned the photograph, my stomach ached. If it was possible, I already missed her. Missed my home.

Missed my girl.

Sensing my pappa was still behind me, I said quietly, "I hate you for doing this to me."

I caught his quick inhale of breath. I turned around, and I saw my mamma standing beside him. Her face was as shocked as my pappa's. I had never treated them this badly. I liked my parents. I had never understood how other teenagers didn't like theirs.

But I did now.

I *hated* them.

I'd never felt such hate toward anyone before.

"Rune—" my mamma began, but I stepped forward and cut her off.

"I will never forgive you, *either* of you, for doing this to me. I hate you both so much right now I can't stand to be near you."

I was surprised at how harsh my voice sounded. It was thick and full with all the anger that was building inside of me. Anger that I hadn't known it was possible to feel. I knew to most people I seemed moody, sullen, but really, I rarely felt anger. Now I felt I was made of it. Only hate ran through my veins.

Rage.

My mamma's eyes filled with tears, but for once, I didn't care. I wanted them to feel as bad as I did right now.

"Rune—" my pappa said, but I turned my back to him.

"What time do we leave?" I barked, interrupting whatever he was trying to say.

"We leave at seven a.m.," he informed me softly.

I closed my eyes; I now had only *hours* with Poppy. In eight hours I would be leaving her behind. Leaving everything behind apart from this rage. I would make sure that traveled with me.

"It won't be forever, Rune. After a while, it'll get easier. You'll meet someone else eventually. You'll move on—"

"*Don't!*" I roared as I whipped around, throwing the lamp from my nightstand across the room. The glass bulb shattered on impact. I breathed hard, heart racing in my chest, as I glared at my pappa. "Don't you ever say anything like that again! I won't move on from Poppy. I love her! Don't you get that? She's my *everything*, and *you're* ripping us apart." I watched his face pale. I stepped forward.

My hands were shaking.

"I have no choice but to come with you, I know that. I'm only fifteen; I'm not stupid enough to believe that I could stay here alone." I clenched my hands into fists. "But I *will* hate you. I will hate *both* of you every single day until we return. You might think that just because I'm fifteen I'll forget Poppy as soon as some slut from Oslo flirts with me. But that will never happen. And I will hate you every single second until I'm with her again."

I paused for breath, then added, "And even then, I'll hate you for taking me away from her in the first place. Because of you, I'll miss out on years of being with my girl. Don't think that just because I'm young I don't recognize what I have with Poppy. I love her. I love her more than you could imagine. And you're taking me away, without even considering how I would feel." I turned my back, walked to my closet, and began pulling down my clothes. "So from now on, I won't give a damn how you feel about anything. I will *never* forgive you for this. Either of you. *Especially* you, Pappa."

I began packing the suitcase my mamma must have placed on my bed. My pappa remained where he was, staring at the floor in silence. Eventually he turned away and said, "Get some sleep, Rune. We're up early."

Every hair on my neck pricked up in annoyance at his dismissal of what I had to say, until he quietly added, "I'm so sorry, son. I *do* know how much Poppy means to you. I tried to leave telling you until now to spare you weeks of hurt. It clearly didn't help. But this is real life, and it's my job. You'll understand one day."

The door closed behind him, and I dropped onto the bed. I dragged my hand down my face, and my shoulders slumped when I stared at my empty closet. But the anger was still there, burning in my stomach. If anything, it was burning hotter than before.

I was pretty sure it was here to stay.

I threw the last of my shirts into the case, not caring how crumpled they got. I made my way to the window and saw Poppy's house was in darkness, all except for the dim nightlight telling me the coast was clear.

After locking my bedroom door, I snuck out the window and rushed across the grass. The window was slightly open, waiting for me. I slid through and closed it tightly behind me.

Poppy was sitting in the center of her bed, her hair down and her face freshly washed. I swallowed when I saw how beautiful she looked in her white nightdress, her arms and legs bare, and her skin so soft and smooth.

I stepped closer to the bed and saw the photo frame in her hand. When she looked up, I could see she'd been crying.

"*Poppymin*," I said softly, my voice breaking at seeing her so upset.

Poppy set the frame on the bed and laid her head on her pillow, patting the mattress beside her. As quickly as I could, I lay down next to her, shifting until we were only inches apart.

As soon as I saw Poppy's bloodshot eyes, the anger inside me seemed to flare. "Baby," I said, covering my hand with hers, "please don't cry. I can't stand to see you cry."

Poppy swallowed. "My mama told me that y'all are leaving real early in the morning."

I dipped my eyes and slowly nodded.

Poppy's fingers ran over my forehead. "So we only have tonight left," she said. I felt a dagger pierce through my heart.

"*Ja*," I replied, blinking up at her.

She was staring at me strangely.

"What?" I asked.

Poppy shuffled her body closer. So close that our chests touched and her lips hovered at my mouth. I could smell minty toothpaste on her breath.

I licked my lips as my heart began pounding hard. Poppy's fingers drifted down my face, over my neck and down over my chest until they reached the bottom of my shirt. I shifted on the bed, needing some space, but before I could move away, Poppy closed in and pressed her mouth to mine. As soon as I tasted her on my lips, I leaned in closer, and then her tongue pushed through to meet mine.

She kissed me slow, deeper than ever before. When her hand lifted my shirt and landed on my bare stomach, I snapped my head back and swallowed hard. I could feel Poppy's hand trembling against my skin. I looked into her eyes, and my heart missed a beat.

"*Poppymin*," I whispered and ran my hand over her bare arm. "What are you doing?"

Poppy moved her hand upward until her hand was on my chest, and my voice was halted by the thickness in my throat.

"Rune?" Poppy whispered as she dipped her head to carefully place a single kiss on the bottom of my throat. My eyes drifted closed as her warm mouth touched my skin. Poppy spoke against my neck. "I...I want you..."

Time stopped. My eyes snapped open. Poppy inched back and tipped her head until her green eyes met mine.

"Poppy, no," I protested, shaking my head, but she laid her fingers over my lips.

"I can't..." She drifted off, then gathered herself and continued, "I can't have you leave me and never know what it's like to be with you." She paused. "I love you, Rune. So much. I hope you know that."

My heart slammed into a new kind of beat, one that knew it had the love of its other half. It was harder and faster. It was infinitely stronger than the one before. "Poppy," I whispered, completely struck by her words. I knew she loved me, because I loved her. But this was the first time we'd ever said it aloud.

She loves me...

Poppy waited silently. Not knowing how to respond in any other way, I ran the tip of my nose down her cheek, pulling back just a fraction to gaze into her eyes. "*Jeg elsker deg.*"

Poppy swallowed, then smiled.

I smiled back. "I love you," I translated into English, just to make sure she completely understood.

Her face grew serious once more, and she moved to sit up in the middle of the bed. Reaching for my hand, she pulled me to sit opposite her. Her hands dropped to the bottom of my shirt.

Taking in a stuttering breath, she pulled it up and over my head. I closed my eyes and felt a warm kiss on my chest. I opened my eyes again to see Poppy giving me a shy smile. I melted at the nervous look on her face.

She'd never looked so beautiful.

Trying to fight through my own nerves, I put my hand on her cheek. "We don't have to do this, Poppy. Just because I'm leaving—you don't need to do this for me. I'll be coming back; I'll make sure of it. I want to wait until you're ready."

"I'm ready, Rune," she said, her voice clear and steady.

"You think we're too young—"

"We'll be sixteen soon."

I smiled, hearing the fire in her voice. "Most people still think that's too young."

"Romeo and Juliet were around our age," she argued. I couldn't help but laugh. I stopped laughing when she edged closer and ran her hand down my chest. "Rune," she whispered, "I've been ready for some time, but I was happy to wait because we had all the time in the world. There was no rush. Now we don't have that luxury. Our time, *this* time, is limited. We only have hours left. I love you. I love you more than anyone could believe. And…and I think you feel the same way about me."

"*Ja,*" I replied instantly. "I love you."

"Forever always," Poppy said on a sigh, then shifted away from me. Without breaking her eyes from mine, she lifted her hand to the strap of her nightdress and pushed it down. She did the same to the other strap, and the nightgown fell away to her hips.

I froze. I couldn't move as Poppy sat in front of me, bared to me. "*Poppymin,*" I breathed, convinced I didn't deserve this girl…this moment.

I moved closer, until I towered right above her. I searched her eyes and asked, "Are you sure, *Poppymin?*"

Poppy threaded her hand through mine, then brought our hands to her bare skin. "Yes, Rune. I'm sure. I want this."

I couldn't hold back any longer, so I let go and kissed her lips. We only had hours. I was going to spend them being with my girl, in every possible way.

Poppy moved her hand from mine and explored my chest with her fingers, never breaking from our kiss. I ran my fingers over her back, pushing her closer to me. She shivered under my touch. I dropped my hand to the hem of her dress at her thigh. My hand traveled upward, until I worried I was going too far.

Poppy broke away and rested her forehead on my shoulder. "Keep going," she instructed breathlessly. I did as she asked, swallowing the nerves building in my throat.

"Rune," she murmured.

I closed my eyes at the sound of her sweet voice. I loved her so damn much. Because of that I didn't want to hurt her. I didn't want to be responsible for pushing her too far. I wanted her to feel special. I wanted her to understand that she was my world.

We stayed like this for a minute, locked in the moment, breathing, waiting for whatever came next.

Then Poppy's hands drifted to the button on my jeans and I opened my eyes. She was studying me closely. "Is this…is this okay?" she asked cautiously. I nodded, speechless. Taking her free hand, she guided me to undress her, until all our clothes had been shed onto the floor.

Poppy sat quietly before me, her hands fidgeting on her lap. Her long brown hair was flowing over one of her shoulders, and her cheeks were flushed with red.

I'd never seen her so nervous.

I'd never been so nervous.

Reaching out my hand, I ran my finger down her hot cheek. At my touch, Poppy's eyes fluttered up, a shy smile pulling on her lips.

"I love you, *Poppymin*," I whispered.

A soft sigh escaped her mouth. "I love you too, Rune."

Poppy's fingers wrapped around my wrist and she carefully lay back on the bed, guiding me forward until I was beside her, my torso moving to cover hers.

Leaning in, I peppered soft kisses over her flushed cheeks and forehead, ending in a long kiss on her warm mouth. Poppy's shaking hand pushed into my hair and pulled me closer.

It felt like only seconds later when Poppy shifted beneath me, breaking the kiss. She placed her palm on my cheek and said, "I'm ready."

Nuzzling my face into her hand, I kissed the fingers resting on my cheek and absorbed her words. Poppy leaned over to the side and took something from the drawer of her nightstand. When she handed me the small packet she'd retrieved, I fought back a sudden rush of nerves.

I stared at Poppy and her cheeks flushed in embarrassment. "I knew this day would come soon, Rune. I wanted to make sure we were prepared."

I kissed my girl until I built up the nerve to do this. It didn't take long, with Poppy's touch calming the storm inside, until I knew I was ready.

Poppy opened her arms, guiding me above her. My mouth fused with hers, and for the longest time, I simply kissed her. I tasted the cherry lip balm on her lips, loving the feeling of her warm bare skin pressing against mine.

I pulled back for air. I met Poppy's gaze and she nodded her head. I could see on her face how much she wanted me, as I wanted her. I kept my eyes locked on hers, and I did not break away once.

Not for a single second...

Afterward, I held her in my arms. We faced each other as we lay under the covers. Poppy's skin was warm to the touch, and her breathing was slowing back to its normal rhythm. Our fingers were linked on the pillow we now shared, our grips tight, hands slightly trembling.

Neither of us had spoken yet. As I studied Poppy watching every move I made, I prayed that she didn't regret what we'd done.

I watched her swallow deeply and she drew in a slow breath. When she exhaled, she dipped her eyes to our clasped hands. As slowly as possible, she ran her lips over our entwined fingers.

I stilled.

"*Poppymin,*" I said, and her eyes lifted up. A long strand of her hair had fallen over her cheek and I gently pushed it back, tucking it behind her ear. She still hadn't said anything. Needing her to know what we'd shared had meant to me, I whispered, "I love you so much. What we just did...being with you like that..." I trailed off, unsure how to express what I wanted to say.

She didn't respond, and my stomach rolled, fearing I'd done something wrong. As my eyes closed in frustration, I felt Poppy's forehead against mine and her lips whisper kisses onto my mouth. I shifted until we were as close as we could possibly get.

"I'll remember this night for the rest of my life," she confided, and the fear I felt was pushed far from my mind.

I blinked my eyes open and tightened my hold around her waist. "Was it…was it special for you, *Poppymin*? As special as it was for me?"

Poppy smiled a smile so wide that the sight stole my breath. "As special as special can be," she softly replied, echoing the words she'd said to me when we were eight years old and I kissed her for the first time. Unable to do anything else, I kissed her with everything I had, pouring out all of my love into the kiss.

When we broke apart, Poppy squeezed my hand, and tears built in her eyes. "Kiss three hundred and fifty-five, with my Rune, in my bedroom… after we made love for the first time." Taking my hand, she laid it on her chest, directly over her heart. I could feel its heavy beats under my palm. I smiled. I knew her tears were tears of happiness, not sadness.

"It was so special that my heart almost burst," she added with a smile.

"Poppy," I whispered, feeling my chest tighten.

Poppy's smile fell, and I watched as her tears began falling to her pillow. "I don't want you to leave me," she said brokenly.

I couldn't stand the pain in her voice. Or the fact that these tears were now sad ones. "I don't want to go," I replied honestly.

We didn't say anything else. Because there was nothing more to say. I combed Poppy's hair through my fingers, while she ran her fingertips up and down my chest. It wasn't long before Poppy's breathing had evened out and her hand had stilled on my skin.

The rhythm of her steady breathing lulled my eyes to a close. I tried to stay awake as long as possible, to savor the time I had left. But before long, I drifted to sleep, a bittersweet mixture of happiness and sadness flowing through my veins.

It seemed like I had only just closed my eyes when I felt the rising sun's warmth kissing my face. I blinked until I opened my eyes, seeing a new day breaking through Poppy's window.

The day I was leaving.

My gut clenched when I saw the time. I was leaving in an hour.

When I glanced at Poppy, sleeping over my chest, I thought she'd never looked more beautiful. Her skin was flushed from the heat of our bodies, and I smiled on seeing our hands still joined on my stomach.

Suddenly nerves flooded through me when I thought of the night before.

She looked so contented as she slept. My biggest fear was that she would wake and regret what we'd done. I wanted her, so badly, to love what we had done as much as I did. I wanted the image of us together to be as ingrained in her memory as it would be in mine.

As if feeling my heavy stare, Poppy slowly opened her eyes. I watched as the recollection of the night before flashed across her face. Her eyes widened as she took in our bodies, our hands. My heart skipped a beat in trepidation, but then a beautiful slow smile spread across her face. Seeing this, I shifted closer to her. Poppy buried her head in my neck as I wrapped her in my arms. I held her close for as long as I possibly could.

When I finally lifted my head and checked the clock again, the anger from yesterday came crashing back.

"*Poppymin*," I whispered, hearing the strained anger in my graveled voice. "I…I have to go."

Poppy stiffened in my arms. When she shifted back, her cheeks were wet. "I know."

I felt tears hitting my cheeks too. Poppy gently wiped them away. I caught her hand and laid a single kiss on the center of her palm. I stayed for a couple more minutes, drinking in every inch of Poppy's face, before forcing myself to leave the bed and get dressed. Without looking back, I slid through the window and ran across the grass, feeling my heart tear with every single step.

I climbed through my window. My bedroom door had been unlocked from the outside. My pappa stood near the bed. For a brief moment my stomach turned at the fact that I'd been caught. But then the fury flared within me and I lifted my chin, daring to him to say something, *anything*.

I welcomed a fight.

I wouldn't let him shame me for spending the night with the girl I loved. The one he was ripping me away from.

He turned and walked away without saying a word.

Thirty minutes passed in a flash. I cast a glance over my room, one last time. Lifting my backpack, I swung it over my shoulder and walked outside, my camera hanging around my neck.

Mr. and Mrs. Litchfield were already on our driveway, standing with Ida and Savannah, hugging my parents with their goodbyes. Seeing me walk out the door, they met me at the bottom of the steps and hugged me goodbye too.

Ida and Savannah ran to me and threw themselves around my waist. I ruffled the hair on their heads. When they stepped aside, I heard a door being opened. I lifted my eyes and saw Poppy running. She had wet hair, clearly having just showered, but she looked more beautiful than ever before as she sprinted to where we all stood, only me in her sights.

When she arrived on our driveway, she stopped briefly to hug my parents and kiss Alton goodbye. Then she turned to face me. My parents got into the car, and Poppy's parents and sisters moved back toward their house, giving us some space. I wasted no time holding out my arms, and Poppy ran into my chest. I squeezed her tight, inhaling the sweet scent from her hair.

I put my finger under her chin and tilted her head up, and then I kissed her for the final time. I kissed her with as much love as I could find inside my heart.

When I broke away, Poppy spoke through streaming tears. "Kiss number three hundred and fifty-six. With my Rune on his driveway...when he left me."

I closed my eyes. I couldn't stand the pain she was in—that *I* was in too.

"Son?" I looked over Poppy's shoulder at my pappa. "We have to go," he said apologetically.

Poppy's hands tightened on my shirt. Her big green eyes were shining with tears, and it seemed like she was trying to memorize every part of my face. Finally releasing my hold on her, I raised my camera and pressed the button.

I captured this rare moment: the exact moment when someone's heart broke.

I walked to the car, my feet feeling like ton weights. As I climbed in the backseat, I didn't even try to stop my tears. I watched Poppy standing to the side of our car, her damp hair blowing in the breeze, watching me leave, waving goodbye.

My pappa started the engine. I opened my window. I held out my hand and Poppy took hold of it. As I gazed into her face one last time, she said, "I'll see you in your dreams."

"I'll see you in my dreams," I whispered back and reluctantly let go of her hand as my pappa drove the car away. I stared back at Poppy through the rear window, watching her wave, until she was out of sight.

I held on to the memory of that wave goodbye.

I vowed to hold on to it until that wave welcomed me home again.

Until it once again stood for "hello."

Silence

Rune
Oslo
Norway

A DAY LATER I WAS BACK IN OSLO, SEPARATED FROM POPPY BY AN OCEAN.

She and I talked every day for two months. I tried to be happy that we at least had that. But as every day ended without her by my side, the anger inside me built. My hatred for my pappa increased, until it broke something inside, and all I could feel was emptiness. I resisted making friends at school, I resisted doing anything that would make this place my home again.

My home was back in Georgia.

With Poppy.

Poppy didn't say anything about my change in mood, if she'd even noticed. I hoped I'd hid it well. I didn't want her worrying about me.

Then one day, Poppy didn't return my calls, emails, or texts.

Or the next day, or the next.

She dropped out of my life.

Poppy simply vanished. No word, no trace.

She left school. She left town.

Her family all upped and left without notice.

For two years she left me completely alone on the other side of the

Atlantic, wondering where she was. Wondering what had happened. Wondering if I'd done something wrong. Making me think that maybe I'd pushed her too far the night before I left.

It was the second moment that defined my life.

A life without Poppy.

No infinity.

No forever always.

Just…nothing.

Lovers Old and Strangers New

Poppy
Blossom Grove, Georgia
Present Day
Aged Seventeen

"HE'S COMING BACK."

Three words. Three words that sent my life into a tailspin. Three words that terrified me.

He's coming back.

I stared at Jorie, my closest friend, clutching my books tightly to my chest. My heart fired off like a cannon, and nerves overwhelmed me.

"What did you say?" I whispered, ignoring the students around us in the hallway, all rushing to their next classes.

Jorie placed her hand on my arm. "Poppy, are you okay?"

"Yes," I replied weakly.

"You sure? You've gone pale. You don't seem okay."

I nodded, trying to be convincing, and asked, "Who…who told you he was coming back?"

"Judson and Deacon," she replied. "I was just in class with them and they were saying that his daddy has been sent back here by his company." She shrugged. "This time, for good."

I swallowed. "To the same house?"

Jorie winced but nodded. "Sorry, Pops."

I closed my eyes and took a calming breath. He was going to be next door again…his room directly opposite mine again.

"Poppy?" Jorie asked, and I opened my eyes. Her gaze was full of sympathy. "You sure you're okay? You've only been back here a few weeks yourself. And I know what seeing Rune will do…"

I forced a smile. "I'll be fine, Jor. I don't know him anymore. Two years is a long time, and we haven't spoken once in that time."

Jorie frowned. "Pop—"

"I'll be fine," I insisted, holding up my hand. "I need to get to class."

I was walking away from Jorie when a question popped into my head. I looked back over my shoulder at my friend, the only friend I had kept in touch with in the past two years. While everyone thought my family had left town to care for my mama's sick aunt, only Jorie knew the truth.

"When?" I mustered the courage to ask.

Jorie's face softened when she realized what I meant. "Tonight, Pops. He arrives tonight. Judson and Deacon are spreading the word for people to go to the field this evening to welcome him back. Everyone's going."

Her words felt like a dagger stabbing my heart. I hadn't been invited. But then again, I wouldn't be. I'd left Blossom Grove without a word. When I came back to this school, without being on Rune's arm, I became the girl I always should have been—invisible to the popular crowd. The weird girl who wore bows in her hair and played the cello.

No one—except for Jorie and Ruby—had even cared I'd been gone.

"Poppy?" Jorie called again.

I blinked myself back to reality and noticed that the hallways were nearly empty. "You'd better get to class, Jor."

She took a step toward me. "Will you be okay, Pops? I'm worried about you."

I laughed a humorless laugh. "I've been through worse."

I dipped my head and rushed to my class before I could see the sympathy and pity on Jorie's face. I entered my math class, sliding into my seat just as the teacher began the lesson.

If someone were to ask me later what the class had been about, I wouldn't have been able to tell them. For fifty minutes all I could think about was the last time I saw Rune. The last time he held me in his arms. The last time he pressed his lips against my lips. How we made love, and the look on his beautiful face as he was driven out of my life.

Idly, I wondered what he looked like now. He was always tall with broad shoulders, well built. But, as for the rest of him, two years was a long time for a person to change at our time of life. I knew that better than anyone.

I wondered if his eyes still appeared crystal blue in the bright sun. I wondered if he still wore his hair long, and I wondered if he still pushed it back every few minutes—that irresistible move that drove all the girls crazy.

And for a brief moment, I let myself wonder if he still thought about me, the girl next door. If he ever wondered what I was doing at any particular moment in time. If he ever thought back to that night. Our night. The most amazing night of my life.

Then dark thoughts hit me hard and fast. The question that made me feel physically sick…had he kissed someone else in the past two years? Had he given anyone his lips, when he'd forever promised them to me?

Or worse: had he made love with another girl?

The shrill call of the school bell tore me from my thoughts. I stood up from my desk, making my way to the hallway. I was thankful it was the end of the school day.

I was tired and I ached. But more than that, I hurt in my heart. Because I knew that Rune would be back in the house next door from tonight, in school the next day, and I wouldn't be able to speak to him. I wouldn't be able to touch him or smile at him, like I'd dreamed about doing since the day I didn't return his calls.

And I wouldn't be able to kiss him sweetly.

I had to stay away.

My stomach churned when I realized he probably wouldn't care about me anymore. Not after the way I simply cut him off—no explanation, nothing.

Pushing through the doors into the cool, fresh air, I inhaled deeply. Feeling instantly better, I tucked my hair behind my ears. Now that it was styled into a short bob, it always felt strange. I missed my long hair.

Beginning my walk home, I smiled up at the blue sky and the birds swooping around the tops of the trees. Nature calmed me; it always had.

I had only made it a few hundred yards when I saw Judson's car, surrounded by Rune's old friends. Avery was the only girl among a crowd of boys. I put my head down and tried to rush past, but she called out my name. I ground to a halt and forced myself to turn in her direction. Avery pushed off from where she had been leaning against the car and stepped forward. Deacon tried to pull her back, but she shrugged off his arm. I saw by her smug expression that she wasn't going to be kind.

"Have you heard?" she asked, a smile on her pink lips. Avery was beautiful. When I arrived back in town, I couldn't believe how beautiful she had become. Her makeup was always perfect and her long blond hair was always neatly styled. She was everything a boy would want in a girl, and everything most girls wanted to be.

I pushed my hair back behind my ear, a habit that showed my nerves. "Heard what?" I asked, knowing exactly what she meant.

"About Rune. He's coming back to Blossom Grove."

I could see the glint of happiness in her blue eyes. I glanced away, determined to keep my composure, and shook my head. "No, Avery, I hadn't heard. I haven't been back long myself."

I saw Ruby, Deacon's girlfriend, walking up to the car, Jorie walking beside her. When they saw Avery talking to me, they hurried to join us. I loved them both for this. Only Jorie knew where I'd been for the past couple of years, *why* I had left. But from the minute I'd returned, Ruby had acted as though I'd never been away. They were true friends, I had realized.

"What's going on here?" Ruby asked casually, but I could hear the edge of protectiveness in her voice.

"I was asking Poppy if she knew Rune was coming back to Blossom Grove tonight," Avery replied tartly.

Ruby looked at me curiously.

"I didn't know," I told her. Ruby smiled sadly at me.

Deacon walked up behind his girlfriend and put an arm around her shoulders. He flicked his chin at me in greeting. "Hey, Pops."

"Hey," I replied.

Deacon turned to Avery. "Ave, Rune hasn't spoken to Poppy in years—I've told you this. She doesn't even know him anymore. Of course she wouldn't know he was coming back; why would he even tell her?"

I listened to Deacon and knew he wasn't being cruel to me. But it didn't mean that his words didn't cut as deeply as a spear through the heart. And now I knew; I knew that Rune never spoke of me. It was obvious he and Deacon had remained close. It was obvious to me that I was nothing to him now. That I was never mentioned.

Avery shrugged. "I just wondered is all. She and Rune were inseparable until he left."

Taking this as my cue to leave, I waved my hand. "I have to go." I quickly turned and headed home. I decided to cut through the park that would lead me to the blossom grove. As I walked through the empty grove, the cherry blossom trees bare of their pretty leaves, a sadness filled me.

These bare branches were as empty as I felt. Yearning for the thing that made them complete, but knowing that no matter how much they wished, they couldn't get them back until spring.

The world simply didn't work that way.

When I got home, my mama was in the kitchen. Ida and Savannah were sitting at the table doing their homework.

"Hey, baby," said my mama. I walked over and gave her a hug, holding on to her waist just that little bit tighter than usual.

My mama tilted up my head, a worried look in her tired eyes. "What's wrong?"

"I'm just tired, Mama. I'm gonna go lie down."

My mama didn't let me go. "You sure?" she asked, laying her palm on my forehead, checking my temperature.

"Yeah," I promised, moving her hand and kissing her cheek.

I made my way to my bedroom. I stared out the window at the Kristiansen house. It was unchanged. No different from the day they had left to return to Oslo.

They hadn't sold it. Mrs. Kristiansen had told my mama that they knew they'd be back at some point, so they kept it. They loved the neighborhood and loved the house. A housekeeper had cleaned and maintained it every few weeks for two years to make sure it would be ready for their return.

Today, all the curtains were drawn back and the windows were open to let in the fresh air. The housekeeper was clearly preparing it for their imminent arrival. The homecoming that I was dreading.

Drawing the curtains that my daddy put up for me when I returned home a few weeks ago, I lay on my bed and closed my eyes. I hated feeling fatigued all of the time. By nature, I was an active person, viewing sleep as a waste of time when it could be spent out in the world, exploring and making memories.

But now I had no choice.

I pictured Rune in my mind's eye, and his face stayed with me as I fell into a dream. It was the dream I dreamed most nights—Rune holding me in his arms, kissing my lips and telling me that he loved me.

I didn't know how long I slept, but when I woke up, it was to the sound of trucks arriving. Loud banging and familiar voices came from across the yard.

Sitting up, I wiped the sleep from my eyes. Realization dawned on me.

He was here.

My heart began to pound. It beat so fast that I gripped myself for fear it would leap out of my chest.

He was here.

He was *here*.

I got out of bed and positioned myself in front of the drawn curtains. I leaned in close so I could hear what was going on. I picked out my mama's and daddy's voices among the drone, along with the familiar sounds of Mr. and Mrs. Kristiansen.

Smiling, I reached out to pull back a curtain. I stopped; I didn't want them to see me. Backing away, I rushed upstairs to my daddy's office. It was the only other window that looked out onto their house, a window where I could hide in plain sight due to the light tint that shielded it from the bright sun.

I moved to the left-hand side of the window, just in case anyone glanced up. I smiled again when my eyes fell upon Rune's parents. They looked barely any different. Mrs. Kristiansen was still as beautiful as ever. Her hair was cut shorter, but apart from that she was exactly the same. Mr. Kristiansen had gone slightly grayer, and he looked like he'd lost some weight, but the difference was small.

A young blond boy ran out the front door, and my hand flew to my mouth when I saw it was little Alton. He would be four now, I calculated. He'd grown so much. And his hair was just like his brother's, long and straight. My heart squeezed. He looked exactly like a young Rune.

I watched the movers refurnish the house with incredible speed. But there was no sign of Rune.

Eventually my parents came back inside, but I kept vigil by the window, waiting patiently for the boy who had been my world for so long that I didn't know where he began and I ended.

Over an hour passed. Night drew in and I was giving up hope of seeing him at all. As I was about to leave the office, I saw movement from behind the Kristiansens' house.

Every one of my muscles tensed as I caught a tiny flicker of light shining in the dark. A white cloud of smoke burst through the air above the patch of grass between our two houses. At first I wasn't sure what I was seeing, until a tall figure, dressed all in black, emerged from the shadows.

My lungs ceased to function as the figure stepped into the glow of the streetlight and stopped dead. Leather biker jacket, black shirt, black drainpipe jeans, black suede boots...and long, bright-blond hair.

I stared and stared, a lump blocking my throat, as the boy with wide shoulders and impressive height lifted his hand and raked it through his long hair.

My heart skipped a beat. Because I knew that movement. I knew that strong jaw. I knew him. I knew him as well as I knew myself.

Rune.

It was *my* Rune.

A cloud of smoke blew from his mouth again, and it took me a few moments to realize what I was actually seeing.

Smoking.

Rune was smoking. Rune didn't smoke; he would never have touched cigarettes. My mamaw had smoked her entire life and died too young from lung cancer. We had always promised each other we would never even try it.

It was clear that Rune had broken that promise.

As I watched him take another drag and push back his hair for the third time in a few minutes, my stomach plummeted. Rune's face tipped upward into the glow of the light as he exhaled a stream of smoke into the cool night breeze.

So here he was. Seventeen-year-old Rune Kristiansen, and he was more beautiful than I could have ever imagined. His crystal-blue eyes were as bright as they had always been. His once-boyish face was now rugged and completely breathtaking. I used to joke he was as handsome as a Norse god. As I studied every part of his face, I was certain his looks surpassed even theirs.

I couldn't tear my eyes away.

Rune finished his cigarette and threw it to the ground, the light from the stub gradually fading to black in the short grass. I waited with bated breath to see what he would do next. Then his pappa came to the edge of the porch and said something to his son.

I watched Rune's shoulders tense and his head snap in the direction of his pappa. I couldn't make out what they were saying, but I heard clearly the raised voices, heard Rune responding aggressively to his pappa in his native Norwegian. His pappa dropped his head in defeat and headed back to the house, clearly hurt at something Rune had said. As Mr. Kristiansen walked away, Rune stuck his middle finger up at his retreating back, only dropping it when the front door of their house slammed shut.

I watched, rigid with shock. I watched as this boy—a boy I once knew so completely—became a stranger before my eyes. Disappointment and sadness washed over me as Rune began to pace across the yard between our two houses. His shoulders were stiff. I could almost feel the anger radiating off him even from this vantage point.

My worst fears had been realized: the boy I knew had gone.

Then I froze, stock still, as Rune stopped pacing and glanced at my bedroom window, directly below where I was standing. A gust of wind blew across the yard, lifting his long blond hair off his face and, in that second, I could see incredible pain, severe longing, in his eyes. The image of his strained face, as he stared at my window, hit me harder than a train. In that lost expression was *my* Rune.

This boy, I recognized.

Rune stepped toward my window, and for a moment, I thought he would try to climb through, the way that he did for all those years. But, abruptly, he stopped and his hands balled at his sides. His eyes closed and his teeth gritted together so tightly that I could see the tension in his jaw from where I stood.

Then, clearly changing his mind, Rune turned on his heel and pounded toward his house. I stayed at the office window, in the shadow. I couldn't move with the shock of what I'd just witnessed.

Rune's bedroom light turned on. I saw him walk around his room, then move to the window and sit on the wide ledge. He cracked it open. He lit another cigarette and blew the smoke through the open gap.

I shook my head in disbelief. Then someone entered the office, and my mama came to my side. When she peered out the window, I knew she'd realize what I was up to.

I felt my cheeks flame with heat at being caught. Finally, my mama spoke. "Adelis said that he's no longer the boy we knew. She said he's given them nothing but trouble since they went back to Oslo. Erik is lost and has no idea what to do. They're real glad Erik got moved back here. They wanted Rune away from the bad crowd he fell in with in Norway."

My gaze fell on Rune again. He threw the cigarette from the window and rolled his head to lean against the glass. His eyes were focused on one thing and one thing only—my bedroom window.

As my mama moved to leave the office, she laid her hand on my shoulder. "Maybe it was a good thing you broke all contact, baby. I'm not real sure he could have handled everything you went through, from what his mamma has said."

Tears filled my eyes as I wondered what had made him this way. Into this boy I didn't know. I had deliberately cut myself off from the world for the past couple of years to save him pain. So that he could live a good life. Because knowing that over in Norway was a boy whose heart was still filled with light made everything I was going through bearable.

But that fantasy was quashed as I studied this doppelgänger of Rune.

This Rune's light was dim; nothing glittered bright. It was obscured by shadow and mired in darkness. It was as though the boy I had loved had been cast aside in Norway.

Deacon's car pulled into the driveway of Rune's house. I saw Rune's cell light up in his hand, and he slowly made his way from his room and sauntered off the porch. He walked with a careless swagger toward Deacon and Judson, who jumped out of the car. He slapped them both on the back in greeting.

Then my heart cracked in two. Avery slid out of the back seat and hugged Rune hard. She was wearing a short skirt and cropped top, showcasing her perfect figure. Rune didn't hug her back—though that did nothing to lessen my pain. Because Avery and Rune, standing side by side, looked so perfect. Both tall and blond. Both beautiful.

They all piled into the car. Rune got in last, taking shotgun, and then they rolled away from our street and out of sight.

I sighed as I watched the taillights fade into the night. When I looked back at the Kristiansen house, I saw Rune's pappa standing at the edge of the porch, gripping the railing, staring in the direction in which his son had just departed. Then he lifted his face to the office window, and a sad smile spread on his lips.

He'd seen me.

Mr. Kristiansen lifted his hand and gave me a small wave. As I waved back, I saw a look of utter sadness etched on his face.

He looked tired.

He looked heartbroken.

He looked like he missed his son.

I returned to my room, lay back on my bed, and pulled my favorite photo frame into my hands. As I stared down at the beautiful boy and the smitten girl staring back, both so in love, I wondered what had happened in the last two years to make Rune as troubled and rebellious as he appeared to be.

Then I cried.

I cried for the boy who was my sun.

I mourned the boy I once loved with everything I had.

I mourned Poppy and Rune—a couple of extreme beauty and even quicker death.

Crowded Hallways and Pierced Hearts

Poppy

"YOU SURE YOU'RE OKAY?" MY MAMA ASKED AS SHE STROKED MY ARM. THE car rolled to a stop.

I smiled and nodded my head. "Yeah, mama, I'm good."

Her eyes were rimmed with red, and tears were building in her eyes. "Poppy. Baby. You don't have to go to school today if you don't want to."

"Mama, I love school. I want to be here." I shrugged. "Plus, I have history fifth period and you know how much I love it. It's my favorite class."

A reluctant smile pulled on her mouth and she laughed, wiping her eyes. "You're just like your mamaw. Stubborn as an ox and always seeing the sunshine behind every cloud. I see her personality shining through your eyes every single day."

Warmth blossomed in my chest. "That makes me real happy, Mama. But I mean it; I'm truly okay," I said sincerely.

When Mama's eyes filled with water again, she shooed me from the car, pushing the doctor's note into my hand. "Here, make sure to hand that in."

I took the paper, but before I shut the car door, I ducked down to say, "I love you, Mama. With my whole heart."

My mama paused, and I saw the bittersweet happiness spread on her face. "I love you too, Pops. With my whole heart."

I shut the door and turned to walk into school. I always thought it was strange, arriving at school late. The place was so quiet and still, kind of apocalyptic, the total opposite from the rowdiness of lunch period or the mad dash of students in between classes.

I made my way to the school office for Mrs. Greenway, the secretary, to process my doctor's note. As she handed me my hall pass, she asked, "How you doing, darlin'? You keeping that pretty head of yours up?"

Smiling at her kind face, I replied, "Yes, ma'am."

She winked at me, making me laugh. "That's my girl."

Checking my watch, I saw that my next class had only been in session fifteen minutes. Moving as quickly as I could to avoid missing anything else, I rushed through two sets of doors until I arrived at my locker. I yanked it open and pulled out the pile of English Lit books that I needed for my class.

I heard the door at the end of the short hallway opening but paid it no mind. Once I had everything I needed, I shut my locker door with my elbow and headed for class, wrestling with my many books. When I looked up, I stopped dead.

I was sure my heart and my lungs stopped working. Standing about eight feet in front of me, seemingly as glued to the spot as I was, was Rune. A towering and fully grown Rune.

And he was staring at me. Crystal-blue eyes held me in their trap. I couldn't have turned away even if I had wanted to.

Finally, I was able to find a breath, and filled my lungs with air. Like a jump lead, the action caused my heart to beat, to beat furiously under the stare of this boy. The one, that if I was being honest with myself, I still loved more than anything in the world.

Rune was dressed as he always had—black muscle T-shirt, black slim-fit jeans, and black suede boots. Only now, his arms were thicker; his waist was toned and leaner, tapering in at his hips. My eyes traveled to his face and my stomach flipped. I thought I had seen all his beauty as he stood under the lamplight last night, but I hadn't.

Older and more mature, he was quite possibly the most beautiful creature I had ever seen. His jaw was strong, perfectly defining his Scandinavian face.

His cheekbones were prominent, but not in any way feminine, and a light dusting of blond stubble graced his chin and cheeks. The constants, I discovered, were those dark-blond eyebrows furrowed over his almond-shaped bright-blue eyes.

The eyes that even the distance of four thousand miles, and a timescale of two years, could never erase from my memory.

But that gaze, the gaze that was currently boring through mine, didn't belong to the Rune I knew. Because it was filled with accusation and hatred. These eyes were glaring at me with unconcealed contempt.

I swallowed back the pain that was clawing up my throat, the pain of being on the receiving end of such a hard stare. Being loved by Rune brought the heady sensation of warmth. Being hated by Rune was like standing on an arctic ice shelf.

Minutes passed by and neither of us moved an inch. The air seemed to crackle around us. I watched as Rune's fist clenched at his side. He seemed to be mentally warring with himself. I wondered what he was fighting inside. The look on his face grew darker still. Then, behind him, the door opened, and William, the hall monitor, walked through.

He looked at Rune and me, serving up the excuse I needed to break free from this too-intense moment. I needed to gather my thoughts.

William cleared his throat. "Can I see your hall passes?"

I nodded and, balancing my books on a raised knee, went to hand mine over, but Rune shoved his in front of mine.

I didn't react to his blatant rudeness.

William checked his pass first. Rune had been picking up his class schedule; that was why he was late. William handed back Rune's pass, but Rune still didn't move. William took hold of mine. He looked at me and said, "I hope you feel better soon, Poppy."

My face paled, wondering how he knew, but then I realized the pass had said I'd been to see my doctor. He was simply being kind. He didn't know.

"Thank you," I said nervously and risked a look up. Rune was watching me, only this time his forehead appeared lined. I recognized his expression of worry. As soon as Rune saw me staring at him, *reading* him correctly, the worry was quickly replaced by the scowl he had previously worn.

Rune Kristiansen was way too handsome to scowl. A face that beautiful should forever wear a smile.

"Go on, you two. Get to class." William's hard voice pulled my attention back from Rune. I pushed past them both and rushed out through the far doors. As soon I was through to the next hallway, I glanced back, only to find Rune staring at me through the large panes of glass.

My hands began to shake at the intensity of his gaze, but then he suddenly moved away, as if he was forcing himself to leave me alone.

It took several seconds to gather some composure, and then I hurried to my class.

I was still shaking an hour later.

———————————

A week passed by. A week of avoiding Rune at all costs. I stayed in my bedroom until I knew he wasn't home. I kept my curtains drawn and my window locked—not that Rune would have tried to come in. The few times I had seen him in school he had either ignored me or glared at me like I was his greatest enemy.

Both hurt in equal measure.

During lunch periods I stayed away from the cafeteria. I ate my lunch in the music room and spent the rest of the time practicing my cello. Music was still my safe haven, the one place where I could escape the world.

When my bow hit the string, I was transported away on a sea of tones and notes. The pain and grief of the last two years disappeared. The loneliness, the tears and anger, all evaporated, leaving a peace I could not find anywhere else.

The previous week, after my awful hallway reunion with Rune, I'd needed to get away from it all. I'd needed to forget the look in his eyes as he glared at me with such hatred. Music was normally my remedy, so I threw myself into intense practice. The only problem? Each time I finished a piece, as soon as the final note faded and I lowered my bow, that devastation cut back through me tenfold. And it stayed. Now, after I finished playing at lunch, the anguish haunted me for the rest of the afternoon. It weighed heavily on my mind as I exited the school building.

The courtyard was bustling with students making their way home. I kept my head down and pushed through the crowd, only to turn the corner and see Rune and his friends sitting on the field in the park. Jorie and Ruby were there too. And so was Avery.

I tried not to stare as Avery sat beside Rune, who was lighting up a cigarette. I tried not to stare as Rune began to smoke, his elbow resting casually on his knee as he leaned back against a tree. And I tried to ignore the flip of my stomach as I hurried by, Rune's narrowed eyes briefly meeting mine.

I quickly averted my eyes. Jorie jumped to her feet and came running after me. I managed to get far enough from Rune and his friends that they wouldn't hear what Jorie had to say to me.

"Poppy," she called as she stopped behind me. I turned to face her, feeling Rune's watchful gaze settle on me. I ignored it.

"How are you doing?" she asked.

"Fine," I replied. Even I heard the slight tremble in my voice.

Jorie sighed. "Have you spoken to him yet? He's been back over a week."

My cheeks blazed. I shook my head. "No. I'm not real sure that's a good idea." I drew in a breath and confided, "I have no idea what I would say anyhow. He doesn't seem to be the boy I knew and loved for all those years. He seems different. Looks like he's changed."

Jorie's eyes flared. "I know. But I think you're the only girl that sees that as a bad thing, Pops."

"What do you mean?" Jealousy sparked in my chest.

Jorie pointed to the girls gathering around where he sat, aiming to appear casual, but failing epically in their endeavor. "He's all anyone is talking about, and I'm pretty sure any girl in this school—except you, me, and Ruby—would sell their soul to the devil for him to even acknowledge them. He was always wanted, Pops, but well, he had you and we all knew he wouldn't leave you for anything or anyone. But now…" She trailed off, and I could feel my heart deflating.

"But now he doesn't have me," I finished for her. "Now he's free to be with whoever he wants."

Jorie's eyes widened when she realized she had once again put her foot in her mouth. She squeezed my arm in support, wincing apologetically. I couldn't be mad at her though, she was always speaking before she'd thought it through. Besides, everything she said was true.

A moment of awkward silence passed, until she asked, "What are you up to tomorrow night?"

"Nothing," I replied. I was itching to leave.

Jorie's face lit up. "Good! You can come to Deacon's house party. Can't have you sitting in alone another Saturday night."

I laughed.

Jorie frowned.

"Jorie, I don't go to parties. No one would invite me anyway."

"I'm inviting you. You'll be my date."

My humor dropped. "I can't, Jor." I paused. "I can't be there when Rune is. Not after everything."

Jorie leaned in closer. "He won't be there," she said quietly. "He's told Deacon he isn't going, that he's going somewhere else."

"Where?" I asked, failing to disguise my curiosity.

She shrugged. "Hell if I know. Rune doesn't really talk much. I think it only adds to why he's attracting groupies like there's no tomorrow." Jorie stuck out her bottom lip and prodded my arm. "Please, Pops. You've been gone so long, and I've missed you. I want to spend as much time with you as I can, but you keep hiding yourself away. We have years to make up for. Ruby will be there too. You know I'd never leave you alone."

My eyes inspected the ground, trying hard to think up an excuse. I looked up at Jorie, and I could see that my refusal was upsetting her.

Chasing away the pangs of doubt in my chest, I relented. "Okay, I'll come with you."

Jorie's face split into a huge smile. "Perfect!" she said. I laughed as she brought me in for a quick hug.

"I need to get home," I said as she released me. "I've got a recital tonight."

"Okay, I'll come get you at seven tomorrow night. Good?"

I waved my hand and began walking home. I had only made it a few hundred yards before I felt someone walking behind me through the blossom grove. When I looked over my shoulder, there was Rune.

My heart kicked into sprint mode as my gaze caught his. He didn't look away from me, but I did from him. I was terrified he would try to talk to me. What if he wanted me to explain everything? Or, worse, what if he wanted to tell me that what we had was nothing?

That would break me.

Quickening my pace, I kept my head down and rushed all the way home. I felt him trailing me the entire way, but he made no move to overtake me.

As I raced up the steps of my porch, I looked to the side and saw him leaning against the side of his house, near his window. My heart flipped as he pushed back his hair. I had to keep my feet rooted to the porch, in case I dropped my bag and ran over to him, to explain why I let him go, why I cut him off so horribly, why I'd give anything for him to kiss me just one more time. Instead, I forced myself to go inside.

My mama's words played heavily on my mind as I walked to my bedroom and lay down...*maybe it was a good thing you broke all contact, baby. I'm not real sure he could have handled everything you went through from what his mamma has said...*

Closing my eyes, I vowed to leave him alone. I wouldn't be a burden to him. I'd protect him from the pain.

Because I still loved him as much as I always had.

Even if the boy I loved no longer loved me back.

7

Lips Betrayed and Painful Truths

Poppy

I FLEXED ONE HAND, BALANCING MY CELLO AND BOW WITH THE OTHER. Every now and again, my fingers grew numb and I had to wait to be able to play again. But as Michael Brown finished up his violin solo, I knew nothing would deter me from sitting center stage tonight. I would play my piece. And I'd savor every second of creating the music I loved so much.

Michael drew back his bow, and the audience burst into rapturous applause. He took a quick bow and exited on the other side of the stage.

The emcee grabbed the mic and announced my name. When the audience heard I was making my long-overdue return, their clapping grew louder, welcoming me back to the musical fold.

My heart raced in excitement at the whistles and support from parents and friends in the auditorium. As many of my peers from the orchestra came to the wings to pat me on the back and wish me words of encouragement, I had to chase back a lump in my throat.

Straightening my shoulders, I forced back the overwhelming onslaught of emotion. I tipped my head to the audience as I walked to take my seat. The spotlight above rained bright light on me.

I positioned myself perfectly, waiting until the clapping died down. As always, I glanced up and found my family sitting proudly in the third row. My mama and daddy were smiling widely. Both sisters gave me little waves.

Smiling back to show them I had seen them, I fought against the slight pain that fluttered in my chest as I spotted Mr. and Mrs. Kristiansen sitting alongside them, Alton waving at me too.

The only person missing was Rune.

I hadn't performed in two years. And before that, he never missed one of my recitals. Even if he had to travel, he was at every single one, camera in hand, smiling his crooked half-smile when our eyes connected in the dark.

Clearing my throat, I closed my eyes as I placed my fingers on the neck of the cello and brought the bow to the string. I counted to four in my head and began the challenging Prelude from Bach's Cello Suites. It was one of my favorite pieces to play—the intricacy of the melody, the fast pace of the bow work, and the perfect tenor sound that echoed around the auditorium.

Each time I sat on this seat, I let the music flow through my veins. I let the melody pour from my heart, and I imagined sitting center stage at Carnegie Hall—my ultimate dream. I imagined the audience sitting before me: people who, like me, lived for the sound of a single perfect note, who thrilled to be carried away on a journey of sound. They felt the music in their hearts and its magic in their souls.

My body swayed to the rhythm, at the change in tempo and the final crescendo…but best of all, I forgot the numbness in my fingertips. For a brief moment, I forgot it all.

As the final note rang in the air, I lifted my bow from the vibrating string and, tipping my head back, slowly opened my eyes. I blinked against the bright light, a smile pulling on my lips in the solace of that silent moment when the note faded to nothing, before the applause of the audience began. That sweet, sweet moment when the adrenalin of the music made you feel so alive you felt you could conquer the world, that you had achieved serenity in its purest form.

And then, the applause began, breaking the spell. Lowering my head, I smiled as I rose from the seat, bowing my head in thanks.

As I gripped the neck of my cello, my eyes automatically searched for my family. Then my eyes traveled along the cheering patrons and skirted along the back wall. At first, I didn't realize what I was seeing. But as my heart slammed against my chest, my eyes were drawn to the very left of the far wall. I caught sight of long blond hair disappearing through the exit door...a tall, toned boy dressed all in black, vanishing from sight. But not before he glanced over his shoulder one last time, and I caught a glimpse of crystal-blue eyes...

My lips parted in shock, but before I could be sure what I was witnessing, the boy was gone, leaving behind a slowly closing door.

Was it...? Would he...?

No, I tried to convince myself, firmly. It couldn't have been Rune. There was no way he would have come to this.

He hated me.

The memory of his cold blue stare in the school hallway confirmed my thoughts—I was simply wishing for things that couldn't possibly be real.

With a final bow, I walked off the stage. I listened to the three remaining performers, then left through the backstage door, only to find my family and Rune's family waiting for me.

My thirteen-year-old sister, Savannah, was the first to see me. "Pops!" she shouted and ran to me, wrapping her arms around my waist.

"Hey, y'all," I replied and squeezed her in return. The next second, Ida, now eleven, was hugging me too. I squeezed them back as tightly as I could. When they drew back, their eyes were shining. I playfully tilted my head. "Hey now, no crying, remember?"

Savannah laughed, and Ida nodded her head. They released me. My mama and daddy both took their turn in telling me how proud they were.

Finally, I turned to Mr. and Mrs. Kristiansen. A sudden wave of nerves crashed through me. This would be the first time I had spoken to them since they had returned from Oslo.

"Poppy," Mrs. Kristiansen said softly and held out her arms. I walked to the woman who had been a second mother to me and fell into her embrace. She held me close and kissed my head. "I've missed you, darling," she said, her accent sounding stronger than I remembered.

My mind drifted to Rune. I wondered if his accent was stronger too.

As Mrs. Kristiansen let me go, I chased this idle thought away. Mr.

Kristiansen hugged me next. When I pulled away, I saw little Alton gripping tightly on to Mr. Kristiansen's legs. I bent down. Alton ducked his head down shyly, glimpsing up at me through the thick strands of his long hair.

"Hey, baby," I said, tickling his side. "Do you remember me?"

Alton stared at me for the longest time, before shaking his head.

I laughed. "You lived right next door to me. Sometimes you would come to the park with me and Rune or, if it was a good day, to the blossom grove!"

I had spoken Rune's name without conscious thought, but it reminded me and everyone around me that Rune and I had once been inseparable. A silence descended on the group.

Feeling an ache in my chest, the kind I got when I fiercely missed my mamaw, I stood up and glanced away from the sympathetic stares. I was about to change the subject, when something pulled on the bottom of my dress.

When I looked down, Alton's big blue eyes were fixed on my face. I ran my hand over his soft hair. "Hey, Alton, you okay?"

Alton's cheeks flushed, but he asked in his sweet voice, "You are friends with Rune?"

That same ache from a moment ago flared, and I cast a panicked look around our families. Rune's mamma winced. I didn't know what to say. Alton pulled on my dress again, waiting for an answer.

Sighing, I kneeled down and said sadly, "He was my very best friend in the whole wide world." I pressed my hand over my chest. "And I loved him with my whole heart, every single inch of it." Leaning in closer, I whispered through a thick throat, "And I always will."

My stomach flipped. Those words were the very truth from my soul, and no matter how Rune and I were now, I would forever hold him in my heart.

"Rune…" Alton suddenly spoke up. "Rune…*spoke* to you?"

I laughed. "Of course, sweetie. He spoke to me all the time. All of his secrets. We talked about everything."

Alton looked back at his daddy and his little eyebrows drew together, etching a scowl on his cute face. "He spoke to Poppy, Pappa?"

Rune's pappa nodded his head. "He did, Alton. Poppy was his best friend. He loved her completely."

Alton's eyes became impossibly wide and he turned back to me. His bottom lip trembled.

"What's wrong, baby?" I asked, rubbing his arm.

Alton sniffed. "Rune doesn't talk to me." My heart sank. Because Rune adored Alton; he had always looked after him, played with him. Alton adored Rune. He admired his big brother so much.

"He ignores me," Alton said, his cracked voice breaking my heart. Alton watched me. He watched me with an intensity that I'd only ever experienced from one other person—the older brother who ignored him. He placed his hand on my arm and asked, "Can you speak to him? Can you ask him to speak to me? If you're his best friend, then he'll listen to you."

My heart fell to pieces. I looked over Alton's head at his mamma and pappa, then at mine. They all appeared hurt by Alton's stark revelation.

When I turned to Alton again, he was still staring, willing me to help. "I would, sweetie," I said softly, "but he doesn't speak to me now either."

I could see Alton's hope deflate like a balloon. I kissed his head, and then he ran back to his mamma. Clearly seeing I was hurting, my daddy quickly changed the subject. He turned to Mr. Kristiansen and invited the Kristiansen family for drinks at our house the next night. I stepped away from them all, drawing in a deep breath as my eyes stared blankly across the parking lot.

The sound of a car engine revving snapped me from my trance. I turned in that direction. I lost all the breath in my lungs when, in the distance, I saw a long-haired blond boy jump into the front seat of a black Camaro.

A black Camaro that belonged to Deacon Jacobs, Rune's best friend.

I looked in the mirror and admired my outfit. My sky-blue skater dress hung to mid-thigh, my bobbed brown hair was pulled up at the side with a white bow, and I wore black ballet flats on my feet.

Reaching for my jewelry box, I pulled out my favorite silver earrings and slipped them into my lobes. They were infinity signs. Rune had given them to me for my fourteenth birthday.

I wore them at every opportunity.

Grabbing my cropped denim jacket, I hurried out of my bedroom and out into the cool night. Jorie had texted me that she was outside. As I climbed into the front seat of her mama's truck, I turned to face my best friend. She was smiling at me.

"Poppy, you look so freakin' cute," she remarked. I ran my hands down my dress, smoothing out the skirt.

"Is it okay?" I asked, worried. "I didn't really know what to wear."

Jorie batted her hand in front of her face as she pulled out of the driveway. "It's fine."

I checked out what she was wearing. Jorie was dressed in a black sleeveless dress and biker boots. She was definitely edgier than me, but I was thankful that our outfits were not poles apart.

"So," she began, as we left my street, "how was the recital?"

"Good," I said evasively.

Jorie glanced at me cautiously. "And how are you feeling?"

I rolled my eyes. "Jorie, I'm good. Please, just let me be. You're as bad as my mama."

Jorie, seemingly stuck for words for once, stuck out her tongue. And just like that, she made me laugh again.

For the remainder of the ride, Jorie filled me in on the gossip that had circled the school about why I'd been gone. I smiled in all the right places and nodded my head at the parts she expected me to, but I wasn't really interested. I never much cared for all the drama that happened at school.

I heard the party before I saw it. Shouting and loud music blasted out of Deacon's house and down the street. His parents were on a short vacation, and in the small town of Blossom Grove that meant one thing: house party.

As we parked near the house, we could see kids spilling out onto the front yard. I swallowed back my nerves. I stayed close behind Jorie as we crossed the street.

Gripping onto her arm, I asked, "Are house parties always this crazy?"

Jorie laughed. "Yeah." She linked my arm with hers and pulled me forward.

When we entered the house, I flinched at how loud the music was. As we pushed our way through the rooms to the kitchen, drunken students staggered by, forcing me to grip on to Jorie until I was convinced I'd be causing her physical pain.

Jorie glanced back at me and laughed. When at last we reached the kitchen, I immediately relaxed on seeing Ruby standing with Deacon. The kitchen was much quieter than the rooms we had struggled through.

"Poppy!" Ruby declared and crossed the kitchen to pull me into her arms. "Do you want a drink?"

"Just a soda," I replied. Ruby frowned.

"Poppy!" she admonished. "You need a *real* drink."

I laughed at her horrified expression. "Ruby, thanks, but I'll stick to soda."

"Boo!" Ruby cried but threw her arm around my neck and led me to the drinks.

"Pops," Deacon greeted as a text came through on his cell.

"Hey, Deek," I replied and took the diet soda Ruby had poured me. Ruby and Jorie led me to the backyard, to the fire pit blazing in the center of the lawn. Surprisingly not many people were out here, which suited me just fine.

It wasn't long before Deacon pulled Ruby back to the party inside, leaving me alone with Jorie. I was staring into the flames, when Jorie said, "I'm sorry about putting my big ole' foot in my mouth yesterday about Rune. It hurt you, I saw it. *Lordy!* I just don't always think before I open my big trap! My daddy's threatening to have it wired shut!" Jorie pushed her hands over her mouth in a mock struggle. "I can't, Pops! This mouth, uncontrollable as it is, is all I've got!"

Laughing, I shook my head. "It's alright, Jor. I knew you didn't mean it. You'd never hurt me."

Jorie dropped her hands from her mouth, her head tipped to the side. "Seriously though, Pops. What do you think of Rune? You know, since he's been back?"

Jorie was watching me curiously. I shrugged. Jorie rolled her eyes. "You're telling me you have no opinion about how the great love of your life looks, now he's older and, in my opinion, beyond smokin' hot!"

My stomach churned and I played with the plastic Solo cup in my hands. Shrugging, I replied, "He's just as handsome as he ever was."

Jorie smirked behind her cup as she took a drink; then she grimaced when we heard the voice of Avery drifting out from inside the house. Jorie lowered her cup. "Ugh, looks like the whore's in the house."

I smiled at the level of disgust on Jorie's face. "Is she really that bad?" I asked. "Is she actually a whore?"

Jorie sighed. "Not really. I just hate how she flirts with all the guys."

Ah, I thought, knowing exactly who she was referring to. "Anyone in particular?" I teased and watched Jorie scowl in response. "Judson, perhaps?" I added, prompting Jorie to throw her empty cup my way.

I laughed as it flew past me in completely the wrong direction. When my laughter had died down, Jorie said, "At least now Rune's back she seems to have backed off Jud, anyway." My good humor evaporated. When Jorie realized what she'd just said, she groaned in exasperation at herself and moved quickly to sit beside me and take hold of my hand. "Crap, Pops. I'm so sorry. I did it again! I didn't mean—"

"It's okay," I interrupted.

But Jorie tightened her grip on my hand. Moments of silence passed by. "Do you regret it, Pops? Do you ever regret cutting him off like that?"

I stared at the fire, lost in the roaring flames, and answered honestly, "Every single day."

"Poppy," Jorie whispered sadly.

I threw her a weak smile. "I miss him, Jor. You have no idea how much. But I couldn't tell him what was happening. I couldn't do that to him. Better he believed that I was no longer interested than to tell him the ugly truth." Jorie laid her head on my shoulder. I sighed. "If he had known, he would have tried everything in his power to come back. But that wouldn't have been possible. His daddy's job was there in Oslo. And I…" I sucked in a breath. "And I wanted him to be happy. I knew that, in time, he'd get past not hearing from me. But I know Rune, Jor; he would *never* have gotten past the alternative."

Jorie lifted her head and kissed my cheek, which made me laugh. But I could still see the sadness on Jorie's face as she asked, "And now? Now he's back, what will you do? Eventually, everyone else will find out."

Inhaling deeply, I replied, "I'm hoping they won't, Jor. I'm not popular at school like you, Ruby, and Rune. If I simply disappear again, no one will notice." I shook my head. "And I doubt the Rune who came home would care anymore. I saw him in the hallway again yesterday, and the look he gave me showed me how he feels. I'm nothing to him now."

An awkward silence followed until my best friend ventured, "But you love him just as much. Am I right?"

I didn't reply. But my lack of response was as loud as a scream.

I did. I still loved him, the same as always.

A loud crash came from the front yard, shattering the intensity of our conversation. I realized a couple of hours must have passed since we arrived. Jorie got to her feet and grimaced. "Pops, I need to pee! Come inside?"

I laughed at Jorie dancing on the spot and followed her inside. Jorie pushed her way through to the bathroom at the back of the house. I waited for her in the hallway, until I heard Ruby and Deacon's voices drifting from the den.

Deciding to go and sit with them while I waited for Jorie, I opened the door and stepped inside. I was barely three steps in when I regretted ever coming to this party. Three couches dominated the small room. Ruby and Deacon occupied one, Judson and some of the football team sprawled over another. But it was the third couch I couldn't tear my eyes off. No matter how much I commanded my feet to move, they refused.

Avery was sitting on the couch, drinking from her cup. An arm was around her shoulders. Avery was tracing patterns on the hand that was hanging over her chest.

I knew what that hand felt like.

I knew how it felt to be under the protective shelter of that arm.

And I felt my heart shatter as I moved my eyes to the boy who sat by her side. As if feeling the heavy weight of my stare, he looked up. His hand stopped, drink halfway to his mouth.

Tears filled my eyes.

Understanding Rune would have moved on from me was hard enough to bear; seeing him like this brought another level of pain that I never ever thought was possible.

"Poppy? Are you okay?" Ruby's concerned voice suddenly rang across the room, forcing me to break away from the car crash I was witnessing.

Forcing a smile toward Ruby, I whispered, "Yes. I'm fine."

Feeling my legs shake from the unwanted attention of everyone in the room, I managed to step away toward the door. But as I did, I saw Avery turn in toward Rune.

Turn in for a kiss.

As the final part of my heart broke, I turned and fled the room before I could witness that kiss. I pushed into the hallway and ran to the nearest room I could find. Frantically turning the handle, I pushed through into the semi-darkness of a laundry room.

I slammed the door and leaned against the washer, unable to keep myself from bending at the waist and letting the tears pour. I fought back the sickness rising up my throat as I desperately fought to wipe the offensive image from my head.

During these past two years, I thought I'd endured all facets of pain. But I was wrong. I was so wrong. Because nothing could compare with the pain of seeing the one you love in the arms of another.

Nothing could compare to a promised lip's betrayal of a kiss.

My hands clutched at my stomach. As I fought to drag in a much-needed breath, the handle of the door began to turn.

"Don't! Go away—" I had started to shout, but before I could turn and force the door shut, someone pushed through, slamming the door in their wake.

My heart raced when I realized I was trapped in this room with someone else. But when I turned around and saw who had entered, all the blood drained from my face. I staggered back until my back hit the wall beside the washer.

The flames from the fire pit outside illuminated the dark room, enough that I could clearly see who had invaded my moment of weakness.

The same boy who caused it.

Rune stood before me, beside the closed door. Reaching out, he flipped the lock. I swallowed as his face turned back to look at me. His jaw was tense and his blue eyes were firmly fixed on me. His stare was ice-cold.

My mouth went dry. Rune took a step forward, his tall, broad body closing in on me. The pounding of my heart swept the blood through my veins, its heady sound roaring in my ears.

As he approached, my eyes lowered to take in Rune's mostly bare arms: his toned, lean muscles were corded by the tension from his balled fists; the black T-shirt showcased his firm torso; his smooth skin still retained the tint of a fading tan. In the signature move that always brought me to my knees, he lifted a hand and raked back his hair from his face.

Swallowing hard, I tried to find the courage to push past him and run away. But Rune walked forward until there was no way out for me—I was trapped.

My eyes were wide as he focused on me. Rune moved forward until we were merely inches apart. This close, I could feel the heat radiating from his body. This close, I could smell his cool scent: the one that always brought me comfort, the one that took me back to lazy summer days spent in the blossom grove. The one that brought back, in full Technicolor, that final night, when we'd made love.

I felt my cheeks flood with heat as he leaned in close. I smelled the faint hint of tobacco on his clothes, and a trace of spearmint on his warm breath. My fingers twitched at my sides as I gazed at the stubble on his jaw and chin. I wanted to reach out and touch it. Truthfully, I yearned to raise my hand and run a finger over his forehead, down his cheeks, and across his perfect lips.

But as soon as I thought of those lips, the pain sliced back through my heart. I turned my head, closing my eyes. He had touched Avery with those lips.

He had *broken* me by giving away those lips—those lips were supposed to be mine forever.

I felt him close in, until our chests almost brushed. I felt his arms rise over my head, landing on the wall above me, crowding every inch of my personal space. And I felt strands of his long hair drift across my cheek.

Rune's breathing was labored, his minty breath ghosting across my face. I squeezed my eyes even tighter. I felt him so impossibly close. But it was no use; of their own accord and ruled by my heart, my eyes slowly opened and I turned my head, our gazes crashing together.

My breath caught in my throat as the shadows from the fire outside flickered over his face. Then my breathing seemed to stop entirely when one of his hands moved from above my head, traveling hesitantly down to stroke over my hair. As soon as I felt him take a strand between his fingers, shivers broke out over my body and butterflies swooped around my stomach.

I sensed he wasn't faring any better; deep exhales and the tensing of his jaw were clear giveaways. I stared at his handsome face as he studied mine, both of us taking in the effects of the last two years: the changes, yet better still, the aspects that were completely familiar.

Then, when I wasn't sure my confused heart could take any more, his gentle touch left the safety of my hair to drift onto my face and pass feather-light fingers over the apples of my cheeks. His fingers stopped as he whispered one word, one emotionally packed word, in the most painfully desperate, gravelly voice…: "*Poppymin.*"

A teardrop escaped from my eye and splashed onto his hand.

Poppymin.

Rune's perfect name for me.

My Poppy.

His girl.

For infinity.

Forever always.

A lump clawed its rapid way up my throat as that sweet word sailed into my ears, piercing my soul. I tried in earnest to chase it down to join the rest of the pain of the last two years, but overpowered and totally defeated, I could not, and a long-caged sob slipped out.

With Rune so close, I never stood a chance.

As the loud cry escaped my lips, Rune's eyes lost their coldness and softened to shine with unshed tears. His head tipped forward, and he pressed his forehead to mine, bringing his fingers down to press over my lips.

I breathed.

He breathed.

And, against my better judgment, I let myself pretend that the last two years had never happened. I let myself pretend that he hadn't moved away. That I hadn't had to move too. That all the pain and the suffering had never been felt. And the bottomless black void that had replaced my heart was filled with light—the brightest light possible.

Rune's love. His touch and his kisses.

But this wasn't our reality. Someone banged at the laundry room door, and reality came crashing back, like a storm-whipped wave dropping on to a rain-lashed beach.

"Rune? Are you in there?" a female voice called, a voice I recognized as Avery's.

Rune's eyes flew open as Avery's knocking grew louder. He immediately drew back, watching me. Lifting my hand, I wiped at my tears. "Please…just let me go."

I tried to sound confident. I wanted to say more. But I had nothing left within me. No strength to keep up this pretense.

I was hurt.

It was written on my face for all to see.

Placing my hand on Rune's hard chest, I pushed him away, needing to get out. He let me move him from my path, only to grip my hand in his just before I reached the door. I closed my eyes, trying to gather the strength to turn to him again. When I did, more tears fell.

Rune was staring at our joined hands, his long dark-blond lashes almost black with restrained tears.

"Rune," I whispered. His eyes snapped up at the sound of my voice. "Please," I begged, as Avery knocked again.

He held on tighter.

"Rune?" Avery called, louder. "I know you're in there."

I took a step closer to Rune. He watched my every move with a deep intensity. As I reached his chest, I looked up, allowing his hand to keep its hold on mine. I met his eyes, recognizing the confusion on his face, and lifted up onto my tiptoes.

I brought my free hand to his mouth and ran the pads of my fingers over his full bottom lip. I smiled with sadness, remembering how they felt pressed against mine. I traced his defined cupid's bow, letting the tears fall as I said, "It killed me when I cut you off, Rune. It killed me not knowing what you were doing on the other side of the Atlantic." I inhaled shakily. "But nothing has ever hurt me like seeing you kiss that girl."

Rune paled, his cheeks becoming ashen. I shook my head. "I have no right to be jealous. This is all my fault. *Everything*, I know that. Yet I'm so jealous, so *hurt*, that I feel like I could die from this pain." I lowered my hand from his mouth. Looking up at him, begging with my eyes, I added, "So, please...*please* let me go. I can't be here, not right now."

Rune didn't move. I could see the shock on his face. Using this to my advantage, I pulled my hand from his and immediately unlocked the door. Without looking back or taking time to pause, I burst through, pushing past Avery, who was waiting angrily in the hallway.

And I ran. I ran past Ruby and Jorie, past Deacon and Judson, who had all gathered in the hallway to watch the unfolding drama. I ran through the many students drunk on their feet. I ran until I burst out the door into the cool night air. And then I ran again. I simply ran as fast as I could, as far away from Rune as I could manage.

"Rune!" I heard a high-pitched voice shrill in the distance, followed by a male voice, which added, "Where're you going, man? *Rune!*" But I didn't let it deter me. Taking a sharp right, I saw the entrance to the park. It was dark, and the park wasn't well lit, but it was the shortcut home.

Right now I'd give anything to be home.

The gate was open. I let my feet lead the way over the dark tree-lined path, carrying me deeper into the center of the park.

My breathing was labored. My feet hurt as the soles pounded the hard asphalt through my ballet flats. I turned left, heading for the blossom grove, when I heard footsteps behind me.

Suddenly frightened, I turned my head. Rune was sprinting after me. My heart raced faster, but this time it had nothing to do with exertion and everything to do with that look of determination on Rune's face. Rapidly, Rune was gaining on me.

I ran for a few more yards, and then I realized it was no use. As I entered the blossom grove, a place I knew so well—a place *he* knew so well—I slowed to a walk, finally bringing myself to a complete stop.

A moment later, I heard Rune enter the grove of empty trees. I heard his hard breath hammering the cool air.

I felt him move behind me.

Slowly, I spun on my heel and faced Rune. Both hands were in his hair, gripping the strands. His blue eyes were haunted, tortured. The air around us crackled with tension as we stared at one another, in silence, chests heaving, cheeks flushed.

Then Rune's gaze dropped to my lips and he inched forward. He took two steps and bit out a single, harsh question: "Why?"

He ground his teeth together as he waited for my answer. I dropped my gaze, tears filling my eyes. I shook my head and begged, "Please...don't..."

Rune ran his hand down his face. That stubborn expression I knew so well spread across his features. "*No!* God, Poppy. Why? *Why* did you do it?"

I was momentarily distracted by the thickness of his accent, a raspier husk in his already low, graveled voice. As a child, he had lost some of his Norwegian accent over the years here. But now his English was overlain by a heavy Nordic edge. It reminded me of the day we met outside his house, aged five.

But as I saw his face redden with anger, I was quickly reminded that right now that didn't matter. We weren't five anymore. Nothing was innocent. Too much had happened.

And I still couldn't tell him.

"Poppy," he insisted, his voice rising in volume as he stepped even closer. "Why the hell did you do it? Why did you never call me back? Why did you all move? Where the hell have you been? What the hell happened?"

Rune began to pace, his muscles bunching under his T-shirt. A cold wind blew through the grove and he raked back his hair. Stopping dead, he faced me and spat out, "You promised. You promised me that you'd wait for me to come back. Everything was fine, until one day I called and you didn't answer. I called and I called, but you never replied. Not a text, nothing!"

He moved until his booted feet were right against mine, towering over me. "Tell me! Tell me right now." His skin was mottled with the redness born of his anger. "I deserve to goddamn know!"

I flinched at the aggression in his voice. Flinched at the venom in his words. Flinched at the stranger standing before me.

The old Rune would never have spoken to me like this. But then I reminded myself this wasn't the Rune of old.

"I—I can't," I stuttered, barely above a whisper. Lifting my eyes, I saw the incredulous look on his face. "Please, Rune," I begged, "Don't push this. Just leave it." I swallowed, then forced myself to say, "Leave us…leave us in the past. We should move on."

Rune's head snapped back as though I had punched him.

Then he laughed. He laughed, but the sound held no humor. It was laced with fury, coated with rage.

Rune stepped one pace backward. His hands shook at his sides and he laughed one more time. Icily, he demanded, "Tell me."

I shook my head, trying to protest. He lifted his hands to his hair in frustration. "*Tell me*," he repeated. His voice had lowered an octave and radiated menace.

This time I didn't shake my head. Sadness had rendered me motionless. Sadness at seeing Rune like this. He was always quiet and withdrawn. His mamma had told me on more than one occasion that Rune had always been a sullen child. She had always feared he would give her trouble. She had told me that his innate predisposition had been to snap at people and to keep himself to himself. Even when he was a child she had noticed an air of moodiness about him, his inclination to be negative instead of positive.

But then he found you, she said. *He found you. You taught him, through your words and actions, that life didn't always have to be so serious. That life was to be lived. That life was one great adventure, to be lived well and to the fullest.*

His mamma had been right all along.

I realized, as I watched the darkness exude from this boy, that this was the Rune Mrs. Kristiansen had expected—no, feared—he would become. This was the innate moodiness she knew was harbored below the surface of her son.

A predilection to darkness, not light.

Staying quiet, I decided to turn away. To leave Rune alone with his rage.

Moonbeam hearts and sunshine smiles. I ran my mamaw's mantra through my head. I squeezed my eyes shut and forced myself to repel the pain trying to flood in. Tried to stave off this ache in my chest, the ache that told me what I didn't want to believe.

That *I* had done this to Rune.

I made to move forward, to leave, self-preservation seizing control. As I did, I felt desperate fingers wrap around my wrist and spin me back around.

Rune's pupils had all but consumed his crystal-blue irises. "No! Stand right here. Stand right here and tell me." He took in a long breath, and, losing all control, he shouted, "*Tell me why the hell you left me all alone!*"

This time, his anger was unbounded. This time, his hard words contained the force of a slap to the face. The blossom grove before me blurred; it took me a while to realize that it was my tears clouding my vision.

A tear fell to my cheek. Rune's dark gaze didn't waver.

"Who are you?" I whispered. I shook my head as Rune continued to stare, a slight tightening at the corner of his eyes the only evidence that my words had any effect. "Who are you right now?" I glanced down at his fingers, still around my wrist. Feeling my throat close, I said, "Where is the boy I love?" Risking one more look at his face, I whispered, "Where is my Rune?"

Suddenly, Rune ripped his fingers from my arm as though my skin were scalding to the touch. A nasty laugh spilled from his lips as he stared me down. His hand lifted to delicately smooth down my hair—a contradictory softness in the gesture compared to the venom with which he spoke. "You want to know where that boy went?" I swallowed as he searched every part of my face—every feature but my eyes. "You want to know where *your* Rune went?" His lip curled in disgust. As if *my* Rune were someone unworthy. As if *my* Rune weren't worth all the love that I had for him.

Leaning in, he met my eyes, his stare so severe that shivers darted down my spine. Harshly, he whispered, "That Rune died when you left him all alone." I tried to turn away, but Rune jumped in my path, making it impossible to escape his scathing cruelty. I dragged in a hurt breath, but Rune wasn't done. I could see in his eyes that he was *far* from done.

"I waited for you," he said. "I waited and waited for you to call, to explain. I called everyone I knew back here, trying to find you. But you'd vanished. Gone to care for some sick aunt I *know* doesn't exist. Your daddy wouldn't talk to me when I tried; you all blocked me out." His lips tightened as he relived the pain. I saw it. I saw it in his every move, his every word; he had been transported back to that painful place.

"I told myself to be patient, that you would explain everything in time. But as the days turned into weeks and the weeks turned into months, I stopped waiting with hope. Instead, I let in the pain. I let in the darkness that *you* created. As a year came and went, and my letters and messages went unanswered, I let the pain take hold of me until there was nothing left of the old Rune. Because I couldn't look in the mirror one more day, couldn't walk in the shoes of *that* Rune for one more damn day. Because that was the Rune that had you. That Rune was the Rune that had *Poppymin*. That Rune was the one with a full heart. Your half and mine. But your half abandoned me. It left, and it allowed what I have now to take root. Darkness. Pain. A shitload of anger."

Rune leaned in until his breath washed over my face. "*You* made me like this, Poppy. The Rune you knew died when you turned into a bitch and broke every promise you ever made."

I staggered backward, unbalanced by his words. His words that were like bullets to my heart. Rune watched me without showing guilt. I saw no sympathy in his glare. Just the cold, hard truth.

He *meant* every word.

Then, taking a lead from him, I let anger take hold. I handed the reins to all the anger I felt. I rushed forward and pushed at Rune's hard chest. Not expecting him to move, I was surprised when he fell back a single step, before quickly regaining his ground.

But I didn't stop.

I flew at him again, hot tears streaming down my face. I pushed and I pushed at his chest. Firmly grounded, Rune didn't budge. So I struck out. A sob escaped from my mouth as I hit at his torso, the muscles bunching beneath his T-shirt as I released everything that had built up inside me.

"I hate you!" I screamed at the top of my lungs. "I hate you for this! I hate this person you are now! I hate *him*, I hate *you*!" I choked on my screams and I stumbled backward, exhausted.

Seeing his glare still firmly aimed at me, I used the very last drop of my energy to shout, "I was saving you!" I breathed deeply for a few moments, then added, quietly, "I was saving you, Rune! I was saving you from the pain. I was saving you from feeling helpless, like everyone else I loved."

Rune's dark-blond eyebrows became a hard line over his eyes. Confusion distorted his beautiful face.

I stepped back one more time. "Because I couldn't see you, couldn't bear the thought of you seeing what was going to happen to me. I couldn't bear to do it to you when you were so far away." Sobs left my throat. So many sobs that my chest began to wheeze through exertion.

I coughed, clearing my throat and moving forward to where Rune was standing still, like a statue. Laying my hand over my heart, I said in a croaked voice, "I had to fight. I had to give it my all. I had to try. And I wanted you along with me more than you could ever imagine." My wet lashes began to dry in the cool breeze. "You would have dropped everything to try to get to me. You already hated your parents, hated your life in Oslo; I could hear it every time we spoke. You had grown so bitter. How could you have ever possibly coped with this?"

My head throbbed, a pounding headache taking hold.

I needed to leave. I needed to leave it all. I backed away. Rune remained deathly still. I wasn't even sure he had blinked.

"I need to go, Rune." I gripped on to my chest, knowing that the last piece of me would break with what I said next. "Let's just leave this here, in the blossom grove we loved so much. Let us end whatever we had...whatever we were." My voice had almost faded to nothing, but with a final push, I whispered, "I'll stay away from you. You stay away from me. We'll finally put us to rest. Because it has to be this way." I ducked my eyes, not wanting to see the hurt in Rune's eyes. "I can't bear all the pain." I laughed weakly.

"I need moonbeam hearts and sunshine smiles." I smiled to myself. "It's what's keeping me going. I won't stop believing in a beautiful world. I won't let it break me." I forced myself to look at Rune. "And I won't be the cause of any more hurt for you."

As I turned my head, I saw a fissure of agony fracture Rune's expression. But I didn't stall. I ran. I ran fast, just managing to pass my favorite tree when Rune grabbed my arm and swung me around again.

"What?" he demanded. "What the hell are you talking about?" He was breathing harshly. "You just explained nothing! You spout about saving me and sparing me. But from what? What did you think I couldn't handle?"

"Rune, please," I begged and pushed him away. He was on me in a flash, hands on my shoulders, anchoring me in place.

"Answer me!" he shouted.

I pushed from him again. "Let me go!" My heart raced with trepidation. My skin prickled with goose bumps. I turned to go again, but his hands held me still. I struggled and struggled, trying to get away, for once trying to flee the tree whose shelter always brought me solace.

"Let me go!" I shouted again.

Rune leaned in. "No, tell me. Explain yourself!" he shouted back.

"Rune—"

"Explain!" he shouted, cutting me off.

I shook my head faster, trying, to no avail, to escape. "Please! Please!" I begged.

"Poppy!"

"NO!"

"EXPLAIN!"

"I'M DYING!" I screamed into the silent grove, unable to take it anymore. "I'm dying," I added breathlessly. "I'm…dying…"

As I clutched my chest, trying to catch my breath, the enormity of what I'd done slowly filtered into my brain. My heart pounded. It pounded from the onslaught of panic. It pounded and raced with the terrifying knowledge of what I'd just admitted…of what I'd just confessed.

I continued to stare at the ground. Somewhere in my brain, it registered that Rune's hands had frozen on my shoulders. As I felt the heat from his palms, I also realized that they were shaking. I heard his breath, dragging and labored.

I forced myself to raise my gaze and lock on to Rune's. His eyes were wide and racked with pain.

At that moment, I hated myself. Because that look in his eyes, that haunted, gutting stare, was the reason I had broken my promise to him two years ago.

It was why I'd had to set him free.

As it turned out, I had only imprisoned him with bars of rage instead.

"Poppy…," he whispered, accent heavy, as his face paled to the whitest of white.

"I have Hodgkin lymphoma. It's advanced. And it's terminal." My voice trembled as I added, "I have a matter of months left to live, Rune. There's nothing anyone can do."

I waited. I waited to see what Rune had to say, but he said nothing. Instead, he backed away. His eyes traveled over my face, searching for any sign of deception. When none was found, he shook his head. A soundless "no" left his mouth. Then he ran. He turned his back on me, and he ran.

It was many minutes before I found the strength to move.

It was ten minutes after that when I walked through the door of my house, where my mama and daddy were sitting with the Kristiansens.

But it was only seconds after seeing me when my mama rushed to where I stood, and I fell into her arms.

Where I broke my heart for the heart I'd just broken.

The one I'd always strived to save.

8

Scattered Breaths and Haunted Souls

Rune

I'M DYING…I'm dying…dying…I have Hodgkin lymphoma. It's advanced. And it's terminal…I have a matter of months left to live, Rune. There's nothing anyone can do…

I sprinted through the darkness of the park as Poppy's words circled around and around my mind. *I'M DYING…I'm dying…dying…I have a matter of months left to live, Rune. There's nothing anyone can do…*

Pain, the like of which I never knew was possible, pierced my heart. It sliced, stabbed and throbbed away at me until my feet skidded to a stop and I fell to my knees. I tried to breathe, but the pain had barely just begun, moving to rip through my lungs until nothing was left. It traveled with lightning speed through my body, taking all, until only pain remained.

I'd been wrong. I'd been so wrong.

I had thought that Poppy cutting me off for two years was the greatest pain I would ever have to endure. It had changed me, fundamentally changed me. Being broken up, simply being frozen out hurt…but this…this…

Falling forward, crippled by the pain in my stomach, I roared into the darkness of the empty park. My hands scratched at the hard earth beneath my palms, twigs slicing at my fingers, ripping up my nails.

But I welcomed it. This pain I could cope with, but the pain inside…

Poppy's face flashed into my mind's eye. Her perfect damn face as she entered the den tonight. Her smiling face finding Ruby and Deacon, and that smile fading from her lips when her eyes found mine. I saw the devastation flash across her face when she saw Avery sitting beside me, my arm around her shoulders.

What she hadn't seen was me watching her from the kitchen window as she sat outside with Jorie. She hadn't seen me arrive when I'd never planned to be there in the first place. When Judson texted me that Poppy had arrived, nothing could hold me back.

She'd ignored me. From the minute I saw her in the hallway last week, she'd never said a word to me.

And it killed me.

I thought when I came back to Blossom Grove there would be answers. I thought I'd discover why she pulled away.

I choked on a strangled sob. I never, ever, in my wildest dreams, thought it could be anything like this. Because it's Poppy. *Poppymin.* My Poppy.

She couldn't die.

She couldn't leave me behind.

She couldn't leave any of us behind.

Nothing made sense if she wasn't around. She had more life to live. She was meant to be with me for eternity.

Poppy and Rune for infinity.

Forever always.

Months? I couldn't…she couldn't…

My body shook as another raw bellow ripped from my throat, the feeling of this pain no less than if I were being hung, drawn, and quartered.

Tears fell freely down my face, pouring on to the dried dirt below my hands. My body was stuck in place, and my legs refused to move.

I didn't know what to do. What the hell was there to do? How did you get past not being able to help?

Tipping my head back to the star-filled sky, I closed my eyes. "Poppy," I whispered as the salt from my tears forced its way into my mouth. "*Poppymin,*" I murmured again, my endearment fading to nothing on the breeze.

In my mind I saw Poppy's green eyes, as real as if she were sitting in front of me...*I have a matter of months left to live, Rune. There's nothing anyone can do...*

This time my cries didn't clog in my throat. They were freed and they were many. My body shuddered with the force of them when I thought of what she must have gone through. Without me. Without me beside her, holding her hand. Without me kissing her head. Without me holding her in my arms when she was sad, when the treatment made her weak. I thought of her facing all of that pain with only half a heart. Half of her soul struggling to cope without its counterpart.

Mine.

I wasn't sure how long I sat in the park. It felt like forever until I was able to stand. And as I walked, I felt like an imposter in my own body. Like I was trapped in a nightmare, and when I woke up I would be fifteen again. None of this would be happening. I would wake up in the blossom grove under our favorite tree, with *Poppymin* in my arms. She'd laugh at me when I woke up, pulling my arm tighter around her waist. She'd tip up her head, and I'd lower my head for a kiss.

And we'd kiss.

We'd kiss and we'd kiss. When I pulled back, with the sunlight on her face, she'd smile at me with her eyes still closed and whisper, "*Kiss two thousand and fifty-three. In the blossom grove, beneath our favorite tree. With my Rune...and my heart almost burst.*" I'd gather my camera in my hands and I'd wait, my eye ready at the lens for the moment she would open her eyes. *That* moment. That magical captured moment, where I'd see in her eyes how much she loved me. And I'd tell her I loved her back as I ran the back of my hand gently down her cheek. Later I'd hang that picture on my wall so I could see it every single day...

The sound of an owl hooting pulled me from my daze. When I blinked back the fantasy, it hit me like a truck—it was exactly that: a fantasy. Then the pain surged back and stabbed me with the truth. I couldn't bring myself to believe that she was dying.

My vision blurred with fresh tears, and it took me a moment to realize that I was at the tree that I'd pictured in my dreams. The one we always sat below. But when I looked up at it in the darkness, with the cool wind whipping through its branches, my stomach turned. The branches bare of leaves, their spindly arms twisting and turning, all reflected this moment in time.

The moment I knew that *my* girl was leaving.

I forced myself to walk; somehow, my feet led me home. But as I walked, my mind was a jumble of uncertainty—scattered, refusing to pin anything down. I didn't know what to do, where to go. Tears poured ceaselessly from my eyes; the pain inside my body was settling into a new home. No part of me was spared.

I did it to save you...

Nothing could save me from this. The thought of her so sick, fighting to keep the light she beamed so bright from fading, destroyed me.

Arriving at my house, I stared across at the window that had captivated me for twelve years. I knew she was on the opposite side. The house was in darkness. But as I moved my feet forward, I slowly ground to a halt.

I couldn't...I couldn't face her...I couldn't—

Turning on my heel, I rushed up the steps to my house and burst through the door. Tears of anger and sadness were ripping through me, both fighting for dominance. I was being torn apart from the inside.

I passed the living room. "Rune!" my mamma called. I instantly heard the catch in her voice.

My feet drew to a stop. When I faced my mamma, who was standing up from the couch, I saw tears tracking down her cheeks.

It hit me like a hammerblow.

She *knew*.

Mamma stepped forward, her hand outstretched. I stared at it, but I couldn't take it. I couldn't...

I rushed for my bedroom. I smashed through the door, and then I just stood there. I stood dead center and looked around, searching for an idea of what to do next.

But I didn't know. My hands lifted to my hair and gripped at the strands. I choked on the sounds leaving my mouth. I drowned in the damn tears tracking down my cheeks, because I didn't know what the hell to do.

I took a step forward, then stopped. I moved to go to my bed; then I stopped. My heart thumped in a slow, lurching beat. I fought to drag air through my clogged lungs. I fought to not fall to the floor.

And then I broke.

I let the waiting anger free. I let it infuse me and carry me forward. Reaching my bed, I bent to grip the frame and, with a loud roar, I lifted it with all my strength, overturning the mattress and the sturdy wooden frame. I moved to my desk and, with one swipe, cleared the top. Catching my laptop before it hit the floor, I spun where I stood and hurled it into the wall. I heard it shatter, but it didn't help. Nothing was helping. The pain was still here. The gut-wrenching truth.

The goddamn tears.

Clenching my fists, I threw back my head and I screamed. I screamed and I screamed until my voice was rough and my throat was raw. Dropping to my knees, I let myself drown in this grief.

Then I heard my door open and I glanced up. My mamma stepped through. I shook my head, raising my hand to ward her off. But she kept coming.

"No," I rasped, trying to move out of her way. But she didn't listen; instead she dropped to the floor beside me. "No!" I spat out harder, but her arms stretched out and wrapped around my neck.

"No!" I fought, but she pulled me to her, and I lost all that fight. I collapsed into her arms and I cried. I screamed and I cried into the arms of the woman I'd barely spoken to in two years. But right now, I needed her. I needed someone who understood.

Understood what losing Poppy would be like.

So I let it all out. I gripped on to her so tight I thought it would leave a bruise. But my mamma never moved; she cried with me. She sat quietly, cradling my head as I lost all strength.

Then I heard movement from the doorway.

My pappa was watching us with tears in his eyes, sadness on his face. And that reignited the flame in my stomach. Seeing the man who took me away, who forced me from Poppy when she was about to need me most, snapped something inside.

Pushing back from my mamma, I hissed at him, "Get out."

My mamma stiffened and I pushed her back farther, glaring at my pappa. He held up his hands, shock now etched across his face. "Rune…," he said in a calm voice.

It only fueled the flames.

"I said get out!" I stumbled to my feet.

My pappa glanced at my mamma. When he looked back at me, my hands were clenched. I embraced the rage burning inside me.

"Rune, son. You're in shock, you're hurting—"

"Hurting? *Hurting?* You have no damn idea!" I roared and stepped an inch closer to where he stood. My mamma jumped to her feet. I ignored her as she tried to move into my path. My pappa reached forward and pushed her behind him and out into the hallway.

My pappa closed the door slightly, blocking her out.

"Get the hell out," I said one last time, feeling all the hatred I had for this man boiling to the surface.

"I'm sorry, son," he whispered, and he let a teardrop fall to his cheek. He had the audacity to stand before me and shed a tear.

He had no friggin' right!

"Don't," I warned, my voice cut and raw. "Don't you dare stand there and cry. Don't you dare stand there and tell me you're sorry. You have no damn right when you were the one who took me away. You took me from her when I didn't want to go. You took me from her while she got sick. And now… now…she's dy—" I couldn't finish the sentence. I couldn't bring myself to say that word. Instead, I ran. I ran at my pappa and slammed my hands on his broad chest.

He staggered back and hit the wall. "Rune!" I heard my mamma shout from the hallway. Ignoring her plea, I fisted my pappa's collar in my hands and brought my face to hover just in front of his.

"You took me away for two years. And because I was gone she cut me off to *save* me. *Me.* Save me from the pain of being so far away and not being able to comfort her or hold her when she was in pain. You made it so I couldn't be with her while she fought." I swallowed but managed to add, "And now it's too late. She has months…" My voice broke. "*Months…*" I threw my hands down and stepped back, more tears and pain taking hold.

With my back to him, I said, "There's no coming back from this. I'll never forgive you for taking me away from her. Never. We're done."

"Rune..."

"Get out," I snarled. "Get the hell out of my room and get the hell out of my life. I'm done with you. So damn done."

Seconds later I heard the door shut, and the house fell into silence. But to me, in this moment, the house sounded like it was screaming.

Pushing the hair from my face, I slumped down on the overturned mattress, then leaned my back against the wall. For minutes, or it could have been hours, I stared at nothing. My room was dark save for the light from a small lamp in the corner of the room that somehow had survived my rage.

I lifted my eyes, and they settled on a photo hanging on the wall. I frowned, knowing I hadn't put it there. My mamma must have hung it today when she unpacked my room.

And I stared.

I stared at Poppy, only days before we left, dancing in the blossom grove, the cherry blossoms she loved so much in full flower around her. Her arms were stretched to the sky as she twirled, her head tipped back as she laughed.

My heart clenched at seeing her this way. Because *this* was *Poppymin*. The girl who made me smile. The girl who would run to the blossom grove, laughing and dancing all the way.

The one who'd told me to stay away from her. *I'll stay away from you. You stay away from me. We'll finally put us to rest...*

But I couldn't. I couldn't leave her. She couldn't leave me. She needed me and I needed her. I didn't care what she had said; there was no way I was leaving her to endure this alone. I couldn't if I tried.

Before I could overthink it, I jumped to my feet and raced to the window. I took one glance at the window opposite mine and let instinct take control. As quietly as possible, I opened my window and climbed through. My heart beat in tandem with my feet as I pounded across the grass. I stopped dead. Then with a deep breath, I placed my hand under the window and pulled up. It moved.

It was unlocked.

It was as if no time had passed. I climbed inside and gently closed the window. A curtain was in the way, something that wasn't there before. Silently pushing it aside, I stepped forward, stopping as I drank in the familiar room.

Poppy's sweet-scented perfume, the one she'd always worn, hit my nose first. I closed my eyes, chasing away the heaviness on my chest. When I opened them again, my eyes fell to Poppy in her bed. Her breathing was soft as she slept, facing me, her body illuminated only by the dull glow of her nightlight.

Then my stomach dropped. How the hell did she think I would ever stay away? Even if she hadn't told me why she cut me off, I would have found my way back to her. Even through all the hurt, pain and anger, I would have been drawn back, like a moth to a flame.

I could never stay away.

But as I drank her in, her pink lips pursed in sleep, her face flushed with warmth, I felt as if a spear had slammed into my chest. I was going to lose her.

I was going to lose the only reason I lived.

I rocked on my feet. I struggled to cope with the thought. Tears fell onto my cheeks, just as an old floorboard creaked beneath me. I squeezed my eyes shut. When my eyes opened, it was to see Poppy staring at me from her bed, her eyes heavy with sleep. Then, clearly seeing my face—the tears on my cheeks, the grief in my eyes—her expression morphed into a mask of pain, and slowly, she opened her arms.

It was instinctive. A primal power that only Poppy held over me. My feet dragged me forward at the sight of those arms; my legs finally gave out as I reached the bed, knees hitting the floor, head falling into Poppy's lap. And, like a dam, I burst. The tears came thick and fast as Poppy wrapped her arms around my head.

Lifting my arms, I wrapped them—iron-tight—around her waist. Poppy's fingers stroked through my hair as, shaking, I fell apart in her lap, tears drenching the nightdress covering her thighs.

"Shh," Poppy whispered, rocking me back and forth. The sweet sound was like heaven to my ears. "It's okay," she added. It struck me hard that she was comforting me. But I couldn't stop the pain. I couldn't stop the grief.

And I held her. I held her so tightly I thought she would ask me to let go. But she didn't, and I wouldn't. I didn't dare let go, in case when I lifted my head she wasn't here.

I needed her to be here.

I needed her to stay.

"It's okay," Poppy soothed again. This time, I lifted my head until our eyes met.

"It's not," I said hoarsely. "Nothing about this is okay."

Poppy's eyes were shining, but no tears fell. Instead, she tipped my face up, one finger under my chin, and she stroked down my wet cheek with another. I watched, not breathing, as a small smile began tugging on her lips.

My stomach flipped, the first sensation I had felt in my body since the numbness that followed her revelation had overtaken me.

"There you are," she said, so quietly I almost missed it. "My Rune."

My heart stopped beating.

Her face melted into pure happiness as she pushed the hair off my forehead and ran her fingertip down my nose and along the edge of my jaw. I stayed completely still, trying to commit this moment to memory—a photo in my mind. Her hands on my face. That look of happiness, that light shining from within.

"I used to wonder what you looked like, older. I wondered if you had cut your hair. I wondered if you had grown taller, changed in size. I wondered if your eyes had stayed the same." The side of her lip twitched. "I wondered if you had grown more handsome, which seemed impossible to me." Her smile fell. "And I see you have. When I saw you in the hallway last week, I couldn't believe you were there, standing in front of me, more beautiful than I could ever have imagined." She pulled playfully on my hair. "With your bright blond hair longer still. Your eyes as vibrant a blue as they'd ever been. And so tall and broad." Poppy's eyes met mine, and she said softly, "My Viking."

My eyes closed as I tried to chase away the lump in my throat. When I opened them, Poppy was watching me like she always did—in complete adoration.

Rising higher on my knees, I leaned closer, seeing Poppy's eyes soften as I pressed my forehead to hers, as carefully as if she were a china doll. As soon as our skin touched, I drew in a long breath and whispered, "*Poppymin.*"

This time it was Poppy's tears that fell to her lap. I pushed my hand into her hair and held her close. "Don't cry, *Poppymin*. I can't stand to see your tears."

"You mistake their meaning," she whispered in return.

I moved my head back slightly, searching her eyes. Poppy's gaze met mine and she smiled. I could see the contentment on her pretty face as she explained, "I never thought I would hear you say that word to me again." She swallowed hard. "I never thought I would feel you this close to me again. I never dreamed I would feel *this* again."

"Feel what?" I asked.

"This," she said and brought my hand to her chest. Right over her heart. It was racing. I stilled, feeling something in my own chest stirring back to life, and she said, "I never thought I'd ever feel fully whole again." A tear fell from her eye and onto my hand, splashing on my skin. "I never thought I'd regain half my heart before I…" She trailed off, but we both knew what she meant. Her smile dropped and her gaze bored through to my own. "Poppy and Rune. Two halves of the same whole. Reunited at last. When it matters most."

"*Poppy*…," I said, but couldn't fend off the whip of pain cracking deep inside.

Poppy blinked, then blinked again, until all her tears were gone. She stared at me, her head dropping to one side, like she was working out a difficult puzzle.

"Poppy," I said, my voice husky and coarse. "Let me stay awhile. I can't…I can't…I don't know what to do…"

Poppy's warm palm landed gently on my cheek. "There's nothing to do, Rune. Nothing to do but weather the storm."

My words became trapped in my throat and I closed my eyes. When they opened again, she was watching me.

"I'm not scared," she assured me confidently, and I could see that she meant it. One hundred percent meant it. My Poppy. Tiny in size but filled with courage and light.

I had never been more proud to love her than I was at that moment.

My attention dropped to her bed—a bed that was bigger than the one she had had two years ago. She seemed too small for the large mattress. As she sat in the center, she looked like a little girl.

Clearly seeing me looking at the bed, Poppy shuffled back. I could detect an edge of wariness in her expression, and I couldn't blame her. I knew I was not the boy she waved goodbye to two years ago. I was changed.

I wasn't sure I could be *her* Rune ever again.

Poppy swallowed, and after a moment's hesitation, she patted the mattress beside her. My heart raced. She was letting me stay. After everything. After everything I'd done since I returned, she was letting me stay.

As I made to stand up, my legs felt unsteady. The tears had stained my cheeks, grated my throat to soreness, and the grief, the surreal revelation about the pain of Poppy's illness...it had left a residual numbness in my body. Every inch of me broken, patched back up with Band-Aids—Band-Aids over open wounds.

Temporary.

Futile.

Useless.

I toed off my boots, then climbed onto the bed. Poppy shifted to lie on her natural side of the bed, and I, awkwardly, lay on mine. In a move so familiar to us both, we turned onto our sides and faced one another.

But it wasn't as familiar as it once was. Poppy had changed. I had changed. Everything had changed.

And I didn't know how to adjust.

Minutes and minutes of silence ticked by. Poppy seemed content to watch me. But I had one question. The one question I had wanted to ask her when the contact stopped. The thought that had burrowed inside of me, turning dark for want of an answer. The one thought that made me feel sick. The one question that still had the potential to rip me apart. Even now, when my world couldn't shatter anymore.

"Ask me," Poppy said suddenly, keeping her voice low so as not to wake her parents. Surprise must have shown on my face, because she shrugged, looking so damn cute. "I may not know the boy you are now, but I recognize that expression. The one that's building up to a question."

I ran my finger over the sheet between us, my attention focused on the movement I was making. "You do know me," I whispered in reply, wanting to believe that more than anything. Because Poppy was the only one who ever truly knew the real me. Even now, buried under all this rage and anger, after the distance of two silent years, she still knew the heart underneath.

Poppy's fingers moved closer to mine in the neutral territory between us. The no-man's-land that separated our bodies. As I watched our two hands, straining for each other, but not quite reaching, I was engulfed with the need to get my camera, a need I hadn't felt for a long time.

I wanted this moment captured.

I wanted this picture. I wanted this moment in time, to hold on to forever.

"I know some of your question, I think," Poppy said, pulling me back from my thoughts. Her cheeks blushed, deep pink spreading over her fair skin. "I'll be honest, since you've returned, I don't recognize much. But there are times that there are glimpses of the boy I love. Enough to inspire hope that he still lies in wait underneath." Her face was determined. "I think, above anything, that I want to see him fight through what has him hidden. I think seeing him again is my biggest wish, before I go."

I turned my head away, unwilling to listen to her talk about leaving, about the letdown I was, about the fact that her time was running out. Then, like a soldier's act of courage, her hand breached the distance between us and her fingertip grazed over mine. I turned my head back around. My fingers opened at her touch. Poppy ran her fingertip along the flesh of my palm, tracing the lines.

The hint of a smile came on her lips. My stomach sank, wondering how many more times I would see that smile. Wondering how she found the strength to smile at all.

Then, slowly retreating to where it had lain before, Poppy's hand grew still. She looked at me, patiently waiting for the question that I still had not asked.

Feeling my heart race in trepidation, I opened my mouth and asked, "Was the silence…was it only about…your illness, or was it…was it because…" Images from our final night flashed into my brain. Me lying over her body, our mouths pressed together in slow, soft kisses. Poppy telling me she was ready. Us losing our clothes, me watching her face as I pushed forward, and afterward as she lay in my arms. Falling asleep beside her, nothing left unsaid between us.

"What?" Poppy asked, wide-eyed.

Taking in a quick breath, I blurted, "Was it because I pushed too far? Did I force you? Pressure you?" Biting the bullet, I asked, "Did you regret it?"

Poppy tensed, her eyes glistening. I wondered for a minute if she was about to cry, confess that what I had feared these past two years was true. That I hurt her. She put her trust in me and I hurt her.

Instead, Poppy rose from the bed and knelt down. I heard her pulling something out from underneath. When she rose to her feet, in her hand was a familiar glass mason jar. A mason jar filled with hundreds of pink paper hearts.

A thousand boy-kisses.

Poppy carefully kneeled on the bed, and tipping the jar in the direction of the nightlight's glow, she opened the lid and began to search. As her hand swilled around the paper hearts, I tracked the ones that traveled past the glass on my side. Most were blank. The jar was coated in dust—a sign it hadn't been opened for a long time.

A mixture of sadness and hope stirred inside me.

Hope that no other boy had touched her lips.

Sadness that the greatest adventure of her life had come to standstill. No more kisses.

Then that sadness cut a hole right through me.

Months. She only had months left, not a lifetime, to fill this jar. She would never write the message on a heart on her wedding day like she wanted. She would never be a mamaw, reading these kisses to her grandchildren. She wouldn't even live out her teens.

"Rune?" Poppy asked when new tears fell down my cheeks. I used the back of my hand to wipe them away. I hesitated to meet Poppy's eyes. I didn't want to make her feel sad. Instead, when I glanced up, all I saw on Poppy's face was understanding, an understanding that quickly changed to shyness.

Nervousness.

In her outstretched hand was a pink heart. Only this heart wasn't blank. It was full, both sides. This heart's ink was pink, practically disguising the message.

Poppy pushed her hand farther out. "Take it," she insisted. I did as she asked.

Sitting up, I shifted into the path of light. I focused hard on the light ink, until I could make out the words:

Kiss three hundred and fifty-five.
   In my bedroom. After I made love to my Rune. My heart almost burst.

I turned the heart over and read the other side.
I stopped breathing.

It was the best night of my life…as special as special can be.

I closed my eyes, yet another wash of emotion flowing through me. If I had been standing, I'm sure it would have brought me to my knees.

Because she loved it.

That night, what we did, it was wanted. I hadn't hurt her.

I choked down on a noise that was slipping up my throat. Poppy's hand was on my arm. "I thought I'd destroyed us," I whispered, looking into her eyes. "I thought you'd regretted us."

"I didn't," she whispered back. With a shaking hand, a gesture rusty from too much time spent apart, she pushed back the fallen strands of hair from my face. I closed my eyes under her touch, then opened them when she said, "When everything happened…," she explained, "when I was seeking treatment"—tears, this time, did slip down her cheeks—"when that treatment stopped working…I thought of that night often." Poppy closed her eyes, her long dark lashes kissing her cheek. Then she smiled. Her hand stilled in my hair. "I thought of how gentle you were with me. How it felt… to be with you, that close. Like we were the two halves of the heart we always called ourselves." She sighed. "It was like home. You and me, together, were infinity—we were joined. In that moment, that moment when our breathing was rough and you held me so tightly…it was the best moment of my life."

Her eyes opened again. "It was the moment I replayed when it hurt.

It is the moment I think of when I slip, when I begin to feel scared. It's the moment that reminds me that I'm lucky. Because in that moment I experienced the love my mamaw sent me on this adventure of a thousand boy-kisses to find. That moment when you know that you are loved so much, that you are the center of somebody's world so wonderfully, that you *lived*... even if it was only for a short time."

Keeping the paper heart in one hand, I reached up with the other and brought Poppy's wrist to my lips. I pressed a small kiss over her pulse, feeling it flutter beneath my mouth. She drew in a sharp breath.

"No one else has kissed your lips but me, have they?" I asked.

"No," she said. "I promised you I wouldn't. Even though we weren't speaking. Even though I never thought I'd see you again, I would never break my promise. These lips are yours. They were only ever yours."

My heart stuttered and, releasing her wrist, I lifted my fingers to press them across her lips—the lips that she had gifted to me.

Poppy's breathing slowed as I touched her mouth. Her lashes fluttered and heat built in her cheeks. My breathing quickened. Quickened because I had ownership of those lips. They were still mine.

Forever always.

"Poppy," I whispered and leaned toward her. Poppy froze, but I didn't kiss her. I wouldn't. I could see that she couldn't read me. She didn't know me.

I hardly knew myself these days.

Instead, I laid my lips on my own fingers—still over her lips, forming a barrier between our mouths—and just breathed her in. I inhaled her scent—sugar and vanilla. My body felt energized simply from being near her.

Then my heart cracked down the center as I moved back and she asked brokenly, "How many?"

I frowned. I searched her face for a clue to what she was asking. Poppy swallowed, and this time, she placed her fingers over my lips. "How many?" she repeated.

I knew then exactly what she was asking. Because she stared at my lips like they were a betrayer. She stared at them like something she once loved, lost, and could never win back.

Ice-coldness ran through me as Poppy pulled her shaking hand away.

Her expression was guarded, her breath held in her chest as though protecting herself from what I would say. But I didn't say anything. I couldn't; that look on her face slew me.

Poppy exhaled and said, "I know about Avery, of course, but were there any others in Oslo? I mean, I know there will have been, but, was it a lot?"

"Does it matter?" I asked, my voice low. Poppy's paper heart was still in my hand, the significance of it almost scalding my skin.

The promise of our lips.

The promise of our halved hearts.

Forever always.

Poppy slowly began to shake her head, but then, shoulders slumping, she nodded once. "Yes," she whispered, "it matters. It shouldn't. I set you free." She dropped her head. "But it does. It matters more than you'd understand."

She was wrong. I understood why it mattered so much. It did to me too.

"I was away a long time," I said. In that moment, I knew that the anger that held me captive had taken back control. Some sick part of me wanted to hurt her like she'd hurt me.

"I know," Poppy agreed, her head still low.

"I'm seventeen," I continued. Poppy's eyes snapped to mine.

Her face had paled. "Oh," she said, and I could hear every hint of pain in that tiny word. "So what I feared is true. You have been with others, intimately...like you were with me. I...I just..."

Poppy moved to the edge of the bed, but I reached out and caught her retreating wrist. "Why does it matter?" I demanded, and saw her eyes glisten with tears.

The anger within me dimmed slightly, but it came back as I thought of those lost years. Years I'd spent drinking and partying away my pain, while Poppy was sick. It almost made me shake with rage.

"I don't know," Poppy said, then shook her head. "That was a lie. Because I do know. It's because you're mine. And despite it all, all the things that have happened between us, I kept a vain hope that you would keep your promise. That it meant that much to you too. Despite everything."

I dropped my hand from her wrist, and Poppy got to her feet. She headed for her door. Just as she reached for the doorknob, I said quietly, "It did."

Poppy froze, her back bunched. "What?"

She didn't turn. Instead, I got to my feet and walked to where she stood. I leaned down, making sure that she would hear my confession. My breath blew her hair from her ear, as I said, so quietly I could barely hear myself, "The promise did mean as much to me. You meant that much to me...you still do. Somewhere, underneath all this anger...there's you and only you. It will always be that way for me." Poppy still hadn't moved. I drew in closer. "Forever always."

She turned, until our chests were touching and her green eyes were staring into mine. "You...I don't understand," she said.

I slowly lifted my hand and pushed it through her hair. Poppy's eyes fluttered to a close as I did so, but they opened again to watch me. "I kept my promise," I admitted and watched the shock cross her face.

She shook her head. "But I saw...you kissed—"

"*I kept my promise,*" I interrupted. "Since the day I left you, I haven't kissed anyone else. My lips are still yours. There's never been anyone else. There never will be."

Poppy's mouth opened, then closed. When it opened again, she said, "But you and Avery..."

My jaw clenched. "I knew you were near. I was pissed. I wanted to hurt you like you hurt me." Poppy shook her head in disbelief. I stepped closer still. "I knew seeing me with Avery would do that to you. So I sat beside her and waited until you appeared. I wanted you to believe that I was about to kiss her...until I saw your face. Until I saw you run from the room. Until I couldn't stand seeing the pain I'd caused."

Tears spilled down Poppy's cheeks. "Why would you do that? Rune, you wouldn't—"

"I would and I did," I said curtly.

"Why?" she whispered.

I smiled humorlessly. "Because you're right. I'm not the boy you knew. I was filled with so much anger when I was taken from you that after a while, it was the only thing I felt. I tried to hide it when we talked, fought against it, knowing I still had you with me even if we were thousands of miles apart. But when you cut me off, I didn't care anymore. I let it consume me. It has consumed me so much since then that it has *become* me." I reached down for Poppy's hand and brought it over my chest.

"I'm half a heart. This, who I am now, was due to a life devoid of you. This darkness, this anger, was born from you not being by my side. *Poppymin*. My adventurer. My girl." And then the pain returned. For that brief few minutes, I had forgotten our new reality. "And now," I said through gritted teeth, "now you tell me you're leaving me for good. I…" I choked on my words.

"Rune," Poppy murmured and threw herself into my arms, wrapping hers tightly around my waist.

Instantly, my arms locked around her like a vise. As her body melted into mine, I breathed. I breathed the first clean breath in a long while. Then it became restricted, strangled, when I said, "I can't lose you, *Poppymin*. I can't. I can't let you go. I can't live without you. You're my forever always. You're meant to walk beside me through this life. You need me and I need you. That's all there is to it." I felt her shaking in my arms. "I won't be able to let you go. Because wherever you go, I have to go too. I've tried living without you; it doesn't work."

Slowly, and as carefully as she could, Poppy lifted her head, separating our bodies just enough to look at me and whisper brokenly, "I can't take you with me where I'm going."

As her words sunk in, I stumbled back, freeing my arms from around her waist. I didn't stop until I sat down on the edge of the bed. I couldn't handle it. *How the hell do I deal with all of this?*

I couldn't understand how Poppy could be so strong.

How did she face this death sentence with such dignity? All I wanted to do was curse at the world, to destroy everything in my path.

My head fell forward. And I cried. I cried tears that I didn't realize I had left. It was my reserve, the last wave of the devastation I was feeling. The tears that acknowledged the truth I didn't want to accept.

That *Poppymin* was dying.

She was really, truly dying.

I felt the bed dip beside me. I smelled her sweet scent. I followed her as she guided me to lie back in bed. I followed her silent instruction to fall into her arms. I released everything that had been pent up inside as she stroked her hands through my hair. I wrapped my arms around her waist and held on, trying my damnedest to memorize how this felt. How she felt in my arms. Her heartbeat strong and her body warm.

I wasn't sure how much time had passed, but, eventually, the tears dried up. I didn't move from Poppy's arms. She didn't stop caressing my back with her fingers.

I managed to wet my throat enough to ask, "How did it all happen, *Poppymin*? How did you find out?"

Poppy was quiet for a few seconds before she sighed. "It doesn't matter, Rune."

I sat up and looked into her eyes. "I want to know."

Poppy ran the back of her hand over my cheek and nodded. "I know you do. And you will. But not tonight. This—us, like this—is all that matters tonight. Nothing more."

I didn't break my gaze from hers, and neither did she. A numb kind of peace had settled between us. The air was thick as I leaned in, wanting nothing more than to press my mouth to hers. To feel her lips against mine.

To add another kiss to her jar.

When my mouth was just a hairsbreadth from Poppy's, I moved to kiss her cheek instead. It was soft and gentle.

But it wasn't enough.

Shifting upward, I pressed another kiss, and another, to every inch of her cheek, over her forehead and across her nose. Poppy shifted beneath me. As I drew back, I guessed from the understanding in her expression that Poppy knew I wasn't pushing things.

Because as much as I didn't want to accept it, we were different people now. The boy and girl who kissed each other as easily as breathing had changed.

A true kiss would come when we'd worked our way back to us.

I planted one more kiss on the end of Poppy's nose, causing a light giggle to spill from her lips. It seemed as if the anger had subsided just enough to allow me to feel its joy take root in my heart.

As I pressed my forehead to Poppy's, I assured her, "My lips are yours. Not for anyone else."

In response, Poppy whispered a kiss on my cheek. I felt the effect of this kiss travel all through my body. I tucked my head in the crook of her neck and allowed myself a small smile when she whispered in my ear, "My lips are yours too."

I rolled to pull Poppy into my arms, and our eyes eventually drifted to a close. I fell asleep quicker than I thought. Tired, heartbroken, and emotionally scarred, I fell asleep quickly. But then it always did when Poppy was by my side.

It was the third moment that defined my life. The night I found out I would lose the girl I loved. Knowing our moments together were numbered, I held on to her tighter, refusing to let go.

She fell asleep doing exactly the same...

...a powerful echo of who we used to be.

The sound of rustling woke me.

I rubbed the sleep from my eyes. Poppy's quiet silhouette drifted toward the window. "*Poppymin*?"

Poppy halted, then finally looked back at me. I swallowed, chasing away the razor blades in my throat, as Poppy came to stand before me. She was wearing a thick parka coat over track pants and a sweater. A backpack lay at her feet.

I frowned. It was still dark.

"What are you doing?"

Poppy made her way back to the window, looking back to playfully ask, "Are you coming?"

She grinned at me and my heart cracked. It splintered at how beautiful she was. My lips curved upward at her infectious happiness, and I asked again, "Where the hell are you going?"

Poppy pulled back the curtain and pointed at the sky. "To watch the sunrise." She cocked her head to the side as she looked at me. "I know it's been a while, but did you forget I did this?"

A wave of warmth flowed through me. I hadn't forgotten.

Getting to my feet, I allowed myself a small huff of a laugh. I immediately stopped. Poppy noticed, and sighing sadly, she walked back to me. I glanced down at her, wanting nothing more than to wrap my hand around the nape of her neck and take her mouth with my own.

Poppy studied my face, then took my hand. Taken aback, I stared down at her fingers, wrapped around mine. They looked so small as they gently squeezed my hand.

"It's okay, you know?" she said.

"What?" I asked, edging closer.

Poppy's grip stayed on my hand as the other lifted toward my face. She rose to her tiptoes and laid her fingertips on my lips.

My heart beat a little faster.

"It's okay to laugh," she said, her voice as soft as a feather. "It's okay to smile. It's okay to feel happy. Or what's the point in life?" What she was saying hit me hard. Because I didn't want to do or feel those things. I felt guilty just thinking about being happy.

"Rune," Poppy said. Her hand drifted down to rest on the side of my neck. "I know how you must be feeling. I've dealt with this for a while now. But I also know how it makes me feel seeing my favorite people in the world, the ones that I love with my whole heart, hurt and upset."

Poppy's eyes shone. It made me feel worse. "Poppy...," I went to say, covering her hand with my own.

"It's worse than any pain. It's worse than facing death. Seeing my illness leech the joy from those I love is the worst thing of all." She swallowed, drew in a soft breath, and whispered, "My time is limited. We all know that. So I want that time to be special..." Poppy smiled. And it was one of her wide, bright smiles. The kind that could make even an angry guy like me see a sliver of light. "As special as special can be."

And so I smiled.

I let her see the happiness she brought out in me. I let her see that those words—the words from our childhood—had broken through the dark.

At least for the moment.

"Freeze," Poppy suddenly said. I did. A slight giggle left her throat.

"What?" I asked, still holding her hand.

"Your smile," she replied and playfully dropped her mouth as if in shock. "It's still there!" she whispered dramatically. "I thought it was a mythical legend like Sasquatch or the Loch Ness monster. But it's there! I've witnessed it with my own eyes!"

Poppy framed her face with her hands and batted her eyelashes in exaggeration.

I shook my head, fighting a real laugh this time. When my laugh had calmed, Poppy was still smiling at me. "Only you," I said. Her smile softened. Inching down, I pulled the collar of her coat closer to her neck. "Only you could make me smile."

Poppy closed her eyes, just for a moment. "Then that's what I'll be doing as much as I can." She looked into my eyes. "I'll make you smile." She rose higher onto her toes, until our faces were almost touching. "And I'll be determined."

A bird chirped outside, and Poppy's gaze drifted to the window. "We have to go if we want to catch it," she urged, then stepped back, breaking our moment.

"Then let's go," I replied and, pulling on my boots, followed her. I picked up her bag and threw it over my shoulder; Poppy smiled to herself as I did.

I slid open the window. Poppy dashed to her bed. When she came back, she was holding a blanket in her hands. She glanced up at me. "It's cold this early."

"That coat won't be warm enough?" I asked.

Poppy held the blanket to her chest. "This is for you." She pointed to my T-shirt. "You'll be cold in the grove."

"You know I'm Norwegian, right?" I asked dryly.

Poppy nodded. "You're a real-life Viking." She leaned in. "And between you and me, you're really good on adventures, as predicted."

I shook my head in amusement. She rested her hand on my arm.

"But, Rune?"

"Yes?"

"Even Vikings get cold."

I nudged my head toward the open window. "Go on or we'll miss the sun."

Poppy slid through the window, still smiling, and I followed behind. The morning was cold, the wind stronger than the night before.

Poppy's hair whipped at her face. Concerned that she was cold, and that it might make her sick, I reached for her arm and pulled her to face me. Poppy looked surprised, until I lifted her heavy hood and pulled it up over her head.

I tied the strings to secure it in place. Poppy watched me the whole time. My actions were slowed under her rapt attention. When the bow was tied, my hands stilled, and I looked deeply into her eyes.

"Rune," she said after several strained seconds of silence. I tipped my chin, quietly waiting for her to continue. "I can still see your light. Beneath the anger, you're still there."

Her words made me step back in surprise. I glanced up at the sky. It was beginning to lighten. I walked forward. "You coming?"

Poppy sighed and rushed to catch up with me. I slipped my hands into my pockets as we made our way in silence to the grove. Poppy was looking all around her on the way. I tried to follow what she was seeing, but it only ever appeared to be birds or trees or grass swaying in the wind. I frowned, wondering what had her so transfixed. But this was Poppy; she'd always danced to her own drumbeat. She'd always seen more going on in the world than anyone else I knew.

She saw the light piercing the dark. She saw the good through the bad.

It was the only explanation I had for why she hadn't told me to leave her alone. I knew she saw me as different, changed. Even if she hadn't told me so, I would have seen it in the way she watched me. Her stare was guarded sometimes.

She would never have looked at me like that before.

When we entered the grove, I knew where we would sit. We walked to the biggest tree—our tree—and Poppy opened her backpack. She pulled out a blanket to sit on.

When she had laid it out, she gestured for me to sit. I did, resting my back against the wide tree trunk. Poppy sat in the center of the blanket and leaned back on her hands.

The wind seemed to have dropped. Untying the bow from the hood's strings, she let the hood fall back, showing her face. Poppy's attention turned to the brightening horizon, the sky now gray, with tints of red and orange pushing through.

Reaching into my pocket, I pulled out my smokes and brought one to my mouth. I struck the lighter, lit the smoke, and drew in a drag, feeling the instant it hit my lungs.

The smoke billowed around me as I exhaled slowly. I caught Poppy watching me closely. Resting an arm on my raised knee, I stared right back at her.

"You smoke."

"*Ja.*"

"You don't want to stop?" she asked. I could hear in her voice that this was a request. And I could see by the flicker of a smile on her lips that she knew I was onto her.

I shook my head. It calmed me. I wouldn't be quitting anytime soon.

We sat in silence, until Poppy looked back at the rising dawn and asked, "Did you ever watch the sunrise in Oslo?"

I followed her gaze to the now-pink horizon. The stars were beginning to disappear in a fan of light.

"No."

"Why not?" Poppy asked, shifting her body to face me.

I took another drag of my smoke and tipped my head back to exhale. I lowered my head and shrugged. "Never occurred to me."

Poppy sighed and turned away once more. "What an opportunity wasted," she said, waving her arm toward the sky. "I've never been out of the U.S., never seen a sunrise anywhere else, and there you were, in Norway, and you never rose early to watch the new day roll in."

"Once you've seen one sunrise, you've seen them all," I replied.

Poppy shook her head sadly. When she looked at me, it was in pity. It made my stomach turn. "That's not true," she argued. "Every day is different. The colors, the shades, the impact on your soul." She sighed and said, "Every day is a gift, Rune. If I've learned anything from the last couple of years, it's that."

I was silent.

Poppy tipped her head back and closed her eyes. "Like this wind. It's cold because it's early winter, and people run from it. They stay inside to keep warm. But I embrace it. I cherish the feeling of the wind on my face, the heat of the sun on my cheeks in the summer. I want to dance in the rain. I dream of lying in the snow, feeling its coldness in my bones." She opened her eyes. The crest of the sun began to inch into the sky. "When I was getting treatment, when I was confined to my hospital bed, when I was in pain and going crazy from every aspect of my life, I would get the nurses to turn my bed to the window. The sunrise each day would calm me. It would restore my strength. It would fill me with hope."

A trail of ash dropped onto the ground beside me. I realized that I hadn't moved since she started talking. She faced me and said, "When I used to look out of that window, when I was missing you so much that it hurt worse than the chemo, I would stare at that breaking dawn and I would think of you. I would think of you watching the sunrise in Norway, and it would bring me peace."

I said nothing.

"Were you happy even once? Was there any part of the last two years where you weren't sad or angry?"

The fire of anger that sat in my stomach flared to life. I shook my head. "No," I replied as I flicked my dead smoke to the ground.

"Rune," Poppy whispered. I saw the guilt in her eyes. "I thought you'd move on, eventually." She lowered her eyes, but when she looked up again, she completely broke my heart. "I did it because we never thought I would last this long." A weak yet strangely powerful smile graced her face. "I've been gifted more time. I've been gifted life"—she breathed in deeply—"and now, to add to the miracles that keep coming my way, you've returned."

I turned my head, unable to keep calm, unable to balance Poppy talking about her death so casually and my return so happily. I felt her move to sit beside me. Her sweet scent washed over me and I closed my eyes, breathing hard when I felt her arm press against mine.

Silence again hung between us, thickening the air. Then Poppy laid her hand over mine. I opened my eyes just as she pointed to the sun, now moving quickly, ushering in the new day. I laid my head back against the rough bark, watching a pink haze flood over the barren grove. My skin shivered with the cold. Poppy lifted the blanket next to her to lie over us both.

As soon as the thick woolen blanket had enveloped us in its warmth, her fingers threaded through mine, joining our hands. We watched the sun, until daylight fully arrived.

I felt the need to be honest. Pushing aside my pride, I confessed, "You hurt me." My voice was coarse and low.

Poppy stiffened.

I didn't look into her eyes, I couldn't. Then I added, "You completely broke my heart."

As the thick clouds cleared, the pink sky turned to blue. As the morning settled in, I felt Poppy move—she was wiping away a tear.

I winced, hating the fact that I had upset her. But she wanted to know why I was pissed 24/7. She wanted to know why I never watched a damn sunrise. She wanted to know why I had changed. That was the truth. And I was learning real fast that sometimes the truth was a bitch.

Poppy sniffed back a sob, and I lifted my arm and wrapped it around her shoulders. I expected her to resist, but instead she fell gently against my side. She let me hold her close.

I kept my attention on the sky, clenching my jaw as my eyes blurred with tears. I held them back.

"Rune," Poppy said.

I shook my head. "It doesn't matter."

Poppy raised her head and turned my face to hers, her hand on my cheek. "Of course it matters, Rune. I hurt you." She swallowed her tears. "It was never my intention. I desperately wanted to save you."

I searched her eyes and I saw it. As much as it had hurt me, as much as her abrupt silence had destroyed me, sent me spiraling into a place I didn't know how to fight free from, I could see that it was because she had loved me. Had wanted me to move on.

"I know," I said, holding her closer.

"It didn't work."

"No," I agreed, then pressed a kiss on her head. When she looked up at me, I brushed the tears off her face.

"What now?" she asked.

"What do you want to happen now?"

Poppy sighed and looked up at me through determined eyes. "I want the old Rune back." My stomach sank and I edged backward. Poppy stopped me. "Rune—"

"I'm not the old Rune. I'm not sure I ever will be again." I dropped my head, but then forced myself to face her. "I still want you the same, *Poppymin*, even if you don't want me."

"Rune," she whispered, "I've just got you back. I don't know this new you. My mind is foggy. I never expected to have you with me through this. I'm...I'm confused." She squeezed my hand. "But at the same time, I feel full with new life. With the promise of us again. With knowing that, for at least the time I have left, I get to have you." Her words danced in the air, as she asked nervously, "Don't I?"

I ran my finger down her cheek. "*Poppymin*, you have me. You'll always have me." I cleared the lump in my throat and added, "I might be different from the boy you knew, but I'm yours." I smirked without humor. "Forever always."

Poppy's eyes softened. She nudged my shoulder then laid her head on it. "I'm sorry," she whispered.

I held her close, as tight as I could. "Christ, *I'm* sorry, Poppy. I don't..." I couldn't finish my words. But Poppy waited patiently until I dropped my head and continued. "I don't know how you're not breaking apart with all this. I don't know how you're not..." I sighed. "I just don't know how you're finding the strength to keep going."

"Because I love life." She shrugged. "I always have."

I felt like I was seeing a new side to Poppy. Or maybe I was being reminded of the girl I always knew she'd grow up to be.

Poppy gestured to the sky. "I'm the girl who wakes up early to watch the sunrise. I'm the girl who wants to see the good in everyone, the one who is taken away by a song, inspired by art." Turning to me, she smiled. "I'm that girl, Rune. The one who waits out the storm simply to catch a glimpse of a rainbow. Why be miserable when you can be happy? It's an obvious choice to me."

I brought her hand up to my mouth and kissed the back of her hand.

Her breathing changed, the tempo racing to double speed. Then Poppy pulled our joined hands to her mouth, twisting them so she could kiss my hand. She lowered them to her lap, tracing small patterns on my skin with the index finger of her free hand. My heart melted when I realized what she was drawing—infinity signs. Perfect figure eights.

"I know what lies ahead for me, Rune. I'm not naïve. But I also have a strong faith that there's more to life than what we have right now, here, on this Earth. I believe that heaven awaits me. I believe that when I take my last breath and close my eyes in this life, I'll awake in the next, healthy and at peace. I believe this with my whole heart."

"Poppy," I rasped, tearing apart inside at the thought of losing her but so damn proud of her strength. She amazed me.

Poppy's finger dropped from our hands and she smiled at me, not a hint of fear on her beautiful face. "It'll be okay, Rune. I promise."

"I'm not sure I'll be okay without you." I didn't want to make her feel bad, but this was my truth.

"You will," she said confidently. "Because I have faith in you."

I didn't say anything in response. What could I say?

Poppy looked at the bare trees around us. "I can't wait for them to bloom again. I miss the sight of pretty pink petals. I miss walking into this grove and feeling like I'm stepping into a dream." She lifted her hand and trailed it along a low-hanging branch.

Poppy flashed me an excited smile, then jumped to her feet, her hair blowing freely in the wind. She stepped onto the grass and stretched her hands into the air. Her head tipped back and she laughed. A laugh that ripped from her throat with pure abandon.

I didn't move. I couldn't. I was transfixed. My eyes refused to move away from watching Poppy as she began to turn, spinning as the wind blew through the grove, her laughter drifting on the wind.

A dream, I thought. She was right. Poppy, bundled up in her coat, spinning in the early morning grove, looked exactly like a dream.

She was like a bird: at its most beautiful when flying free.

"Can you feel it, Rune?" she asked, her eyes still closed as she soaked up the warming sun.

"What?" I asked, finding my voice.

"Life!" she called, laughing harder as the wind changed direction, almost knocking her off her feet. "Life," she said quietly, as she grew still, rooting her feet in the dry grass. Her skin was flushed and her cheeks windburned. Yet she'd never looked more beautiful.

My fingers twitched. When I glanced down I immediately knew why. The urge to capture Poppy on film gnawed inside me. A natural urge. Poppy had once told me I was born with it.

"I wish, Rune," Poppy said, causing me to glance up, "I wish that people realized how this felt every day. Why does it take a life ending to learn how to cherish each day? Why must we wait until we run out of time to start to accomplish all that we dreamed, when once we had all the time in the world? Why don't we look at the person we love the most like it's the last time we will ever see them? Because if we did, life would be so vibrant. Life would be so truly and completely *lived*."

Poppy's head drifted slowly forward. She glanced back at me over her shoulder and rewarded me with the most devastating smile. I looked at the girl I loved most like it was the very last time I would see her, and it made me feel alive.

It made me feel like the most blessed person on the planet, because I had her. Even though, right now, things were still awkward and fresh, I knew I had her.

And she definitely had me.

My legs stood up of their own accord, discarding the blanket onto the grassy floor of the grove. Slowly, I walked to Poppy, drinking in every part of her.

Poppy watched me approach. As I stood in front of her, she ducked her head, a flush of embarrassment traveling up her neck to rest upon the apples of her cheeks.

As the wind wrapped around us, she asked, "Do you feel it, Rune? Truly?"

I knew she was referring to the wind on my face and the sun's rays shining down.

Alive.

Vibrant.

I nodded, replying to a completely different question. "I feel it, *Poppymin*. Truly."

And it was at that moment that something inside of me shifted. I couldn't think of the fact she only had months to live.

I had to focus on the moment.

I had to help her feel as alive as possible, while I had her back by my side.

I had to win back her trust. Her soul. Her love.

Poppy stepped closer to me, running her hand down my bare arm. "You're cold," she announced.

I didn't care if I was suffering from hypothermia. Pushing my hand to the nape of her neck, I leaned in, watching her face for a sign this move wasn't wanted. Her green eyes flared, but it wasn't in resistance.

Spurred on, seeing her lips part and her eyes flutter to a close, I tipped my head to the side, bypassing her mouth, to run the tip of my nose down her cheek. Poppy gasped, but I kept going. Kept going until I reached the pulse in her neck; it was racing.

Her skin was warm from dancing in the wind yet shivering at the same time. I knew it was because of me.

Closing in the rest of the way, I pressed my lips over her galloping pulse, tasting her sweetness, feeling my own heartbeat race in tandem.

Alive.

Life being so truly and completely lived.

A soft whimper escaped Poppy's lips and I drew back, gradually meeting her gaze. Her green irises were bright, her lips pink and full. Dropping my hand, I stepped back and said, "Let's go. You need sleep."

Poppy looked adorably bewildered. I left her on that spot as I gathered our things. When I finished, I found her exactly where I had left her.

I flicked my head in the direction of our houses, and Poppy walked beside me. With each step, I mulled over the last twelve hours. About the roller coaster of emotions, about the fact that I'd got half my heart back, only to discover it was temporary. I thought about kissing Poppy's face, about lying in bed beside her.

Then I thought about her jar. The half-empty jar of a thousand boy-kisses. For some reason that flash of blank paper hearts bothered me the most. Poppy loved that jar. It was a challenge set by her mamaw. A challenge blunted by my two-year absence.

I flicked a look to Poppy, who was staring at a bird in a tree, smiling as it sang from the topmost branch. Feeling my stare, she turned to me and I asked, "You still like adventures?"

Poppy's ear-splitting grin immediately answered that question. "Yes," she replied, "Lately, every day is an adventure." She lowered her eyes. "I know the next few months will be an interesting challenge, but I'm ready to embrace it. I'm trying to live every day to the fullest."

Ignoring the pain this remark ignited in me, a plan formed in my mind. Poppy stopped; we had reached the patch of grass between our homes.

Poppy turned to me as we stood in front of her window. And she waited, waiting for what I'd do next. Inching closer to where she stood, I placed the bag and blanket on the ground and straightened up, hands by my sides.

"So?" Poppy asked, a tinge of humor in her voice.

"So," I replied. I couldn't keep from smiling at the twinkle in her eyes. "Look, Poppy," I started, and rocked on my feet, "you believe you don't know the guy I am now." I shrugged. "So, give me a chance. Let me show you. Let's start a new adventure."

I felt my cheeks heat up with embarrassment, but Poppy suddenly took hold of my hand and placed it in hers. Bemused, I stared at our hands; then Poppy shook them up and down twice. With the biggest smile on her face, her dimples deep and proud, she declared, "I'm Poppy Litchfield and you're Rune Kristiansen. This is a handshake. My mamaw told me it's what you do when you don't know somebody. Now we're friends. *Best* friends."

Poppy looked up at me through her lashes and I laughed. I laughed as I recalled the day I met her. When we were five, and I saw her climb through her window, blue dress covered in mud and a big white bow in her hair.

Poppy moved to take back her hand, but I held on tightly. "Go out with me tonight."

Poppy stilled.

"On a date," I continued awkwardly. "A real date."

Poppy shook her head in disbelief. "We never really went on a date before, Rune. We always just…*were*."

"Then we'll start now. I'll pick you up at six. Be ready."

I turned and headed for my window, assuming that her answer was yes. Truth was, no way was I giving her a chance to say no. I was going to do this for her.

I was going to do my damnedest to make her happy.

I'd win her back.

I'd win her back as the Rune I was now.

There was no choice.

This was us.

This was our new adventure.

One that would make her feel alive.

9

First Dates and Dimpled Smiles

Poppy

"You're going on a date?" Savannah asked as she and Ida lay on my bed. They watched my reflection in my mirror. Watched as I looped my infinity earrings through my ears. Watched as I applied a final layer of mascara.

"Yeah, a date," I replied.

Ida and Savannah glanced at each other with wide eyes. Ida turned back to look at me. "With *Rune?* Rune Kristiansen?"

This time, I turned to face them. The shock on their faces was unsettling. "Yes, with Rune. Why are y'all so surprised?"

Savannah sat up, hands braced on the mattress. "Because the Rune Kristiansen that everyone's been talking about wouldn't go on *dates*. The Rune who smokes and drinks at the field. The one who doesn't speak, the one who scowls instead of smiles. The bad boy that returned a different person from Norway. *That* Rune."

I stared at Savannah and picked out the concern on her face. My stomach rolled, listening to what people had obviously been saying about Rune.

"Yeah, but all the girls like him," Ida butted in, flashing me a smile. "People were jealous of you when you were with him before he left. They're gonna freakin' die now!"

As those words slipped from her lips, I saw Ida slowly lose her smile. She glanced down, then looked back up. "Does he know?"

Savannah was now wearing the same sad look. So sad that I had to turn away. I couldn't bear that expression on their faces.

"Poppy?" said Savannah.

"He knows."

"How did he take it?" Ida inquired tentatively.

I smiled through the flash of pain in my heart. I faced my sisters, the two of them watching me as though I could disappear from their eyes any second. I shrugged. "Not well."

Savannah's eyes began to glisten. "I'm sorry, Pops."

"I shouldn't have cut him off," I stated. "It's why he's so angry all the time. It's why he's so standoffish. I hurt him, deeply. When I told him, it seemed to destroy him, but then he asked me on a date. *My* Rune, finally taking me on a date, after all these years."

Ida quickly wiped her cheek. "Do Mama and Daddy know?"

I grimaced, then shook my head. Savannah and Ida looked at each other, then at me, and in seconds we were all laughing.

Ida rolled on her back, holding her stomach. "Oh my Lord, Pops! Daddy's gonna flip! All he's talked about since the Kristiansens got back is how much Rune has changed for the worse, how he's disrespectful because he smokes and shouts at his pappa." Flipping around, she sat up. "He isn't gonna let you go."

My laughter stopped. I knew my mama and daddy were concerned about Rune's attitude, but I hadn't known how badly they judged him.

"Is he coming to our door?" Savannah asked.

I shook my head, although I was unsure what he would do.

Suddenly the doorbell rang.

We all looked at one another, wide-eyed. I frowned. "This can't be Rune," I exclaimed in surprise. He always came to my window. He was never formal; it just wasn't us. Certainly it wasn't him.

Savannah read the clock on my nightstand. "It's six o'clock. Isn't that the time he was coming?"

With one final look in the mirror, I grabbed my jacket and rushed through my bedroom door, my sisters hard on my heels. As I rounded the hallway, I saw my daddy open the door, his face dropping when he saw whoever was there.

I skidded to a halt.

Savannah and Ida stopped beside me. Ida grabbed my hand when we heard a familiar voice say, "Mr. Litchfield."

At the sound of his voice, my heart stuttered mid-beat. I watched as my daddy drew back his head in confusion. "Rune?" he asked. "What are you doing here?"

My daddy was being his usual polite self, but I could hear a wariness in his tone. I could hear a slight edge of worry, maybe even a deeper concern.

"I'm here for Poppy," Rune told my daddy. My daddy's hand tightened on the doorknob.

"For Poppy?" he clarified. I peeked around the wall, hoping to catch a glimpse of Rune. Ida squeezed my arm.

I looked at my sister. *"OMG!"* she mouthed dramatically.

I shook my head while silently laughing at her. She refocused her attention on my daddy, but I stared at her excited face for a fraction longer. It was moments like this, the carefree moments where we were just three sisters gossiping about dates, that struck me the hardest. Feeling a pair of eyes watching me, I turned my head toward Savannah.

Without words, she told me she understood.

Savannah's hand pressed on my shoulder as I heard Rune explain, "I'm taking her out, sir." He paused. "On a date."

My daddy's face blanched, and I pushed forward. As I moved toward the door to rescue Rune, Ida whispered in my ear, "Poppy, you're my new hero. Look at Daddy's face!"

I rolled my eyes and laughed. Savannah grabbed Ida and pulled her back, out of sight. But they'd still be watching. They wouldn't miss this for the world.

A flush of nerves swept through me as I approached the door. I saw my daddy begin to shake his head. Then his gaze fixed on me.

His confused eyes surveyed my dress, the bow in my hair and the makeup on my face. He turned a whiter shade of pale.

"Poppy?" my daddy asked. I lifted my head high.

"Hey, Daddy," I replied. The door still blocked Rune, but I could see his blurred dark figure through the stained-glass panel. I could smell his fresh scent drifting in on the cool breeze that filtered through the house.

My heart raced in anticipation.

Daddy pointed at Rune. "Rune here seems to think he's taking you out." He said it as though it couldn't possibly be true, but I heard the doubt in his voice.

"Yes," I confirmed.

I heard the hushed whispers of my sisters coming from behind us. I saw my mama watching from the shadow of the living room.

"Poppy—" My daddy went to speak, but I stepped forward, cutting him off.

"It's okay," I assured him. "I'll be fine." It seemed like my daddy couldn't move. I used this awkward moment to walk around the door and greet Rune.

I felt my lungs seize and my heart stop dead.

Rune was dressed all in black: T-shirt, jeans, suede boots, and leather biker jacket. His long hair was down. I savored the moment when he lifted his hand and pushed it through his hair. He was leaning against the doorway, an air of arrogance radiating from his casual stance.

When his eyes, bright under frowning dark-blond brows, fell on me, I saw light flare in his gaze. His eyes slowly tracked over my body, over my long-sleeved yellow dress, down my legs, and back up to the white bow holding up one side of my hair. His nostrils flaring and his pupils enlarging were the only evidence that he liked what he saw.

Blushing under his heavy stare, I dragged in a breath. The air was thick and full. The tension between us was palpable. I realized in that moment that it was possible to miss someone fiercely even though mere hours had passed since you'd last been together.

The clearing of my daddy's throat hurled me back to reality. I glanced back. Putting a reassuring hand on his arm, I said, "I'll be back later Daddy, okay?"

Not waiting for his response, I ducked under his arm that was leaning on the door and out onto the porch. Rune slowly pushed his body away from the doorframe and turned to follow me. When we reached the end of the driveway, I turned to him.

His intense gaze was already on me, his jaw clenching as I waited for him to speak. Peering over his shoulder, I saw my daddy watching us leave, that worried expression still marring his face.

Rune looked back but didn't react. He didn't say a single word. Reaching into his pocket, he pulled out a set of keys. He flicked his chin toward his mamma's Range Rover. "I got the car" was all he said as he walked forward.

I followed him, heart thudding as I made my way to the car. I focused on the ground to steady my nerves. When I looked up, Rune had opened the passenger door for me. Suddenly, all of my nerves slipped away.

There he stood, like a dark angel, watching me, waiting for me to climb inside. Smiling at him as I passed, I jumped in the car, blushing with happiness as he gently closed the door and got in the driver's side.

Rune started the engine without a word, his attention fixed on my house through the windshield. There was my daddy, still as a rock, watching us leave. Rune's jaw clenched once more.

"He's just protective is all," I explained, my voice breaching the silence. Rune cast me a sideways look. With a dark glare at my daddy, Rune pulled out of the street, a thick silence gradually intensifying the farther we drove.

Rune's hands gripped the steering wheel tightly, knuckles white. I could feel the anger rolling off him in waves. It made me feel so sad. Never before had I seen anyone harbor so much rage.

I couldn't imagine living like this every day. Couldn't imagine feeling that barbed coil forever in my stomach, that aching of the heart.

Inhaling, I turned to Rune and tentatively asked, "Are you okay?"

Rune exhaled harshly through his nose. He nodded his head once, then pushed back his hair. My eyes fell to his biker jacket and I smiled.

Rune arched his right brow. "What?" he asked, the sound of his deep voice rumbling through my chest.

"Just you," I replied evasively.

Rune darted his gaze to the road, then back to me. When he repeated it several more times, I could tell it was because he was desperate to know what I was thinking.

Reaching out, I let my hand drift over the distressed leather on the arm of his jacket. Rune's muscles bunched under my palm.

"I can see why all the girls in town have a crush on you." I said. "Ida was telling me all about it tonight. How all of them would be jealous that I was on a date with you."

Rune's eyebrows drew down. I laughed, truly laughed, at the lines on his forehead. He rubbed his lips together as I giggled louder, but I could see the sparkle in his eyes. I could see him disguising his amusement.

Sighing lightly, I wiped my eyes. I noticed that Rune's hands had slackened some on the wheel. His jaw wasn't so tense and his eyes weren't so narrowed.

Taking the opportunity while I could, I explained, "Since I got sick, Daddy got more protective. He doesn't hate you, Rune. He just doesn't know this new you. He didn't even know we'd been speaking again."

Rune sat still, saying nothing.

This time I didn't try to talk. It was clear that Rune had slipped back into a mood. But nowadays, I wasn't sure how to bring him out of it. If I even could. I turned to watch the world outside as we drove. I had no idea where we were going, the excitement making it impossible to sit still.

Suddenly hating the quiet in the car, I leaned over to the radio and switched it on. I flicked the dial to my favorite channel; the harmonies of my favorite girl band filled the car.

"I love this song," I said happily, sitting back in my seat as the slow piano melody began filling every corner of the car. I listened to the opening bars, singing along quietly to the stripped-back acoustic version of the song. My favorite version.

I closed my eyes, letting the heartbreaking lyrics flow into my mind and out through my lips. I smiled when the string section struck up in the background, deepening the emotion with its dulcet sounds.

This was why I loved music.

Only music had the ability to steal my breath and give life to the song's story so flawlessly. So profoundly. I opened my eyes and found Rune's face had lost all anger. His blue eyes were watching me, as much as they could. His hands were tighter on the wheel, but there was something else in his expression.

My mouth grew dry as he glanced at me again, his face unreadable. "It's about a girl who desperately loves a boy, with her whole heart. They keep their love a secret, but she doesn't want it to be that way. She wants the world to know that he's hers and she's his."

Then, to my utter surprise, Rune rasped, "Keep singing."

I saw it on his face; I saw his need to hear me.

So I did.

I wasn't a strong singer. So I sang it soft, I sang it true. I sang the lyrics, embracing every word. As I sang the song about love requited, I sang them with heart. These lyrics, these passionate pleas, I had lived.

Still lived.

They were Rune and me. Our separation. My foolish plan: to keep him out of my life, to save him from pain, unexpectedly wounding both of us in the process. Loving him from here in America, him loving me from Oslo, in return, in secret.

When the last lyric faded, I opened my eyes, my chest aching from the rawness of the emotions. Another song began to play, one I didn't know. I could feel Rune's watchful gaze boring into me, yet I couldn't lift my head.

Something was making it impossible.

I let my head roll against the headrest, and I stared out the window. "I love music," I said, almost to myself.

"I know you do," Rune answered. His voice was firm, strong and clear. But in that tone, I caught a hint of tenderness. Of something gentle. Caring. I rolled my head to face him. I didn't say anything as our eyes met. I simply smiled. It was small and timid, but Rune let out a slow breath as I did.

We made a left and another left, taking us down a dark country road. My eyes never left Rune. I thought about how truly beautiful he was. I let myself imagine how he would look in ten years' time. He'd be broader, I was sure. I wondered if his hair would still be long. I wondered what he'd be doing with his life.

I prayed that it would be something to do with photography.

Photography brought the same soul-enhancing peace to him as my cello did to me. Since he'd returned, though, I hadn't seen his camera once. He said it himself; he didn't take photos anymore.

That made me sadder than anything.

Then, I did the one thing I had told myself long ago I would never allow—I imagined what *we* would look like in ten years' time, together. Married, living in an apartment in SoHo, New York. I would be cooking in our cramped kitchen. I'd be dancing to music playing from the radio in the background. And Rune would be sitting at the counter watching me, taking photos as he documented our lives. And he'd reach out from behind his lens to run his finger down my cheek. I'd swat his hand away playfully and I'd laugh. That would be when he'd click the button on the camera. That would be the shot I'd see later that night waiting for me on my pillow.

His perfectly captured moment in time.

His perfect second. Love in still life.

A tear fell from my eyes as I held on to that image. The image that could never be us. I allowed myself a moment of feeling the pain, before I hid it deep. Then I let myself feel happy that he would get the opportunity to fulfill his passion and become a photographer. I'd be watching on from my new home in heaven, smiling with him.

As Rune concentrated on the road, I let myself whisper, "I've missed you…I've missed you so, so much."

Rune froze, every part of his body becoming still. Then he hit the turn signal and pulled over onto the edge of the road. I sat up, wondering what was happening. The engine purred beneath us, but Rune's hands slipped from the wheel.

His eyes were downcast, hands lying on his lap. He momentarily gripped his jeans; then he turned his head to face me. His expression was haunted.

Torn.

But it softened when he fixed his gaze on me and said in a rough whisper, "I've missed you too. So damn much, *Poppymin*."

My heart lurched forward, taking my pulse along with it. They both raced; they both made my head dizzy as I drank in the honesty in his graveled voice. The beautiful look on his face.

Not knowing what else to say, I laid my hand on the center console. My palm was facing up, fingers open. After several silent seconds, Rune slowly placed his hand in mine and we linked our fingers tightly together. Shivers ghosted through my body at the feel of his large hand holding mine.

Yesterday confused us both, neither one knowing what to do, where to go, how to find our way back to us. This date was our start. These joined hands, a reminder. A reminder that we were Poppy and Rune. Somewhere under all the hurt and pain, under all the new layers we'd acquired, we were still here.

In love.

Two halves of one heart.

And I didn't care what anyone said about it. My time was precious but, I realized, not as precious to me as Rune. Without breaking our hands, Rune put the car into drive and we pulled back out onto the road. After a moment, I could see where we were going.

The creek.

I smiled wide as we pulled into the old restaurant, its deck adorned with strings of blue lights, large heaters warming the outdoor tables. The car drew to a halt and I turned to Rune. "You brought me to the creek for our date? To Tony's Shack?"

My mamaw would bring Rune and me here when we were kids. On a Sunday night. Just like tonight. She lived for their crawfish. She happily traveled all this way to get them.

Rune nodded. I tried to pull my hand away, and he frowned. "Rune," I teased, "we have to get out of the car at some point. To do that, we have to break hands."

Rune reluctantly let go, his eyebrows pulling down as he did. I grabbed my coat and climbed out of the car. As soon as I shut the door, Rune was by my side. Reaching down, not seeking permission, he took hold of my hand again.

By his grip, I was convinced he'd never let go.

A gust of wind blew in from the water as we walked toward the entrance. Rune stopped. Silently, he took my coat from my hand and unclasped our linked fingers. Shaking the coat, he held it out for me to put on.

I went to protest, but a dark look passed over Rune's face and I sighed. Turning around, I pushed my arms into my parka, turning back when Rune's arm guided me before him. Focusing intently on the task, he zipped up my coat until the cold night air was held at bay.

I waited for Rune's hands to drop from my collar, but instead, they lingered. His minty breath drifted over my cheeks. He glanced up momentarily, catching my eyes. My skin bumped at the flash of shyness those eyes held. Then, latching his gaze on mine, he inched closer and said softly, "Did I tell you how beautiful you look tonight?"

My toes curled in my boots at the thickness of his accent. Rune may have looked calm and aloof, but I knew him. When his accent was thicker, so were his nerves.

I shook my head. "No," I whispered. Rune glanced away.

When he looked back, his hands had tightened on my collar, drawing me closer. Hovering his face an inch before mine, he said, "Well you do. Real damn beautiful."

My heart leaped, it soared. In response, I could only smile. But that seemed enough for Rune. In fact, it seemed to floor him.

As he leaned in just that little bit more, Rune's lips brushed past my ear. "Stay warm, *Poppymin*. I couldn't bear for you to get sicker."

His act of putting on my coat suddenly made sense. He was protecting me. Keeping me safe.

"Okay," I whispered back. "For you." He inhaled a quick breath, his eyes closing just a fraction too long for it to be a blink.

He stepped back and took my hand in his. Without speaking, he led me into Tony's Shack and requested a table for two. The hostess led us around back to the patio overlooking the creek. I hadn't been here in years, but it hadn't changed one bit. The water was quiet and still, a piece of heaven hidden away among the trees.

The hostess stopped at a table at the back of the busy patio. I smiled, about to take my seat, when Rune said, "No." My eyes flew to Rune, as did the hostess's. He pointed to the farthest table on the deck, one right on the edge of the water. "That one," he demanded curtly.

The young hostess nodded. "Certainly," she replied, slightly flustered. She led us across the patio to the table.

Rune took the lead, his hand still clutching mine. As we threaded our way through the tables, I noticed girls staring at him. Rather than be upset by their attention, I followed their gazes, trying to see him with fresh eyes. I found that difficult. He was so ingrained in my every memory, so carved into the fabric of who I was, that it made it almost impossible. But I tried and tried, until I saw what they must have seen.

Mysterious and brooding.

My very own bad boy.

The hostess left the menus on the wooden table and turned to Rune. "Is this okay, sir?" Rune nodded, a scowl still etched on his face.

Flushing, the hostess told us our server would be here soon and hurriedly left us alone. I glanced at Rune, but his eyes were looking over the creek. I broke my hand away from his, so I could take my seat, and as soon as I did, his head snapped around and his brow furrowed.

I smiled at his grouchiness. Rune dropped to the chair overlooking the water, and I sat in the seat opposite. But as soon as I sat down, Rune reached around and gripped the arm of my chair. I shrieked as he pulled on the chair, dragging it toward him. I jerked in the seat as it moved, clutching on to the arms until he'd repositioned it.

Repositioned it, next to him.

Right beside him, so my chair now overlooked the creek too.

Rune didn't react to the slight blush on my cheeks as my insides warmed at this simple gesture. In fact, he didn't even seem to notice. He was too busy retaking possession of my hand. Too busy locking our fingers in place. Too busy never letting me go.

Reaching forward, Rune adjusted the heater above us to its highest setting, only relaxing back in his chair when the flames roared higher behind their iron guard. My heart melted when he brought our joined hands to his mouth, the back of my hand brushing back and forth over his lips in a hypnotic motion.

Rune's eyes were fixed on the water. Even though I adored the trees embracing the water in a protective cocoon, as much as I loved to watch the ducks dip and dive, the cranes swoop and soar above the surface, I could only watch Rune.

Something had changed in him from last night. I didn't know what. He was still abrupt and surly. There was darkness in his personality; his aura warned almost all to stay well clear.

But now there was a new edge of possession with regard to me. I could see the fierceness of that possession in his stare. I could feel it in his grip on my hand.

And I liked it.

As much as I missed the Rune I knew, I watched this Rune with renewed fascination. Right now, sitting beside him in a place that meant so much to us both, I was perfectly content to be in the company of *this* Rune.

More than content.

It made me feel alive.

The server arrived: a guy, maybe in his twenties. Rune's hold tightened on my hand. My heart swelled.

He was jealous.

"Hey, y'all. Can I get y'all started with some drinks?" the server asked.

"Can I get a sweet tea, please?" I replied, feeling Rune stiffen beside me.

"Root beer," Rune barked. The server quickly retreated. When he was out of earshot, Rune snapped, "He couldn't keep his eyes off you."

I shook my head and laughed. "You're crazy."

Rune's forehead lined with frustration. This time it was his turn to shake his head. "You have no idea."

"About what?" I asked, moving my free hand to trace a couple of new scars on Rune's knuckles. I wondered where they were from. I heard his breathing hitch.

"About how beautiful you are," he replied. He was watching my finger as he said it. When my finger stopped he looked up.

I stared at him, lost for words.

Finally, Rune's lip hooked at the side into a crooked half-smile. He shifted closer to me. "Still drinking sweet tea, I see."

He remembered.

Gently nudging his side, I said, "Still on the root beer, I see."

Rune shrugged. "Can't get it back in Oslo. Now I'm back, I can't get enough of the stuff." I smiled and began retracing his hand. "Turns out I can't get enough of a few things I couldn't get back in Oslo."

My finger stopped moving. I knew exactly what he was talking about: me.

"Rune," I said, the guilt lying thick within me.

I looked up to try and apologize again, but as I did, the server arrived, placing our drinks on the table. "Y'all ready to order?"

Without breaking my gaze, Rune said, "Two crawfish boils."

I felt the server hanging by, but after a tense few seconds, he said, "I'll get that to the kitchen then," and edged away.

Rune's eyes moved from my face to my ears, where that flicker of a smirk remerged. I wondered what had caused him this moment of happiness. Rune leaned forward, and with the backs of his fingers he pushed the hair from my face, tucking it behind my ear.

His fingertip traced down the outline of my ear, and then he let out a comforting sigh. "You still wear them."

The earrings.

My infinity earrings.

"Always," I confirmed. Rune looked up at me with heavy eyes. "Forever always."

Rune dropped his hand, but he caught the ends of my hair between his finger and thumb. "You cut your hair."

It sounded like a statement, but I knew it was a question.

"My hair grew back," I said. I saw him stiffen. Not wanting to break tonight's magic with talk of illness or treatment, things that I paid no mind to anyhow, I leaned in and pressed my forehead to his.

"I lost my hair. Fortunately, hair grows." Drawing back, I playfully flicked at my bob. "Plus, I kinda like it. I think I suit it. Lord knows it's easier to handle than the mountain of frizz I fought against all those years."

I knew it had worked when Rune huffed a single quiet laugh. Continuing the joke, I added, "Plus, only Viking men should wear their hair long. Vikings and bikers." I scrunched up my nose as I pretended to study Rune. "Unfortunately you don't have a bike…" I trailed off, laughing at the hard look on Rune's face.

I was still laughing when he pulled me into his chest and, with his mouth at my ear, said, "I could get a bike, if that's what you want. If that's what it would take to win back your love."

He said it as a joke.

I knew he did.

But it brought me up short. So short that I stilled, the humor draining out of me. Rune noticed the shift. His Adam's apple bobbed and he swallowed whatever he was going to say.

Letting my heart rule my actions, I lifted my hand and dropped my palm to lie upon his face. Making sure I had his undivided attention, I whispered, "It wouldn't take a bike to do that, Rune."

"No?" he questioned, his voice husky.

I shook my head.

"Why?" he asked nervously. Redness blossomed on his cheeks. I could see what that question had cost his heavily fortified pride. I could see that Rune didn't ask anything anymore.

Closing the gap between us, I said in a hushed voice, "Because I'm pretty sure you never lost it."

I waited. I waited with bated breath to see what he would do next.

I wasn't expecting tender and soft. I wasn't expecting for my heart to sigh and my soul to melt.

Rune, with the most careful of movements, moved forward and kissed me on my cheek, only inching back to drag his lips across mine. I held my breath in anticipation of a kiss on the lips. A real kiss. A kiss I yearned for. But instead, he bypassed my mouth for my other cheek, giving it the kiss my lips longed to gain.

When Rune pulled away, my heart was beating like a drum. A loud bass in my chest. Rune sat back, but his hand, in my hand, had tightened a fraction.

A secret smile took refuge behind my lips.

A sound from over the creek pulled my attention—a duck taking flight into the dark sky. When I glanced at Rune, I saw he was watching it too. When he looked my way, I teased, "You're already a Viking. You don't need no bike."

This time Rune smiled. The merest hint of teeth showed through. I beamed with pride.

The server approached, carrying our crawfish, and placed the buckets on the paper-covered table. Rune reluctantly released my hand, and we started ripping into the mountain of seafood. I closed my eyes when I tasted the meaty flesh on my tongue, a burst of lemon hitting my throat.

I groaned at how good it was.

Rune shook his head, laughing at me. I threw a broken bit of shell into his lap and he scowled. Wiping my hand on the napkin, I tipped my head back toward the night sky. The stars were bright in their cloudless blanket of black.

"Have you ever seen anything so beautiful as this little creek?" I asked. Rune looked up, then out along the quiet creek, the reflection of blue-stringed lights twinkling back at us.

"I'd say yes," he answered in a matter-of-fact tone, then pointed to me. "But I get what you're saying. Even when I was back in Oslo, I would sometimes picture this place, wondering if you had been back."

"No, this is the first time. Mama and Daddy aren't real big crawfish fans; it was always Mamaw." I smiled, picturing her sitting beside us at this table, after sneaking us away. "Do you remember"—I laughed—"she would bring her flask full of bourbon with her, to slip into her sweet tea?" I laughed harder. "Do you remember her putting her finger over her lips and saying, *Now don't y'all be telling your folks about this. I had the good grace to bring y'all here, rescuing y'all from church. So no loose lips!*?" Rune was smiling too, but his eyes were watching me laugh.

"You miss her," he said.

I nodded my head. "Every day. I wonder what other adventures we could have been on together. I often wonder if we would have gone to Italy to see Assisi, just like we talked about. I wonder if we would have gone to Spain, to run with the bulls." At that thought I laughed again. A peace settled over me, and then I added, "But, the best part of all this is I'll see her again soon." I met Rune's eyes. "When I return home."

Like my mamaw had taught me, I never ever thought of what would happen to me as dying. The end. It was the beginning of something great. My soul would be returning home where it belonged.

I hadn't realized I had upset Rune, until he rose from his chair to walk along the small pier next to our table, the pier that led to the middle of the creek.

The server came over. I watched Rune light a cigarette as he disappeared into the dark, only a cloud of smoke betraying where he stood.

"Shall I clear up, ma'am?" the server inquired.

I smiled and nodded. "Yes, please." I stood, and he looked puzzled, seeing Rune on the deck. "Can we have the check as well, please?"

"Yes, ma'am," he replied.

I walked out onto the deck to meet Rune, following the tiny speck of his lit cigarette. When I arrived at his side he was leaning over the railing, staring absently at nothing.

A soft crease was marring his forehead. His back was tense; it tensed even more when I stopped beside him. He took in a long drag of his cigarette and released it into the gentle breeze.

"I can't deny what's happening to me, Rune," I said cautiously. He remained silent. "I can't live in a fantasy. I know what's coming. I know how this will go."

Rune's breathing was ragged and his head dropped. When he lifted his eyes, he said brokenly, "It's not fair."

My heart cried for his pain. I could see it racking his face, see it in the bunching of his muscles. Leaning forward on the railing, I inhaled the cool air. When Rune's breathing had settled, I said, "It would have been really unfair had we not been gifted the next precious months."

Rune's forehead fell slowly to rest upon his hands.

"Don't you see a bigger picture for us both here, Rune? You came back to Blossom Grove only a few weeks after I was sent home to live out the rest of my life. To enjoy the limited few months granted by medication." I looked at the stars again, feeling the presence of something greater smiling down on us. "For you it's unfair. I believe the opposite. We came back together for a reason. Perhaps it's a lesson we may struggle to learn until it's learned."

I turned and pushed back the long hair covering his face. In the moonlight, underneath the glittering stars, I saw a tear tumble down his cheeks.

I cleared it with a kiss.

Rune turned into me, tucking his head into the crook of my neck. I wrapped my hand around his head, holding him close.

Rune's back rose with a deep inhale. "I brought you here tonight to remind you of when we were happy. When we were inseparable, best friends and more. But—"

He cut his words off. I gently pushed back his head to look at his face "What?" I asked. "Please, tell me. I promise I'm okay."

He searched my eyes, then stared across the still water. When his gaze returned to me, he asked, "But what if this is the last time we ever get to do this?"

Pushing myself between him and the railing, I took the cigarette from his hand and threw it into the creek. Standing on my tiptoes, I took both his cheeks in my hands. "Then we had tonight," I asserted. Rune's face winced at my words. "We've had this memory. We've had this cherished moment." My head tipped to the side and a nostalgic smile pulled on my lips. "I used to know a boy, a boy I loved with my whole heart, who lived for a single moment. Who told me that a single moment could change the world. It could change someone's life. That one moment could make someone's life, in that brief second, infinitely better or infinitely worse."

He closed his eyes, but I continued to speak. "This, tonight, being at this creek with you again," I said, feeling a sense of peace fill my soul, "remembering my mamaw and why I loved her so much…it has made my life infinitely better. *This* moment, given to me by *you*, I will remember always. I will take it with me to…wherever I go."

Rune's eyes opened. I pulled him down farther. "You gave me tonight. You've returned. We can't change the facts, we can't change our fates, but we can still *live*. We can live as hard and as fast as we can while we have these days before us. We can be us again: Poppy and Rune."

I didn't think he would say anything in return, so it surprised me and filled me with incredible hope when he said, "Our final adventure."

The perfect way to phrase it, I thought. "Our final adventure," I whispered into the night, an unprecedented joy infusing my body. Rune's arms snaked around my waist. "With one amendment," I said. Rune frowned.

Smoothing the crease on his forehead, I said, "*This* life's final adventure. Because I know, with unwavering faith, that we'll be together again. Even when this adventure is over, a greater one awaits us on the other side. And Rune, there would be no heaven if you weren't back in my arms someday."

All six feet four of Rune Kristiansen braced against me. And I held him. I held him until he calmed. When he pulled back, I asked, "So, Rune Kristiansen, Viking from Norway, are you with me?"

Despite himself, Rune laughed. Laughed when I held out my hand for him to shake. Rune, my Scandinavian bad boy with a face made by the angels, slipped his hand into mine and we shook on our promise. Twice. Like my mamaw taught me.

"I'm with you," he said. I felt his vow all the way to my toes.

"Ma'am, sir?" I looked over Rune's shoulder to see the server holding our check. "We're closing up," he explained.

"You okay?" I asked Rune, signaling to the server that we were coming.

Rune nodded, his heavy brows pushing his face back into his familiar scowl. I imitated how he looked by scrunching my face. Rune, unable to resist, gave me his good-humored smirk. "Only you," he said, more to himself than to me, "*Poppymin*." Slipping his hand back into mine, he slowly guided me to the front of the shack.

When we were back in the car, Rune turned on the engine and said, "We have one more place to go."

"Another memorable moment?"

As we pulled out onto the road, Rune took my hand in his across the console and replied, "I hope so, *Poppymin*. I hope so."

It took us a while to drive back to town. We didn't talk much. I had come to understand that Rune was quieter than he used to be. Not that he'd exactly been an extrovert before. He was always introverted and quiet. He fit nicely the image of the brooding artist, head always juggling places and landscapes he wanted to capture on film.

Moments.

We had traveled only a mile or so down the road when Rune turned the radio on. He told me to pick any station I wanted. And when I quietly sang, his fingers tightened just that bit more in mine.

A yawn escaped my mouth as we approached the edge of town, but I fought to keep my eyes open. I wanted to know where he was taking me.

When we stopped outside the Dixon Theater, my pulse took flight. This was the theater I had always dreamed of performing at. It was the theater I had always wanted to return to when I was older, as part of a professional orchestra. To my hometown.

Rune cut the engine, and I stared up at the impressive stone theater. "Rune, what are we doing here?"

Rune released my hand and opened his door. "Come with me."

Frowning, but my heart racing so impossibly hard, I opened my door to follow him. Rune took my hand and led me to the front entrance.

It was late on a Sunday night, but he led us straight through the front doors. As soon as we entered the dim foyer, I heard the faint sounds of Puccini playing in the background.

My hand tightened in Rune's. He glanced down at me, a smirk on his lips. "Rune," I whispered, as he led me up the opulent staircase. "Where are we going?"

Rune pressed his finger over my lips, signaling for me to be quiet. I wondered why, but then he led me to a door…the door that led to the dress circle of the theater.

Rune opened the door, and music washed over me like a wave. Gasping at the sheer volume of the sound, I followed Rune to the front row of seats. Down below was an orchestra, their conductor leading them. I recognized them instantly: the Savannah Chamber Orchestra.

I was transfixed, staring at the musicians focusing so intently on their instruments, swaying in time to the beat. Whipping my head to Rune, I asked, "How did you do this?"

Rune shrugged. "I was looking to take you to see them perform properly, but they're traveling overseas tomorrow. When I explained to the conductor how much you loved them, he said we could drop in on their rehearsal."

No words passed through my lips.

I was speechless. Completely and utterly speechless.

Failing to adequately express my feelings, my sheer gratitude for this surprise, I laid my head on his shoulder and cuddled into his arm. The smell of leather filled my nose as my eyes focused on the orchestra below.

I watched in fascination. I watched as the conductor expertly guided the musicians through their rehearsal: the solos, the decorative passages, the intricate harmonies.

Rune held me close as I sat, mesmerized. Occasionally, I felt his eyes on me: him watching me, me watching them.

But I couldn't tear my eyes away. Especially from the cello section. When the deep tones rang clear and true, I let my eyes drift to a close.

It was beautiful.

I could picture myself, so clearly, sitting among fellow musicians, my friends, staring into this theater, full of the people I knew and loved. Rune sitting, watching with his camera around his neck.

It was the most perfect of dreams.

It had been my biggest dream for as long as I could remember.

The conductor called for the musicians to quiet. I watched the stage. I watched as all but the principal cellist lowered their instruments. The woman, who looked to be in her thirties, pulled her chair to center stage. No audience except for us.

She positioned herself, her bow poised on the string, to start. She concentrated on the conductor. As he raised his baton, instructing her to begin, I heard the first note play. And as I did, I became completely still. I didn't dare breathe. I didn't want to hear anything but the most perfect melody ever in existence.

The sound of "The Swan" from *Carnival of the Animals* drifted up to our seats. I watched the cellist become lost in the music, her facial expressions betraying her emotions with each new note.

I wanted to be her.

In that moment, I wanted to be the cellist playing this piece so perfectly. I wanted to be gifted that trust, the trust of giving this performance.

Everything faded away as I watched her. Then I closed my eyes. I closed my eyes and let the music take hold of my senses. I let it take me on its journey. As the tempo picked up, the vibrato echoing beautifully off the theater's walls, I opened my eyes.

And the tears came.

The tears came as the music demanded.

Rune's hand tightened in mine, and I felt his gaze on me. I could sense he was worried that I was upset. But I wasn't upset. I was soaring. Heart-soaring in the blissful melody.

My cheeks grew wet, but I let the tears flow. This was why music was my passion. From wood and string and bow, this magical melody could be created, stirring life into a soul.

And I stayed that way. I stayed that way until the last note drifted to the ceiling. The cellist raised her bow. Only then did she open her eyes, guiding her spirit to its resting place inside her. Because that's what she was feeling, I knew. The music had transported her to a distant place, somewhere only she knew. It had moved her.

For a time, the music had graced her with its power.

The conductor nodded and the orchestra walked backstage, leaving silence to occupy the now-empty stage.

But I didn't turn my head. Not until Rune sat forward, with a hand placed gently upon my back. "*Poppymin?*" he whispered, his voice guarded and unsure. "I'm sorry," he said under his breath, "I thought this would make you happ—"

I faced him, clasping both his hands between mine. "No," I said, interrupting his apology. "No," I reiterated. "These are tears of joy, Rune. Absolute joy."

He exhaled, releasing one of his hands to wipe at my cheeks. I laughed, my voice echoing around us. I cleared my throat, chasing away an excess of emotion, and explained, "That's my favorite piece, Rune. 'The Swan,' from the *Carnival of the Animals*. The principal cellist, she just played my favorite piece. Beautifully. Perfectly."

I took a deep breath. "It's the piece I was planning to play when I auditioned for Julliard. It's always been the piece I pictured myself playing at Carnegie Hall. I know it inside out. I know every note, every shift in tempo, every crescendo…everything." I sniffed and wiped my eyes. "Hearing it tonight," I said, squeezing his hand, "sitting next to you…it was a dream come true."

Rune, too lost for words, placed his arm around my shoulders and pulled me close. I felt his kiss on my head. "Promise, Rune," I said. "Promise me that when you're in New York, when you're studying at Tisch, you'll go and see the New York Philharmonic play. Promise me you'll watch the principal cellist play this piece. And promise me that when you do, you'll think of me. Imagine me playing up on that stage, fulfilling my dream." I breathed deeply, content with that picture. "Because that would be enough for me now," I explained. "Simply knowing that I'd at least get to live out that dream, even if it is only in your mind's eye."

"Poppy," Rune said, painfully. "Please, baby..." My heart leapt as he called me "baby." It sounded as perfect as the music to my ears.

Raising my head, I lifted his chin with my finger and insisted, "Promise me, Rune."

He turned his gaze away from me. "Poppy, if you're not going to be in New York with me, why the hell would I ever go?"

"Because of your photography. Because like this dream was mine, yours was to study photography at NYU."

Concern cut through me when Rune's jaw clenched. "Rune?" I questioned. After a long moment, he turned slowly back to face me. I searched his beautiful face. I slumped back in my seat at what I saw in his expression.

Refusal.

"Why don't you take pictures anymore, Rune?" I asked. Rune looked away. "Please, don't ignore me."

Rune sighed in defeat. "Because without you, I didn't see the world the same way anymore. *Nothing* was the same. I know we were only young, but without you, nothing made sense. I was angry. I was drowning. So I gave up my passion because the passion within me had died out."

Out of anything he could have done or said, this saddened me most of all. Because the passion had been so strong within him. And his pictures, even though he was fifteen, were like nothing I'd ever seen.

I stared at Rune's hard features, his eyes lost in a trance as he stared blankly at the empty stage. His wall was back up and the tension in his jaw was back. The sullen expression had returned.

Needing to leave him be, not to push him too far, I leaned my head back against his shoulder and smiled. I smiled, still hearing that piece drift into my ears.

"Thank you," I whispered, as the lights on the stage faded.

Lifting my head, I waited for Rune to look at me. Eventually he did.

"Only you could have known that this—" I gestured to the auditorium—"would mean so much to me. Only my Rune."

Rune pressed a soft kiss on my cheek.

"It *was* you at my recital the other night, wasn't it?"

Rune sighed, then eventually nodded his head. "I was never going to miss you play, *Poppymin*. I never will."

He got to his feet. He was silent as he held out his hand. He was silent as I gave him my hand and he led us to the car. He was silent as we journeyed home. I thought I must have hurt him somehow. I worried that I had done something wrong.

When we arrived home, Rune left the car and walked around the hood to open my door. I took his proffered hand as I jumped down. I kept tight hold as Rune walked me back to my house. I expected to go to the door. Instead, he led me to my window. I frowned when I saw the frustrated look on his face.

Needing to know what was wrong, I ran my hand down his face. But as my finger landed on his cheek, something in him seemed to snap. He backed me against the side of my house. His body pressed against mine, and he cupped my face with his hands.

I was breathless—breathless at his closeness. Breathless at the intensity in his dark expression. His blue eyes searched every part of my face. "I wanted to do this right," he said. "I wanted to take this slow. This date. Us. Tonight." He shook his head, his forehead creasing as he fought whatever he was battling inside. "But I can't. I won't."

I opened my mouth to answer, but his thumb drifted to graze my bottom lip, his attention on my mouth. "You're my Poppy. *Poppymin*. You know me. Only *you* know me." Taking my hand, he laid it over his heart. "You know me—even under this anger, you know me." He sighed, edging so close that we shared the same air. "And I know you." Rune paled. "And if we only have limited time, I'm not going to waste it. You're mine. I'm yours. To hell with anything else."

My heart fluttered like an arpeggio in my chest. "Rune" was all I managed to say. I wanted to shout that *yes*, I was his. That he was mine. Nothing else mattered. But my voice failed me. I was too overcome with emotion.

"Say it, *Poppymin*," he demanded. "Just say *yes*."

Rune took a final step, trapping me, his body flush with my own, his heart beating in tandem with mine. I dragged in a breath. Rune's lips brushed against mine, hovering, waiting, primed to possess them completely.

As I looked into Rune's eyes, his black pupils all but eliminating the blue, I let go and whispered, "Yes."

Warm lips suddenly crashed to mine, Rune's familiar mouth taking them with single-minded determination. His warmth and minty taste drowned out my senses. His hard chest kept me pinned to the wall, trapped, as he owned me with his kiss. Rune was showing me to whom I belonged. He was giving me no other choice but to submit to him, to give myself back to him after withdrawing for too many years.

Rune's hands threaded through my hair, keeping me in place. I moaned as his tongue pushed through to meet mine—soft, hot, and desperate. As he lifted my hands up his wide back, they landed in his hair. Rune growled into my mouth, kissing me deeper, taking me further and further from any fear or trepidation I harbored at his return. He kissed me until there was no part of me that didn't know who it belonged to. He kissed me until my heart again fused with his—two halves of one whole.

My body began to weaken under his touch. As he felt me completely surrender to him, Rune's kiss slowed to soft, gentle caresses. Then he broke away, our breathing heavy, an arc of tension above us. Rune's swollen lips kissed my cheeks, my jaw, and my neck. When he finally withdrew, his quick breaths blew against my face. His hands slackened their grip on me.

And he waited.

He waited, watching me with his intense gaze.

Then my lips parted, and I whispered, "Kiss three hundred and fifty-seven. Against the wall of my house…when Rune took possession of my heart." Rune stilled, his hands tensed, and I finished with, "And my heart almost burst."

Then it came. Rune's pure smile. It was bright, it was wide, and it was true.

My heart soared at the sight.

"*Poppymin*," he whispered.

Gripping his shirt, I whispered back, "*My Rune.*"

Rune's eyes closed as I spoke those words, a soft sigh falling from his mouth. His hands gradually loosened their grip on my hair and he took a reluctant step back. "I'd better go in," I whispered.

"*Ja,*" he answered back. But he didn't look away. Instead he pressed against me again, taking my mouth quickly and softly, before pulling back. Then he stepped back several spaces, putting a good distance between us.

I lifted my fingers to my lips and said, "If you keep kissing me like this, I'll fill my jar in no time at all."

Rune turned away to walk to his house but stopped to glance over his shoulder. "That's the idea, baby. One thousand kisses from *me.*"

Rune rushed back to his house, leaving me to watch him go, leaving me with a dizzying lightness flowing through me like a rapid. When my feet finally moved, I walked into my house and straight to my room.

I pulled out the jar from under my bed and wiped off the dust. Opening the jar, I took the pen from my nightstand and wrote down tonight's kiss.

An hour later I was lying in bed when I heard the window opening. Sitting up, I saw my curtain be pushed aside. My heart leapt into my mouth when Rune stepped in.

I smiled as he walked forward, shucking off his shirt and throwing it on the floor. My eyes widened when I drank in the sight of his bare chest. Then my heart almost exploded when he raked his hand through his hair, pushing it from his face.

Rune walked slowly to my bed, standing to wait by its side. Shuffling back, I lifted the cover and Rune climbed in, immediately wrapping his arms around my waist.

As my back nestled perfectly against his front, I sighed in contentment. I closed my eyes. Rune pressed a kiss just below my ear and whispered, "Sleep, baby. I got you."

And he did.

He had me.

Just like I had him.

Clasped Hands and Awakened Dreams

Rune

I WOKE TO POPPY STARING UP AT ME.

"Hey," said Poppy. She smiled and nuzzled further into my chest. I let my hands wander through her hair, before tucking my hands under her arms, pulling her up until she lay above me, her mouth opposite mine.

"Morning," I replied, then pressed my lips against hers.

Poppy sighed into my mouth as her lips parted and worked against my own. When I pulled back, she glanced out the window and said, "We missed the sunrise."

I nodded. But when she looked back at me, her expression didn't show any sadness. Instead she kissed my cheek and admitted, "I think I'd trade all the sunrises if it meant I got to wake up like this, with you."

My chest concaved at those words. Taking her by surprise, I flipped her on her back, hovering over where she lay. Poppy giggled as I trapped her hands on the pillow above her head.

I scowled. Poppy tried—unsuccessfully—to stop her laughter.

Her cheeks were pink with excitement. Needing to kiss her more than breathe, I did.

I released Poppy's hands and she grasped my hair. Her laugh began to fade as the kiss grew deeper, and then there was a loud knock on the door. We froze, our lips still joined and our eyes wide open.

"Poppy! Time to get up, sweetheart!" Poppy's daddy's voice drifted into the room. I could feel Poppy's heart racing, echoing through my chest, flush against hers.

Poppy shifted her head to the side, breaking the kiss. "I'm awake!" she shouted back. We didn't dare move until we heard her daddy walking away from the door.

Poppy's eyes were huge when she faced me again. "Oh my God!" she whispered, bursting into a fresh set of giggles.

Shaking my head, I rolled to the side of the bed, grabbing my shirt off the floor. As I pulled the black material over my head, Poppy's hands landed on my shoulders from behind. She sighed. "We slept too late this morning. We almost got caught."

"It won't happen again," I said, not wanting her to have any excuse to end this. I had to be with her at night. I had to. Nothing happened—we kissed, we slept.

That was enough for me.

Poppy nodded in agreement, but when her chin rested on my shoulder, her arms wrapping around my waist, she said, "I liked it."

She laughed again and I turned my head slightly, catching the bright look on her face. She nodded playfully. Poppy sat back and took my hand and pressed it over her heart. It was beating fast. "It made me feel alive."

Laughing at her, I shook my head. "You're crazy."

Standing up, I slid on my boots. Poppy sat back on her bed. "You know, I've never done anything naughty or bad before, Rune. I'm a good girl, I suppose."

I frowned at the thought of corrupting her. But Poppy leaned forward, and said, "It was fun." I pushed my hair back from my face and leaned down over the bed and gave her one last kiss, soft and sweet.

"Rune Kristiansen, maybe I'll like this bad-boy side to you after all. You're sure gonna make the next few months entertaining." She sighed dramatically. "Sweet kisses and troublemaking antics…I'm in!"

As I made my way to the window, I heard Poppy move behind me. Just as I went to sneak out of her window, I glanced back. Poppy was filling out two blank hearts from her jar. I allowed myself to watch her. Watch as she smiled at whatever she was writing.

She was so beautiful.

As she placed the completed hearts back in her jar, she turned and stopped. She'd caught me watching. Her gaze softened. She opened her mouth to say something, when the knob on her door began to turn. Her eyes widened and she flicked her hands in a shooing motion.

As I jumped from the window and ran from the house, I heard her laughter following behind. Only something that pure could chase away the darkness in my heart.

I had barely made it back through my window before I had to jump in the shower for school. The steam billowed around the bathroom as I stood under the hot spray.

I leaned forward, the powerful jets pelting water onto my head. My hands rested against the slick tiles in front of me. Every day when I woke, anger consumed me. It was so consuming that I could almost taste its bitterness on my tongue, feel the heat of it coursing through my veins.

But this morning was different.

It was Poppy.

Lifting my head from the water, I switched it off and grabbed my towel. I slipped on my jeans and opened the bathroom door. My pappa was standing in the doorway of my room. When he heard me behind him, he turned to face me.

"Morning, Rune," he greeted. I pushed past him to walk to my closet. I grabbed a white T-shirt and pulled it over my head. When I reached for my boots, I noticed my pappa was still standing in the doorway.

Stopping mid-motion, I met his eyes and snapped, "What?"

He edged into the room, holding a coffee in his hand. "How was your date with Poppy last night?"

I didn't respond. I hadn't told him anything about it, which meant my mamma had. I wouldn't answer him. The prick didn't deserve to know.

He cleared his throat. "Rune, after you left last night, Mr. Litchfield came over to see us."

And then it came back, rushing through me like a torrent. The anger. I remembered Mr. Litchfield's face as he opened the door last night. As we drove away out of the street. He was pissed. I could see he hadn't wanted

Poppy to come with me. Hell, he'd looked like he was one second away from forbidding her to go.

But when Poppy walked outside, I could see that he wouldn't say no to whatever she wanted. How could he? He was losing his daughter. It was the only thing that stopped me from saying exactly what I thought of his objection to her being with me.

My pappa walked to stand in front of me. I kept my eyes to the floor as he said, "He's worried, Rune. He's worried that you and Poppy getting back together might not be such a good thing."

I gritted my teeth. "Not good for who? Him?"

"Poppy, Rune. You know...you know she doesn't have long—"

I whipped my head up, rage burning in my stomach. "Yeah, I get that. It's not too hard to forget. You know, the fact that the girl I love is dying."

My pappa paled. "James just wants Poppy's final days to be trouble-free. Peaceful. Enjoyable. No stress."

"And let me guess, I'm trouble, right? I'm that stress?"

He sighed. "He's asked that you stay away from her. Just let her go without a scene."

"Not happening," I bit out, grabbing my backpack off the floor. I slid my leather jacket on and walked around him.

"Rune, think of Poppy," my pappa pleaded.

I stopped dead and turned back to him. "She's *all* I'm thinking of. You have no idea what it's like for us, so how about you stay the hell out of my business. James Litchfield too."

"She's his daughter!" my pappa argued, his voice sterner than before.

"Yeah," I argued back, "and she's the love of my life. And I'm not walking away from her, even for a second. And there's nothing either of you can do about it."

I stormed through my bedroom doorway as my pappa shouted, "You're not good for her, Rune. Not like this. Not with all the smoking and drinking. Your attitude. The chip on your shoulder about everything in your life. That girl worships you, she always has. But she's a good girl. Don't be her ruin."

Stopping in my tracks, I glared at him over my shoulder and said, "Well I have it on good authority that she wants a little more bad boy in her life."

With that, I pounded past the kitchen, only briefly looking at my mamma and Alton, who waved at me as I passed. I slammed the front door and walked down the steps, lighting a smoke as soon as I hit the grass. I leaned back against the railings of our porch. My body was like a live wire at what my pappa had said. At what Mr. Litchfield had done. Warning me off his daughter.

What the hell did he think I was going to do to her?

I knew what they all thought of me, but I would never hurt Poppy. Not in a million years.

The front door of Poppy's house opened. Savannah and Ida rushed through, Poppy following right behind. They were all talking at once. Then, as if he felt my heavy gaze, Poppy's eyes drifted to the side of my house and focused on me.

Savannah and Ida looked over at what held her attention. When they saw me, Ida laughed and waved. Savannah, like her daddy, stared at me with quiet concern.

I flicked my chin at Poppy, telling her to come over. Poppy made her way to me slowly, Ida and Savannah on her heels. She looked beautiful, as always. Her red skirt came to mid-thigh, black tights covering her legs, small pixie boots on her feet. Her navy coat was covering her top half, but I could just see her white shirt underneath, a black tie around the collar.

She was so damn cute.

Poppy's sisters dropped back as Poppy stood in front of me. Needing to reassure myself that I had her, that she had me, I pushed myself off the railing, throwing my smoke to the ground. Cupping Poppy's cheeks with my hands, I pulled her to my lips, crashing my mouth to hers. This kiss wasn't gentle. I hadn't planned it to be. I was branding her, marking her as mine.

And me as hers.

This kiss was a strong flick of the middle finger to anyone who tried to get in our way. When I pulled back, Poppy's cheeks were flushed and her lips wet. "That kiss better be going in your jar," I warned.

Poppy nodded, dumbstruck. Giggles came from behind us. When I looked, Poppy's sisters were laughing. At least Ida was; Savannah was pretty much just gaping.

Reaching down for Poppy's hand, I clasped it in mine. "You ready?"

Poppy stared at our hands. "We're going to school like this?"

I frowned. "Yeah. Why?"

"Then everyone will know. They'll all talk, and—"

I smashed my lips to hers again, and, when I pulled back, said, "So let them talk. You never cared before. Don't start now."

"They'll think we're boyfriend and girlfriend again."

I scowled. "We are," I said plainly. Poppy blinked and blinked again. Then, extinguishing my anger completely, she smiled and fell into my side. Her head rested on my bicep.

Looking up, she said, "Then, yes, I'm ready."

I let myself hold Poppy's gaze for a few seconds longer than normal. Our kiss may have been a middle finger to anyone who didn't want us together, but her smile was a middle finger to the darkness in my soul.

Poppy's sisters ran to our side and joined us as we started walking toward our schools. Just before we turned toward the blossom grove, I glanced back over my shoulder. Mr. Litchfield was watching us go. I stiffened when I saw the stormy look on his face. But I gritted my teeth. This was one fight he was definitely going to lose.

Ida chatted the entire way to her school, Poppy laughing fondly at her youngest sister. I understood why. Ida was a miniature Poppy. Even down to the dimples on her cheeks.

Savannah was a different personality altogether. She was more introverted, a deep thinker. And clearly protective of Poppy's happiness.

With a quick wave goodbye, Savannah left us to go into the junior high school. As she walked away, Poppy said, "She was real quiet."

"It's me," I replied. Poppy looked at me, shocked.

"No," she argued. "She loves you."

My jaw tensed. "She loves who I used to be." I shrugged. "I get it. She's worried I'll break your heart."

Poppy pulled me to stop beside a tree near the entrance of our school. I glanced away. "What's happened?" she asked.

"Nothing," I replied.

She stepped into the path of my stare. "You won't break my heart," she stated with one hundred percent conviction. "The boy who took me to the creek, and then to listen to an orchestra, could never break my heart."

I remained silent.

"Plus, if my heart breaks, so does yours, remember?"

I huffed at that reminder. Poppy pushed me until my back was against the tree. I saw students beginning to enter the school, most of them looking at us. The whispers were already beginning.

"Would you hurt me, Rune?" Poppy demanded.

Defeated by her tenacity, I placed a hand on the nape of her neck, and assured her, "Never."

"Then to hell with what anyone else thinks."

I laughed at her fire. She smiled and put her hand on her hip. "How was that for attitude? Bad-girl enough?"

Taking her by surprise, I spun her until her back was against the tree. Before she had a chance to argue, I closed in and kissed her. Our lips were slow-moving, the kiss was deep, Poppy's lips parting to let in my tongue. I tasted the sweetness in her mouth, before pulling away.

Poppy was breathless. Combing through my damp hair with her fingers, she said, "I know you, Rune. You wouldn't hurt me." She scrunched her nose and joked, "I'd bet my life on it."

An ache tried to form in my chest. "That wasn't funny."

She held her finger and thumb about an inch apart. "It was. A little bit."

I shook my head. "You do know me, *Poppymin*. Only you. *For* you. *For* you *only*."

Poppy studied me. "And maybe that's the problem," she concluded. "Maybe if you let other people in. Maybe if you showed those you love that you're still *you* underneath all the dark clothes and broodiness, they wouldn't judge you so harshly. They'd love you for whoever you chose to be, because they'd see your true soul."

I stayed silent, and then she said, "Like Alton. How's your relationship with Alton?"

"He's a kid," I replied, not understanding what she meant.

"He's a little boy who worships you. A little boy who's upset you don't speak to him or do anything with him."

I felt those words tunnel a pit into my stomach. "How do you know?"

"Because he told me," she said. "He got upset."

I pictured Alton crying, but I quickly chased it away. I didn't want to think of it. I may not have much to do with him, but I didn't want to see him cry.

"There's a reason he has long hair, you know? There's a reason he pushes it from his face like you do. It's real cute."

"He has long hair because he's Norwegian."

Poppy rolled her eyes. "Not every Norwegian boy has long hair, Rune. Don't be silly. He has long hair because he wants to be like you. He imitates your habits, your idiosyncrasies, because he wants to be like *you*. He wants you to notice him. He adores you."

My head dropped to face the ground. Poppy guided it back with her hands. She searched my eyes. "And your pappa? Why don't you—"

"*Enough*," I spat out harshly, refusing to talk about him. I would never forgive him for taking me away. This one topic was off-limits, even for Poppy. Poppy seemed neither hurt nor offended by my outburst. Instead, all I saw was sympathy in her face.

I couldn't bear that either.

Taking her hand, and without another word, I pulled her toward the school. Poppy gripped my hand tightly when other students stopped looking and started staring. "Let them stare," I said to Poppy as we entered the school gates.

"Okay," she replied and edged closer to my side.

When we walked into the hallway, I saw Deacon, Judson, Jorie, Avery and Ruby all gathered near their lockers. I hadn't spoken to any of them since the party.

None of them knew of this development.

It was Jorie who turned first, her eyes widening when her gaze fell to Poppy's and my joined hands. She must have said something under her breath, because in seconds, all our friends turned to look at us. Confusion was all over their faces.

Turning to Poppy, I urged, "Come on—we'd better speak to them."

I moved to go forward, when Poppy pulled me back. "They don't know about..." she whispered, for only me to hear. "No one does except our families and the teachers. And you."

I nodded slowly. Then she said, "And Jorie. Jorie knows too."

That bit of information slammed into my gut. Poppy must have seen the hurt on my face, because she explained, "I needed someone, Rune. She was my closest friend except for you. She helped me with schoolwork and things like that."

"But you told her and not me," I said, fighting the urge to walk away and get some air.

Poppy held on tightly to me. "She didn't love me like you did. And I don't love her like I love you."

As Poppy said those words, my anger faded... *And I don't love her like I love you...*

Stepping closer to Poppy, I wrapped an arm around her shoulder. "They're going to find out at some point."

"But not yet," she said firmly.

I smirked at the determination in her eyes. "But not yet."

"Rune? Get the hell over here, you've got some explaining to do!" Deacon's loud voice rang out over the bustle of the hallway.

"You ready?" I asked Poppy.

She nodded. I steered us to meet our group of friends. Poppy's arm was wrapped firmly around my waist. "So you're back together?" Deacon asked.

I nodded, my lip curling in disgust as Avery's face beamed with jealousy. Clearly seeing me notice, she quickly assumed her usual cynical mask. I didn't care; she was never anything to me.

"So it's Poppy and Rune, together again?" Ruby clarified.

"Yes," Poppy confirmed, smiling up at me. I kissed her forehead, holding her close.

"Well, it seems the world has righted itself again," Jorie announced, reaching out to squeeze Poppy's arm. "It wasn't right, y'all not being together. The universe just kinda felt...off."

"Thanks, Jor," Poppy said, and they held each other's gazes for a second longer, communicating in silence. I noticed Jorie's eyes begin to water. As they did, she exclaimed, "Well, I gotta get to class. I'll catch y'all later!"

Jorie walked away. Poppy moved to her locker. I ignored all the stares. When Poppy had retrieved her books, I backed her against the closed door and said, "See? It wasn't so bad."

"Not so bad," Poppy echoed, but I saw her watching my lips.

Leaning in, I pressed my chest against hers and took her mouth with mine. Poppy whimpered when my hand dropped to her hair, clasping it tight. When I pulled back, her eyes were bright and her cheeks were flushed.

"Kiss three hundred and sixty. Against my locker door at school. Showing the world we're together again…and my heart almost burst."

I moved away, leaving Poppy to catch her breath.

"Rune?" she called as I headed to my math class. I turned and flicked my chin. "I'm gonna need more of these moments to fill my jar."

Heat speared through me at the thought of kissing her at every opportunity. Poppy flushed at the intensity on my face. Just as I turned again, she called, "And Rune?"

I smirked and answered, "*Ja?*"

"Where's your favorite place to go here in Georgia?" I couldn't quite make out the expression on her face, but something was going on in that head of hers. She was planning something, I just knew it.

"The blossom grove, when it's spring," I replied, feeling my face soften just at the thought.

"And when it's not spring?" she probed.

I shrugged. "The beach probably. Why?"

"No reason," she trilled, then headed in the opposite direction.

"See you at lunch," I shouted.

"I gotta practice my cello," she shouted back.

Standing still, I told her, "Then I'll be watching."

Poppy's face brightened and she repeated, gently, "Then you'll be watching."

We stood, on opposite sides of the hallway, just staring. Poppy mouthed, "*For infinity.*"

And I mouthed back, "*Forever always.*"

The week passed in a blur.

I'd never cared about time before—whether it went fast or slow. Now I did. Now I wanted a minute to last an hour, an hour to last a day. But, despite my silent pleas to whoever the hell was up there, time was rushing by too fast. Everything was moving too damn fast.

At school, the collective interest at me and Poppy being back together settled down after a few days. Most people still didn't get it, but I paid that no mind. In our little town, I knew that people talked. Most of the gossip was about how and why we got back together.

I didn't give a damn about that either.

The doorbell rang as I lay on my bed, and I rolled to stand, grabbing my jacket off my chair. Poppy was taking me out.

She was taking *me* out.

This morning when I left her bed, she told me to be ready at ten. She wouldn't tell me why or what we were doing, but I did as she asked.

She knew I would.

As I walked out of my door and down the hallway, I heard the sound of Poppy's voice. "Hey, little man, how're you doing?"

"Good," Alton replied shyly.

Rounding the corner, I stopped when I saw Poppy crouching down to meet Alton's eyes. Alton's long hair was shielding his face. I watched as he nervously pushed his hair from his face with his hand…just like I did. Poppy's words from last week came crashing into my mind…

He has long hair because he wants to be like you. He imitates your habits, your idiosyncrasies, because he wants to be like you. He wants you to notice him. He adores you…

I watched my baby brother rock shyly on his feet. I couldn't help curling my lip in amusement. He too was quiet, like me. Didn't really speak unless he was spoken to first.

"What are you up to today?" Poppy asked him.

"Nothing," Alton replied sullenly.

Poppy's smile faded. Alton asked, "Are you going out with Rune again?"

"Yeah, baby," she replied quietly.

"Does he talk to you now?" Alton asked. And I heard it. I heard the tone of sadness in his quiet voice, the one that Poppy had told me about.

"Yeah, he does," Poppy said, and like she did to me, she ran her finger down his cheek. Alton dipped his head in embarrassment, but I caught a little smirk through the gaps in his long hair.

Poppy looked up and saw me leaning against the wall, watching intently. She slowly straightened and I walked forward, reaching for her hand and pulling her forward for a kiss.

"You ready?" she asked.

I nodded my head, eying her suspiciously. "You still not telling me where we're going?"

Poppy pursed her lips and shook her head, teasing me. She took my hand in hers and led me out the door. "Bye, Alton!" she called over her shoulder.

"Bye, *Poppymin*," I heard him say quietly in response. I came to a dead stop as my pet name for Poppy left his lips. Poppy's hand went over her mouth, and I saw her practically melting on the spot.

She stared at me, and in that stare I knew she wanted me to say something to my brother. Sighing, I turned to Alton and he said, "Bye, Rune."

Poppy's hand squeezed mine, urging me to respond. "Bye, Alt," I replied awkwardly. Alton's head lifted, and a huge smile spread on his lips. All because I'd said bye.

That smile lighting up his face made something tighten in my chest. I led Poppy down the steps and toward Poppy's mama's car. As we reached the car, Poppy refused to release my hand until I looked up at her. When I did, she tipped her head to the side and declared, "Rune Kristiansen, I'm real freakin' proud of you right now."

I glanced away, not comfortable with that kind of praise. With a heavy sigh, Poppy finally released my hand and we climbed into the car. "You going to tell me where we're going yet?" I inquired.

"Nope." Poppy backed the car out of the drive. "Though you'll guess soon enough."

I tuned the radio to Poppy's usual station and sat back in my seat. Poppy's soft voice began to fill the car, singing along to another pop song I didn't know. It wasn't long before I stopped watching the road and simply watched her. Like when she played the cello, her dimples deepened as she sang along to her favorite songs, smiling through the lyrics she loved. Her head swayed and her body moved in time to the beat.

My chest constricted.

It was a constant battle. Seeing Poppy so carefree and happy filled me with the brightest of lights, but knowing these moments were limited, finite, *running out*, brought only darkness.

Patches of pitch black.

And anger. The ever-present unwound coil of anger that waited to strike.

As if she could see me breaking, Poppy stretched out her hand and laid it on my lap. When I glanced down, her hand was palm-up, her fingers ready to intertwine with mine.

I let out a long exhale and slipped my hand through hers. I couldn't look at her. I wouldn't do it to her.

I knew how Poppy felt. Even though cancer was draining her of life, it was the pain of her family members and those who loved her that was killing her. When I got quiet, when I got upset, it was the only time her bright green eyes would dim. When I let the anger consume me, I could see the tiredness on her face.

Tired of being the cause of so much hurt.

Keeping her hand tightly in mine, I turned to look out the window. We drove along the twists and turns out of town. Bringing our joined hands to my mouth, I pressed kisses to Poppy's soft skin. When we passed a sign for the coast, the heaviness lifted from my chest and I turned to Poppy.

She was already smiling.

"You're taking me to the beach," I stated.

Poppy nodded her head. "Yep! Your second-favorite place."

I thought of the cherry blossoms in bloom in the grove. I envisioned us sitting under our favorite tree. And, as unlike me as it was, I sent a prayer that she would make it that long. Poppy had to see the trees in their full flower.

She simply had to hold on that long.

"I will," Poppy suddenly whispered. I met her eyes, and she squeezed my hand like she was hearing my silent plea. "I'll see them. I'm determined."

The silence stretched out between us. A lump lodged in my throat as I silently counted the months to when the trees would be in blossom. About four months.

No time at all.

Poppy's hand had become rigid. When I searched her face, I saw the pain again. The pain silently telling me that she was hurting, because I was hurting.

Forcing the lump aside, I said, "Then you will. God knows not to stand in your way when you're determined."

And like a switch, her pain faded and pure happiness shone through.

I settled back in my seat, watching the world outside flash by in a blur. I was lost in my own thoughts when I heard, "Thank you." It was a tiny sound, barely a fraction of a whisper. But I closed my eyes, feeling Poppy's hand relax.

I didn't respond. She wouldn't want me to.

Another song began on the radio, and as if nothing had even happened, Poppy's soft voice filled the car, and it didn't let up. For the remainder of the journey I held on to her hand as she sang.

Making sure I drank in every note.

When we arrived at the coast, the first thing I saw was the tall, white lighthouse sitting on the edge of the cliff. The day was warm, the cold snap seemed to have passed, and the sky was bright.

There was barely a cloud in the sky as the sun sat high, beaming its rays over the still water. Poppy parked the car and cut the engine. "I agree. It's my second-favorite place," she said.

I nodded, watching the several families scattered around the soft sand. There were kids playing; seabirds circling, waiting for discarded food. Some adults were slumped against the dunes reading. Some were relaxing, eyes closed, lapping up the warmth.

"You remember coming here in the summer?" Poppy asked, joy lacing her soft voice.

"*Ja*," I rasped.

She pointed underneath the pier. "And there, kiss seventy-five." She turned to me and laughed at the memory. "We sneaked off from our families to stand under the pier, just so you could kiss me." She touched her lips, her eyes unfocused, lost in thought. "You tasted of salt from the seawater," she said. "Do you remember?"

"*Ja*," I replied. "We were nine. You wore a yellow bathing suit."

"Yes!" she said through a giggle.

Poppy opened the door. She looked back, excitement on her face, and asked, "Are you ready?"

I got out of the car. The warm breeze blew my hair over my face. Taking a rubber band from my wrist, I pushed my hair back off my face into a loose bun and walked to the trunk to help Poppy with whatever she'd brought.

When I glanced inside the large trunk, I saw she'd brought a picnic basket and another backpack. I had no idea what she had in that.

I reached forward to take everything from her when she tried to carry it all herself. She released them for me to hold; then she stopped, motionless.

Her stillness forced me to look up. I frowned, seeing her studying me. "What?" I asked.

"Rune," she whispered and touched my face with her fingertips. She skirted them over my cheeks and along my forehead. Finally, a huge smile broke out on her lips. "I can see your face."

Lifting onto her tiptoes, Poppy reached up and playfully tapped my hair, trapped in the bun. "I like this," she declared. Poppy's eyes tracked over my face one more time. Then she sighed. "Rune Erik Kristiansen, do you realize how utterly beautiful you are?"

I ducked my head. Hands ran down my chest. When I looked up, she added, "Do you realize how deeply I feel about you?"

I slowly shook my head, needing her to tell me. She placed my hand over her heart and her hand over mine. I felt its steady beat under my palm, the steady beat that got faster as my eyes locked on hers. "It's like music," she explained. "When I look at you, when you touch me, when I see your face… when we kiss, my heart plays a song. It sings that it needs you like I need air. It sings to me that I adore you. It sings that I've found its perfect missing part."

"*Poppymin*," I said softly, and she pressed a finger over my lips.

"Listen, Rune," she said, and she closed her eyes. I did too. And I heard it. I heard it as loudly as if it were next to my ear. The steady beats, the rhythm of us. "When you're near, my heart doesn't sigh, it soars," she whispered, as if she didn't want to disturb the sound. "I think hearts beat a rhythm like a song. I think that, just like music, we're drawn to a particular melody. I heard your heart's song, and yours heard mine."

I opened my eyes. Poppy stood, her dimples deep as she smiled and swayed to the beat. When her eyes opened, a sweet giggle slipped from her lips. I pushed forward and crushed our lips together.

Poppy's hands went to my waist, holding tightly to my T-shirt as I moved my lips slowly against hers, backing us up until she rested against the car, my chest flush against her body.

I felt the echo of her heartbeat in my chest. Poppy sighed as I slipped my tongue to slide against hers. Her hands tightened on my waist. When I drew back, she whispered, "Kiss four hundred and thirty-two. At the beach with my Rune. My heart almost burst."

I breathed heavily as I tried to gather myself. Poppy's cheeks were flushed, and she was breathing just as hard as me. We stayed that way, simply breathing, until Poppy pushed off the trunk and placed a kiss on my cheek.

Turning, she lifted the backpack and put it over her shoulder. I went to take it from her, but she said, "I'm not too weak yet, baby. I can still carry some of the weight."

Her words contained a double meaning. I knew she wasn't just talking about the bag but about my heart.

The darkness within me, that she was incessantly trying to fight.

Poppy moved away, allowing me to gather everything else. I followed her to a secluded spot on the far side of the beach, next to the pier.

When we stopped, I spotted the post where I had kissed her all those years ago. A strange feeling spread in my chest, and I knew that before we left to return home, I was going to kiss her there again. Kiss her as a seventeen-year-old.

Another kiss for her jar.

"Is here okay?" Poppy asked.

"*Ja*," I replied, placing the things on the sand. Seeing the umbrella, and concerned that Poppy shouldn't get too much sun, I quickly planted it in the sand and opened it to give her some shade.

As soon as the umbrella spread open and a blanket was on the sand, I nudged my chin to Poppy, indicating for her to move beneath it. She did, quickly kissing my hand as she passed.

And my heart didn't sigh. It soared.

My eyes were drawn to the quietly rolling ocean. Poppy sat down. Closing her eyes, she inhaled deeply.

Watching Poppy embrace nature was like watching an answered prayer. The joy in her expression seemed limitless, the peace in her spirit humbling.

I lowered myself to the sand. I sat forward, arms draping over my bent legs. I stared at the sea. I stared at the boats in the distance, wondering where they were going.

"What adventure do you think they're on?" Poppy asked, reading my mind.

"I don't know," I replied honestly.

Poppy rolled her eyes and said, "I think they're leaving it all behind. I think they woke up one day and decided there's more to life. I think they decided—a couple in love, a boy and a girl—that they wanted to explore the world. They sold their possessions and bought a boat." She smiled and lowered her chin, cradling it in her hands, her elbows resting on her bent knees. "She loves to play music, and he loves to capture moments on film."

I shook my head and glanced at her from the side of my eye.

She didn't seem to care, instead adding, "And the world is good. They'll travel to far-off places, create music, art and pictures. And along the way they'll kiss. They'll kiss, they'll love, and they'll be happy."

She blinked as the gentle breeze whispered through our shade. When she looked at me again, she asked, "Doesn't that sound like the most perfect adventure?"

I nodded. I couldn't speak.

Poppy looked at my feet, and shaking her head, shuffled along the blanket until she was at the end of my legs. I raised an eyebrow in question.

"You have boots on, Rune! It's a wonderfully sunny day and you have boots on." Poppy then set to unzipping my boots, pulling each one off. She rolled my jeans up to my ankles and nodded her head. "There," she said proudly. "That's a slight improvement."

Unable not to find the humor in her sitting there so smugly, I reached forward and pulled her over me, lying down so she lay above me.

"There," I repeated. "That's a slight improvement."

Poppy giggled, awarding me a swift kiss. "And now?"

"A huge improvement," I joked dryly. "A massive, asteroid-sized improvement."

Poppy laughed harder. I rolled her over to lie beside me. Her arm stayed over my waist, and I ran my fingers down her soft exposed skin.

I stared silently at the sky. Poppy was quiet too, until she suddenly said, "It wasn't long after you left that I began feeling tired, so tired that I couldn't get out of bed."

I grew still. She was finally telling me. Telling me what happened. Telling me it *all*.

"My mama took me to the doctor and they did some tests." She shook her head. "To be honest, everyone thought I was acting different because you had left." I closed my eyes and inhaled. "I did too," she added, holding me tighter. "For the first few days, I could let myself pretend you'd just gone on vacation. But after weeks began to pass, the void you left within me began to hurt so bad. My heart was completely broken. On top of that, my muscles ached. I would sleep too much, unable to find any energy."

Poppy fell silent. Then she continued. "We ended up having to go to Atlanta for more tests. We stayed with Aunt DeeDee while they figured out what was wrong."

Poppy lifted her head and, with a hand on my cheek, guided my eyes to meet hers. "I never told you, Rune. I kept up the pretense that I was okay. Because I couldn't bear to hurt you more. I could see you weren't doing real well. Every time we video-chatted, I could see you getting angrier and angrier at being back in Oslo. The things you said were just not *you*."

"So that visit to your Aunt DeeDee's," I cut in, "it was because you were sick. It wasn't just a visit like you told me?"

Poppy nodded and I saw the guilt in her green eyes. "I knew you, Rune. And I saw you were slipping. You were always sullen in attitude. You were always darker in nature. But when you were with me, you weren't. I could only imagine what finding out I was sick would do to you."

Poppy's head gently fell back to rest on my chest. "It wasn't long before I received my diagnosis: advanced Hodgkin lymphoma. It rocked my family. At first, it rocked me. How could it not?" I held her closer, but Poppy inched back. "Rune, I know I've never looked at the world like everyone else. I have always lived each day to the fullest. I know I've always embraced aspects of the world no one else does. I think, in some way, it was because I knew I wouldn't have the time to experience them like everyone else. I think, deep down, my spirit knew. Because when the doctor told us I would only have a couple of years, even with medication and treatment, I was okay."

Poppy's eyes began to shine with tears. Mine did too.

"We all stayed in Atlanta; we lived with Aunt DeeDee. Ida and Savannah started new schools. Daddy traveled for his work. I was home-schooled, or tutored in the hospital. My mama and daddy prayed for a miracle. But I knew there was none to be had. I was okay. I kept my chin up. The chemo was hard. Losing my hair was tough." Poppy blinked, clearing her vision, then confided, "But cutting you off almost killed me. It was my choice. The blame lies with me. I just wanted to save you, Rune. Save you from seeing me that way. I saw what it was doing to my parents and sisters. But you, I could protect. I could give you what my family didn't get: Life. Freedom. The chance to move on without pain."

"It didn't work," I managed to say.

Poppy lowered her gaze. "I know that now. But believe me, Rune. I thought of you every single day. I pictured you, prayed for you. Hoped that the darkness I saw sprouting within you had faded with my absence."

Poppy rested her chin on my chest once more. "Tell me, Rune. Tell me what happened to you."

My jaw clenched, not wanting to let myself feel what I did then. But I could never say no to my girl. It was impossible. "I was angry," I said, pushing her hair from her pretty face. "No one could tell me where you went. Why you cut me off. My parents wouldn't get off my back. My pappa pissed me off 24/7. I blamed him for everything. I still do."

Poppy opened her mouth to speak, but I shook my head. "No," I bit out. "*Don't.*"

Poppy closed her mouth. I closed my eyes and forced myself to continue. "I went to school, but it wasn't long before I fell in with people just as pissed at the world as me. It wasn't long before I began to party. To drink, to smoke—to do the opposite of anything my pappa told me."

"Rune," Poppy said sadly. She didn't say anything else.

"That became my life. I threw my camera away. Then I packed away everything that reminded me of you." I barked out a laugh. "Shame I couldn't pull out my heart and pack it away too. Because that prick wouldn't let me forget you, no matter how much I tried. And then we returned. Back here. And I saw you in the hallway, and all that anger I still carried in my veins turned into a tidal wave."

I rolled onto my side, opened my eyes, and ran my hand down Poppy's face. "Because you looked so beautiful. Any image I had in my head of what you would look like at seventeen was blown out of the water. The minute I saw this brown hair, those big green eyes fixed on mine, I knew that any effort I'd made over the past two years to push you away was ruined. By one look. Ruined."

I swallowed. "Then when you told me about…" I trailed off, and Poppy shook her head.

"No," she said. "Enough now. You've said enough."

"And you?" I asked. "Why did you come back?"

"Because I was done," she said with a sigh. "Nothing was working. Each new treatment made no difference. The oncologist told us straight out: nothing would work. That was all I needed to make up my mind. I wanted to go home. I wanted to live out my remaining days at home, on palliative treatment, with those I loved most."

Poppy shuffled closer, kissing my cheek, my head, and finally, my mouth. "And now I have you. As I know now it was meant to be. This is where we were meant to be at this precise moment in time—home."

I felt a stray tear escape my eye. Poppy quickly brushed it away with her thumb. She leaned over me, across my chest, and said, "I have come to understand that death, for the sick, is not so hard to endure. For us, eventually, our pain ends, we go to a better place. But for those left behind, their pain only magnifies."

Poppy took my hand and held it to her cheek. "I really believe that tales of loss don't always have to be sad or sorrowful. I want mine to be remembered as a great adventure that I tried to live as best as I possibly could. Because how dare we waste a single breath? How dare we waste something so precious? Instead, we should strive for all those precious breaths to be taken in as many precious moments as we can squeeze into this short time on Earth. That's the message I want to leave behind. And what a beautiful legacy to leave for those I love."

If, as Poppy believed, a heartbeat was a song, then right now, in this moment, my heart would be singing with pride...of the complete admiration I had for the girl I loved, at the way she saw life, at the way she tried to make me believe—make me believe that there could be a life beyond her.

I was sure that wasn't the case, but I could see that Poppy was determined. That determination never failed.

"So now you know," Poppy declared and rested her head on my chest. "Now, let's say no more about it. We have our future to explore. We won't be slaves to the past." I closed my eyes, and she pleaded, "Promise me, Rune?"

Finding my voice, I whispered, "I promise."

I fought back the emotions slicing me inside. I wouldn't show her any sign that I was sad. She would see only happiness from me today.

Poppy's breathing evened out as I stroked her hair. The warm breeze flowed over us, taking with it the heaviness that had surrounded us.

I let myself begin to drift off, thinking Poppy had too, when she murmured, "What do you think heaven's like, Rune?"

I tensed, but Poppy's hands began to circle over my chest, ridding my body of the heaviness her question brought back.

"I don't know," I said. Poppy didn't offer anything, just stayed exactly where she was. Shifting slightly to bring her tighter into my arms, I said, "Somewhere beautiful. Somewhere peaceful. Somewhere where I'd see you again."

I felt Poppy smile against my shirt. "Me too," she agreed softly and turned to kiss my chest.

This time I was sure Poppy slept. I looked across the sand and watched as an old couple sat down near us. Their hands were clasped tightly. Before the woman could sit, the man spread a blanket on the sand. He kissed her cheek before helping her to sit down.

A pang of jealousy shot through me. Because we would never have that.

Poppy and I would never grow old together. Never have kids. Never have a wedding. Nothing. But as I glanced down at Poppy's thick brown hair and her delicate hands splayed on my chest, I let myself be grateful that at least I had her now. I didn't know what lay ahead. But I had her *now*.

I'd had her since I was five.

I now realized why I had loved her so hard from being so young—so I had this time with her. Poppy believed her spirit always knew she'd die young. I was starting to think that maybe mine did too.

Over an hour passed. Poppy was still sleeping. I gently lifted her from my chest and sat up. The sun had moved; waves lapped the shore.

Feeling thirsty, I opened the picnic basket and pulled out one of the bottles of water Poppy had packed. As I drank, my eyes rested on the backpack Poppy had carried from the trunk.

Wondering what was inside, I hauled it over and gently opened the zipper. At first all I saw was another black bag. This bag was padded. I pulled it out, and my heart kicked into a sprint when I realized what I was holding.

I sighed and closed my eyes.

I lowered the bag to the blanket and rubbed my hands over my face. When I lifted my head, I opened my eyes and blankly stared out over the water. I watched the boats in the distance, Poppy's words filtering into my mind…

I think they're leaving it all behind. I think they woke up one day and decided there's more to life. I think they decided—a couple in love, a boy and a girl—that they wanted to explore the world. They sold their possessions and bought a boat… She loves to play music, and he loves to capture moments on film…

My eyes left the camera bag that I knew so well. I understood where she got her theory about the boats.

He loves to capture moments on film…

I tried to be angry with her. I gave up taking pictures two years ago; it wasn't who I was anymore. It was no longer my dream. NYU wasn't in my plans. I didn't want to pick the camera back up. But my fingers began to twitch, and, despite being pissed at myself, I lifted the lid off the case and peered inside.

The old black-and-chrome vintage Canon that I had treasured stared up at me. I felt my face blanch, the blood moving to rush through to my heart, which slammed against my ribs. I had thrown this camera away. I had discarded it and all that it meant.

I had no idea how the hell Poppy had gotten hold of it. I wondered if she'd tracked down another and bought it. I lifted it from the bag and turned it over. There, scratched into the back, was my name. I had scraped it there on my thirteenth birthday, when my mamma and pappa gave me this camera.

It was the exact one.

Poppy had found my camera.

Flipping the back, I saw a full roll of film inside. In the bag lay the lenses. The ones I knew so well. Despite the years, I still instinctively knew which one would work best for any given shot—landscape, portrait, nighttime, daylight, natural setting, studio…

Hearing a soft rustle from behind me, I glanced over my shoulder. Poppy was sitting, watching me. Her eyes fell to the camera. Nervously inching forward, she said, "I asked your pappa about it. Where it had gone. He told me that you threw it away." Poppy's head tilted to the side. "You never knew, and he never told you, but he found it. He saw you had thrown it away. You had broken parts of it. The lenses were cracked, and other things." I was clenching my jaw so tightly it ached.

Poppy's finger traced the back of my hand that was resting in the blanket. "He had it repaired without you knowing. He's kept it safe for the past couple of years. He's kept up hope that you would find your way back to photography. He knew how much you loved it. He also blames himself for the fact that you gave it up."

My instinct was to open my mouth and hiss out that it was his fault. Everything was. But I didn't. For some reason the twist in my stomach kept my mouth shut.

Poppy's eyes glistened. "You should have seen him last night, when I asked him about it. He was so emotional, Rune. Even your mamma didn't know he'd kept it. He even had reels of film ready. Just in case you ever wanted it back."

I averted my gaze from Poppy's, instead refocusing on the camera. I didn't know how to feel about all that. I tried for angry. But, to my surprise, anger refused to come. For some reason I couldn't get the image from my head, of my pappa cleaning the camera and getting it fixed, on his own.

"He even has the darkroom ready and waiting for you, at your house."

I closed my eyes when Poppy added the last part. I was silent. Completely silent in response. My head was racing with too many thoughts, too many images. And I was conflicted. I had vowed never to take another picture.

But vowing it had been one thing. Holding the object of my addiction in my hands compromised everything I had sworn to fight against. To rebel against. To throw away, just like my pappa had cast aside my feelings when he chose to return to Oslo. The pit of heat in my stomach began to spread. This was the anger I anticipated. This was the blast of fire I was expecting.

I inhaled deeply, bracing for the darkness to overwhelm me, when, suddenly, Poppy jumped to her feet. "I'm going to the water," she announced and walked past me without another word. I watched her walk off. I watched her sink her feet into the soft sand, the breeze flicking up her short hair. I stayed, mesmerized, as she skipped to the water's edge, allowing the breaking waves to lap over her feet. She held her dress higher on her legs to avoid the splashes.

Her head tipped back to feel the sun on her face. Then, she glanced back to where I sat. She glanced back and she laughed. Free, with abandon, like she had no cares in the world.

I was transfixed, even more so when a reflected ray of sun from the sea cast a golden sheen on the side of her face, her green eyes emerald in this new light.

I lost my breath, actually fought for breath at how stunning she looked. Before I had even thought it through, I had my camera in my hand. I felt the weight transfer into my hands, and closing my eyes, I let the urge succeed.

Opening my eyes, I lifted the camera to my eye. Uncapping the lens, I found the most perfect angle of my girl dancing in the waves.

And I clicked.

I clicked the button on the camera, my heart stuttering at every snap of the shutter, sure in the knowledge that I was capturing Poppy in this moment—happy.

Adrenalin surged through me at the thought of how these pictures would develop. It was why I used the vintage camera. The anticipation of the darkroom, the delayed gratification of seeing the wonder that you had caught. The skill it took to work the camera to achieve that perfect shot.

A split second of serenity.

A moment of magic.

Poppy, in her own world, ran along the shore, her cheeks flushing pink with the warmth of the sun. Lifting her hands into the air, she let the hem of her dress fall and dampen with splashes from the water.

Then she turned to face me. As she did, she grew perfectly still, as did my heart in my chest. My finger waited, poised over the button, waiting for the right shot. And then it came. It came as a look of pure bliss spread across her face. It came as her eyes closed and her head tilted back, as if it were a relief, as if uncensored happiness possessed her.

I lowered the camera. Poppy held out her hand. Feeling high from the rush of having my passion sprung upon me, I jumped to my feet and walked across the sand.

When I took Poppy's hand, she pulled me close and pressed her lips on mine. I let her take the lead. I let her show me how much this meant to her. *This* moment. And I let myself feel it too. I allowed myself, for this brief moment, to push aside the heaviness I always carried like a shield. I allowed myself to get lost in the kiss, lifting the camera up high. Even with my eyes closed and no direction, I was convinced I had captured the best picture of the day.

Poppy stepped back and silently guided me back to the blanket, sitting us down, resting her head on my shoulder. I lifted my arm over her warm, sun-kissed shoulders and pulled her in close to my side. Poppy glanced up as I lazily placed a kiss to her head. When I met her eyes, I sighed and pressed my forehead to hers.

"You're welcome," she whispered as she looked away to stare out over the sea.

I hadn't felt like this in so long. I hadn't felt this peace inside since before we parted. And I was thankful to Poppy.

More than thankful.

Suddenly a quiet, awed gasp escaped Poppy's mouth. "Look, Rune," she whispered, pointing into the distance. I wondered what she wanted me to see; then she said, "Our footprints in the sand." She lifted her head and smiled a beaming smile. "Two sets. Four prints. Just like the poem."

I pulled my eyebrows down in confusion. Poppy's hand lay over my bent knee. With her head tucked under the shelter of my arm, she explained. "It's my favorite poem, Rune. It was my mamaw's favorite too."

"What does it say?" I asked, smiling slightly at the tiny size of Poppy's footprint next to my own.

"It's beautiful. And it's spiritual, so I'm not sure what you'll think of it." Poppy sent me a teasing look.

"Tell me anyway," I urged, just to hear her voice. Just to hear that reverence in her tone when she shared something she adored.

"It's more of a story really. About someone who has a dream. In the dream they are on a beach just like this. But they're walking beside the Lord."

My eyes narrowed and Poppy rolled her eyes. "I told you it was spiritual!" she said, laughing.

"You did," I replied and nudged her head with my chin. "Keep going."

Poppy sighed, and with her finger, she traced lazy patterns in the sand. My heart kind of cracked when I saw it was another infinity sign.

"As they're walking on the beach, in the dark sky above the person's life is played out for them to see. As each scene is played, like a movie reel, the person notices that two sets of footprints were left in the sand behind them. And as they continued, every new scene brought with it a trail of their footprints."

Poppy's attention honed in on our footprints. "When all the scenes had been played, the person looks back on the trail of footprints and notices something strange. They notice that during the saddest, or most despairing times of their life, there was only one set of footprints. For happier times there were always two sets."

My eyebrows furrowed, wondering where the story was headed. Poppy lifted her chin and blinked in the bright glare of the sun. With watery eyes, she looked at me and continued. "The person is really troubled by this. The Lord said that, when a person dedicates their life to Him, He would walk with them through all the ups and downs. The person then asked the Lord: why, at the worst points of their life, did He abandon them? Why did He leave?"

An expression of deep comfort washed over Poppy's face. "And what?" I prompted. "What does the Lord say?"

A single tear fell from her eye. "He tells the person that He *had* walked with them their whole life through. But, He explains, the times where there is only a single set of footprints were not when He walked beside them, but instead, when He carried them."

Poppy sniffed and said, "I don't care if you're not religious, Rune. The poem is not only for the faithful. We all have people who carry us through the worst of times, the saddest of times, the times that seem impossible to break free from. In one way or another, whether it's through the Lord or a loved one or both, when we feel like we can't walk on anymore, someone swoops in to help us…someone carries us through."

Poppy rested her head on my chest, wrapping herself up in my waiting arms.

My eyes got lost in a blurred haze as I stared at our footprints embedded in the sand. At that moment, I wasn't sure who was helping who. Because as much as Poppy insinuated that it was me who was helping her through her final months, I was beginning to believe that she was somehow saving me.

A single set of footprints on my soul.

Poppy shifted to face me, her cheeks wet with tears. Happy tears. Awed tears…*Poppy tears.* "Isn't it beautiful, Rune? Isn't it the most beautiful thing you've ever heard?"

I just nodded. Right now wasn't the time for words. I couldn't compete with what she'd just recited, so why would I even try?

I let my focus drift around the beach. And I wondered…I wondered if anyone else had just heard something so moving that it rocked their very core? I wondered if the person they loved more than any other on the planet had opened up to them so purely, with such raw emotion?

"Rune?" Poppy said quietly from beside me.

"Yeah, baby?" I replied softly. She turned her pretty face to me and cast me a weak smile. "You okay?" I asked, grazing my hand down her face.

"I'm getting tired," she admitted reluctantly. My heart cracked. Over the past week, I had begun to see tiredness gradually creeping into her face when she'd done too much.

And worse still, I could see how much she hated it. Because it prevented her from enjoying all life's adventures.

"It's okay to be tired, *Poppymin*. It's not a weakness."

Poppy's eyes dipped in defeat. "I just hate it. I've always been of the opinion that sleep is a waste of time."

I laughed at the cute pout that had formed on her lips. Poppy watched me, waiting for me to speak. Sobering, I said, "The way I see it, if you sleep when you need to, it means we can do more when you're strong." I brushed the tip of my nose over hers and said, "Our adventures will be that much more special. And you know I like you sleeping in my arms. I've always thought you look kind of perfect there."

Poppy sighed, and with one last glance at the sea, whispered, "Only you, Rune Kristiansen. Only you could give reason to my biggest hate so beautifully."

Kissing her warm cheek, I stood and gathered our things. When everything was packed, I looked over my shoulder at the pier, then back at Poppy. Holding out my hand, I said, "Come on, sleepyhead. For old times' sake?"

Poppy looked at the pier, and an unrestrained giggle leapt from her throat. I pulled her to standing, and we walked slowly, hand in hand, underneath the pier. The hypnotic sounds of the soft waves crashing against the old wooden beams cocooned where we stood.

Without wasting any time, I crowded Poppy back against the wooden post, cupping her cheeks and bringing our lips together. My eyes closed as the warm skin of her cheeks heated up under my palms. My chest heaved, breathless, as our lips kissed, slow and deep, while the cooling breeze rushed through Poppy's hair.

Pulling away, I rolled my lips, savoring the taste of sun and cherries bursting on my mouth.

Poppy's eyes fluttered open. Seeing how tired she appeared, I whispered for her, "Kiss four hundred and thirty-three. With *Poppymin* under the pier." Poppy smiled shyly, waiting for what had to come next. "My heart almost burst." The hint of teeth showing under her smile almost did make it burst, making it the perfect time to add, "Because I love her. I love her more than I could ever explain. My single set of footprints in the sand."

Poppy's beautiful green eyes widened at my confession. They immediately shimmered, and tears spilled over and tracked down her cheeks. I tried to brush them away with my fingers as my heart pounded in my chest. But Poppy gripped my hand, softly nuzzling her cheek into my palm. Keeping my hand in place, she met my eyes and whispered back, "I love you too, Rune Kristiansen. I never, ever stopped." She rose on tiptoes and brought my face down to stay opposite hers. "My soul mate. My heart…"

A calmness settled over me. A restfulness as Poppy fell into my arms, her light breathing seeping through my shirt.

I held her. I held her close, embracing this new feeling, until Poppy yawned. I tilted her head up to mine and said, "Let's get you home, beautiful."

Poppy nodded and, folding herself to my side, let me walk her back to our things, then up to the car. Reaching into the pocket of her purse, I took the car keys and opened the passenger-side door.

Placing both hands on her waist, I lifted her to the seat, reaching across her to click the seatbelt into the socket. As I pulled back, I placed a gentle kiss on Poppy's head. I heard her breathing hitch at my touch. I went to straighten up, when Poppy took hold of my arm, and with thick tears on her cheeks, whispered, "I'm sorry, Rune. I'm so sorry."

"What for, baby?" I asked, my voice breaking at how sad she sounded.

I pushed her hair back from her face as she said, "For pushing you away."

My stomach hollowed out. Poppy's eyes searched for something in mine, before her face contorted in pain. Fat tears poured down her paling face, and her chest shuddered as she fought to calm her suddenly erratic breathing.

"Hey," I said, planting my hands on her cheeks.

Poppy looked up at me. "We could have been like this if I hadn't been silly. We could have found a way for you to come back. You could have been with me the whole time. With me. Holding me…loving me. You loving me and me loving you so fiercely." Her voice stuttered, but she managed to finish. "I'm a thief. I stole our precious time—two years of you and me—for nothing."

It felt like my heart physically tore as Poppy cried, gripping tightly to my arm as if, frightened, I would turn away. How had she not realized by now that nothing could tear me away?

"Shh," I soothed, moving my head to rest against hers. "Breathe, baby," I said softly. I placed Poppy's hand over my heart, as she locked her gaze on mine. "Breathe," I repeated and smiled as she followed the rhythm of my heart to calm herself.

I wiped her damp cheeks with my hands, melting when she sniffed, her chest jerking every so often through the sobs she'd set free. Seeing I had her attention, I said, "I won't take the apology, because there's nothing to apologize for. You told me that the past no longer matters. That it's these moments that are important now." I steeled my emotions, to say, "Our final adventure. Me, giving you chest-bursting kisses to complete your jar. And you...you just being you. Loving me. Me loving you. For infinity..." I trailed off.

I stared intently and patiently into Poppy's eyes, smiling wide when she added, "Forever always."

I closed my eyes, knowing I'd broken through her pain. Then when my eyes opened, Poppy giggled hoarsely.

"There she is." I pressed one kiss onto each of the apples of her cheeks.

"Here I am," she echoed, "so completely in love with you."

Poppy lifted her head and kissed me. When she lay back in the seat, her eyes closed, called by sleep. I watched her for a second, before moving to shut the door. Just as the door closed, I caught Poppy whispering, "Kiss four hundred and thirty-four, with my Rune at the beach...when his love came home."

I could see through the window that Poppy had already drifted to sleep. Her cheeks were red from crying, but even in sleep, her lips were tilted upward, giving the appearance of a smile.

I wasn't sure how someone so perfect even existed.

Moving around to the hood of the car, I pulled my smokes out of the back pocket of my jeans and struck the lighter. I inhaled a much-needed drag. I closed my eyes as the hit of nicotine calmed me down.

I opened my eyes and stared at the sunset. The sun was fading on the horizon, flashes of orange and pink in its wake. The beach was almost empty but for the old couple I had seen before.

Only this time when I watched them, still so in love after all these years, I didn't let myself feel grief. As I glanced back at Poppy sleeping in the car, I felt a...happiness. Me. I felt happy. I let myself feel happy even through all this hurt. Because...*here I am...so completely in love with you...*

She loved me.

Poppymin. My girl. She loved me.

"That's enough," I said to the wind. "That's enough for right now."

Throwing the smoke's butt to the ground, I quietly slid into the driver's seat and turned the key. The engine sprang to life and I drove away from the beach, sure we'd be here again.

And if we didn't, like Poppy said, we'd had this moment. We had this memory. She had her kiss.

And I had her love.

––––––––––––

When I pulled into her driveway, dusk had fallen, the stars beginning to wake. Poppy had slept all the way home, her light, rhythmic breathing a comforting sound as I drove us down the dark roads toward home.

Putting the car in park, I got out and walked around to her side. I opened the door as quietly as I could, undoing the seatbelt and scooping Poppy into my arms.

She felt as if she weighed nothing as she instinctively curled into my chest, her warm breath drifting over my neck. I walked to her door. As I reached the top step, the front door opened. Mr. Litchfield was standing in the hallway.

I continued forward and he moved out of my way, allowing me to carry Poppy to her bedroom. I saw Poppy's mama and sisters sitting in the living room, watching TV.

Her mama got to her feet. "Is she okay?" she whispered.

I nodded. "She's just tired."

Mrs. Litchfield leaned forward and kissed Poppy's forehead. "Sleep tight, baby," she whispered. My chest tightened at the sight; then she nodded for me to take Poppy to her room.

I walked her down the hallway and through to her bedroom. As gently as I could, I placed her on her bed, smiling when Poppy's arm naturally searched for me on the side of the bed in which I slept.

When Poppy's breathing had evened out once again, I sat down on the side of her bed and ran my hand down her face. Leaning forward, I kissed her soft cheek and whispered, "I love you, *Poppymin*. Forever always."

Rising from the bed, I froze when I caught sight of Mr. Litchfield in the doorway, watching…listening.

My jaw clenched as he stared me down. Inhaling a calming breath through my nose, I walked silently past him, down the hallway, and back out to the car to get my camera.

I returned to the house to leave the car keys on the table in the hallway. As I entered, Mr. Litchfield walked from the living room. I stopped, rocking awkwardly until he reached out his hand for the keys.

I dropped them in his hand and went to turn to walk away. Before I could, he asked, "Did y'all have a good time?"

My shoulders tensed. Forcing myself to respond, I met his eyes and nodded. Throwing a wave to Mrs. Litchfield, Ida, and Savannah, I walked out the door and down the steps. As I reached the bottom step, I heard, "She loves you too, you know."

Mr. Litchfield's voice brought my feet to a stop, and without looking back, I replied, "I know."

I crossed the grass to my house. I went straight to my room and tossed the camera onto the bed. I intended to wait out the next few hours before I went to Poppy. But the more I stared at the camera bag, the more I wanted to see how the photos had turned out.

The pictures of Poppy dancing in the sea.

Without giving myself the chance to walk away, I grabbed the camera and sneaked down to the darkroom in the basement. As I reached the door and turned the knob, I flicked on the light. I sighed, a strange feeling settling within me.

Because Poppy had been right. My pappa had prepared this room for me. My equipment was exactly where it would have been two years ago. The lines and pegs were ready and waiting.

The process of developing the pictures felt as if I'd never been away. I enjoyed the familiarity of each step. Nothing was forgotten, like I had been born with the ability to do this.

Like I had been given this gift. Poppy recognized that I had needed this in my life, when I was too blinded by the past to see it.

The smell of the chemicals hit my nose. An hour passed, and I eventually

185

stood back, the pictures on their pegs forming into shapes, second by second revealing the moment caught on film.

The red light didn't stop me from seeing the wonders that I'd captured. As I walked along the lines of hanging images, of life in its glory, I couldn't stave off the excitement burning in my chest. I couldn't stop the smile—for this work—playing on my lips.

Then I stopped.

I stopped at a picture that held me captive. Poppy, holding on to the hem of her dress, dancing in the shallow water. Poppy, with a carefree smile and windblown hair, laughing wholeheartedly. Her eyes bright and her skin flushed as she looked over her shoulder, right at me. The sun lighting her face in an angle so pure and beautiful it was as if it was a spotlight on her happiness, attracted by her magnetic joy.

I lifted my hand, keeping it a centimeter away from the picture, and traced my finger over her beaming face, over her soft lips and rosy cheeks. And I felt it. Felt the overwhelming passion for this craft burst back to life inside me. This picture. This one picture cemented what I had secretly known all along.

I was meant to do this with my life.

It made sense that this picture brought this message home—it was of the girl that *was* my home. A knock sounded at the door, and without taking my gaze from the picture, I answered, "*Ja?*"

The door opened slowly. I felt who it was before I looked. My pappa entered the darkroom, by only a few steps. I looked at him, but I had to turn away again at the expression on his face as he drank in all the pictures hanging from the pegs across the room.

I didn't want to confront what that feeling in my stomach meant. Not yet.

Minutes passed by in silence, before my pappa said softly, "She's absolutely beautiful, son." My chest constricted when I saw his eyes on the photo that I was still standing before.

I didn't respond. My pappa stood awkwardly in the doorway, saying nothing else. Finally, he moved to leave. As he went to shut the door, I forced myself to say a sharp "Thank you...for the camera."

In my peripheral vision, I saw my pappa pause. I heard a slow, ragged intake of breath, and then he replied, "You have nothing to thank me for, son. Nothing at all."

With that he left me in my darkroom.

I stayed longer than I intended, replaying my pappa's response in my mind.

Clutching two photographs in my hands, I climbed the steps of the basement and headed for my room. As I passed the open door of Alton's bedroom, I saw him sitting on his bed, watching TV.

He hadn't seen me, standing there in his doorway, and I carried on to my room. But as I heard him laugh at whatever he was watching, my feet stuck to the floor, and I made myself turn back.

As I entered his room, Alton turned to me, and in a move that made me feel a crack in my chest, the biggest smile spread on his cute face.

"*Hei*, Rune," he said quietly, and he sat further up in bed.

"*Hei*," I replied. I walked toward his bed and nodded toward the TV. "What are you watching?"

Alton looked at the TV, then back to me. *Swamp Monsters.* His head tipped to the side, and then he pushed his long hair from his face. Something in my stomach tugged as he did. "You want to watch it with me for a while?" Alton asked nervously, then dropped his head.

I could tell he thought I would say no. Surprising both him and myself, I replied, "Sure."

Alton's blue eyes widened to the size of saucers. He lay stiffly on his bed. When I stepped forward, he shuffled to the side of the narrow mattress.

I lay down beside him, kicking up my feet. Then Alton leaned against my side and continued watching his show. I watched it with him, only looking away when I caught him staring up at me.

When I met his eyes, his cheeks flushed with red and he said, "I like you watching this with me, Rune."

Breathing through the unfamiliar feeling his words brought out, I ruffled his long hair and replied, "Me too, Alt. I like this too."

Alton leaned back against my side. He lay there until he fell asleep, the timer on his TV kicking in and plunging the room into darkness.

Rising off the bed, I passed my mamma, who had been watching silently from the hallway. I nodded my head at her as I entered my room, turning and shutting the door behind me. I flipped the lock, placed one of the photos on the desk, and climbed through my window and ran across to Poppy's.

When I entered her room, Poppy was still sleeping. Taking off my shirt, I walked around the side of her bed to where she slept. I placed the photo of us kissing by the water on her pillow for her to see as soon as she woke up.

I climbed into her bed, Poppy automatically finding me in the dark, laying her head against my chest and wrapping her arm around my waist.

Four footprints in the sand.

Soaring Wings and Fading Stars

Poppy
Three Months Later

"WHERE'S MY POPPY-GIRL?"

I wiped sleep from my eyes, sitting up on my bed, excitement zipping through me at the sound of a voice I loved.

"Aunt DeeDee?" I whispered to myself. I tried to listen harder, making sure I really had heard her voice. Muffled voices came from the hallway, and then suddenly the door flew open. I rose on my arms, the darn things shaking after I pushed my weakening muscles too far.

I lay back down as Aunt DeeDee appeared in the doorway. Her dark hair was pulled into a bun, and she was wearing her flight attendant uniform. Her makeup was perfectly in place, as was her infectious smile.

Her green eyes softened when they landed on me. "There she is," she said gently, walking to my bed. She sat down on the edge of the mattress and leaned down to wrap me in her arms.

"What are you doing here, DeeDee?"

My aunt smoothed my hair back from its sleep-induced disarray and whispered conspiringly, "Blowing you from this joint."

My eyebrows drew together in confusion. Aunt DeeDee had spent Christmas and New Year's with us, and then a whole week with us, just two weeks ago. I knew she had a busy schedule over the next month.

Which was why I was so confused about her being back now.

"I don't understand," I said, swinging my legs off the mattress. For the past few days I had mostly been stuck in bed. After my hospital check-up at the beginning of the week, we found my white blood cell count was too low. I had been given blood and medication to help. And it had helped some, but it made me tired for a few days. Kept me inside so infections were kept at bay. My doctors had wanted me to stay in the hospital, but I'd refused. I wasn't missing a second of my life by being back in that place. Not now that I could see that my cancer was increasing its grip on me. Every second was becoming more and more precious.

Home was my happy place.

Having Rune beside me, kissing me sweetly, was my safety.

It was all I needed.

Glancing at the clock, I saw it was nearing four p.m. Rune would be around soon. I had made him attend school these past few days. He hadn't wanted to go if I couldn't. But this was his senior year. He needed the grades to get into college. Even though he protested that right now he didn't care.

And that was okay. Because I would care for the both of us. I wouldn't let him put his life on hold for me.

Aunt DeeDee jumped to her feet. "Okay, Poppy-girl, jump in the shower. We have an hour before we have to set off." She looked at my hair. "Don't bother washing your hair; I got a girl that can take care of that when we get there."

I shook my head, about to ask more questions, but my aunt swept out of my bedroom. I got to my feet, stretching out my muscles. Taking in a deep breath, I closed my eyes and smiled. I felt better than I had these past few days. Felt a little stronger.

Strong enough to leave the house.

Grabbing my towel, I made quick work of having a shower. I applied a light layer of makeup. I tied my unwashed hair back in a side bun, my white bow firmly in place. I dressed in a hunter-green dress, sliding a white sweater over the top.

I was placing my infinity earring in my earlobe when my bedroom door suddenly opened. I caught the buzz of raised voices, my daddy's voice in particular.

Turning my head, I smiled when Rune entered, his blue eyes immediately colliding with mine. Searching, checking, before brightening with relief.

Rune silently cut across the room, only stopping when he had threaded his arms around my shoulders and pulled me to his chest. I let my arms hold his waist and breathed in his fresh scent.

"You look better," Rune said above me.

I held him a little tighter. "I feel better."

Rune stepped back and placed his hands on my face. He searched my eyes, before his lip curled up and he pressed the sweetest of soft kisses to my mouth. When we broke away, he sighed. "I'm glad. I was worried that we wouldn't be able to go."

"Where?" I asked, my heart kicking into a steady run.

This time Rune smiled and, moving his mouth to my ear, announced, "On another adventure."

My racing heart increased to a gallop. "Another adventure?"

With no more explanation, Rune led me out of my bedroom. His hand, so tightly gripping mine, was the only indication he gave of how concerned he had been over the past few days.

I knew though. I saw the fear in his eyes every time I moved in bed and he asked if I was okay. Every time he sat with me after school, watching me, studying me...waiting. Waiting to see if this was it.

He was petrified.

The progression of my cancer didn't frighten me. The pain and the near future didn't scare me. But seeing Rune look at me this way, so desolate, so desperate, had begun to make me afraid. I loved him so much, and I could see he loved me beyond measure. But this love, this soul-searing connection, had begun to anchor the heart I had set free to this life.

I had never feared death. My faith was strong; I knew there was a life after this. But now fear had started to creep into my consciousness. Fear of leaving Rune. Fear of his absence...fear of not feeling his arms around me and his kisses on my lips.

Rune glanced back as if sensing my heart beginning to tear. I nodded. I wasn't sure I had been convincing; I still detected concern in his expression.

"She isn't going!" My daddy's forceful voice carried down the hallway.

Rune pulled me to his side, lifting his arm until I was safely underneath. When we arrived at the doorway, my mama, daddy, and Aunt DeeDee were standing at the mouth of the living room.

My daddy's face was red. My aunt had her arms crossed over her chest. My mama ran her hand down my daddy's back, attempting to calm him.

My daddy lifted his head. He forced a smile. "Poppy," he said and came closer. Rune didn't let go of me. My daddy picked this up and shot him a glare that should have eviscerated him on the spot.

Rune didn't even flinch.

"What's wrong?" I asked, reaching for my daddy's hand.

My touch seemed to have rendered him speechless. I glanced at my mama. "Mama?"

Mama stepped forward. "It's been planned since your aunt came a few weeks ago." I looked to Aunt DeeDee, who smiled mischievously.

"Rune here planned to take you away. He asked your aunt to help plan it." Mama sighed. "We never expected your levels to fall this soon." Mama placed her hand on my daddy's arm. "Your daddy doesn't think you should go."

"Go where?" I asked.

"It's a surprise," Rune announced from beside me.

Daddy stepped an inch back and met my eyes. "Poppy, your white blood cell levels have dropped. It means the chance of infection is high. With your immune system being at risk, I don't think you should travel on a plane—"

"A plane?" I interrupted.

I looked up at Rune. "A plane?" I repeated.

He curtly nodded his head once but didn't explain any further.

Mama placed her hand on my arm. "I asked your specialist and he said"—she cleared her throat—"he said, at this point in your illness, if you want to go, then you should go." I heard the underlying current of her words. *Go before it got too late to travel anywhere.*

"I want to go," I said with unwavering certainty, gripping onto Rune's waist. I wanted him to know I wanted this. I glanced up at him; he met my eyes. Smiling, I said, "I'm with you."

Rune, surprising me, but at the same time not surprising me at all, kissed me. Kissed me hard and quick right in front of my family. Rune broke free from me and moved next to my aunt. Beside DeeDee there was a suitcase. Without another word, he took the suitcase to the car.

My heart was beating a staccato rhythm of excitement.

Daddy squeezed my hand. His touch brought me back to his worry, his fear. "Poppy," he said sternly.

Before he could say any more, I leaned forward and kissed him on his cheek. I looked him in the eye. "Daddy, I understand the risks. I've been fighting this a long time. I know you're worried. I know you don't want me to be hurt. But staying trapped in my room like a caged bird for one more day...that is what will hurt me. I've never been one to stay inside. I want this, Daddy. I *need* this." I shook my head, feeling a sheer sheen of water fill my eyes. "I can't spend whatever time I have left locked away for fear it'll make me worse. I need to live...I need this adventure."

He sucked in a stuttering breath. But, eventually, he nodded his head. A light dizziness flooded through me. I was going!

Jumping on the spot, I wrapped my arms around my daddy's neck. He hugged me back.

I kissed my mama then looked to my aunt. She had her hand held out. I took hold of it, just as my daddy said, "I'm trusting you to look after her, DeeDee."

My aunt sighed. "You know this girl is my heart, James. You think I'd let anything happen to her?"

"And they stay in separate rooms!"

I simply rolled my eyes at that.

My daddy began talking to my aunt. But I didn't hear it. I didn't hear anything as my gaze went through the open door and down to the boy dressed all in black who was leaning against the railing of our porch. The boy in a leather jacket who was casually bringing a cigarette to his mouth, all the time watching me. His crystal-blue eyes not once straying from mine.

Rune blew out a cloud of smoke. Casually tossing the butt to the ground, he flicked his chin and held out his hand.

Releasing Aunt DeeDee's hand, I closed my eyes for a brief moment, committing to memory how he looked, right at this moment.

My Norwegian bad boy.

My heart.

Opening my eyes, I rushed through the door. Reaching the top step, I then jumped into Rune's open arms. He enveloped me in his embrace. I giggled, feeling the breeze on my face. Holding me tightly, my feet still off the ground, Rune asked, "You ready for that adventure, *Poppymin*?"

"Yes," I replied breathlessly.

Rune pressed his forehead to mine and closed his eyes. "I love you," he whispered after a long pause.

"I love you too," I said, just as quietly.

I was rewarded with a rare smile.

He carefully lowered me to the ground, took my hand, and asked again, "You ready?"

I nodded, then turned to my parents, who were standing on the porch. I waved goodbye.

"Come on, kids," said DeeDee. "We got a flight to catch."

Rune led me to the car, holding my hand as always. As we settled in the backseat, I looked out the window as we pulled away. I stared up at the clouds, knowing that soon I'd be soaring above them.

On an adventure.

An adventure with my Rune.

"New York," I said breathlessly, reading the screen at our gate.

Rune smirked. "We always planned to go. It'll just be briefer than we'd always thought."

Completely speechless, I wrapped my arms around his waist and rested my head on his chest. Aunt DeeDee returned from speaking to the woman at the desk.

"Come on, you two," she said, waving her hand toward the entrance to the plane. "Let's get you on board."

We followed DeeDee. My mouth fell open when she showed us to the two front seats in first class. I looked at her and she shrugged. "What's the point of being in charge of the first-class cabin if I can't use the perks to spoil my favorite niece?"

I hugged DeeDee. She held on a little longer than normal. "Go on, now," she said and shooed me to my seat. Aunt DeeDee quickly disappeared behind the curtain of the attendants' section. I stood, watching her go. Rune took my hand.

"She'll be okay," he soothed, then pointed to the window seat. "For you," he added. Unable to stop the excited giggle leaping from my throat, I sat down and stared out of the window at the people working on the ground below.

I watched them until the plane was fully boarded and we began to roll away. Sighing happily, I turned to Rune, who was watching me. Wrapping his fingers in mine, I said, "Thank you."

"I wanted you to see New York." He shrugged. "I wanted to see it with you."

Rune leaned in to kiss me. I stopped his lips with my fingers. "Kiss me at thirty-nine thousand feet. Kiss me in the sky. Kiss me among the clouds."

Rune's minty breath ghosted over my face. Then he silently sat back. I laughed as the plane suddenly gained speed and we soared into the air.

When the plane leveled off, I suddenly found my lips being brought flush to Rune's. His hands clasped my head as he took my mouth with his own. Needing something to keep me grounded, I gripped on to his shirt. I sighed against his mouth as his tongue dueled softly against mine.

When he pulled back, his chest heaving and skin warm, I whispered, "Kiss eight hundred and eight. At thirty-nine thousand feet. With my Rune...my heart almost burst."

By the end of the flight I had lots of new kisses to add to my jar.

"This is for us?" I asked incredulously. I stared at the penthouse of the ridiculously expensive hotel in Manhattan my aunt had brought us to.

I looked up at Rune and I could tell, even through his ever-neutral expression, that he too was floored.

Aunt DeeDee stopped beside me. "Poppy, your mama doesn't know this yet. But well, I've been dating someone for a while now." A loving smile spread on her lips and she continued. "Let's just say this room was his gift to you both."

I stared up at her in amazement. But then a warmth filled me. I had always worried about Aunt DeeDee. She was on her own often. I could see in her face how happy this man had made her.

"He paid for this? For us? For me?" I asked.

DeeDee paused, then explained, "Technically, he doesn't really have to pay for it. He owns the joint."

My mouth, if possible, dropped further, until Rune playfully shut it with his finger under my chin. I stared at my boyfriend. "You knew?"

He shrugged. "She helped me plan all this."

"So you knew?" I repeated. Rune shook his head at me, then carried our suitcases into the master bedroom to the right. He was clearly ignoring my daddy's instruction of separate rooms.

As Rune disappeared through the doorway, my aunt said, "That boy would walk on broken glass for you, Pops."

My heart filled with light. "I know," I whispered. But that slight edge of fear I had begun to feel seeped into me.

Aunt DeeDee's arm slipped around me. As I squeezed her back, I said, "Thank you."

She kissed my head. "I didn't do anything, Pops. It was all Rune." She paused. "I don't think, in all my life, that I've ever seen two kids love each other so hard so young, and even harder as teens."

Aunt DeeDee pulled me back to meet my eyes. "Cherish this time with him, Pops. That boy, he loves you. You'd have to be blind not to see it."

"I will," I whispered.

DeeDee moved to the door. "We're here for two nights. I'll be with Tristan in his suite. Call my cell if you need anything. I'll only be minutes away."

"Okay," I replied.

Turning, I drank in the splendor of the room. Its ceilings were so high that I had to bend my head back just to see the pattern in the white plaster.

The room was so big that it would dwarf most people's houses. I walked to the window and beheld a panoramic view of all of New York.

And I breathed.

I breathed as my gaze fell upon the familiar sights that I had only ever seen in pictures or on film: the Empire State Building, Central Park, the Statue of Liberty, the Flatiron Building, Freedom Tower...

There was so much to see that my heart raced in anticipation. This was where I was meant to have lived my life. I would have been at home here. Blossom Grove would have been my roots; New York would have been my wings.

And Rune Kristiansen would forever have been my love. By my side through it all.

Noticing a door to my left, I walked over and pushed down the handle. I gasped as a cold breeze hit me, and then I truly let myself take in the sight.

A garden.

An outdoor terrace with winter flowers, benches and, better still, the view. Zipping up my coat to keep warm, I stepped out into the coldness. Flurries of light snowflakes settled on my hair. Needing to feel them on my face, I tipped my head back. Cold flakes landed on my eyelashes, tickling my eyes.

I laughed as my face grew damp. Then I walked forward, running my hands over the glistening evergreens until I was standing at the wall that offered a panorama of Manhattan on a plate.

I breathed in, letting the cold air fill my bones. Suddenly, warm arms were around my waist and Rune's chin rested on my shoulder. "You like it, baby?" Rune asked softly. His voice was barely above a whisper so as not to intrude into our little haven of tranquility.

I shook my head in disbelief and turned back slightly until I faced him. "I can't believe you've done all this," I replied. "I can't believe you've given me this." I pointed to the sprawling city below. "You've given me New York."

Rune kissed my cheek. "It's late, and we have lots to do tomorrow. I want to make sure you're rested enough to see everything I have planned."

A thought sprang into my mind. "Rune?"

"*Ja?*"

"Can I take you somewhere tomorrow too?"

He frowned, creasing his forehead. "Of course," he agreed. I could see him searching my eyes, trying to discover what I was up to. But he didn't question me. And I was happy about that. He'd refuse if he knew ahead of time.

"Good," I said proudly and smiled to myself. Yes, he had given me this trip. Yes, he had things planned. But I wanted to show him something, to remind him of his dreams. Dreams he could still achieve even after I was gone.

"You need to sleep, *Poppymin*," Rune said and lowered his mouth to kiss my neck.

I threaded my hand through his. "With you beside me in bed."

I felt him nod against my neck, before kissing it one more time. "I've run you a bath and I've ordered food. You bathe, then we'll eat, then we'll sleep."

I turned in his arms and lifted onto my tiptoes to place my hands on his cheeks. They were cold. "I love you, Rune," I said softly. I said it often. And I always felt it with my whole heart. I wanted him to know, at all times, how much I adored him.

Rune sighed and kissed me slowly. "I love you too, *Poppymin*," he said against my lips, barely breaking away.

Then he led me inside, where I bathed. We ate. And then we slept.

I lay in his arms in the center of a huge four-poster bed. With his warm breath drifting across my face. His bright blue eyes watching my every move.

I fell asleep, cradled in his embrace, with a smile both in my heart and on my lips.

12

Heart Songs and Beauty Found

Poppy

I THOUGHT I HAD FELT A BREEZE THROUGH MY HAIR BEFORE. BUT NOTHING compared to the breeze that whipped through my tresses at the top of the Empire State Building.

I thought I'd been kissed in every way there was to be kissed. But nothing compared to Rune's kisses under the fairy-tale castle in Central Park. To his kiss in the crown of the Statue of Liberty. In the center of Times Square, the bright lights flashing as people rushed around us like they had no time left in the world.

People were always rushing even though they had plenty of time. Although I had very little, I made sure everything I did was slow. Measured. Meaningful. I made sure to savor any new experience. To take a deep breath and drink in every new sight, smell, and sound.

To simply stop. Breathe. Embrace.

Rune's kisses varied. They were slow and soft, gentle and feather-light. Then they were hard, fast, and ravishing. Both left me breathless. Both made it into the jar.

More kisses sewn onto my heart.

After eating a late lunch at the Stardust Diner, somewhere I decided may just be my third-favorite place on Earth, I led Rune outside and around the corner.

"Is it my turn now?" I asked, as Rune took hold of my collar and pulled it close around my neck. Rune checked his watch. I eyed him curiously, wondering why he kept checking the time. Rune saw me watching him in suspicion.

Wrapping his arms around me, he replied, "You have the next couple of hours; then it's back to my schedule."

I scrunched my nose at his strict attitude and playfully stuck out my tongue. Heat flared in Rune's eyes as I did. He dived forward and pressed his mouth to my lips, his tongue immediately stroking against mine. I squealed and held on tight as he dipped me back, before breaking the kiss.

"Don't tempt me," he said teasingly. But I still saw that heat in his eyes. My heart skipped a beat. Since Rune had been back in my life, we had done nothing more than kiss. Kiss and talk, and hold each other so impossibly close. He never pushed for more, but as the weeks had rolled on, I had begun to want to give myself to him again.

Memories of our night, two years ago, ran like a show reel in my mind. The scenes were so vivid, so filled with love, that my lungs seized. Because I still remembered that look in his eyes when he moved above me. I still remembered the way his eyes watched mine. The way heat flooded through me as I felt him, so warm, in my arms.

And I remembered his gentle touches on my face, my hair, and my lips. But best of all, I remembered his face in the afterglow. The incomparable expression of adoration. The look that told me that, though we were young, what we had done had changed us forever.

Joined us in body, mind, and soul.

Truly made us infinity.

Forever always.

"Where are we going, *Poppymin?*" Rune asked, pulling me from my reverie. He held the back of his hand against my burning cheek. "You're hot," he said, his accent strong, the perfect sound running through me like a cool breeze.

"I'm fine," I said coyly. Taking his hand, I tried to lead him down the street. Rune pulled on my hand and made me face his concern head on.

"Poppy—"

"I'm fine," I interrupted, pursing my lips so he would know I meant it.

Groaning in exasperation, Rune slung his arm around my shoulder and led me forward. I searched for the street name and block, working out where to go from here.

"Are you going to tell me what we're doing?" Rune asked.

Ensuring we were heading in the right direction, I shook my head. Rune pressed a kiss to the side of my head as he lit up a cigarette. As he smoked, I took the opportunity to look around me. I loved New York. I loved everything about it. Eclectic people—artists, suits, and dreamers—all woven into the giant patchwork quilt of life. The busy streets, car horns, and shouts the perfect symphonic soundtrack to the city that never sleeps.

I breathed in the fresh scent of snow on the cold, crisp air and hugged closer into Rune's chest. "We would do this," I said and smiled, briefly closing my eyes.

"What?" Rune asked, the now-familiar scent of his cigarette smoke billowing before us.

"This," I said, "us, walking down Broadway. We would walk the city, heading to meet friends, to our schools or our apartment." I nudged his arm over my shoulder. "You would hold me just like this and we would talk. You'd tell me about your day, and I'd tell you about mine." I smiled at the normalcy of the picture. Because I didn't need grand gestures or fairy tales; a normal life with the boy I loved would have always been enough.

Even in this moment, it was worth everything.

Rune didn't say anything. I had learned that when I spoke like this, so candidly about things that would never come to pass, Rune found it best to say nothing at all. And it was okay. I understood why he had to protect his already breaking heart.

If I could protect it for him I would, but I was the cause.

I just prayed, to all that was good, that I could also be the remedy.

Seeing the banner on the old building, I looked up at Rune and said, "We're nearly there."

Rune looked around in confusion, and I was glad. I didn't want him to see where we were. I didn't want him to be angry at a gesture kindly meant. I didn't want him to hurt at being forced to see the future that could be his.

I steered Rune left toward a building. Rune threw his finished cigarette to the ground and took my hand in his. Walking to the register, I asked for our tickets.

Rune pushed my hand from my purse when I tried to pay. He paid, not yet knowing where we were. I reached up and kissed him on the cheek. "Such a gentleman," I teased and watched as he rolled his eyes.

"I'm not sure your daddy thinks that way about me."

I couldn't contain my laugh. As I giggled freely, Rune stopped and watched me, holding out his hand. I placed mine in his and let him pull me to him. His mouth landed just above my ear, and he said, "Why is it when you laugh like that I desperately need to take your picture?"

I looked up, my laughter fading. "Because you capture all aspects of the human condition—the good, the bad, the truth." I shrugged and added, "Because despite how much you protest and exude an aura of darkness, you strive for happiness, you wish to be happy."

"Poppy." Rune turned his head. As always, he didn't want to embrace the truth, but it was there, locked deep in his heart. All he had ever wanted was to be happy—just him and me.

For me, I wanted him to learn to be happy alone. Even though I would walk beside him every day in his heart.

"Rune," I urged softly. "Please come with me."

Rune stared at my outstretched hand before relenting and clasping our hands tightly together. Even then he stared at our joined hands with a hint of pain behind his guarded eyes.

Bringing those hands to my lips, I kissed the back of one hand and brought them both to my cheek. Rune exhaled through his nose. Finally, he pulled me under the protection of his arm. Wrapping my arm around his waist, I led him through the double doors, revealing the show on the other side.

We were greeted with a vast, open space, famous pictures framed by the high walls. Rune stilled, and I looked up just in time to see his surprised yet impassioned reaction on seeing his dream showcased before him. An exhibition of pictures that had shaped our time.

Pictures that had changed the world.

Perfectly captured moments in time.

Rune's chest expanded slowly as he inhaled deeply, then exhaled with guarded calmness. He glanced down at me and opened his lips. Not a sound came out. Not a single word formed.

Rubbing my hand across his chest, under the camera that was hanging around his neck, I said, "I found out this exhibition was on last night and wanted you to see it. It'll be here for the year, but I wanted to be here, with you, in this moment. I…I wanted to share this with you."

Rune blinked, his expression neutral. The only reaction he displayed was the clenching of his jaw. I wasn't sure if that was a good thing or a bad thing.

Slipping from below his arm, I loosely held his fingers. Consulting the guidebook, I brought us to the first picture in the exhibition. I smiled, seeing the sailor in the center of Times Square dipping the nurse back to kiss her on the lips. "*New York City. August 14, 1945.* V-J Day in Times Square *by Alfred Eisenstaedt,*" I read. And I felt the lightness and the excitement of the celebration through the image displayed before me. I felt I was there, sharing that moment with all who were there.

I looked up at Rune, and I saw him studying the picture. His expression hadn't changed, but I saw his jaw slacken as his head tilted slightly to one side.

His fingers twitched in mine.

I smiled again.

He wasn't immune. And no matter how much he resisted, he loved this. I could feel it as easily as I could feel the snow hit my skin outside. I led him to the second picture. My eyes widened as I took in the dramatic sight. Tanks rolling forward in convoy, a man standing directly in their path. I quickly read the information, heart racing. "*Tiananmen Square, Beijing. June 5, 1989. This picture captured one man's protest to stop the military suppression of continuing protests against the Chinese government.*"

I stepped closer to the picture. I swallowed. "It's sad," I said to Rune. Rune nodded his head.

Every new picture seemed to evoke a different emotion. Looking at these captured moments, I truly understood why Rune loved to take photographs. This exhibition demonstrated how capturing these images impacted society. They showed humanity at its best and at its worst.

They highlighted life in all its nakedness and in its purest form.

When we stopped at the next picture, I immediately glanced away, unable to look properly. A vulture patiently waiting, hovering over an emaciated child. The image immediately made me feel full of sorrow.

I moved to walk away, but Rune stepped closer to the image. My head snapped up and I watched him. I watched him study every part of the picture. I watched as his eyes flared and his hands clenched at his side.

His passion had broken through.

Finally.

"This picture is one of the most controversial pictures ever taken," he informed me quietly, still focused on the image. "The photographer was covering the famine in Africa. As he was taking his pictures, he saw this child walking for help, and this vulture waiting by, sensing death." He took a breath. "This picture showed, in one image, the extent of the famine more than all the previous written reports ever did." Rune looked at me. "It made people sit up and pay attention. It showed them, in all its brutal severity, how bad the famine had grown." He pointed back at the child, crouched on the ground. "Because of this picture, aid work increased, the press covered more of the people's struggles." He took a deep breath. "It changed their world."

Not wanting to stop his momentum, I walked him to the next one. "Do you know what this one is about?"

Most of the photographs, I struggled to look at. Most were of pain, most were of suffering. But to a photographer, although graphic and heart-wrenchingly difficult to view, they held a certain type of poetic grace. They held a deep and endless message, all captured in a single frame.

"It was a protest—the Vietnam war. A Buddhist monk set himself on fire." Rune's head dipped and tipped to the side, studying the angles. "He never flinched. He took the pain to make a statement that peace should be achieved. It highlighted the plight and the futility of that war."

And the day rolled on, Rune explaining almost every picture. When we reached the final shot, it was a black-and-white picture of a young woman. It was old; her hair and makeup seemed to be from the sixties. She appeared to be around twenty-five in the picture. And she was smiling.

It made me smile too.

I looked to Rune. He shrugged, silently telling me that he didn't know the picture either. The title simply read *"Esther."* I searched the guidebook for the information, my eyes immediately brimming with water when I read the inspiration. When I read why this picture was here.

"What?" Rune asked, his eyes flashing with worry.

"Esther Rubenstein. The late wife of the patron of this exhibition." I blinked and finally managed to finish, *"Died aged twenty-six, of cancer."* I swallowed the emotion in my throat and stepped closer to Esther's portrait.

"Placed in this exhibition by her husband, who never remarried. He took this picture and hung it in this exhibition. It reads that even though this picture didn't change the world, Esther changed his."

Slow tears trickled down my cheeks. The sentiment was beautiful; the honor was breathtaking.

Wiping my tears away, I glanced back at Rune, who had turned away from the picture. My heart sank. I moved before him. His head was hanging low. I pushed back the hair from his face. The tortured expression that greeted me tore me in two.

"Why did you bring me here?" he asked through a thick throat.

"Because this is what you love." I gestured around the room. "Rune, this is NYU Tisch. This is where you wanted to attend. I wanted you to see what you could achieve one day. I wanted you to see what your future could still hold."

Rune's eyes closed. When they opened, he caught my stifled yawn. "You're tired."

"I'm fine," I argued, wanting to address this now. But I *was* tired. I wasn't sure I could do much more without some rest.

Rune threaded his hand through mine and said, "Let's go rest before tonight."

"Rune," I tried to argue, to talk about this more, but Rune swung around and quietly said, *"Poppymin,* please. No more." I could hear the strain in his voice. "New York was *our* dream. There's no New York without you. So please…" He trailed off, then sadly whispered, "Stop."

Not wishing to see him so broken, I nodded. Rune kissed my forehead. This kiss was soft. It was thankful.

We left the exhibition, and Rune hailed a cab. In minutes we were en route back to the hotel. As soon as we got into the suite, Rune lay down with me in his arms.

He didn't speak as I drifted to sleep. I fell asleep with the image of Esther in my mind, wondering how her husband had healed after she had returned home.

Wondered if he had even healed at all.

"*Poppymin?*"

Rune's soft voice called me from sleep. I blinked into the darkness of the room, only to feel Rune's gentle finger running down my cheek.

"Hey, baby," he said quietly when I rolled over to face him. Reaching out, I turned on the lamp. When the light flickered on, I focused on Rune.

A smile tugged on my lips. He wore a tight white T-shirt under a brown blazer. His black skinny jeans were on his legs, familiar black suede boots on his feet. I tugged on the lapels of his blazer. "You're looking real smart, baby."

Rune's lips molded into a half-smile. He leaned forward and took my mouth gently with his. When he pulled back, I noticed his hair was freshly washed and dried. And unlike every other day, today he'd run a comb through it, the golden strands feeling silky between my fingers.

"How're you feeling?" he asked. I stretched out my arms and legs.

"A little tired and sore from all the walking, but I'm okay."

Rune's forehead lined with worry. "You sure? We don't have to go tonight if you're not feeling up to it."

Shuffling farther forward on my pillow, I stopped just an inch before Rune's face and said, "Nothing could keep me from tonight." I ran my hand down his soft brown blazer. "Especially with you looking all spiffed up. I have no idea what you have planned, but if it got you out of your leather jacket, it must be something real special."

"I think so," Rune replied after a pregnant pause.

"Then I'm definitely fine," I said confidently, allowing Rune to help me up to a sitting position when this simple task became too much of a struggle.

Remaining crouched down, Rune searched my face. "I love you, *Poppymin.*"

"I love you too, baby," I replied. As I stood, with Rune's help, I couldn't help but flush. He was becoming more handsome with each passing day, but looking like this, he made my heart gallop in my chest.

"What should I wear?" I asked Rune. He led me to the living area of the suite. A lady was waiting in the center of the room, hair and makeup equipment spread out around her.

Astounded, I glanced up at Rune. He nervously pushed his hair from his face. "Your aunt organized it all." He shrugged. "So you'd look perfect. Not that you don't anyway."

The lady in the room waved and tapped the seat in front of her. Rune lifted my hand to his mouth and kissed it. "Go—we have to leave in an hour."

"What do I wear?" I asked breathlessly.

"We have that organized too." Rune led me to the seat and I sat down, briefly stopping to introduce myself to the stylist.

Rune moved to sit on the couch across the room. I was filled with happiness when he took his camera from its bag on the side table. I watched Rune raise the camera to his eye as Jayne, the stylist, began working on my hair. And for the next forty minutes, he captured those moments.

I couldn't have been happier if I tried.

Jayne leaned down, checking my face, and, with a final brushstroke on my cheek, moved back and smiled. "There we go, girl. All done." She stepped away and began packing her things. When she was finished, she kissed me on the cheek. "Have a good night, lady."

"Thank you," I replied and walked her to the door.

When I turned around, Rune was standing before me. He lifted his hand to my newly curled hair. "*Poppymin,*" he rasped. "You look beautiful."

I ducked my head. "Do I?"

Rune lifted his camera and snapped the button. Lowering it again, he nodded. "Perfect."

Rune reached down for my hand and led me through to the bedroom. Hanging on the door was a black empire-waist dress. Low-heeled shoes rested on the plush carpeted floor.

"Rune," I whispered as I ran my hand over the soft material. "It's so pretty."

Rune lifted the dress and placed it on the bed. "Get dressed, baby; then we have to go."

I nodded my head, still in a daze. Rune left the bedroom and shut the door. In minutes I'd dressed and slipped my feet into the heels. I moved to the bathroom mirror, and a stunned gasp left my mouth when I stared at the girl looking back. My hair was curled, and not a strand was out of place. My makeup boasted a light smoky eye, and best of all, my infinity earrings were shining bright.

A knock came from the bedroom door. "Come in!" I shouted. I couldn't tear myself away from my reflection.

Rune moved behind me, and my heart melted when I saw his reaction in the mirror…the floored look on his handsome face.

He placed his hands on my arms. As he leaned down, one hand lifted to pull back my hair as he kissed the spot just below my ear. I felt short of breath at his touch, at his eyes still fixed on mine in the mirror.

My black dress plunged slightly at the front, showing my chest and neck, wide straps lying on the edge of my shoulders. Rune kissed down my neck, before moving his hand to my chin to turn my mouth to his. His warm lips melted against mine and I sighed, with pure happiness, into his mouth.

Rune reached over to the counter and lifted my white bow in his hands. He slipped it into my hair. Casting me a shy smile, he said, "Now you're perfect. Now you're my Poppy."

My stomach flipped at the huskiness in his voice; then it completely turned over when he took my hand and led me from the room. A dress coat waited in the room and, like a true gentleman, he held it out and guided it over my shoulders.

Turning me to face him, Rune asked, "You ready?"

I nodded and allowed Rune to lead me into the elevator and then out the door. A limousine was waiting for us, the smartly dressed driver opening the door for us to get in. I turned to Rune to ask him how he'd arranged everything, but before I even could, he answered, "DeeDee."

The driver closed the door. I held tightly on to Rune's hands as we pulled into the bustling streets. I watched Manhattan whirr past the window, and then we came to a stop.

I saw the building before I left the limousine, my heart hammering in excitement. I whipped my head to Rune, but he had already gotten out. He appeared at my door, opening it for me and holding out his hand.

I stepped out onto the street and looked up at the huge building before us. "Rune," I whispered. "Carnegie Hall." My hand slipped over my mouth.

Rune shut the door and the limousine drew away. He pulled me close and said, "Come with me."

As we walked to the entrance, I tried to read all of the signs to get an indication about the performance. But no matter how hard I searched, I couldn't discover who was performing tonight.

Rune pushed through the large doors, and a man greeted us on the inside and pointed out the way to go. Rune led me forward until we had passed the foyer and entered the main auditorium. If I was breathless before, it was nothing to how I felt at this moment—standing in the hall that had been my dream since I was a little girl.

When I had drunk in the vast, impressive space—the gold balconies, the plush red of the chairs and carpets—I frowned, realizing we were completely alone. There was no audience. There was no orchestra.

"Rune?"

Rune rocked nervously on his feet and pointed to the stage. I followed his hand. In the center of the large stage was a single chair and a cello resting on its side with its bow lying on top.

I tried to fathom what I was seeing, but I couldn't comprehend it. This was Carnegie Hall. One of the most famous concert venues in the whole wide world.

Without a word, Rune led me down the aisle toward the stage, stopping at a set of temporary steps. I turned to face him, and Rune met my eyes. "*Poppymin*, if things had been different…" He sucked in a breath but managed to compose himself enough to continue. "If things had been different, you would have played here as a professional one day. You would have played here as part of an orchestra, the orchestra that you've dreamed about being a part of." Rune's hand squeezed mine. "You would have performed the solo you've always wanted to perform on this stage."

A tear spilled out from Rune's eye. "But because that can't happen, because life is so damn unfair...I still wanted you to have this. To have known what this dream would feel like. I wanted you to have your chance in the spotlight. A spotlight that, in my opinion, you deserve, not only as the person I love most in the entire world but as the best cellist. The most gifted musician."

Realization dawned. The magnitude of what he had done for me began to set in, drifting slowly to rest on my exposed heart. Feeling my eyes fill with water, I stepped closer to Rune, splaying my hands on his chest. I blinked up at him, trying to rid the tears from my eyes. Unable to hold back my emotions, I tried to ask, "Have you...how did you...do this...?"

Rune pulled me forward and guided me up the stairs until I was standing on the stage that had been my life's greatest ambition. Rune's hand squeezed mine again, in place of words. "Tonight you have the stage, *Poppymin*. I'm sorry I'm the only one who will witness your performance, but I just wanted you to have this dream fulfilled. I wanted you to play in this hall. I wanted your music to fill this auditorium. I wanted your legacy to be imprinted on these walls."

Stepping closer to me, Rune placed his hands on my cheeks and wiped away my tears with the pads of his thumbs. Pressing his forehead to mine, he whispered, "You deserve this, Poppy. You should have had more time to see this dream realized, but...but..."

I gripped my hands around Rune's wrists as he struggled to finish. My eyes squeezed shut, expelling the remaining tears from my eyes. "Don't," I hushed out, and I lifted Rune's wrist to kiss his racing pulse. Resting it on my chest, I added, "It's okay, baby." I inhaled, and a watery smile spread on my lips. The scent of wood filled my nostrils. If I closed my eyes tightly enough, it felt as though I could hear the echo of all the musicians who had stepped onto this wooden stage, the master musicians who had graced this hall with their passion and genius.

"We're here now," I finished and stepped back from Rune. Opening my eyes, I blinked in the view of the auditorium from my heightened position. I imagined it full of people, all dressed for a concert. Men and women who love to feel the music in their hearts. I smiled, seeing the picture so vibrantly in my mind.

When I turned back to the boy who had arranged this moment for me, I was speechless. I had no words to accurately express what this gesture had done to my soul. The gift Rune had given me so purely and sweetly...my biggest dream come true.

So I didn't speak. I couldn't.

Instead, I released his wrists and walked to the solitary seat that awaited me. I ran my hand over the black leather, feeling the texture under my fingertips. I walked to the cello, the instrument that had always felt like an extension of my body. An instrument that filled me with a joy that one can never explain until it is truly experienced. A joy that is all-encompassing and carries with it a higher form of peace, of tranquility, of serenity; a delicate love like no other.

Unbuttoning my coat, I slipped it off my arms, only for two familiar hands to lift it, then skirt gently over my skin. I glanced back at Rune, who silently left a kiss on my bare shoulder, then left the stage.

I didn't see where he sat, for as he left the stage, the spotlight from directly above the seat moved from a dim glow to a potent shine. The house lights were brought down. I stared at the brightly illuminated chair with a heady mix of nervousness and excitement.

One foot stepped forward, the heels from my shoes causing an echo to rebound off the walls. The sound shook my bones, setting ablaze my weakening muscles, rejuvenating them with life.

Bending down, I lifted the cello and felt its neck in my grasp. I held the bow in my right hand, its slender wood fitting perfectly into my fingers.

I lowered myself to the chair, tipping the cello to move the spike to my perfect height. Righting the cello, the most beautiful cello I had ever seen, I closed my eyes and brought my hands to the strings, plucking each one to check it was in tune.

Of course, it was pitch-perfect.

I shuffled to the edge of the seat, planting my feet down on the wooden floor until I felt ready and primed.

Then I allowed myself to look up. I tilted my chin to the spotlight as if it were the sun. Inhaling a deep breath, I closed my eyes, then connected my bow to the string.

And I played.

The first notes of the Bach Prelude flowed from my bow to the string and out to the hall, rushing forth to fill the large room with the heavenly sounds. I swayed as the music took me in its embrace, pouring from me, exposing my soul for everyone to hear.

And in my head the hall was packed. Every seat was occupied as aficionados listened to me play. Listened to music that demanded to be heard. Played such melodies that not a dry eye could be found in the house. Exuded such passion that all hearts would be filled and spirits would be touched.

I smiled under the heat of the light, which was warming my muscles and extinguishing their pain. The piece drew to a close. Then I struck up another. I played and I played until so much time had passed that I could feel my fingers beginning to ache.

I lifted the bow, a gaping silence now shrouding the hall. I let a tear fall as I thought of what to play next. What I knew I would play next. What I *must* play next.

The one piece of music that I dreamed I would play on this prestigious stage. The one piece that spoke to my soul like no other. The one piece that would have a presence here long after I was gone. The one I would play as a farewell to my passion. After hearing its perfect echo in this magnificent hall, I would not, could not, play it ever again. There would be no more cello for me.

This had to be where I left this part of my heart. This would be where I said goodbye to the passion that had kept me strong, that had been my savior in the times I grew lost and alone.

This would be where the notes were left to dance in the air for eternity.

I felt a tremble in my hands as I paused before I began. I felt the tears flowing thick and fast, but they weren't in sadness. They were for two fast friends—the music and the life that created it—telling one another that they had to part, but that one day, *someday*, they would be together again.

Counting myself in, I placed the bow on the string and let "The Swan" from *Carnival of the Animals* begin. As my now-steady hands began to create the music I adored so much, I felt a lump fill my throat. Each note was a whispered prayer, and each crescendo was a loudly sung hymn, to the God who gave me this gift. Gave me the gift of playing music, of feeling it in my soul.

And these notes were my grateful thanks to the instrument for allowing me to play its glory with such grace.

Allowing me to love it so much that it became a part of who I was—the very fabric of my being.

And finally, as the delicate bars of the piece flowed so softly into the room, they signaled my eternal gratitude to the boy sitting silently in the dark. The boy as gifted at photography as I was at music. He was my heart. The heart freely given to me as a child. The heart that made up one half of my own. The boy who, though breaking inside, loved me so deeply that he gave me this farewell. Gave me, in the present, the dream that my future never could.

My soul mate who captured moments.

My hand shook as the final note rang out, my tears splashing to the wood. I held my hand in the air, the end of the piece suspended until the final echo of its whispered top note drifted to the heavens to take its place among the stars.

I paused, letting the farewell sink in.

Then as quietly as possible, I stood. And, smiling, I pictured the audience and their applause. I bowed my head and lowered the cello to the floor of the stage, laying the bow on top just as it had been found.

I tipped my head back into the tunnel of light from above one last time, then stepped into the shadow. My heels created a dull drum beat as I left the stage. When I reached the bottom step, the house lights came on, ushering away the remnants of the dream.

I took in a deep breath as I ranged my gaze over the empty red chairs, then cast a glance back to the cello still positioned exactly as it was on the stage, waiting patiently for the next young musician to be blessed with its grace.

It was done.

Rune slowly rose to his feet. My stomach lurched as I saw his cheeks reddened by emotion. But my heart skipped a much-needed beat when I saw the expression on his handsome face.

He understood me. He understood my truth.

He understood it was the final time I would play. And I could see, with crystal clarity, the mixture of sorrow and pride set in his eyes.

When he reached me, Rune didn't touch the tear stains on my cheeks, as I left his untouched. Closing his eyes, Rune took my mouth in a kiss. And in this kiss I felt his outpouring of love. I felt a love that, at seventeen, I was blessed to have received.

A love that knew no boundaries.

The kind of love that inspires music that lasts through the ages.

A love that should be felt and meant and treasured.

When Rune pulled back and stared into my eyes, I knew that this kiss would be handwritten on a pink paper heart with more devotion than any of those that had gone before.

Kiss eight hundred and nineteen was the kiss that changed it all. The kiss that proved that a long-haired brooding boy from Norway and a quirky girl from the Deep South could find a love to rival the greats.

It showed that love was simply the tenacity to make sure that the other half of your heart knew he, or she, was adored in every way. In every minute of every day. That love was tenderness in its purest form.

Rune inhaled deeply, then whispered, "I have no words right now…in either of my languages."

I offered a weak smile in return. Because I didn't either.

This silence was perfection. It was far better than words.

Taking Rune's hand, I guided him up the aisle and out of the foyer. The cold blast of the New York February wind was a welcome relief from the heat of the building within. Our limousine was waiting at the curb; Rune must have called the driver.

We slipped into the back seat. The driver pulled out into the traffic, and Rune pulled me to his side. I fell willingly, breathing in the fresh scent of him on his blazer. With each turn the driver took, my heart rate increased. When we arrived at the hotel, I took Rune's hand and walked inside.

Not a single word had been uttered on the drive here, not a single sound made as the elevator reached the top floor. The sound of the card opening the electronic lock sounded like thunder in the hushed hallway. I opened the door, my footsteps clicking on the wooden floor, and stepped through and into the living room.

Without stopping, I walked to the doorway of the bedroom, only glancing back to make sure Rune followed. He stood at the doorway, watching me leave.

Our gazes crashed, and needing him more than air, I slowly lifted my hand. I wanted him. I needed him.

I had to love him.

I watched Rune pull in a deep breath, then step toward me. He walked carefully to where I waited. He slid his hand into mine, his touch sending flares of light and love through my body.

Rune's eyes were dark, almost black, his dilated pupils blotting out the blue. His need was as strong as mine, his love proven and his trust so complete.

A calm flooded through me like a river. I let it in and led Rune into the bedroom and closed the door. The atmosphere thickened around us. Rune's intense, assessing eyes watched my every move.

Knowing I had his unwavering attention, I released his hand and stepped back. Lifting my trembling fingers, I began unfastening the large buttons of my coat, our locked gazes never wavering as the coat opened and I slowly let it drop to the floor.

Rune's jaw tensed as he watched, his fingers opening and closing at his sides.

I slipped off my shoes, my bare feet sinking into the plush carpet. Taking a fortifying breath, I stepped across the carpet and over to where Rune stood, waiting. When I stopped before him, I lifted my eyes, lids heavy with the onslaught of feelings within me.

Rune's broad chest rose and fell, the tight white T-shirt under his blazer showcasing his toned chest. Feeling a flush coat my cheeks, I gently laid my palms over his chest. Rune stilled as my warm hands touched him. Then, keeping my eyes locked on his, I slid my hands to his shoulders, freeing him from his blazer. The jacket fell to the floor at his feet.

I breathed in three times, fighting to control the nerves suddenly racing through me. Rune didn't move. He remained completely still, letting me explore; I ran my hand down over his stomach, over to his arm, and took his hand with my own. I lifted our clasped hands to my mouth, and in a move so familiar to us both, I kissed our intertwined fingers.

"This is how they should always be," I whispered, gazing at our woven fingers.

Rune swallowed and nodded his head in silent agreement.

My feet stepped back, and back again. I led us toward the bed. The comforter was pulled back, turned down by the maid service. And the closer I got to this bed, the more my nerves settled and a peace set within me. Because this was right. Nothing, *no one*, could tell me this was wrong.

Pausing before the edge of the bed, I released our hands. Driven by desire, I took hold of the hem of Rune's shirt and slowly brought it over his head. Helping me, Rune threw the T-shirt to the floor, leaving him standing with his torso bare.

Rune slept like this every night, but there was something about the charged static in the atmosphere and the way he'd made me feel with tonight's surprise that made this different.

It was different.

It was poignant.

But it was *us*.

Lifting my hands, I pressed my palms to his skin and ran my fingertips over the peaks and valleys of his abdominals. Rune's skin bumped in my wake, his labored breath hissing through his slightly parted lips.

As my fingers explored his broad chest, I leaned forward and pressed my lips over his heart. It was racing like a hummingbird's wings.

"You're perfect, Rune Kristiansen," I whispered.

Rune's fingers rose to thread through my hair. He guided my head up. I kept my eyes lowered until the final second, when I finally looked up and met his crystal-blue gaze. His eyes were glistening.

Rune's full lips opened and he whispered, "*Jeg elsker deg.*"

He loved me.

I nodded to show that I'd heard him. But my voice had been stolen by the moment. By the preciousness of his touch. I stepped back, Rune's eyes tracking my every move.

I wanted them to.

Lifting my hand to the strap on my shoulder, I steeled my nerves and dropped it down my arm. Rune's breathing stuttered as I freed the other strap, the silk dress pooling at my feet. I forced my arms down by my side, most of my body revealed to the boy I loved beyond anything else in the world.

I was bared, showing the scars I'd obtained over the course of two years. Showing all of me—the girl he'd always known, and the battle scars from my unwavering fight.

Rune's gaze dropped to run over me. But there was no disgust in his eyes. I saw only the purity of his love shining through. I saw only want and need and, above all, his whole heart exposed.

Just for my eyes.

As always.

Rune edged closer and closer, until his warm chest pressed against mine. With a feather-light touch, he brushed my hair behind my ear and then drifted his fingertips down my bare neck and on to my side.

My eyes fluttered at the sensation. Shivers ran down my spine. The scent of Rune's minty breath filled my nose as he leaned forward and dragged his soft lips along my neck, peppering delicate kisses on my exposed skin.

I held on to his strong shoulders, anchoring myself to the ground. "*Poppymin*," Rune whispered hoarsely as his mouth passed by my ear.

Inhaling deeply, I whispered, "Make love to me, Rune."

Rune was still for a moment; then, shifting until his face hovered above mine, he briefly caught my eyes before laying his lips against my own. This kiss was as sweet as this night, as soft as his touch. This kiss was different—it was the promise of what lay ahead, Rune's vow to be gentle...his vow to love me just as I loved him.

Rune's strong hands lay on the nape of my neck as his mouth worked slowly against mine. Then, when I was breathless, his hands dropped to my waist and carefully lifted me onto the bed.

My back hit the soft mattress, and I watched from the center of the bed as Rune shed the remainder of his clothes, never taking his eyes off mine as he crawled on the bed to lie beside me.

The intensity on Rune's handsome face melted me, causing my heart to thud in a staccato rhythm. Rolling on my side to face him, I ran my fingers down his cheek and whispered, "I love you too."

Rune's eyes closed as if he needed to hear those words more than his next breath. He moved above me, his mouth taking mine. My hands ran over his strong back and up through his long hair. Rune's hands ran down my side, then freed me of the remainder of my clothes and dropped them on the floor to join the rest.

I was breathless as Rune towered over me. Breathless as he met my eyes and asked, "Are you sure, *Poppymin?*"

Unable to contain my smile, I replied, "More than I have been about anything in my life."

My eyes fluttered closed as Rune kissed me again, as his hands explored my body—all of the once-familiar parts. And I did the same. With every touch and every kiss, my nerves fell away, until we were Poppy and Rune— there was no beginning to us and no end.

The air became heavy and warm the more we kissed and explored, until finally, Rune shifted above me. Not once breaking eye contact, he took me as his again.

My body filled with life and light as he made us one. My heart filled with such love that I feared it would not contain all the happiness flooding in.

I held him as we fell back to earth, holding him tightly in my arms. Rune's head lay in the crook of my neck, his skin glistening and warm.

I kept my eyes closed, unwilling to break away from this moment. This perfect moment. Eventually, Rune lifted his head. Seeing the vulnerable expression on his face, I kissed him gently. As gently as he had taken me. As gently as he handled my fragile heart.

His arms cradled my head, keeping me safe. When I broke from the kiss, I met his loving gaze and whispered, "Kiss number eight hundred and twenty. With my Rune, on the most amazing day of my life. After we made love…my heart almost burst."

Rune's breath hitched in his throat. With a final brief kiss, he rolled beside me and wrapped me in his arms.

My eyes closed and I drifted off into a light sleep. So light that I felt Rune kiss me on my head then shift from the bed. As the door to the bedroom closed, I blinked in the dark room, catching the sound of the door to the terrace slipping open.

Pushing the comforter aside, I put on the robe that was hanging on the back of the door and the slippers that lay neatly on the floor. As I walked through the room, I smiled, still smelling the scent of Rune on my skin.

I entered the living room, heading in the direction of the door to outside, but immediately stopped in my tracks. Because through the wide window I could see Rune on the ground, sitting on his knees. Falling apart.

It felt as if my heart physically ripped in two as I watched him, out in the cold night air, clothed in only his jeans. Tears streamed from his eyes as his back shook with body-shuddering pain.

Tears blurred my vision as I stared at him. My Rune. So broken and alone as he sat in the lightly falling snow.

"Rune. *Baby*," I whispered to myself as I forced my feet to the door, making my hand turn the handle and ordering my heart to brace itself for the grief causing this scene.

My feet crunched on the thin, crisp layer of snow beneath my feet. Rune didn't seem to hear. But I heard him. I heard his uncontrolled breathing. But worse still, I heard his racking sobs. I heard the pain overwhelm him. I saw it in the way he lurched forward, palms planted to the floor beneath him.

Failing to hold back my cries, I rushed forward and wrapped my arms around him. His bare skin was freezing to the touch. Seeming not to notice the cold, Rune collapsed into my lap, his long, broad torso seeking the comfort of my arms.

And he broke. Rune completely broke apart: floods of tears flowed down his cheeks, coarse breaths ghosted to white puffs of smoke as they hit the freezing air.

I rocked back and forth, holding him close. "Shh," I soothed, trying in earnest to breathe through my own pain. The pain of seeing the boy I loved falling apart. The pain of knowing I had to pass soon, yet wanting to resist home's call with all of my heart.

I had come to terms with my fading life. Now I wanted to fight to stay with Rune, *for* Rune, even knowing it was useless.

I wasn't in control of my fate.

"Rune," I whispered, my tears becoming lost in the long strands of his hair in my lap.

Rune looked up, his expression devastated, and asked hoarsely, "Why? Why do I have to lose you?" He shook his head and his face contorted in pain. "Because I can't, *Poppymin*. I can't watch you leave. I can't bear the thought of not having you like this for the rest of our lives." He choked on a sob but managed to say, "How can a love like ours be broken? How can you be taken away so young?"

"I don't know, baby," I whispered, glancing away in an effort to hold myself together. The lights of New York sparkled in my line of sight. I chased away the grief that came with his asking those questions.

"It just is, Rune," I said sadly. "There's no reason why it's me. Why not me? No one deserves this, yet I have to..." I trailed off but managed to add, "I *have* to trust that there's a bigger reason, or I would crumble with the pain of leaving all I love behind." I sucked in a breath and said, "With leaving you, especially after today. Especially after making love to you tonight."

Rune stared into my tear-filled eyes. Gathering some composure, he got to his feet and lifted me into his arms. I was glad, because I felt too weak to move. I wasn't sure I could have stood up from the cold, damp ground if I'd tried.

Linking my arms around Rune's neck, I laid my head on his chest and closed my eyes as he carried me back inside and back to the bedroom. Pushing the comforter back, he placed me underneath, following behind and wrapping his arms around my waist as we faced one another on my pillow.

Rune's eyes were red, his long hair was damp from the snow, and his skin was mottled with the depth of his sadness. Lifting my hand, I ran it down his face. His skin was freezing.

Rune turned his face in to my palm. "Up on that stage tonight, I knew you were saying goodbye. And I..." His voice stuck, but he coughed and finished, "It made this all too real." His eyes glossed with new tears. "It made me realize, this was really happening." Rune held my hand and brought it to his chest. He squeezed it tightly. "And I can't breathe. I can't breathe when I try to imagine living without you. I've tried it once, and it didn't go well. But...but at least you were alive, out there, somewhere. Soon...soon..." He cut off his words as the tears fell. He turned his head from my gaze.

I caught his retreating cheek. Rune blinked. "Are you scared, *Poppymin*? Because I'm terrified. I'm terrified of what the hell life looks like without you."

I paused. I truly thought about his question. And I let myself feel the truth. I let myself be honest. "Rune, I'm not scared of dying." I ducked my head, and the pain that had never taken me before suddenly filled my every cell. I let my head drop to his and whispered, "But since I got you back, since my heart regained its beat—you—I've been feeling all kinds of things that I hadn't before. I pray for more time, just so I can live more days in your arms. I pray for longer minutes so you can gift me more kisses." Dragging in a much-needed breath, I added, "But worst of all, I'm beginning to feel fear."

Rune inched closer, his arm tightening around my waist. I lifted my shaking hand to his face. "I feel fear over leaving you. I'm not scared of dying, Rune. But I'm terrified of going anywhere new without you." Rune's eyes shut and he hissed as though in pain.

"I don't know me without you," I said quietly. "Even when you were in Oslo, I pictured your face, and I would remember how your hand felt holding mine. I would play your favorite songs and I would read the kisses in my jar. Just like my mamaw told me to. And I would close my eyes and feel your lips on mine." I allowed myself to smile. "I would remember the night we first made love and the feeling in my heart at that moment—fulfilled...at peace."

I sniffed and quickly wiped at my damp cheeks. "Though you weren't with me, you were in my heart. And that was enough to sustain me, even though I wasn't happy." I kissed Rune's mouth, just to savor his taste. "But now, after this time back together, it's made me fearful. Because who are we without each other?"

"Poppy," Rune rasped.

My tears fell with reckless abandon, and I cried, "I've hurt you by loving you so much. And now I have to go on an adventure without you. And I can't bear how much it hurts you. I can't leave you so lonely and in pain."

Rune pulled me to his chest. I cried. He cried. We shared our fears of loss and love. My fingers rested on his back, and I took comfort in his warmth.

When our tears had slowed, Rune gently pushed me back and searched my face. "Poppy," he asked huskily, "what does heaven look like to you?"

I could see in his face that he desperately wanted to know. Gathering my composure, I declared, "A dream."

"A dream," Rune echoed, and I saw his lip hook up at the corner.

"I read once that when you dream each night, it's actually a visit home. *Home*, Rune. Heaven." I began feeling the warmth that that vision brought at my toes. It began to travel over my whole body. "My heaven will be you and me in the blossom grove. Like always. Forever seventeen."

I took a strand of Rune's hair between my fingers, studying the golden color. "Do you ever dream a dream so vividly that when you wake you believe it was real? It feels like it is real?"

"*Ja*," Rune said quietly.

"That's because it was, Rune, in a way. So at night, when you close your eyes, I'll be there, meeting you in our grove."

Inching closer, I added, "And then when it's time for you to come home too, it'll be me who greets you. And there'll be no worry or fear or pain. Just love." I sighed happily. "Imagine that, Rune. A place where there's no pain or hurt." I closed my eyes and smiled. "When I think about it that way, I'm not so scared anymore."

Rune's lips brushed over mine. "It sounds perfect," he said, his accent thick, voice graveled. "I want you to have that, *Poppymin*."

I fluttered my eyes open and saw the truth and acceptance on Rune's handsome face.

"It will be like that, Rune," I said with unwavering certainty. "We won't end. We never will."

Rune rolled me until I lay on his chest. I closed my eyes, lulled by the hypnotic rhythm of Rune's deep breathing. As I was about to drift away to sleep, Rune asked, "*Poppymin?*"

"Yes?"

"What do you want out of the time left?"

I thought about his question, but only a few things sprang to mind. "I want to see the cherry blossoms bloom one final time." I smiled against Rune's chest. "I want to dance at prom with you"—I tilted my head up and caught him smiling down at me—"with you in a tux and your hair combed back off your face." Rune shook his head in amusement at that.

Sighing at the peaceful happiness we had now found, I said, "I want to see a final perfect sunrise." Sitting up higher, I met Rune's eyes and finished, "But more than anything, I want to return home with your kiss on my lips. I want to pass on to the next life still feeling your warm lips on mine."

Settling back down onto Rune's chest, I closed my eyes and whispered, "That's what I pray for most. To last long enough to achieve these things."

"They're perfect, baby," Rune whispered, stroking my hair.

And that's how I fell asleep, under Rune's protection.

Dreaming that I'd see all my wishes fulfilled.

Happy.

13

Dark Clouds and Blue Skies

Rune

I DREW LAZY CIRCLES ON MY PAPER AS THE TEACHER DRONED ON ABOUT chemical compounds. My mind was occupied with Poppy. It always was, but today was different. We had been back from New York for four days now, and with each passing day she had grown quieter.

I constantly asked what was wrong. She would always tell me it was nothing. But I knew there was something. This morning, it was worse.

Her hand felt too weak in mine as we walked to school. Her skin was too hot to the touch. I had asked if she was feeling sick, but she just shook her head and smiled.

She thought that smile could stop me in my tracks.

It normally could, but not today.

Something felt off. My heart dropped every time I thought back to lunch, when we had been sitting with our friends and she lay in my arms. She never spoke, instead just traced her fingertip over my hand.

The afternoon had dragged, and every minute was filled with worry that she wasn't okay. That the time she had left was coming to a close. Sitting up quickly, I tried to stave off the panic that image brought. But it was no use.

When the final bell sounded, signaling the end of the school day, I jumped from my seat and rushed to the hallway, darting to Poppy's locker. When I arrived, Jorie was standing there.

"Where is she?" I asked curtly.

Jorie took a surprised step back and pointed to the back door. As I quickly made my way to the exit, Jorie shouted, "She didn't look too good in class, Rune. I'm real worried."

Shivers ran down my spine as I burst into the warm air. My eyes scanned the courtyard until I found Poppy standing at a tree in the park opposite. I pushed past my fellow students and ran over to her.

She didn't notice me as she stared straight ahead, seemingly caught in a trance. There was a light sheen of sweat covering her face, and the skin on her arms and legs seemed pale.

I stood directly in her path. Poppy's dull eyes were sluggish as they blinked and focused slowly on mine. She forced a smile. "Rune," she whispered weakly.

I pressed my hand against her forehead, my eyebrows pulled together in concern. "Poppy? What's wrong?"

"Nothing," she said unconvincingly. "I'm just tired."

My heart slammed against my ribs as I took in her lie. Knowing I had to get her back to her parents, I gathered her under my arm. As the nape of her neck almost scalded my arm, I bit back a curse.

"Let's go home, baby," I said softly. Poppy wrapped her arms around my waist. Her hold was weak, but I could tell she was using my body to hold herself straight. I knew she would protest if I tried to carry her.

I closed my eyes for a second as we stepped onto the pathway of the park. I tried to quell the fear taking hold of me inside. The fear of her being sick. Of this being…

Poppy was silent but for her breathing, which grew deeper and wheezier the farther we walked. As we entered the blossom grove, Poppy's steps faltered. I looked down, only to feel her body lose all its strength.

"Poppy!" I called out and caught her just before she hit the ground. Looking down at her in my arms, I stroked back the damp hair from her face. "Poppy? Poppy, baby, what's wrong?"

Poppy's eyes began to roll, losing focus, but I felt her hand take hold of mine and grip it as hard as she could manage. It was a barely a squeeze.

"Rune," she tried to say, but her breathing became too fast; she struggled to retain enough air to push out her voice.

Reaching into my pocket, I pulled out my cell and hit 911. As soon as the operator answered, I reeled off Poppy's address and informed them of her illness.

Scooping Poppy into my arms, I was about to set into a run when Poppy's weak palm landed on my face. I glanced down, only to see a tear roll down her cheek. "I'm…I'm…not ready…" she managed to tell me, before her head flopped back and she fought for consciousness.

Despite the tear ripping through my heart at Poppy's broken spirit and failing body, I leapt into a sprint, pushing myself harder and faster than ever before.

As I passed by my house, I saw my mamma and Alton in the driveway.

"Rune?" my mamma called, then whispered, "No!" when she saw Poppy hanging limply in my arms.

The sound of the ambulance's siren blared in the distance. Wasting no time, I kicked through the front door of Poppy's house.

I ran into the living room; no one was there. "Help!" I screamed as loudly as I could. Suddenly, I heard footsteps running in my direction.

"Poppy!" Poppy's mama came barreling around the corner as I lowered Poppy to the couch. "Oh my God! Poppy!" Mrs. Litchfield crouched down beside me, pushing her hand over Poppy's head.

"What happened? What's wrong?" she asked.

I shook my head. "I don't know. She just collapsed in my arms. I've called for an ambulance."

Just as those words left my mouth, I heard the sound of the ambulance turning into the street. Poppy's mama ran out of the house. I watched her go, ice replacing the blood in my veins. I ran my hands through my hair, not knowing what to do. A cold hand landed on my wrist.

I snapped my eyes back to Poppy and saw her fighting for breath. My face fell at the sight. Dropping down closer, I kissed her hand and whispered, "You'll be okay, *Poppymin*. I promise."

Poppy gasped for breath, but managing to place her palm on my face, she said, almost inaudibly, "Not…going home…yet…"

I nodded my head and kissed her hand, gripping it tightly with my own.

Suddenly, the sound of the EMTs entering the house came from behind me, and I stood up to let them past. But as I did, Poppy's hand tightened on my own. Tears leaked from her eyes. "I'm right here, baby," I whispered. "I won't leave you."

Poppy's eyes showed me her thanks. The sound of crying came from behind me. As I turned, I saw Ida and Savannah standing to the side, watching, crying in each other's arms. Mrs. Litchfield moved to the other side of the couch and kissed Poppy's head. "You'll be okay, baby," she whispered, but as she looked up at me, I could see she didn't believe her own words.

She thought the time had arrived too.

The EMTs put an oxygen mask over Poppy's face and gathered her onto a gurney. Poppy's hand still held mine; she refused to let go. As the EMTs moved her out of the house, she never loosened her grip on my hand, her eyes never leaving mine as she fought to keep them open.

Mrs. Litchfield ran behind, but when she saw Poppy's hand clutching mine so tightly, she said, "You go with Poppy, Rune. I'll follow straight behind with the girls."

I could see the conflict on her face. She wanted to be with her daughter.

"I'll bring them, Ivy—you go with Poppy and Rune," I heard my mamma say from behind me. I climbed into the back of the ambulance; Mrs. Litchfield joined me.

Even when Poppy's eyes closed en route to the hospital, she didn't release my hand. And, as Mrs. Litchfield collapsed into tears beside me, I gave her my other hand.

———

I stayed by Poppy's side as she was wheeled into an oncology room. My heart beat as quickly as the doctors and nurses moved—a blur, a mass of activity.

I fought back the lump blocking my throat. I held the numbness inside me at bay. Poppy was being poked and prodded—blood taken, temperature taken, too many things to count. And my baby fought. As her chest became erratic with her inability to breathe properly, she stayed calm. As

unconsciousness tried to pull her down, she forced her eyes to remain open...
she forced her eyes to stay fixed on mine, mouthing my name whenever she
almost slipped under.

I stayed strong for Poppy. I wouldn't let her see me fall.

She needed me to be strong.

Mrs. Litchfield was beside me, holding my hand. Mr. Litchfield came
running in, briefcase in hand, his tie in disarray.

"Ivy," he said in a hurried voice, "what happened?"

Mrs. Litchfield chased her tears away from her cheeks and took her
husband's hand. "She collapsed on Rune, on the way home from school. The
doctors believe it's an infection. Her immune system is so low she can't fight
it."

Mr. Litchfield looked to me as Mrs. Litchfield added, "Rune carried
Poppy in his arms all the way home. He ran and called for an ambulance. He
saved her, James. Rune saved our girl."

I swallowed hard as I heard Mrs. Litchfield's words. Mr. Litchfield
nodded, I assumed in thanks, then ran toward his daughter. I saw him
squeeze her hand, but the doctors quickly ushered him out of the way.

It was five minutes before a doctor spoke to us. He stood still, his face
blank. "Mr. and Mrs. Litchfield, Poppy's body is trying to fight off an infection. As you know, her immune system is severely compromised."

"Is this it?" Mrs. Litchfield prompted, her throat tight with grief.

The doctor's words seeped into my brain. I turned my head away from
him as I sensed a pair of eyes watching me.

The doctors had cleared a space, and through that space, I saw Poppy's
pretty face covered in a mask, IVs in her arms. But her green eyes, those
green eyes I adored, were on me. Her hand hung out to the side.

"We'll do all that we can. We'll give her a moment before we put her
under."

I heard the doctor say they were putting her into a medically induced
coma to help her try to fight the infection. And that we had to see her before
they did. But my feet were already moving. Her hand was held out for me.

As soon as I took Poppy's hand, I saw her eyes searching for mine, and
her head shook weakly. I briefly closed my eyes, but when they opened I

couldn't stop the tear escaping down my cheek. Poppy made a noise below her oxygen mask, and I didn't need to take it off to know what she had said. She wasn't leaving me yet. I could see the promise in her eyes.

"Rune, son," Mr. Litchfield said. "Can we have a moment with Poppy, to kiss her and speak with her some?"

I nodded and went to move aside, when Poppy made a sound and shook her head again. She squeezed my hand again. Because she didn't want to let me go.

Leaning forward, I pressed a kiss on her head, feeling her warmth on my lips, inhaling her sweet scent. "I'll be just over there, *Poppymin*. I won't leave you, I promise."

Poppy's eyes tracked me as I stepped away. I watched as Mr. and Mrs. Litchfield spoke quietly to their daughter, kissing her and gripping her hand.

I leaned against the wall of the small room, clenching my fists as I fought to hold myself together. I had to be strong for her. She hated tears. She hated to burden her family with all this.

She wouldn't see me break.

Mrs. Litchfield disappeared from the room. When she came back in, Ida and Savannah followed. I had to turn away when I saw the pain in Poppy's eyes. She adored her sisters; she wouldn't want them to see her like this.

"Poppy," Ida cried and rushed to her side. Poppy's weak hand drifted down her younger sister's face. Ida kissed Poppy on her cheek, then stepped back into Mrs. Litchfield's waiting arms. Savannah went next. Savannah broke down on seeing her sister, her hero, this way. Poppy held her hand, and Savannah whispered, "I love you, PopPops. Please...please don't leave, not yet."

Poppy shook her head, then looked back my way, her hand struggling to move in my direction. I walked over, feeling like every step was a mile. Inside of me was a flurried storm of darkness, but as soon as my hand slipped into hers, the storm calmed. Poppy blinked up at me, her long dark lashes fluttering on her cheeks. Sitting on the edge of the bed, I leaned down and pushed the hair back from her face.

"*Hei, Poppymin*," I said quietly, with as much strength as I could muster. Poppy's eyes closed on hearing my words. I knew that under the mask she'd be smiling. When her eyes fixed on mine, I said, "They need to put you under for a while to help you fight off this infection." Poppy's head nodded in understanding. "You'll get to dream, baby," I said and made myself smile. "Go visit with your mamaw awhile, while you gather the strength to come back to me." Poppy sighed, a tear escaping her eye. "We have things you want to do before you go home, remember?"

Poppy nodded lightly and I kissed her cheek. When I pulled back, I whispered, "Sleep, baby. I'll stay right here, waiting for you to come back to me."

I stroked back Poppy's hair until her eyes closed and I knew she had given herself to sleep.

The doctor entered a second later. "If you all go wait in the family room, I'll be through with an update when we have her all set up."

I heard her family leaving, but as I stared at her hand in mine, I didn't want to let go. A hand landed on my shoulder, and I looked up to find the doctor looking at me. "We'll take care of her son, I promise."

Pressing a final kiss to her hand, I forced myself to let go and leave the room. As the doors shut behind me, I looked up to see the family room opposite. But I couldn't go in. I needed air. I needed...

I rushed toward the small garden at the end of the hallway and burst through the door. The warm wind drifted over my face, and seeing I was alone, I staggered to the bench in the center of the garden. Dropping to the seat, I let the sadness take me.

My head fell forward and landed in my hands. The tears dropped down my face. I heard the sound of the door opening. When I looked up, my pappa was hovering near the door.

I waited for the usual anger to hit me when I saw his face. But it must have been buried under a mass of grief. My pappa didn't say anything. Instead, he walked forward and sat beside me. He made no move to comfort me. He knew I wouldn't welcome his touch. Instead, he just sat there while I fell apart.

A part of me was glad. I would never tell him. But as much as I wouldn't admit it, I didn't want to be alone.

I wasn't sure how much time passed, but eventually I straightened and pushed the hair back from my face. I wiped my hand down over my face.

"Rune, she—"

"She'll be fine," I said, cutting off whatever he was trying to say. I glanced down at my pappa's hand lying on his knee, clenching and unclenching like he was debating whether to reach out and touch me.

My jaw tensed. I didn't want that.

Time with Poppy was running out, and it was his fault that I would have only had… The thought trailed off. I didn't know how long I had left with my girl.

Before my pappa could do anything, the door opened again, and this time Mr. Litchfield walked out. My pappa got to his feet and shook his hand. "I'm so sorry, James," my pappa said.

Mr. Litchfield clapped him on the shoulder, then asked, "Do you mind if I speak to Rune for a minute?"

I stiffened, every muscle in me bracing for his anger. My pappa glanced back at me but nodded. "I'll leave you both alone."

Pappa left the garden, and Mr. Litchfield strode slowly to where I sat, then lowered himself onto the bench beside me. I held my breath, waiting for him to speak. When he didn't, I said, "I'm not leaving her. Don't even ask me to leave, because I'm not going anywhere."

I knew I sounded angry and aggressive, but my heart slammed against my ribs at the thought of him telling me I had to go. If I wasn't with Poppy, I *had* nowhere to go.

Mr. Litchfield tensed, then asked, "Why?"

Surprised by his question, I turned to him and tried to read his face. He was looking at me square on. He truly wanted to know. Without breaking his gaze, I said, "Because I love her. I love her more than anything in the world." My voice cut through my tight throat. Taking a deep inhale, I managed to say, "I made a promise to her that I would never leave her side. And even if that weren't the case, I wouldn't be able to leave. My heart, soul, everything, is connected to Poppy." My hands fisted at my sides. "I can't leave her now, not when she needs me most. And I won't leave her until she forces my hand."

Mr. Litchfield sighed and ran his hand over his face. He sat back against the bench. "When you came back to Blossom Grove, Rune, I took one look at you and couldn't believe how you'd changed. I felt disappointed," he admitted. I felt my chest tighten at that blow. He shook his head. "I saw the smoking, the attitude, and assumed you bore no resemblance to the boy you were before. The one that loved my daughter as much as she loved him. The boy that—I would have bet my life—would have walked through fire for my baby girl.

"But who you are now, I never would have expected you to love her in the way she deserves." Mr. Litchfield's voice grew husky with pain. Clearing his throat, he said, "I fought against you. When I saw how you two had connected again, I tried to warn her off. But you two have always been like magnets, drawn together by some unknown force." He huffed a laugh. "Poppy's mamaw said that you were both thrust together for a greater meaning. One we would never know until it presented itself. She said that great loves were always destined to be together for some great reason." He paused, and turning to me, stated, "And now *I know*."

I looked him straight in the eye. Mr. Litchfield's firm hand landed on my shoulder. "You were meant to be together, so you could be her guiding light through all of this. You were created perfectly for her, to make this time for my girl special. To make sure her remaining days were filled with things her mama and I could never have given her."

Pain sliced through me and I closed my eyes. When I opened them again, Mr. Litchfield dropped his hand but made me face him still. "Rune, I was against you. But I could see how much she loved you. I just wasn't sure you loved her back."

"I do," I said hoarsely. "I never stopped."

He nodded his head. "I didn't know until the trip to New York. I didn't want her to go." He inhaled and said, "But when she came back I could see that there was a new peace within her. Then she told me what you did for her. Carnegie Hall?" He shook his head. "You gave my girl her biggest dream, for no other reason than you wanted her to achieve it. To make her happy… because you loved her."

"She gives me more," I replied and bowed my head. "Just by being her, she gives me that tenfold."

"Rune, if Poppy comes out of this—"

"When," I interrupted. "*When* she comes out of this."

I lifted my head to see Mr. Litchfield looking at me. "When," he said with a hopeful sigh. "I won't stand in your way." He leaned forward to rest his face on his hands. "She was never right after you left, Rune. I know you've struggled with not having her in your life. And I'd have to be a fool not to see that you blame your pappa for all of this. For you leaving. But sometimes life doesn't go the way you expect. I never expected to lose my daughter before I left. But Poppy has taught me that I can't be angry. Because, son," he said and looked me in the face, "if Poppy isn't angry about having a short life, how dare any of us be angry for her?"

I stared back silently. My heart beat faster at his words. Images of Poppy twirling in the blossom grove filled my mind, her smile wide as she breathed in the scented air. I saw that same smile as I remembered her dancing in the shallow water at the beach, her hands in the air as the sun kissed her face.

Poppy was happy. Even with this diagnosis, even with all the pain and disappointment of her treatment, she was happy.

"I'm glad you returned, son. You're making Poppy's final days, in her words, 'as special as special can be'."

Mr. Litchfield got to his feet. In a move I'd only ever seen from his daughter, Poppy, he tipped his face to the setting sun and closed his eyes.

When he brought his head back down, he walked back toward the door, looking back to say, "You're welcome here as much as you like, Rune. I think with you by her side, Poppy will come out of this. She'll come out of this just so she can spend a few extra days with you. I saw that look in her eyes as she lay on that bed; she isn't going anywhere just yet. You know as well as I do, if she's determined to see something through, then she'll damn well see it through."

My lips lifted into a small smile. Mr. Litchfield left me alone in the garden. Reaching into my pockets, I pulled out my smokes. As I went to light the end, I stopped. As Poppy's smile filled my head, her disapproving scrunched nose every time I smoked, I pulled the cigarette from my mouth and threw it to the ground.

"Enough," I said aloud. "No more."

Taking a long breath of the fresh air, I got to my feet and went back inside. As I entered the family room, Poppy's family was sitting on one side and, on the other, my mamma, pappa and Alton. As soon as my baby brother saw me, he lifted his head and waved.

Doing what Poppy would have wanted me to do, I sat down beside him. "*Hei*, buddy," I said, and I almost lost it when he crawled onto my lap and pushed his arms around my neck.

I felt Alton's back shaking. When he pulled back his head, his cheeks were wet. "Is *Poppymin* sick?"

Clearing my throat, I nodded. His bottom lip wobbled. "But you love her," he whispered, cracking my heart in the process. I nodded again, and he laid his head against my chest. "I don't want *Poppymin* to go anywhere. She made you speak to me. She made you be best friends with me," he sniffed. "I don't want you to be angry again."

I felt each of his words like a dagger to my chest. But those daggers only let in light when I thought of how Poppy had guided me to Alton. I thought of how disappointed she'd be if I ignored him now.

Holding Alton closer, I whispered, "I won't ignore you again, buddy. I promise."

Alton lifted his head and wiped at his eyes. When he raked his hair back, I couldn't help but smirk. Alton smiled in reply and hugged me tighter. He didn't let go of me until the doctor entered the room. He told us we could go in and see her two at a time.

Mr. and Mrs. Litchfield went in first; then it was my turn. I pushed through the door and froze in my tracks.

Poppy lay in a bed in the middle of the room. Machines were hooked up all around her. My heart cracked. She looked so broken lying there, so quiet.

No laughter or smiles on her face.

I walked forward and sat down on the chair beside her bed. Taking hold of her hand, I brought it to my lips and pressed down a kiss.

I couldn't stand the silence. So I began to tell Poppy about the first time I'd kissed her. I told her about every kiss I could remember since we were eight—how they felt, how she made me feel—knowing that if she could hear me, she'd love every word of what I had to say.

Reliving every single kiss that she held so dear.

All nine hundred and two that we'd achieved so far.

And the ninety-eight we'd still collect.
When she woke up.
Because she would.
We had a vow to fulfill.

Blossoms Bloomed and Peace Restored

Rune
One Week Later

"HEY, RUNE."

I looked up from the paper I was writing to see Jorie at the door to Poppy's room. Judson, Deacon, and Ruby were standing behind her in the hallway. I flicked my chin in their direction, and they all walked in.

Poppy was still in her bed, still in her coma. After a few days, the doctors had said the worst of her infection had passed, and other visitors had been allowed in.

My Poppy had done it. Just as she'd promised, she'd fought to keep the infection from taking her down. I knew she would. She'd held my hand when she'd made that promise. She'd met my eyes.

It was as good as done.

The doctors were planning on bringing her slowly out of her coma over the next few days. They were going to gradually lessen the dosage of anesthetic, beginning later tonight. And I couldn't wait. This week had felt like an eternity without her; everything felt wrong and out of place. So much had changed in my world by her being gone, yet by contrast, nothing on the outside really had.

The only real development was that the entire school now knew that Poppy didn't have much time left. From what I'd heard they were all predictably shocked; everyone was sad. We had been at school with most of these people since kindergarten. Although they didn't know Poppy like our small group of friends did, it had still rocked the town. People from her church had gathered to pray for her. To show their love. I knew if Poppy knew about it, it would warm her heart.

The doctors weren't sure how strong she would be when she woke up. They were reluctant to estimate how long she had left, but her doctor told us this infection had severely weakened her. He told us we had to be prepared: when she finally woke up, we could be facing only weeks.

As much as that blow hurt, as much as it tore my heart from my chest, I tried to take joy in the small victories. I would have weeks to help fulfill Poppy's final wishes. I would have the time I needed to truly say goodbye, to hear her laugh, see her smile, and kiss her soft lips.

Jorie and Ruby entered the room first, going to the opposite side of the bed to where I sat to squeeze Poppy's hand.

Deacon and Judson stopped bedside me, laying their hands on my shoulder in support. The minute word had spread about Poppy, my friends had cut school to come see me. As soon as I'd laid eyes on them rushing through the hallway, I knew that everyone knew. I knew that *they* knew. They'd been by my side ever since.

They were upset that Poppy and I hadn't said a thing to any of them except for Jorie. But in the end they understood why Poppy didn't want a fuss. I think they loved her even more for that. They saw her true strength.

Over the past week, when I hadn't been in school, it was my friends who had brought my assignments from my teachers. They had looked out for me, as I had done for Poppy. Deacon and Judson said they were determined I didn't flunk out when we'd all reached our senior year together. It was the furthest thing from my mind, but I appreciated their concern.

In fact, this week showed me how much they meant to me. Even though Poppy was my entire life, I realized that I had love elsewhere. I had friends who would walk through fire for me. My mamma also came every day. As did my pappa. He didn't seem to care that I mostly ignored him. He didn't seem to care if we sat in silence. I thought he only cared that he was here, that he was beside me.

I wasn't sure what to do with that yet.

Jorie looked up, catching my eye. "How is she today?"

I rose from my chair and sat on the edge of Poppy's bed. I linked her fingers through mine and held on tight. Leaning forward, I brushed the hair back from her face and kissed her on her forehead. "She's getting stronger each day," I said softly, and then for Poppy's ears only, I whispered, "Our friends are here, baby. They've come to see you again."

My heart lurched when I thought I saw the flickering of her lashes, but when I stared longer, I realized it must have been my imagination. I'd been desperate to see her again for too many hours to count. Then I relaxed, knowing that, over the next few days, seeing these things wouldn't simply be in my imagination. They'd be real.

My friends sat down on the couch near the large window. "The doctors have decided to start gradually bringing her out of her coma tonight," I said. "It might take a couple of days for her to be fully conscious, but bringing her around slowly is what they believe is best. Her immune system has strengthened as much as they think it will. The infection has gone. She's ready to come back to us." I exhaled and added quietly, "Finally. I'll finally be able to see her eyes again."

"That's good, Rune," Jorie replied and gave me a weak smile. There was an expectant silence; my friends all glanced at each other.

"What?" I asked, trying to read their faces.

It was Ruby who replied. "What will she be like when she wakes?"

My stomach tightened. "Weak," I whispered. Turning back to Poppy, I stroked down her cheek. "But she'll be here again. I don't care if I have to carry her everywhere we go. I just want to see her smile. I'll have her back with me, where she belongs...at least for a little while."

I heard a sniff and saw Ruby crying. Jorie held her close.

I sighed in sympathy but said, "I know you love her, Ruby. But when she wakes, when she finds out everyone knows, act normal. She hates seeing those she loves upset. It's the worst part of all of this for her." I squeezed Poppy's fingers. "When she wakes we need to make her happy, like she does everyone else. We can't show her that we're sad."

Ruby nodded her head, then asked, "She won't ever be coming back to school again, will she?"

I shook my head. "Neither will I. Not until..." I trailed off, unwilling to finish off with those words. I wasn't ready to say them yet. I wasn't ready to face all of this.

Not yet.

"Rune," Deacon said, a serious tone to his voice. "What are you doing next year? For college? Have you even applied anywhere?" He wrung his hands together. "You've got me concerned. We're all leaving. And you haven't even mentioned a thing. We're just real worried."

"I'm not even thinking that far ahead," I replied. "My life is here, right now, in this moment. All that will come later. Poppy's my focus. She's only ever been my focus. I don't give a damn about next year or what I'll do."

A silence descended on the room. I saw in Deacon's face that he wanted to say more, but he didn't dare.

"Will she make prom?"

My heart sank as Jorie gazed sadly at her best friend. "I don't know," I replied. "She wanted to, so badly, but it's still six weeks out." I shrugged. "The doctors just don't know." I turned to look at Jorie. "It was one of her last wishes. To go to her senior prom." I swallowed and turned back to Poppy. "In the end all she wants to do is be kissed and see out prom. That's all she's asking for. Nothing grand, nothing life-changing...just those things. With me."

I gave my friends a moment as Jorie and Ruby began to cry quietly. But I didn't break. I just silently counted down the hours until she came back to me. Imagining the moment I would see her smile once more. Look up at me.

Squeeze my hand in hers.

After an hour or so, my friends stood up. Judson dropped papers on the small table beside Poppy's bed that I used as a desk. "Math and geography, man. The teachers wrote everything on there for you. Hand-in dates and such." I stood and said goodbye to my friends, thanking them for coming. When they left, I moved to the table to complete the homework. I'd finish this work, then take my camera outside. My camera, which I hadn't removed from my neck in weeks.

The camera that was a part of me again.

Hours must have passed as I ducked in and out of the room, capturing the day outside. Later that evening, Poppy's family began filing into the room, Poppy's doctors following closely behind. I jumped from my seat and rubbed the tiredness from my eyes. They had arrived to begin bringing her out from the coma.

"Rune," Mr. Litchfield greeted. He walked over to where I was standing and embraced me. A happy truce had settled between us since Poppy had been in her coma. He understood me, and I understood him. Because of that, even Savannah had begun to trust me with not breaking her sister's heart.

And because I hadn't left, not once, since Poppy had been admitted. If Poppy was here, so was I. My dedication must have showed that I loved her more than any of them had ever believed.

Ida came over to where I stood and wrapped her arms around my waist. Mrs. Litchfield kissed me on my cheek.

Then we all waited for the doctor to finish his exam.

When he turned to us, he said, "Poppy's white blood cell count is as good as we can hope for in this stage of her illness. We'll gradually reduce the anesthetic and bring her around. As she gets stronger, we'll be able to unhook her from some of these machines." My heart beat fast, my hands clenching at my sides.

"Now," the doctor continued. "Poppy, at first, will slip in and out of consciousness. When she is conscious, she may be delirious, out of sorts. That will be from the medication still in her system. But eventually, she should begin to rouse for longer periods of time and, all being well, in a couple of days, show us her usual happy self." The doctor held up his hands. "But Poppy will be weak. Until we assess her in her conscious state, we won't be able to determine just how much this infection has weakened her. Only time will tell. But she may have limited movement that restricts the things she can do. It is unlikely that she will regain full strength."

I closed my eyes, praying to God that she would be okay. And if she wasn't, I promised that I would help her through—anything to give me just a little more time. No matter what it took, I'd do anything.

The next couple of days dragged by. Poppy's hands began to move slightly, her eyelashes fluttered, and on day two, her eyes began to open.

It was only for a few seconds at a time, but it was enough to fill me with a mixture of excitement and hope.

On day three, a team of doctors and nurses came into the room and began the process of unhooking Poppy from the machines. I watched, heart pounding, as the breathing tube was removed from her throat. I watched as machine after machine was carted away, until I saw my girl again.

My heart swelled.

Her skin was pale, her usually soft lips chapped. But seeing her free from all of those machines, I was sure she'd never looked so perfect to me.

I sat patiently in the chair by her bed, holding her hand in mine. My head was tipped back as I stared in a trance at the ceiling, when I felt Poppy's hand weakly squeezing mine. My breathing paused. My lungs froze. My eyes darted to Poppy on the bed. Her fingers on her free hand moved, softly twitching.

Reaching over to the wall, I slammed the call button for the nurses. When one entered, I said, "I think she's waking up." Poppy had made slight movements over the past twenty-four hours, but never this many and for this long.

"I'll get the doctor," she replied and left the room. Poppy's parents came rushing in shortly after, having just arrived for their daily visit.

The doctor entered seconds later. As he approached the bed, I stepped back to stand beside Poppy's parents, letting the assisting nurse check her vitals.

Poppy's eyes began to flutter under her lids; then they slowly rolled open. I inhaled as her green eyes sleepily took in her surroundings.

"Poppy? Poppy, you're okay," the doctor said soothingly. I saw Poppy try turn her head in his direction, but her eyes couldn't focus. I felt a tug somewhere inside me when her hand reached out. She was searching for me. Even in a confused state, she was searching for my hand.

"Poppy, you've been asleep for a while. You're okay, but you're going to feel tired. Just know that you're okay."

Poppy made a sound like she was trying to speak. The doctor turned to the nurse. "Get her some ice for her lips."

I couldn't stay back any longer, and I rushed forward, ignoring Mr.

Litchfield's call for me to stop. Moving to the other side of the bed, I leaned down and wrapped my hand around Poppy's. The minute I did, her body calmed and her head softly rolled in my direction. Her eyes fluttered open. Then she looked right at me.

"*Hei, Poppymin*," I whispered, fighting the tightness in my throat.

And then she smiled. It was small, barely a trace, but it was there. Her weak fingers squeezed mine with all the strength of a fly, and then she slipped back to sleep.

I blew out a long breath. But Poppy's hand never released mine. So I stayed where I was. Sitting on the chair beside her, I stayed exactly where I was.

Another day passed with an increasing number of moments of consciousness from Poppy. She wasn't really lucid when she was awake, but she smiled at me when she focused her attention my way. I knew a part of her, although confused, was aware I was here with her. Her weak smiles made sure there was nowhere else I'd ever be.

Later that day, when a nurse came into the room to do her hourly checks, I asked, "Can I move her bed?"

The nurse stopped what she was doing and raised her brow. "To where, darlin'?"

I walked to the wide window. "Here," I said. "So when she wakes properly she can see outside." I huffed a quiet laugh. "She loves to watch the sunrise." I glanced back. "Now she's not hooked up to anything but her IV, I thought it might be okay?"

The nurse stared at me. I could see the sympathy in her eyes. I didn't want her sympathy. I just wanted her to help me. I wanted her to help me give this to Poppy.

"Sure," she said eventually. "I can't see that being a problem." My body relaxed. I moved to the side of Poppy's bed, the nurse at the other, and we rolled it to sit in front of the view of the pediatric oncology garden outside. A garden which sat under a clear blue sky.

"This okay?" the nurse asked and pushed the brakes down.

"Perfect," I replied and smiled.

When Poppy's family came in a short time later, her mama hugged me.

"She'll love it," she said. As we sat around the bed, Poppy stirred from time to time, shifting where she lay, but for no longer than a few seconds.

Over the past couple of days, her parents had taken turns staying overnight in the family room across the hallway. One stayed at home with the girls. More often than not it was her mama who stayed here.

I stayed in Poppy's room.

I lay beside her in her small bed every night. Slept with her in my arms, waiting for the moment she woke up.

I knew her parents weren't exactly thrilled with it, but I figured they allowed it because, why not? They wouldn't disallow it. Not now. Not in this circumstance.

And I sure as hell wasn't leaving.

Poppy's mama was talking to her sleeping daughter about her sisters. She was telling her about how they were doing at school—mundane things. I sat, half-listening, when there was a soft knock at the door.

When I glanced up, I saw my pappa open the door. He gave Mrs. Litchfield a small wave, then looked at me. "Rune? Can I see you for a second?"

I tensed, my eyebrows pulling into a frown. My pappa waited by the door, never breaking our stare. Blowing out a breath, I rose from my seat. My pappa backed away from the door as I approached. As I left the room, I saw he held something in his hand.

He rocked on his feet nervously.

"I know you didn't ask me to, but I developed your films for you."

I froze.

"I know you asked me to take them home. But I've seen you, Rune. I've watched you take these photographs, and I know they're for Poppy." He shrugged. "Now Poppy's waking up more and more, I thought you might want to have them with you, for her to see."

Without saying anything else, he handed over a photo album. It was filled with print after print of all the things I'd captured while Poppy was asleep. It was all the captured moments she'd missed out on.

My throat began to close. I hadn't been home. I hadn't been able to develop these in time for her...but my pappa...

"Thank you," I rasped, then dropped my eyes to the ground.

In my peripheral vision, I saw my pappa's body relax, releasing its tension. He raised his hand, as if to touch my shoulder. I stilled as he did. My pappa's hand paused in mid-air, but clearly deciding to commit, he placed his hand on my shoulder and squeezed.

I closed my eyes as I felt his hand on me. And for the first time in a week, I felt like I could breathe. For a second, as my pappa showed me he was with me, I actually breathed.

But the longer we stood there, the more I didn't know what to do. I hadn't been like this with him for so long. Hadn't let him get this close.

Needing to get away, unable to deal with this again, I nodded my head and went back into the room. I shut the door and sat down, the album on my lap. Mrs. Litchfield didn't ask what it was; I didn't tell her. She continued reciting her stories to Poppy until it was late.

When Mrs. Litchfield had left the room, I slipped off my boots, and like I did every night, I opened the curtains and moved to lie beside Poppy.

I remembered looking at the stars, and then the next thing I knew, I felt a hand stroking over my arm. Disoriented, I blinked my eyes open, the early rays of a new day seeping into the room.

I tried to clear the fog of sleep from my head. I felt hair tickling my nose and warm breath drifting across my face. Glancing up, I blinked the sleep from my eyes, and my gaze collided with the prettiest pair of green eyes I'd ever seen.

My heart missed a beat, and a smile spread on Poppy's lips, her deep dimples sinking in on her pale cheeks. Lifting my head in surprise, I held her hand and whispered, "*Poppymin?*"

Poppy blinked, blinked again, and then her gaze ranged around the room. She swallowed, wincing as she did. Seeing her lips were dry, I reached over and took the glass of water from the side table. I brought the straw to her mouth. Poppy drank a few small sips, then pushed the glass aside.

She sighed in relief. Lifting her favorite cherry lip balm from the table, I smoothed a thin layer on her lips. Poppy slowly rubbed her lips together. Not breaking my gaze, she smiled, a wide, beautiful smile.

Feeling my chest expand with light, I leaned down and pressed my lips against hers. It was brief, barely a kiss, but when I pulled back, Poppy swallowed and whispered hoarsely, "Kiss number…" Her brow furrowed as confusion played on her face.

"Nine hundred and three," I finished for her.

Poppy nodded. "When I came back to Rune," she added, holding my gaze and weakly squeezing my hand, "just like I promised I would."

"Poppy," I whispered in reply and lowered my head until I tucked it into the crook of her neck. I wanted to hold her as close as I could, but she felt like a fragile doll: easy to break.

Poppy's fingers landed in my hair, and in a move as familiar as breathing, they ran through the strands, Poppy's light breath flowing over my face.

I raised my head and stared down at her. I made sure to drink in every part of her face, her eyes. I made sure to cherish this moment.

The moment when she returned to me.

"How long?" she asked.

I stroked back the hair from her face. "You were under a week. You've been waking up gradually for the past few days."

Poppy's eyes closed momentarily, then opened again.

"And how long…left?"

I shook my head, proud of her strength, and answered honestly, "I don't know."

Poppy nodded her head, the movement barely there. Feeling a warmth on the back of my neck, I turned and looked out the window. I smiled. Facing Poppy again, I said, "You rose with the sun, baby."

Poppy frowned, until I moved out of the way. When I did, I heard her sharp intake of breath. When I looked at her face, I saw the orange rays kissing her skin. I saw her eyes close, then open again, as a smile pulled on her lips.

"It's beautiful," she whispered. I lay on her pillow beside her, watching the sky lighten with the arrival of the new day. Poppy didn't say anything as we watched the sun rise in the sky, bathing the room in its light and warmth.

Her hand squeezed mine. "I feel weak."

My stomach fell. "The infection hit you hard. It's taken its toll."

Poppy nodded in understanding, and then became lost once more in the morning view. "I've missed these," she said, pointing her finger to the window.

"Do you remember much?"

"No," she replied softly. "But I know I missed them all the same." She glanced down to her hand and said, "I remember feeling your hand in mine, though... It's strange. I don't remember anything else, but I remember that."

"*Ja?*" I asked.

"Yes," she replied softly. "I think I'd always remember the feel of your hand holding mine."

Reaching out beside me, I lifted up the photo album my pappa brought, placed it on my lap and opened it. The first photo was of the sun rising through thick clouds. The rays split through the branches of the pine tree leaves, capturing the pink hues perfectly.

"Rune," Poppy whispered and ran her hand over the print.

"It was the first morning you were here." I shrugged. "I didn't want you to miss your sunrise."

Poppy's head moved until it rested against my shoulder. I knew then I'd done right. I felt the happiness in her touch. It was better than words.

I flicked through the album. Showed her the trees beginning to flower outside. The raindrops against the window on the day it poured. And the stars in the sky, the full moon, and the birds nesting in the trees.

When I closed the album, Poppy shifted her head back and stared into my eyes. "You captured the moments I've missed."

Feeling my cheeks heat up, I lowered my head. "Of course. I always will."

Poppy sighed. "Even when I'm not here... You need to capture all these moments." My stomach rolled. Before I could say anything, she lifted her hand to my cheek. It felt so light. "Promise me," she said. When I didn't respond, she insisted, "Promise me, Rune. These pictures are too precious to have never been taken." She smiled. "Think of what you can capture in the future. Just think of the possibilities that lie ahead."

"I promise," I replied quietly. "I promise, *Poppymin*."

She exhaled. "Thank you."

Leaning over, I kissed her cheek. When I pulled back, I rolled to face her on the bed. "I've missed you, *Poppymin*."

Smiling, she whispered back, "I've missed you too."

"We've got a lot to do when you get out of this place," I told her, watching the excitement flare in her eyes.

"Yes," she answered. Her lips rubbed together and she asked, "How long until the first bloom?"

My heart tore when I knew what she was thinking. She was trying to assess how much time she had left. And if she would make it. If she would live to see her few remaining wishes come true.

"They think about a week, if that."

This time, there was no masking the utter happiness radiating from her wide smile. She closed her eyes. "I can make it that long," she stated confidently and held my hand just that little bit tighter.

"You'll last longer," I promised and watched as Poppy nodded.

"To one thousand boy-kisses," she agreed.

Stroking my hand down her cheek, I said, "Then I'll draw them out."

"Yes," Poppy smiled. "For infinity."

Poppy was discharged from hospital a week later. The true extent of how much the infection had affected her had become apparent after a few days. Poppy couldn't walk. She'd lost all strength in her legs. Her doctor informed us that if her cancer had been cured, over time she would have recovered that strength. But, as things were, she would never walk again.

Poppy was in a wheelchair. And, being Poppy, she didn't it let affect her one bit. "As long as I can still go outside and feel the sun on my face, I'll be happy," she said when her doctor had told her the bad news. She looked up at me and added, "As long as I can still hold Rune's hand, I really don't care if I ever walk again."

And just like that, she melted me where I stood.

Clutching the new photos in my hand, I ran across the grass between our two houses to Poppy's window. As I climbed through, I saw she was asleep on her bed.

She had been brought home just that day. She was tired, but I had to show her this. It was my surprise. My welcome home.

One of her wishes come true.

As I entered the room, Poppy's eyes blinked open and a smile graced her lips. "The bed was cold without you," she said and ran her hand over the side where I usually lay.

"I had to get something for you," I said, sitting down on the bed. Leaning over, I kissed her lips. I kissed her deeply, smiling as her cheeks flushed in the aftermath. Leaning over, Poppy took a blank paper heart from her jar and scribbled something down.

I stared at the almost-full jar as she dropped the heart inside.

We were nearly there.

Turning back, Poppy shifted to a sitting position. "What's in your hand?" she asked, excitement in her voice.

"Photos," I announced and watched as her face lit with happiness.

"My favorite gift," she said, and I knew that she meant every word. "Your magical captured moments."

I handed over the envelope; Poppy opened it. She gasped when her eyes fell on the subject. She searched through every photo with excitement, then turned to me with hopeful eyes. "First bloom?"

I smiled back and nodded. Poppy placed her hand over her mouth and her eyes shone with happiness. "When were these taken?"

"A few days ago," I replied and watched her hand drop and her lips curve into a smile.

"Rune," she whispered and reached for my hand. She brought it to my face. "That means…"

I stood up.

Moving to her side of the bed, I scooped her up in my arms. Poppy's hands went around my neck, and I lowered my lips to hers. When I pulled back, I asked, "Are you with me?"

Sighing happily, she replied, "I'm with you."

I placed her gently in her wheelchair, pulled the blanket over her legs, and moved to the handles. Poppy tipped her head back as I was about to push her into the hallway. I looked down at her.

"Thank you," she whispered.

I kissed her upturned mouth. "Let's go."

Poppy's infectious giggles echoed through the house as I pushed her down the hallway and out into the fresh air. I carried her down the steps. Once she was safely back in her chair, I pushed her over the grass toward the grove. The weather was warm, the sun shining down from a clear sky.

Poppy tipped her head back to soak in the warmth of the sun, her cheeks filling with life as she did. When Poppy's eyes opened, I knew she had smelled the scent before she'd even seen the grove. "Rune," she said as she gripped the arms of the wheelchair.

My heart beat faster and faster as we drew closer. Then, as we turned the corner and the blossom grove came into view, I held my breath.

A loud gasp slipped from Poppy's mouth. Taking my camera from around my neck, I walked out to stand by her side until I had the perfect view of her face. Poppy didn't even notice me pressing the button over and over; she was too lost in the beauty before her. Too mesmerized as she reached up her hand and delicately stroked a feather-light touch along a freshly born petal. Then she dropped her head back, eyes closed, arms in the air, as her laughter rang out around the grove.

I held the camera, braced on the button for the moment I prayed would follow next. And then it came. Poppy opened her eyes, completely enraptured by this moment, and then looked at me. My finger pressed down—her smiling face was alive with life, the backdrop a sea of pink and white.

Poppy's hands slowly lowered, and her smile softened as she stared at me. I lowered the camera as I returned that stare, the cherry blossoms full and vibrant around where she sat—her symbolic halo. Then it hit me. Poppy, *Poppymin*—she was the cherry blossom.

She was my cherry blossom.

An unrivaled beauty, limited in its life. A beauty so extreme in its grace that it can't last. It stays to enrich our lives, then drifts away in the wind. Never forgotten. Because it reminds us we must live. That life is fragile, yet in that fragility, there is strength. There is love. There is purpose. It reminds us that life is short, that our breaths are numbered and our destiny is fixed, regardless of how hard we fight.

It reminds us not to waste a single second. Live hard, love harder. Chase dreams, seek adventures…capture moments.

Live beautifully.

I swallowed as these thoughts swirled in my mind. Then Poppy held out her hand. "Take me through the grove, baby," she asked softly. "I want to experience this with you."

Lowering the camera to rest around my neck, I moved behind her wheelchair and pushed her along the dried dirt path. Poppy breathed in, slow and measured. The girl that I loved drank it all in. The beauty of this moment. A wish fulfilled.

Arriving at our tree, its branches bustling with pastel pinks, I took a blanket from the back of her chair and placed it on the ground. I lifted Poppy into my arms and set us down beneath our tree, the view of the grove spread before us.

Poppy laid her back against my chest. And she sighed, she held my hand that lay over her stomach, and she whispered, "We made it."

Shifting her hair from her neck, I placed a kiss on her warm skin. "We did, baby."

She paused for a minute. "It's like a dream...it's like a painting. I want heaven to look exactly like this."

Instead of feeling hurt or sad at her comment, I instead found myself wanting it for Poppy. Wanting so badly for her to have this, forever.

I could see how tired she was. I could see that she was in pain. She never said so, but she didn't need to. She spoke to me without words.

And I knew. I knew she was staying until I was ready to let her go.

"Rune?" Poppy's voice pulled me around. Leaning back against the tree, I lifted Poppy to lie over my legs so I could see her. So I could commit to memory every single second of this day.

"*Ja?*" I answered and ran my fingers down her face. Her forehead was lined with worry. I sat a little straighter.

Poppy took a deep breath, and said, "What if I forget?"

My heart cracked right down the center as I watched fear cross her face. Poppy didn't feel fear. But she did about this.

"Forget what, baby?"

"Everything," she whispered, her voice breaking slightly. "You, my family... all the kisses. The kisses I want to relive until I get you back again one day."

Forcing myself to stay strong, I assured her, "You won't."

Poppy glanced away. "I once read that souls forget their life on Earth when they pass. That they have to forget or else they would never be able to move on, to be at peace in heaven." Her finger began tracing patterns on my fingers. "But I don't want that," she added, almost inaudibly. "I want to remember everything."

Looking up at me, she said with tears in her eyes, "I never want to forget you. I need you with me, always. I want to watch you live your life. The exciting life I know you'll have. I want to see the pictures you'll take." She swallowed. "But most of all, I want my thousand kisses. I never want to forget what we shared. I want to remember them always."

"Then I'll find a way for you to see them," I said, and with the breeze that wrapped around us, Poppy's sadness floated away.

"You will?" she whispered, hope clear in her gentle voice.

I nodded. "I promise. I don't know how, but I will. Nothing, not even God, will stop me."

"As I wait in our grove," she said, with a dreamy, distant smile.

"*Ja.*"

Settling back down in my arms, Poppy whispered, "That'll be nice." Tipping her head, she said, "But wait a year."

"A year?"

Poppy nodded her head. "I read it takes a soul a year to pass on. I don't know if that's true, but in case it is, wait a year to remind me of our kisses. I don't want to miss it…whatever you do."

"Okay," I agreed, but I had to stop talking. I didn't trust that I wouldn't fall apart.

Birds flew from tree to tree, becoming lost from view in the blossom. Clasping our hands together, Poppy said, "You gave me this, Rune. You gave me this wish."

I couldn't respond. My breathing hitched as she spoke. I wrapped her tighter in my arms, then with my finger under her chin, brought her to my mouth. The sweetness was still there on her soft lips. When I drew back, she kept her eyes closed, and said, "Kiss nine hundred and thirty-four. In the blossom grove with the blossoms full. With my Rune…my heart almost burst."

I smiled. As I did, I felt an ache of happiness for my girl. We were almost there. The end of her adventure was in sight.

"Rune?" Poppy called.

"Mm?" I replied.

"You've stopped smoking."

Exhaling, I answered, "*Ja.*"

"Why?"

Pausing to compose my answer, I admitted, "Someone I love taught me life is precious. She taught me not to do anything to jeopardize the adventure. And I listened."

"Rune," Poppy said, a catch in her throat. "It is precious," she whispered, "so very precious. Don't waste one single second of it."

Poppy lazed against me, watching the beauty of the grove. As she inhaled a deep breath, she quietly confided, "I don't think I'll see prom, Rune." My body stilled. "I'm feeling real tired." She tried to hold on to me tightly, and she repeated, "Real tired."

I squeezed my eyes shut and pulled her close. "Miracles can happen, baby," I replied.

"Yes," Poppy said breathlessly, "they can." She brought my hand up to her mouth and kissed each of my fingers. "I would have loved to see you in a tux. And I would have loved to dance with you, under the lights, to a song that made me think of you and me."

Feeling Poppy begin to tire in my arms, I held back the pain this image conjured up and said, "Let's get you home, baby."

As I went to stand, Poppy reached for my hand. I glanced down. "You'll stay by my side, won't you?"

Crouching down, I cupped her cheeks. "Forever."

"Good," she whispered. "I'm not quite ready to let you go, not just yet."

As I pushed her home, I sent a silent prayer to God, asking Him to give her just two more weeks. He could bring my girl home after that; she was ready, I'd be ready. Just after I gave her all her dreams.

Just let me give her this final wish.

I had to.

It was my final thank-you for all the love she'd given me.

It was the only gift I could give.

15

Moonbeam Hearts and Sunshine Smiles

Poppy
Two Weeks Later

I SAT IN MY CHAIR, IN MY MAMA'S BATHROOM, AS SHE COATED MY LASHES with mascara. I watched her like I'd never watched her before. She smiled. I watched, making sure I had etched every part of her face in my memory.

The truth was, I was fading. I knew it. I think deep down we all knew it. Every morning that I woke, Rune curled by my side, I felt just a little more tired, just a little weaker.

But in my heart, I felt strong. I could hear the call from home getting stronger. I could feel the peace of its calling flow through me, minute by minute.

And I was almost ready.

As I watched my family over the past few days, I knew they would be fine. My sisters were happy and strong, and my parents loved them fiercely, so I knew they would be okay.

And Rune. My Rune, the person I found it hardest to leave…he had grown. He had not yet realized that he was no longer the moody, broken boy who had returned from Norway.

He was vibrant.

He smiled.

He was taking pictures again.

But better still, he loved me openly. The boy who'd returned hid behind a wall of darkness. Not anymore; his heart was open. And because of that, he had let in light to his soul.

He would be okay.

Mama went to the closet. When she returned to the bathroom, she was holding out a beautiful white dress. Reaching out, I ran my hand down the material. "It's beautiful," I said and smiled up at her.

"Let's get it on you, shall we?"

I blinked, confused. "Why, Mama? What's happening?"

Mama batted her hand in dismissal. "Enough with the questions, baby girl." She helped me dress, slipping white shoes onto my feet.

The sound of the bedroom door opening made me look around. When I did, my aunt DeeDee stood in the doorway, her hand upon her chest.

"Poppy," she said, tears filling her eyes. "You look beautiful."

DeeDee glanced over to my mama and held out her hand. My mama held her sister, and they stood there, looking at me. Smiling at the look on their faces, I asked, "Can I see?"

My mama pushed my chair in front of the mirror, and I stilled at the sight of my reflection. The dress looked so pretty, prettier than I could have imagined. And my hair...my hair was pulled to the side in a low bun, my favorite white bow pinned in place above it.

As always, my infinity earrings stood out, loud and proud.

I ran my hands down the dress. "I don't understand...it looks like I'm dressed for prom—"

My eyes darted to my mama and DeeDee in the mirror. My heart lost control of its beat. "Mama?" I asked. "Am I? But it's not for two weeks! How—"

My question was cut short by the ringing of the doorbell. Mama and DeeDee looked at one another, and Mama ordered, "DeeDee, you go answer the door."

DeeDee went to move, but Mama held out her hand and stopped her with a hand on her arm. "No, wait, you take the chair; I have to carry Poppy down the stairs."

Mama lifted me onto her bed. DeeDee left the room, and I heard my daddy's voice downstairs, muffled with others. Thoughts were scrambling through my head, but I dared not get my hopes up. Yet I wanted so badly for those hopes to come true.

"You ready, baby?" my mama asked.

"Yes," I replied breathlessly.

I hung on to my mama as we walked down the stairs and made for the front door. As we rounded the corner, my daddy and my sisters, who were gathered in the hall, all looked my way.

Then, although I felt weak, my mama brought me to the door. There, leaning against the doorway, was Rune. He had a spray of cherry blossoms in his hand…and he was wearing a tux.

My heart splintered with light.

He was giving me my wish.

As soon as our eyes met, Rune straightened. I watched him swallow as my mama placed me in my chair. When she stepped away, Rune crouched down, not caring who else was there, and whispered, "*Poppymin.*" My breathing paused when he added, "You look so beautiful."

Reaching out my hand, I tugged on the bottom of his blond hair. "It's combed back so I can see your handsome face. And you're wearing a tux."

A crooked smile pulled on his mouth. "I told you I would," he replied.

Rune took my hand and, as gently as he could, pushed my corsage onto my wrist. I ran my hand over the blossom leaves. I couldn't help but smile.

Looking up into Rune's blue eyes, I asked, "Is this real?"

Leaning forward, he kissed me and whispered, "You're going to prom."

A tear escaped my eye, blurring my vision. I watched Rune's face drop, but I laughed and told him, "They're good tears, baby. I'm just so happy."

Rune swallowed and I reached out and touched his face. "You've made me so impossibly happy."

I hoped he heard the deeper meaning of those words. Because I didn't just mean tonight. It meant he had always made me the happiest girl on the planet. He had to know.

He had to have felt the truth of that fact.

Rune lifted my hand and kissed it. "You've made me so damn happy too."

And I knew he'd understood.

The sound of my daddy's voice unlocked our stare. "Right, kids, you'd better get going." I caught the gruffness in my daddy's tone. I knew he wanted us gone because it was all too much for him to handle.

Rune stood and moved around to the back of my chair. "You ready, baby?"

"Yes," I replied confidently.

All of the weakness I had felt vanished in an instant. Because Rune had somehow made this wish come true for me.

I wasn't going to waste a single second.

Rune pushed me to my mama's car. He lifted me from the wheelchair and placed me on the front seat. I was smiling so big. In fact, I never stopped smiling during the entire drive.

When we pulled up at the school, I heard the music from inside drifting out into the night. I closed my eyes, savoring every image: the parade of limos arriving one after the other, the students dressed so smartly, all entering the school gym.

With so much care, as always, Rune lifted me out of the car and onto my chair, then moved before me and kissed me. He kissed me like he meant it. Like he knew that these kisses were as limited as I knew they were.

It made every touch and taste that much more special. We had kissed almost one thousand times, yet the final few that we were taking, they were the most special. When you know that something is finite, it makes it that much more meaningful.

When he pulled back, I cupped his handsome face and said, "Kiss nine hundred and ninety-four. At my senior prom. With my Rune...my heart almost burst."

Rune took a deep breath and pressed a final kiss on my cheek. He began to push me toward the gym. The teachers who were chaperoning saw us arrive. Their reactions to me warmed my heart. They smiled, they embraced me—they made me feel loved.

The music blared from inside the hall. I was desperate to see how the room looked. Rune reached for the door, and as he wrenched it open, the school gym came into view...a view that was dressed in pastel whites and pinks. Beautifully decorated, perfectly themed with my favorite flower.

My hand moved to my mouth. Lowering it, I whispered, "Cherry blossom–themed."

I looked back at Rune. He shrugged. "What else?"

"Rune," I whispered as he pushed me into the hall. The kids dancing nearby stopped when I entered. For a minute I felt awkward when I was met with their stares.

This had been the first time most of them had seen me since… But the awkwardness was quickly forgotten when they began to come over, greeting me and wishing me well. After a while, clearly seeing I was overwhelmed, Rune pushed me to a table overlooking the dance floor.

I smiled when I saw all of our friends sitting at the table. Jorie and Ruby saw me first. They jumped to their feet and ran our way. Rune stepped back as my friends embraced me.

"Holy crap, Pops. You look so beautiful," Jorie cried. I laughed and gestured at her blue dress.

"So do you, sweetie." Jorie smiled in return. Judson came up behind her, taking her hand. As I stared at their hands, I smiled again.

Jorie met my eyes and shrugged. "I think it was always going to happen eventually." I was happy for her. I liked knowing that she was with someone she adored. She had been an amazing friend to me.

Judson and Deacon hugged me next, then Ruby. When all of our friends had greeted me, Rune pushed in to take his place at the table. Of course he took the seat beside me, immediately taking hold of my hand.

I saw him watching me, his eyes never leaving my face. Turning to him, I asked, "Are you okay, baby?"

Rune nodded, then leaned in to say, "I don't think I've ever seen you looking so beautiful. I can't take my eyes off you."

My head angled to the side as I drank in his look. "I like you in a tux," I announced.

"It's okay, I guess." Rune reached up and fidgeted with the bow tie. "This was near impossible to put on."

"But you managed," I teased.

Rune looked away, then looked back. "My pappa helped me."

"He did?" I asked quietly.

Rune gave a curt nod.

"And you let him?" I persisted, noticing that stubborn tilt of his chin. My heart raced as I waited for the answer. Rune didn't know that my secret wish was that he would mend his relationship with his pappa.

He'd need him soon.

And his pappa loved him.

It was the final hurdle I wanted Rune to overcome.

Rune sighed. "I let him."

I couldn't stop the smile forming on my lips. I reached over and laid my head on his shoulder. Glancing up, I said, "I'm real proud of you, Rune."

Rune's jaw clenched, but he had nothing to say in reply.

Lifting my head, I surveyed the room, watching our classmates dancing and having fun. And I loved it. I looked at each person I had grown up with, wondering what they would make of themselves when they grew up. Who'd they marry, if they'd have kids.

Then my eyes stopped at a familiar face looking at me from across the room. Avery was sitting with another group of friends. When I caught her eyes, I held up my hand and gave a small wave. Avery smiled and waved back.

When I looked back to the table, Rune was glaring at Avery. When my hand landed on his arm, he sighed and shook his head at me. "Only you," he said. "Only you."

As the night passed, I watched on, completely content as our friends danced the night away. I treasured this time. I treasured seeing everyone look so happy.

Rune's arm came around my shoulder. "How did you do this?" I asked.

Rune pointed to Jorie and Ruby. "It was them, *Poppymin*. They wanted you to have this. They did it all. Moved the date forward. The theme, everything."

I eyed him skeptically. "Why do I get the feeling it wasn't just them?"

A blush flared on Rune's cheeks as he shrugged casually. I knew he'd done a lot more than he'd let on.

Inching closer, I took his face in my hands and said, "I love you, Rune Kristiansen. I love you, so, so much."

Rune's eyes closed for a second too long. He breathed in deeply through his nose, then opening his eyes, declared, "I love you too, *Poppymin*. More than I think you'll ever know."

As I cast my eyes around the gym, I smiled. "I know, Rune…I *know*."

Rune held me closer. He asked me to dance, but I didn't want to take my chair out onto the crowded floor. I was happily watching everyone else dance when I saw Jorie walk to the DJ.

She looked over at me. I couldn't read the look in her eye, but then I heard the opening chords of One Direction's "If I Could Fly" flood the room.

I stilled. I had once told Jorie that this song made me think of Rune. It made me think of when Rune was away from me in Norway. And more than anything, it made me think of how my Rune was with me in private. A sweetheart. Only for me. *For my eyes only*. When he told the world that he was bad, he only ever told me he was in love.

He was loved.

So completely.

I had dreamily told her that if we ever married, it would be our song. Our first dance. Rune slowly got to his feet; it seemed like Jorie had told Rune.

As Rune leaned down, I shook my head, not wanting to take my chair on the dance floor. But then to my surprise, with a move that completely stole my heart, Rune took me in his arms and swept me to the floor.

"Rune," I protested weakly, wrapping my arms around his neck. Rune shook his head, not saying a single word, and began to dance with me in his arms.

Refusing to look anywhere else, I stared into his eyes, knowing he could hear every lyric, seeing clearly in his face why he knew this song was for us.

He held me close, swaying gently to the music. And, like it always had for Rune and me, the rest of the world fell away, leaving only us two. Dancing among the blossoms, completely in love.

Two halves of one whole.

As the song hit its crescendo, slowly bringing it to a close, I leaned forward and asked, "Rune?"

"*Ja?*" he rasped back.

"Will you take me somewhere?"

His dark-blond eyebrows furrowed, but he nodded in agreement. As the song ended, he pulled me in for a kiss. His lips shook slightly against mine. Feeling overcome with emotion too, I allowed myself a solitary tear before taking a deep breath and shooing it away.

As Rune withdrew, I whispered, "Kiss nine hundred and ninety-five. With my Rune. At prom as we danced. My heart almost burst."

Rune's forehead pressed to mine.

As Rune moved us to leave, I glanced to the center of the floor. Jorie was standing still, watching me, tears in her eyes. Capturing her gaze, I placed my hand over my heart and mouthed, *"Thank you… I love you… I'll miss you."*

Jorie's eyes closed. When they opened again, she mouthed back, *"I love you and I'll miss you too."*

She held her hand up in a small wave, and Rune met my eyes.

"Ready?"

I nodded, and then he placed me in my chair and took me from the hall. When he had placed me in my seat and gotten into the car, he looked over to me.

"Where are we going, *Poppymin?*"

Sighing in complete happiness, I revealed, "The beach. Let me see the sunrise from the beach."

"Our beach?" Rune queried as he started up the car. "It'll take us a while to get there, and it's already late."

"I don't care," I replied, "As long as we make it before the sun." I sat back, taking Rune's hand in my own as we began our ultimate adventure to the coast.

———

By the time we arrived at the beach, the night had drawn on. Sunrise was only a couple of hours away. And I was content with that.

I wanted this time with Rune.

As we pulled into a parking spot, Rune looked over to me. "Do you want to sit on the sand?"

"Yes," I said hastily, staring up at the bright stars in the sky.

He paused. "It might be cold for you."

"I have you," I replied and watched as his expression softened.

"Wait here." Rune slipped out of the car, and I heard him taking things from the trunk. The beach was dark, lit only by the bright moon above. In the moonbeams, I saw Rune laying a blanket on the sand, a few extra blankets from the trunk beside him.

As he walked back, he reached up and undid his bow tie, then snapped open several buttons of his shirt. As I stared at Rune, I asked myself how I had gotten so lucky. I was loved by this boy, loved so fiercely that other loves paled in comparison.

Though my life had been short, I had loved long. And in the end, this was enough.

Rune opened the car door, and reaching in, he took me in his strong arms. I giggled as he cradled me. "Am I heavy?" I asked as he shut the car door.

Rune met my eyes. "Not at all, *Poppymin*. I've got you."

Smiling, I pressed a kiss to his cheek and laid my head on his chest as he walked us to the blanket. The sound of crashing waves filled the night air, a gentle warm breeze blew through my hair.

When we arrived at the blanket, Rune dropped to his knees and gently laid me down. I closed my eyes and inhaled the salty air, filling my lungs.

The sensation of wool covering my shoulders made me open my eyes; Rune was wrapping me up warm in the blankets. I tipped my head back, watching him behind me. Noticing my smile, he kissed the tip of my nose. I giggled, suddenly finding myself held tightly in Rune's protective arms.

Rune's legs straightened to box me in. My head fell back to rest against his chest. I let myself relax.

Rune pressed kisses to my cheek. "Are you okay, *Poppymin*?" he asked.

I nodded. "I'm perfect," I replied.

Rune's hand pushed the hair back from my face. "Are you tired?"

I went to shake my head, but wanting to be honest, I answered, "Yes. I'm tired, Rune."

I felt as well as heard his deep sigh. "You made it, baby," he said proudly. "The blossom trees, the prom…"

"All that's left are our kisses," I finished for him. I felt him nod against me. "Rune?" I said, needing him to hear me.

"*Ja?*"

Closing my eyes, I lifted my hand to my lips. "Remember, the one thousandth kiss is to be when I go home." Rune tensed against me. Holding his arm tighter around me, I asked, "Is that still okay?"

"Anything," Rune replied. But I could tell by the hoarseness of his voice that the request had hit him hard.

"I can't imagine a more peaceful and beautiful send-off than your lips on mine. The end of our adventure. The adventure we've been on for nine years."

Looking back at him, I held his intense eyes and smiled. "And I want you to know that I've never regretted a day, Rune. Everything about you and me has been perfect." Gripping his hand, I said, "I want you to know how much I have loved you."

I turned my shoulder so I was staring Rune straight in the eye. "Promise me that you'll go on adventures around the world. Visit other countries and experience life."

Rune nodded. I waited, waited for the sound of his voice.

"I promise," he replied.

Nodding, I released a pent-up breath and rested my head against his chest.

Minutes and minutes passed in silence. I watched the stars as they twinkled in the sky. Living this moment.

"*Poppymin?*"

"Yes, baby?" I replied.

"Have you been happy? Have you…" He cleared his throat. "Have you loved your life?"

Answering with one hundred percent honesty, I said, "I've loved my life. Everything. And I've loved you. As clichéd as this sounds, it was always enough. You were always the best part of my every day. *You* were the reason for my every smile."

I closed my eyes and replayed our lives in my mind. I remembered the times I hugged him and he hugged me harder. I remembered how I kissed him and he kissed me deeper. And best of all, I remembered how I would love him and he would always strive to love me more.

"Yes, Rune," I said with complete certainty. "I've loved my life."

Rune exhaled a breath, as if my answer had freed a burden from his heart. "Me too," Rune agreed.

My eyebrows pulled down. Looking back at him, I said, "Rune, your life isn't over."

"Poppy, I—"

I cut short whatever Rune was about to say with a gesture of my hand. "No, Rune. Listen to me." I drew in a deep breath. "You may feel you'll lose half of your heart when I go, but that doesn't give you permission to live half of a life. And half your heart will not be gone. Because I'll always be walking beside you. I'll always be holding your hand. I'm woven into the fabric of who you are—just as you will always be attached to my soul. You'll love and laugh and explore…for both of us."

I held Rune's hand, imploring him to listen. He glanced away, then turned to look into my eyes, as I wanted. "Always say yes, Rune. Always say yes to new adventures."

Rune's lip hooked up in the corner as I stared at him with hard eyes. He ran his finger down my face. "Okay, *Poppymin*. I will."

I smiled at his amusement but then said, in all seriousness, "You have so much to offer the world, Rune. You're the boy who gave me kisses, made real my last wishes. That boy doesn't stop because he suffers loss. Instead, he rises, just as sure as the sun rises each new day." I sighed. "*Weather the storm*, Rune. Then remember one thing."

"What?" he asked.

Losing my frustration, I smiled and said, "*Moonbeam hearts and sunshine smiles.*"

Unsuccessfully holding back his laughter, Rune set it free…and it was beautiful. I closed my eyes as the rich baritone washed over me. "I know, *Poppymin*. I know."

"Good," I said triumphantly and leaned back against him. My heart clenched when I saw the dawn beginning to flare on the horizon. Reaching down, I silently took hold of Rune's hand and held it in mine.

This sunrise needed no narration. I had told Rune everything I had to say. I loved him. I wanted him to live. And I knew I would see him again.

My peace was made.

I was ready to let go.

As if sensing the completion in my soul, Rune held me so impossibly tight as the crest of the sun broke over the blue waters, chasing the stars away.

My eyelids began to become heavy as I sat so contentedly in Rune's arms.

"*Poppymin?*"

"Mm?"

"Have I been enough for you too?" The gruff tone of Rune's voice caused my heart to break, but I nodded softly.

"More than anything," I confirmed and, with a smile, added just for him, "You've been *as special as special can be.*"

Rune sucked in a breath at my response.

As the sun rose to her place to watch protectively over the sky, I said, "Rune, I'm ready to go home."

Rune squeezed me one last time, then moved to get to his feet. As he moved, I weakly lifted my hand and held on to his wrist. Rune looked down at me and blinked back his tears. "I mean…I'm ready to go *home.*"

Rune's eyes closed for a moment. He crouched down and cradled my face in his hands. When his eyes opened, he nodded. "I know, baby. I felt it the moment you decided."

I smiled. I took one last glance at the panoramic view.

It was time.

Rune gently lifted me into his arms, and I watched his beautiful face as he walked back over the sand. He held my gaze.

As I turned one more time to face the sun, my eyes dropped to the golden sand. And then my heart filled with such impossible light when I whispered, "Look, Rune. Look at your footprints in the sand."

Rune's eyes left mine to observe the beach. His breath caught and his gaze came back to me. Lip quivering, I whispered, "You carried me. In my hardest times, when I couldn't walk…you carried me through."

"Always," Rune managed to reply hoarsely. "Forever always."

Taking a deep breath, I laid my head against his chest and hushed out, "Take me home, baby."

As Rune drove, chasing the day, I didn't move my eyes from him once.
I wanted to remember him just like this.
Always.
Until he was back in my arms for good.

Dreams Promised and Captured Moments

Rune

IT WAS TWO DAYS LATER.

Two days of lying beside Poppy in bed, committing her every feature to memory. Holding her, kissing her—reaching our nine hundred and ninety-ninth kiss.

When we returned from the beach, Poppy's bed had been pulled to the window, just like in the hospital. With each hour, she weakened, but, just like Poppy, with each passing minute she was filled with happiness. Her smiles reassuring us all that she was okay.

I was so damn proud of her.

As I stood at the back of the room, I watched as each of her family members kissed her goodbye. I listened as her sisters and DeeDee told her they would see her again. I stayed strong as her parents held their tears for their girl.

When her mama stepped aside, I saw Poppy's hand reach out. She was reaching out for me. Inhaling deeply, I forced my leaden feet to push forward to her bed.

She still took my breath away with how beautiful she was. "*Hei, Poppymin,*" I said and sat on the edge of her bed.

"Hey, baby," she replied, her voice now barely above a whisper. I brought my hand to hers and pressed a kiss to her mouth.

Poppy smiled and melted my heart. A loud gust of wind blew past the window, whistling against the glass. Poppy inhaled sharply. I turned to see what she was seeing.

A mass of blossom petals went sailing in the wind.

"They're leaving..." she said.

I closed my eyes briefly. It was apt that Poppy left the same day that the cherry blossoms lost their petals too.

They were guiding her soul home.

Poppy's breathing hollowed and I leaned forward, knowing this was it. I pressed my forehead to hers, just one last time. Poppy lifted her soft hand to my hair. "I love you," she whispered.

"I love you too, *Poppymin*."

As I pulled back, Poppy looked into my eyes and said, "I'll see you in your dreams."

Trying to hold back my emotions, I rasped back, "I'll see you in my dreams."

Poppy sighed, a peaceful smile gracing her face. Then Poppy closed her eyes, tilting her chin up for her final kiss, her hand squeezing mine.

Lowering myself to her mouth, I pressed the softest, most meaningful kiss to her soft lips. Poppy breathed out through her nose, her sweet scent engulfing me...and she never breathed again.

Reluctantly pulling back, I opened my eyes, now witnessing Poppy in eternal sleep. She was as beautiful then as ever she was in life.

But I couldn't tear myself away, and I pressed another kiss to her cheek. "One thousand and one," I whispered aloud. I pressed another, and another. "One thousand and two, one thousand and three, one thousand and four." Feeling a hand on my arm, I looked up. Mr. Litchfield was shaking his head sadly.

So many emotions rushed around within me that I didn't know what to do. Poppy's now-stilled hand remained in mine, and I didn't want to let go. But when I looked down, I knew she had returned home.

"*Poppymin*," I whispered and looked out the window at the fallen petals racing by. As I glanced back, I saw her jar of kisses on her shelf, a single blank paper heart and pen lying beside it. I got to my feet, scooped them all up, and rushed out onto the porch. As soon as the air hit my face, I fell back against the wall, trying to blink away the tears streaming down my face.

Slumping to the floor, I rested the heart on my knee and wrote.

Kiss 1000
  With Poppymin.
  When she returned home.
  My heart completely burst

Opening the jar, I placed the now-complete heart inside and sealed it shut. Then…

I didn't know what to do. I searched all around me for something to help, but there was nothing. I placed the jar beside me and my arms around my legs and rocked back and forth.

A creak on the step rang out. When I looked up, my pappa was standing there. I met his eyes. This was all he needed to see that Poppy had gone. My pappa's eyes immediately filled with water.

I couldn't hold back my tears anymore, so I released them, full force. I felt arms wrap around me. I tensed, then looked up to see my pappa holding me in his arms.

But this time I needed it.

I needed him.

Giving up the final traces of anger I still harbored, I fell into my pappa's arms and set free all of my pent-up emotions. And my pappa let me. He stayed with me on that porch as day gave way to night. He held me without uttering a single word.

It was the fourth and final moment that defined my life—losing my girl. And, knowing it, my pappa simply held me.

I was sure that if I'd listened closely to the howling wind rushing by, I would have heard Poppy's lips break into a wide smile as she danced her way home.

———

Poppy was laid to rest a week later. The service was just as beautiful as she deserved. The church was small, the perfect send-off for a girl who loved her family and friends with all her heart.

After the service, I decided against the wake at Poppy's parents' house and came back to my room. Less than two minutes later, a knock sounded on my door and my mamma and pappa walked in.

In my pappa's hand was a box. I frowned when he laid it on my bed.

"What's this?" I asked, confused.

My pappa sat down beside me and put his hand on my shoulder. "She asked us to give this to you after her funeral, son. She prepared it quite a while before she passed."

My heart thundered in my chest. My pappa tapped the sealed box. "There's a letter in there I was told to tell you to read first. Then a few boxes. They're numbered in the order you have to open them."

My pappa got to his feet. As he went to leave, I gripped his hand. "Thank you," I said hoarsely. Pappa leaned forward and kissed my head.

"Love you, son," he said softly.

"Love you too," I replied, and I meant every word. Things this week had been easier between us. If Poppy's short life had taught me anything, it was that I had to learn to forgive. I had to love and I had to live. I'd blamed my pappa for so much for so long. In the end my anger caused only pain.

Moonbeam hearts and sunshine smiles.

My mamma kissed me on my cheek. "We'll be outside if you need us, okay?" She was worried about me. But there was also a part of her that had relaxed. I knew it was the bridge I'd built with my pappa. I knew it was the release of all my harbored anger.

I nodded and waited until they had gone. It took fifteen minutes until I could bring myself to open the box. Immediately, I saw the letter on top.

It took me ten minutes more to break its seal:

Rune,

Let me start by saying how much I love you. I know you knew that; I don't think there is a person on the planet who didn't see just how perfect we were for each other.

However, if you're reading this letter, it means I am home. Even as I write this, know that I'm not scared.

I guess the last week has been bad for you. I imagine it has been an effort to even take a breath, to get out of bed each day—I know, because that's how I would feel in a world devoid of you. But even though I understand, it pains me that my absence will do this to you.

The hardest part was watching those I love crumble. The worst part for me, with you, was watching the anger burn within. Please, do not allow that to happen again.

If only for me, continue to be the man you have become. The best man I know.

You will see that I have given you a box.

I asked your pappa to help me weeks and weeks ago. I asked him to help me—he did so without a second thought. Because he loves you so very much.

I hope you know this now too.

In the box there will be another large envelope. Please open it now. Then I will explain.

My heart raced as I gently placed Poppy's letter on my bed. With shaking hands, I reached into the box and pulled out the large envelope. Needing to see what she had done, I quickly broke the seal. Reaching inside, I pulled out a letter. My eyebrows pulled down in confusion; then I saw the letterhead, and my heart completely stopped:

NEW YORK UNIVERSITY. TISCH SCHOOL OF THE ARTS.

My eyes scanned down the page, and I read:

Mr. Kristiansen, On behalf of the admissions committee, it is my honor and privilege to share with you that you have been admitted to our Photography & Imaging program...

I read the entire letter. I read it twice.

Not understanding what was happening, I scrambled to find Poppy's letter and read on.

Congratulations!

I know that right now you will be confused. Those dark-blond eyebrows I adore so much will be pulled down and that scowl that you wear so well will be etched on your face.

But it's okay.

I expect you to be shocked. I expect you to resist at first. But, Rune. You won't. This school has been your dream since we were kids, and just because I am no longer there to live my dream alongside you, it does not mean that you should sacrifice yours.

Because I know you so well, I also know that in my final weeks, you will have abandoned everything to stay by my side. I love you for that more than you will ever understand. The way you cared for me, protected me…the way you held me in your arms and kissed me so sweetly.

There is nothing I would change.

But I know that your love would sacrifice your future.

I couldn't let that happen. You were born to capture those magical moments, Rune Kristiansen. I have never seen a talent like yours. I have also never seen someone so passionate about anything. You are meant to do this.

I had to make sure it happened.

This time, I had to carry you.

Before I ask you to look at something else, I want you to know that it was your pappa who helped me assemble your portfolio to secure your place. He has also paid for the first semester's tuition as well as your dorms. Even when you continued to hurt him, he did this so selflessly it brought me to tears. He did this with so much pride in his eyes that it floored me.

He loves you.

You are loved beyond measure.

Now, please open box number one.

Swallowing back fraying nerves, I took hold of the labeled box and pulled it open. Inside was a portfolio. I flicked through the pages. Poppy and my pappa had pulled together picture after picture of landscapes, sunrises, sunsets. In truth, the work I was most proud of.

But then, when I reached the last page, I stilled. It was Poppy. It was the picture of Poppy on the beach with me all those months ago. The one where she had turned to me at the most perfect moment, allowing me to capture her on film—a picture that spoke to her beauty and grace more than any words could do.

My favorite photo of all time.

Chasing back the tears from my eyes, I ran my finger over her face.

She was so perfect to me.

Slowly setting the portfolio down, I picked her letter back up and continued.

Impressive, hey? You are gifted beyond words, Rune. I knew when we sent in your work that you would be accepted. I may be no expert on photography, but even I could see how you manage to capture images no one else could. How you have a style that is so completely unique.

So special…as special as special can be.

The picture at the end is my favorite. Not because it is of me, but because I knew the passion that picture reignited. I saw, that day on the beach, the fire inside spark back to life.

It was the first day that I knew you would be okay when I was gone. Because I started to see the Rune I know and love breaking back through. The boy who will live a life for us both. The boy now healed.

Glancing back at Poppy's face, looking up at me from the picture, I couldn't help but think of the exhibition at NYU. She must have already known that day that I had been accepted.

Then I thought of the final picture. *Esther.* The picture that the patron had exhibited as the final piece. The picture of his late wife who died too young. The picture that didn't change the world but showed the woman who had changed his.

Nothing described this picture, currently staring back at me, more than this explanation. Poppy Litchfield was just a seventeen-year-old girl from a small town in Georgia. Yet, from the day I had met her, she tipped my world on its head. And even now, after her death, she was still changing my world. Enriching and filling it with a selfless beauty that would never be rivaled.

Picking the letter back up, I read:

This brings me to my final box, Rune. The one I know you will protest about most, but the one that you must follow through.

I know right now you are confused, but before I let you go, I need you to know something.

Being loved by you was the biggest accomplishment of my life. I didn't have long and I had nowhere near enough time to be with you how I wanted. But in those years, in my final months, I knew what real love was. You showed me that. You brought smiles to my heart and light to my soul.

But best of all, you brought me your kisses.

As I write this and reflect on the past several months since you came back into my life, I can't be bitter. I can't be sad that our time is limited. I can't be sad that I won't get to live out my life by your side. Because I had you for as long as I could, and that was perfect. To be loved so fiercely, so intensely, once again, was enough.

But it won't be for you. Because you deserve to be loved, Rune.

When you found out I was sick, I know you struggled with not being able to cure me. To save me. But the more I think about it, the more I believe that it wasn't you who was meant to save me. Rather, I was meant to save you.

Maybe through my passing, through our journey together, you found your way back to you. The most important adventure I'd ever have.

You broke through the darkness and let in the light.

And that light is so pure and strong that it will carry you through… it will lead you to love.

As you read this, I can picture you shaking your head. But, Rune, life is short. However, I have learned that love is limitless and the heart is big.

So open your heart, Rune. Keep it open and allow yourself to love and to be loved.

In a few moments I want you to open the final box. But first, I simply want to say thank you.

Thank you, Rune. Thank you for loving me so much that I felt it every minute of every day. Thank you for my smiles, your hand so tightly holding mine…

For my kisses. All one thousand. Every one was cherished. Every one was adored.

As were you.

Know that even though I'm gone, Rune, you will never be alone. I'll be the hand forever holding yours.

I'll be the footprints walking beside you in the sand.

I love you, Rune Kristiansen. With all of my heart.

I cannot wait to see you in your dreams.

Dropping the letter, I felt the silent tears trickling down my face. Lifting my hand, I brushed them away. I took a deep breath, before lifting the final box onto my bed. It was larger than the rest.

I carefully opened the lid and pulled out the contents. My eyes closed as I realized what it was. Then I read Poppy's handwritten message tied around the lid:

Say yes to new adventures

Forever Always,
Poppy x

I stared at the large mason jar in my hand. I stared at the many blue paper hearts gathered inside. Blank paper hearts, pushing against the glass. The label on the jar read:

A Thousand Girl Kisses

Clutching the jar to my chest, I lay back on my bed and just breathed. I wasn't sure how long I lay there, staring at the ceiling, reliving every moment I'd ever had with my girl.

But when the night drew in and I thought of everything she'd done, a happy smile spread on my lips.

A peace filled my heart.

I wasn't sure why I felt it in that moment. But I was sure that, somewhere, out there in the unknown, Poppy was watching me with a dimpled smile on her pretty face…and a big white bow in her hair.

One Year Later
Blossom Grove, Georgia

"You ready, buddy?" I asked Alton as he ran down the hallway and put his hand in mine.

"*Ja,*" he said and smiled up at me with a gap-toothed grin.

"Good—everyone should be there by now."

I lead my brother out the door and we walked toward the blossom grove. The night was perfect. The sky was crystal clear and filled with glittering stars and, of course, the moon.

My camera hung around my neck. I knew I would need it tonight. I knew I would have to capture this sight to keep forever.

I had made *Poppymin* a promise.

The sounds of people gathered in the grove hit us first. Alton looked up at me, all wide-eyed. "That sounds like a lot of people," he said nervously.

"One thousand," I replied as we turned into the grove. I smiled; the pink and white petals were in full bloom. I momentarily closed my eyes, remembering the last time I was here. Then I opened them again, feeling a warmth spread through my body at this townspeople's gathering; they had packed themselves into the small space.

"Rune!" The sound of Ida's loud call brought me back to the here and now. I smiled as she ran through the crowd, only stopping when she plowed into my chest and wrapped her arms around my waist.

I laughed when she looked up at me. For a minute I saw Poppy in her young face. Her green eyes were filled with happiness as she flashed me a smile—it was dimpled too. "We've missed you so much!" she said and stepped back.

When I lifted my head, Savannah was before me, hugging me gently. Mr. and Mrs. Litchfield came next, followed by my mamma and my pappa.

Mrs. Litchfield kissed me on my cheek, and then Mr. Litchfield shook my hand before bringing me in for a hug. When he stepped back, he smiled.

"You look good, son. Real good."

I nodded. "You do too, sir."

"How's New York?" Mrs. Litchfield asked.

"Good," I said. Seeing them waiting for more, I confessed, "I love it. Everything about it." I paused, then added quietly, "She would have loved it too."

Tears shone in Mrs. Litchfield's eyes, and then she gestured at the crowd behind us. "She'll love *this*, Rune." Mrs. Litchfield nodded and wiped the tears from her cheeks. "And I have no doubt she'll see it up there in the heavens."

I didn't reply. I couldn't.

Moving to let me pass, Poppy's parents and sisters fell into step behind me as my pappa placed his arm around my shoulders. Alton was still gripping my hand tightly. He'd refused to let go of me since I'd arrived home for this visit.

"Everyone's ready, son," my pappa informed me. Seeing a small stage in the center of the grove, a mic waiting, I made my way over, just as Deacon, Judson, Jorie and Ruby stepped into my path.

"Rune!" Jorie exclaimed with a big smile and gave me a hug. As did everyone else.

Deacon's hand slapped my back. "Everyone's ready, just waiting for your signal. It didn't take much to get the word out you were doing this. We got more volunteers than we needed."

I nodded and surveyed the townspeople waiting with their Chinese lanterns in hand. On those lanterns, in large black writing, was every kiss I'd ever given Poppy. My eyes focused to read those nearest...

...Kiss two hundred and three, in the rain in the street, my heart almost burst... Kiss twenty-three, in my yard under the moon, with my Rune, my heart almost burst... Kiss nine hundred and one, with my Rune in bed, my heart almost burst...

Swallowing the intense emotion from my throat, I stopped when I saw a lantern waiting for me on the side of the stage. I glanced around the grove looking for who had left it. As the crowd parted, I saw my pappa watching me closely. I met his gaze, and then he lowered his eyes before walking away.

The one thousandth kiss…*with my Poppy. When she returned home…my heart completely burst…*

It was right that I sent this one up to my girl. Poppy would want me to send this to her myself.

Climbing on the stage, Alton beside me, I lifted the mic and the grove fell into silence. I closed my eyes, gathering the strength to do this, and then raised my head. A sea of Chinese lanterns being held up, ready to fly, stared right back at me. It was perfect. More than I could have ever dreamed.

Raising the mic, I took a deep breath and said, "I won't speak long. I'm not real good with speaking in public. I just wanted to thank you all for gathering here tonight…" I trailed off. My words had dried up. I raked my hand through my hair and, gathering my composure, managed to say, "Before she passed, my Poppy asked me to send these kisses to her in a way that she would see them in heaven. I know most of you didn't know her, but she was the best person I knew…she would have treasured this moment." My lip hooked into a crooked smile at the thought of her face when she saw them.

She would love it.

"So please, light your lanterns and help my kisses reach my girl."

I lowered the mic. Alton gasped when lighters all around the grove lit the lanterns and sent them soaring into the night sky. One after the other, they floated into the darkness, until the entire sky was glowing with lights sailing upward.

Bending down, I took the lantern beside us and held it in the air. Looking to Alton, I said, "You ready to send this to *Poppymin*, buddy?"

Alton nodded, and I lit the lantern. The minute the flame caught, we released the one thousandth—and final—kiss. Standing straight, I watched as it sailed into the air to chase the others, rushing to its new home.

"Wow," Alton whispered and put his hand in mine again. His fingers squeezed mine tight.

Closing my eyes, I sent a silent message: *Here are your kisses, Poppymin. I promised they would come to you. That I'd find a way.*

I couldn't take my eyes from the light show above, but Alton pulled on my hand. "Rune?" he asked and I glanced down to where he stood, watching me.

"*Ja?*"

"Why did we have to do it here? In this grove?"

"It was *Poppymin*'s favorite place," I replied softly.

Alton nodded. "But why did we have to wait for the cherry blossoms to come out first?"

Taking a deep breath, I explained, "Because *Poppymin* was just like the cherry blossom, Alt. She only had a short life, like they do, but the beauty that she brought in that time will never ever be forgotten. Because nothing so beautiful can last forever. She was a blossom petal, a butterfly…a shooting star…she was perfect…her life was short…but she was mine."

I took in a breath and whispered finally, "Just as I was hers."

Epilogue

Rune
Ten Years Later

I BLINKED AS I AWOKE, THE BLOSSOM GROVE COMING INTO CLEAR VIEW. I COULD *feel the bright sun on my face, smell the richness of the blossom leaves filling my lungs.*

I took a deep breath and lifted my head. The dark sky towered above, a sky filled with lights. One thousand Chinese lanterns, sent years ago, floating in the air, perfectly fixed in place.

Sitting up, I searched the grove to check that every blossom was in full bloom. It was. But then it always was. Beauty lasted forever here.

As did she.

The sound of gentle singing came from the entrance to the grove, and my heart began to race. I pushed to my feet and waited with bated breath for her to appear.

And then she did.

My body filled with light as she came around the corner, her hands lifting to brush gently against the full trees. I watched as she smiled at the blooms. Then I watched as she noticed me in the center of the grove. I watched as a huge smile spread on her lips.

"Rune!" she called in excitement and ran straight to me.

Smiling back, I lifted her in my arms as she wrapped her arms around my neck. "I've missed you!" she whispered into my ear, and I held her just that little bit closer. "I've missed you so, so much!"

Pulling back to drink in her beautiful face, I whispered, "I've missed you too, baby."

A blush set on Poppy's cheeks, her deep dimples completely on show. Reaching down, I took her hand in mine. Poppy sighed as I did; then she drifted her gaze to me. I looked at my hand in hers. My seventeen-year-old hand. I was always seventeen when I came here in my dreams. Just as Poppy had always wished.

We were exactly as we were.

Poppy lifted up onto her tiptoes, pulling my focus to her once more. Placing my hand on her cheek, I leaned down and brought her lips to mine. Poppy sighed against my mouth and I kissed her deeply. I kissed her softly. I didn't ever want to let her go.

When I finally pulled back, Poppy's eyes fluttered open. I smiled as she guided us to sit under our favorite tree. When we sat down, I held her in my arms, her back pressed against my chest. Brushing her hair off her neck, I pressed light kisses all along her sweet skin. When I was here, when she was in my arms, I touched her as much as I could, I kissed her...I held her knowing soon I'd have to leave.

Poppy sighed in happiness. When I looked up, I saw her watching the bright lanterns in the sky. I knew she did this a lot. These lanterns made her happy. These lanterns were our kisses, gifted just for her.

Settling against me, Poppy asked, "How are my sisters, Rune? How's Alton? My parents and yours?"

I held her tighter. "They're all good, baby. Your sisters and parents are happy. And Alt, he's perfect. He's got a girlfriend he loves more than life, and his baseball is going well. My parents are great too. Everyone is okay."

"That's good," Poppy replied happily.

Then she grew silent.

I frowned. In my dreams Poppy always asked me about my work—all the places I'd visited and how many of my pictures had recently been published, had helped save the world. But tonight she didn't. She stayed contentedly in my arms. She felt more at peace, if that was possible.

Poppy shifted where she sat, then asked curiously, "Have you ever regretted never finding someone else to love, Rune? Have you ever regretted, in all this time, *never kissing anyone else but me? Never loving anyone else? Never filling the jar I gave you?"*

"No," I replied honestly. *"And I have* loved, *baby. I love my family. I love my work. I love my friends and all the people that I've met on my adventures. I have a good and happy life,* Poppymin. *And I love, and I have* loved with a full heart… *you, baby. I've never stopped loving you. You were enough to last a lifetime." I sighed. "And my jar was filled…it was filled along with yours. There were no more kisses to be collected."*

Turning Poppy's face to look at me, my hand under her chin, I said, "These lips are yours, Poppymin. *I promised them to you years ago; nothing's changed."*

Poppy's face broke into a contented smile and she whispered, "Just as these lips are yours, Rune. They were always yours and yours alone."

As I shifted on the soft ground, as I placed a palm on the floor, I suddenly realized that the grass beneath me felt more real than any of my visits before. When I came to Poppy in my dreams, the grove always felt like I was in a dream. I felt the grass but not the blades, I felt the breeze but not the temperature, I felt the trees but not the bark.

As I lifted my head, tonight, *in this* dream, *I felt the warm breeze cross over my face. I could* feel *it, as real as I did when I was awake. I felt the grass beneath my hands, the blades and the roughness of the dirt. And as I leaned down to kiss Poppy's shoulder, I felt the warmth of her skin on my lips, saw her skin bump in its wake.*

Feeling Poppy's intense gaze on me, I looked up to see her watching me with wide, expectant eyes.

Then it hit me.

I realized why all of this felt so real. My heart beat faster in my chest. Because if it was real…if I had judged this correctly…

"Poppymin?" I asked and took a deep breath. *"This isn't a dream…is it?"*

Poppy shifted to kneel before me and placed her gentle hands on my cheeks. "No, baby," she whispered and searched my eyes.

"How?" I whispered in confusion.

Poppy's gaze softened. "It was quick and it was peaceful, Rune. Your family are okay; they are happy you're in a better place. You lived a short but full life. A good life, the one I always dreamed you would have."

I froze, then I asked, "You mean…?"

"Yes, baby," Poppy replied. "You've come home. You've come home to me."

A huge smile spread across my lips, and a flood of pure happiness washed over me. Unable to resist, I crashed my lips to Poppy's waiting mouth. The minute I tasted her sweet taste on my lips, a deep peace filled me from within. Pulling back, I pressed my forehead to hers.

"I get to stay here with you? Forever?" I asked, praying it was true.

"Yes," Poppy answered gently, and I could hear the complete serenity in her voice. "Our next adventure."

This was real.

It was real.

I kissed her again, slow and soft. Poppy's eyes remained closed afterward; then as a blush spread on her beautiful dimpled cheeks, she whispered, "A forever kiss with my Rune…in our blossom grove…when he finally came home."

She smiled.

I smiled.

Then she added, "…and my heart almost burst."

Bonus Scene

Rune
Blossom Grove, Georgia
One Year After Poppy's Death…

I COULD STILL SEE THE FLICKER OF THE CHINESE LANTERNS AS THEY disappeared high into the midnight sky. I rested my head against the windowpane, unable to take my eyes off the visual representation of all the kisses that we had cherished. They drifted away, joining the stars and moon and my girl.

Another moment that meant so much to us both yet was impossibly out of reach.

I took a deep breath, fighting the tightness in my throat. My sight blurred with tears. But after two minutes, I let the salty water tip over the rims and run down my cheeks. I blinked, trying to rid myself of the tears, but they kept coming. In the past year since losing Poppy, so many tears had been shed. I used to fight them, feeling like I was failing her for being sad, for missing her so much that I felt like I couldn't breathe, couldn't *live*. But now, I let them flow. She was my soulmate, and forever would be. I had survived a year without her, and it had been hard.

But I was here. I had done it. I was *still* doing it. I had to see that as progress.

A light went on in Poppy's home. I caught sight of Mr. Litchfield heading into the hallway. But my eyes only focused on the window that I had climbed through more times than I could remember.

As if the past were an apparition before me, I saw a thirteen-year-old me rushing across the grass in the dead of night, and Poppy ducking her head through the curtains, casting me the widest dimpled smile that she always gave as I snuck into her room and held her all night.

Warmth spread through my tight chest, slackening the muscles. It always helped—remembering her smiles, her laughter, her love for life. It erased the one image that had haunted me more than any other for the past twelve months. Of her lying on the bed, gone, never to look at me again with those big green eyes, never to hold my hand, or kiss my lips…

I closed my eyes and forced myself to release the echo of pain I felt stabbing in my chest. When I opened my eyes, I ran my hand down the windowpane, seeing the last of the lanterns fade far from view and said, "I hope you love them, baby."

Then, I went to bed, and like every night, hoped I would dream of Poppymin again.

"Come on in, guys," Mrs. Litchfield said as she ushered us inside their home. I looked around the house that was once as familiar as my own. It looked the same, but for the new pictures that had been added to the already-full walls. Photographs capturing Ida at school events, and one of Savannah reading under the tree in the Blossom Grove that Poppy and I had loved so much—the one that now held Poppy's grave.

Poppy had been laid to rest in our favorite place.

I stopped dead when I saw the picture of Poppy that had been added to the wall while I'd been away at college. The picture I'd taken of her on the beach when I'd moved back to Georgia, the one that she had added into my portfolio to get into NYU.

I didn't realize Mrs. Litchfield was beside me until she spoke, breaking me from my trance. "I think that's my favorite picture that's ever been taken of her," she said, and I caught the hitch in her voice. Her arm threaded through mine, tightly. "It was only right that it was you that took it," she said, patting her palm over the back of my hand. "You always saw her for how special she was. Saw her true heart." I tore my eyes from the picture and looked at Poppy's mama. She met my eyes. "I love my husband more than life itself. But I didn't understand what a soulmate truly was until I saw you two together, especially toward the end... when she was most sick." Mrs. Litchfield's eyes glistened. "But I worry about you, Rune."

"You do?" I asked, voice hoarse as I fought to hold back the barrage of emotions that were trying to fight through.

She squeezed my hand—her fingers were trembling. "You loved my daughter so much, so hard, and with everything you had, from such a young age. I worry now she's gone it'll be too hard for you to move on..." She trailed off, and took a deep inhale, clearly to keep her composure. She cast a wary gaze toward the family room where everyone must have gone.

Again, I looked at the picture of Poppy dancing on the beach. I let the memory of that day wash over me. Felt the serenity she exuded as she danced in the waves. The happiness and love that consumed me as I watched her—I finally had my girl back, even if it had been temporarily. "She was everything to me," I said quietly. "I loved her more than I can ever explain."

"You don't need to explain, Rune. I saw it. We all did." A stray tear fell down Mrs. Litchfield's cheek.

"There's no need to worry about me," I said and met her watery gaze. "Because I love her more now than ever." I smiled at the picture. "And now I intend to live... for us both. Just like she wanted." A tear fell down Mrs. Litchfield's cheek and she hastily wiped it away.

"Everything okay?" Mr. Litchfield appeared at the doorway, his concern melting from his face when he saw his wife, arm in mine, and staring up at a still shot of the most beautiful girl in the world.

"Yes, yes," Mrs. Litchfield said, pulling her arm from mine, and kissing me on the cheek. She subtly wiped her tears away and brushed her hands down her dress. "Okay, dinner!" she said and quickly left the room. I imagined it was mostly in self-preservation. I could barely imagine what this anniversary was doing to them. Their first daughter, gone for good...

"Okay, son?" Mr. Litchfield said. I tore my eyes from Poppy and nodded my head. Sometimes I didn't know if I was, but there was no choice but to keep going. Mr. Litchfield patted me on my shoulder, then beckoned me with a wave to follow him into the living room.

I took in a deep breath, then trailed behind.

Alton ran straight over to me, fixing himself to my side as he always did when I came home to visit. I scuffed my hand in his long blond hair, my little brother smiling up at me with a huge toothless grin. I still fought hard to forgive myself for how I'd ignored him in Norway when we had been forced to leave Georgia, years back. But I was trying as hard as I could to make that up to him now.

"Hey Rune!" Ida, Poppy's youngest sister came toward me and gave me a tight hug. It always hurt a little looking at Ida. It was like being thrust back in time, like I was looking at Poppy when we were younger, from the dark hair right down to the dimples.

I was proud of Ida. As young and grief-stricken as she was when Poppy passed, she held steadfastly onto the spark that lived inside her—that same spark that never faded in her oldest sister, too. Poppy always let it shine through, even on her hardest days.

"How's school?" I asked.

"Good!" she said. "I made the dance team, so I'm pretty much living at practice these days." I pressed a kiss to her head. She was doing real good. Poppy was always worried about her sisters and how they would be with her gone—a protective big sister right down to her final breath.

As mine and Poppy's parents headed toward the fully-dressed dining table, I searched the room for Savannah. "She'll be out soon," Ida said, clearly picking up on my silent questioning of her sister's absence. A worried expression grew on Ida's usually happy face. Ida clasped her hands together, displaying nervousness in the gesture. "She still struggles, you know?"

I did know what that was like, but I didn't realize Savannah was struggling so badly. Ida inched closer. "She's homeschooling now," Ida said in a low voice. "Couldn't take school no more. It got too hard for her, being around people after Pops left us…"

My heart plummeted. Just at that moment, Savannah came down the hallway from her bedroom. I watched her walk slowly, head down, dressed in black and wearing sadness like a cloak.

"Hey Sav," I said when she was near, forcing my voice to stay strong.

Like I'd ripped her from a trance, Savannah lifted her head. "Oh, hey, Rune. I didn't see y'all out here." She looked tired, *so* tired. Savannah had always been the quieter Litchfield sister. She was always happy to laugh at her louder sisters from a distance, happy to just *be* amongst their infectious personalities, watching and smiling along with them. But I could see the grief she was living with screaming out loud in her sloped shoulders, her obvious weight loss, and the racking pain that had taken up residence in her eyes.

I walked toward her and gave her a hug. "How're you doing?" I asked, feeling her stiffen in my arms.

She pulled back but left her gaze on the floor. "I'm good, thank you," she said, dismissing my suspicious eyes, the lie slipping easily from her lips.

I opened my mouth to say something else—to ask her what I could do to help, *anything*—when Mrs. Litchfield announced, "Dinner's ready! Let's take our seats."

In minutes, we were all sat down. Mr. Litchfield sat at the head of the table and cleared his throat. "Thank y'all for coming tonight." He took a deep breath, then shook his head. "I can't believe my baby has been gone for a year already." Mr. Litchfield was staring down at his plate, voice tight. He reached out beside him and held his wife's hand—she clutched onto it like, at that moment, it was all that was keeping her together.

It gutted me.

I felt a small hand wrap around mine. Alton. I squeezed it, smiling at him looking up at me with worry and confusion on his face. He was so young when Poppy passed, and he still didn't quite grasp the concept of death and grief. He just saw everyone was sad. He missed her, too, but didn't really comprehend that she wasn't ever coming back to us.

I felt my mamma's hand lay on my forearm. Looking up, Ida was staring at her daddy, eyes shining. But it was Savannah I focused on most. She was staring at the saltshaker, hands balled on the floral table linen, like keeping focused on something directly in her sight was all that held her together.

"She was a tornado," Mr. Litchfield said, chuckling, a moment of joy sneaking out from behind his pain. A small smile pulled on my lips. *A tornado…* she was. "My little girl was so happy, so positive…especially given the circumstances, when most people would have fallen apart. Her strength…" He trailed off, unable to continue, throat closed, and eyes squeezed shut.

"She was as special as special can be," Pappa added on for Mr. Litchfield, saving him from the heavy silence we'd all adopted. Pappa looked at me and smiled. "And I know she's looking down on us all—on *you* all—and is so proud of how you've coped."

I lowered my head then, a lump the size of Texas stopping me from breathing. Mamma took hold of my hand and leaned closer to me, to hold me up, to keep me from falling.

"She'll see the lanterns," a soft voice said, breaking through the fog of sorrow that had clogged the room. Ida. "She'll be seeing them from heaven right this second and smiling so big that it would rival the Georgia sun."

I held my breath, seeing that scene so vividly in my head. Ida's thread of optimism chased some of the darkness away, and Mrs. Litchfield said, "She will. I just know it."

"I miss her," I said, lifting my eyes and looking at everyone I loved around the table. I released an affectionate laugh. "She'd love this," I said, pointing around the table at us all. "Love that we're all here, together. All her favorite people in one place." I felt Poppy then. Felt her presence sneak through with the truth of those words. I could almost feel her sit beside me, resting her head on my shoulder, her all-consuming love wrapping around us like a blanket.

"She would," Mrs. Litchfield said, a vein of happiness in her tone. "And she'd be real mad that we're all here sad and crying."

"Moonbeam hearts and sunshine smiles," Ida said, and that black fog of grief began to dissipate around us. A sprinkle of nostalgic laughter filled the room. "She would always say that. Would never let me mope when I was down. Tell me, '*Ida, girl, we're so lucky in our lives. Don't let little things get you down.*'"

I nodded, smiling, seeing Poppy saying just that in my mind. Ida sounded just like her, and for a moment, I heard her again. I heard Poppymin.

"'*Papa, the birds are singing real loud today,*'" Mr. Litchfield said, reminiscing about what Poppy had once said to him. "*What a beautiful, perfect sound!*"

My heart clenched. I'd never met anyone with more optimism than Poppymin. Everyone went around the table, repeating something she had said. Even Alton. "She would sneak me candy and tell me, '*Sweets for the sweetest little boy in the world.*'"

I stared off at nothing, seeing Poppy so vividly in mind. The table got quiet, but it was light, *happy* at remembering our girl and what made her shine. "'*I'm not sure there's anyone who has loved anyone quite as much as I have loved you,*'" I said, remembering what Poppy had whispered to me the day before she died. When it had been just her and I in the bedroom, watching the cherry blossom trees sway in the breeze from her window as we laid on the bed together. My smile fell as that memory resurfaced. I hadn't meant to say it out loud, but maybe it was Poppy pushing me to share.

"It was true," Mr. Litchfield said. I looked at Poppy's daddy. "I'm not sure anyone loved one another like y'all did." An echo of gutting pain threatened to take me under. But I held it back.

Everyone looked to Savannah next. She was the only one left to say something. Her head was still downcast, but her chest was rising up and down in quick movements, her fists were clenched harder than before. Her mama went to speak to her, but before she could, Savannah pushed her chair back and walked from the room.

I sat up to follow, but Mr. Litchfield shook his head. "She's still trying to work through things. Some days are better than others. We have to let her process this in her own way."

"She's found this week especially hard," Mrs. Litchfield added. Poppy's mama stood and began taking the tops off the covered dishes. "Let's eat, before this gets cold."

We ate and I told Poppy's family all about NYU, and about living in New York. Ida talked about her dance team. Night fell, the stars came out, and we moved to the living room for after dinner drinks. I got up from the couch to go to the bathroom. I was halfway down the hall when I saw a light turn on on the porch. I saw a flicker of movement off to the side.

I opened the door and saw Savannah sitting on a chair, blanket pulled over her, holding a notepad in her hands, clutching it tightly to her chest.

No... not a notepad. Realization dawned—the journal Poppy had left

Savannah. The one she'd been writing in her final months. I didn't even know what was inside.

It was solely for Savannah's eyes.

The sound of crickets filled up the spring night. Savannah stared out into the darkness. I shut the door and moved to sit beside her. For several minutes, she didn't say anything, until, "I still haven't read it." Her voice was barely above a whisper. If possible, she squeezed the journal even tighter to her chest. "I just… I *can't*…" Her voice cut out and my heart broke for her.

"You have to read it in your own time," I said. I didn't know what else to say. Savannah was hurting. I was hurting too. I didn't feel qualified to give her any kind of advice. But Poppy would. She would have known exactly what to say. It was her superpower.

"How do you do it?" Savannah said, finally looking my way. I tensed at the question. "How do you get up each day without her? How have you managed to move away and live some kind of normal life without her by your side?" I knew she wasn't angry at me or questioning anything I'd done. She was genuinely asking me how I even took a breath without her sister beside me.

I thought about my answer, because it was complicated. No one had prepared me for what my life would feel like after Poppy. I hadn't known the depth of pain that would follow her leaving me—the hurt, the gut-wrenching sadness, the potent anger with losing the love of my life, the disbelief that she was really gone, the dropping to my knees in the middle of the night and begging God to just bring her home to me, even if it was just for one more day.

"Some days, I honestly don't know," I said, my voice broken and hoarse. I leaned forward, my hair falling forward to shield my face. I rubbed my hands together. My breath was stuttered, chest impossibly tight. "I have days I can't even get out of bed, Sav." I shook my head. "When I look at people on the street, holding hands, in love…I want to scream out loud to the heavens, asking why *my* soulmate was wrenched away from me. Why some bad people have long lives, but then the most perfect girl in the world died before she even got out of her teens."

I lost my breath. I heard sniffing from beside me. I turned to see tears falling down Sav's cheeks. "But then I hear Poppy," I said, and Savannah frowned in confusion. I shrugged. "I can't explain it." I looked out toward the blossom grove, to where my baby waited for me. "Somedays, I feel her with me, like she's not gone at all." I smiled a little. "I can talk to her like she's right there, beside me, talking with me too." I ran my hand through my hair. "I can hear her voice, hear her infectious laugh. Hear her playing the cello…feel her love wrapping around me, keeping me company on the days when missing her is so tough that I can't even move."

I put my hand over my heart. "I've never been a spiritual person, yet I believe she's with me, always." Savannah's breathing was heavy. "I believe she's still with me, every minute of every day." My body was enveloped by sudden, comforting warmth. *There she is,* I thought. "And I believe I'll be with her again. I know I'll see my baby again. I know it with everything I am." I cleared my throat. "That helps…" I exhaled slowly, deeply. "That helps to keep me going, especially when I think I can't."

Silent tears streamed down Savannah's face. I leaned over and took her hand in mine. She let me, and I sat with her in silence. As I did, memories of Poppy ran through my head like a show reel. The first day I met her, our first kiss, the first time I heard her play cello, the first picture I'd taken of her, the blossom grove, the smiles, the first time we made love, then the final kiss, the stillness…her finally being free of pain and at peace…

Savannah pulled her hand back and got to her feet. "I'm gonna head inside," she whispered. Her cheeks were red from crying. She passed by me, then stopped as she opened the door. "Thank you, Rune." I nodded, not quite sure what she was thankful for. I felt like I hadn't helped her at all. The Poppy-sized wound that had been left in our lives when she passed seemed so impossible to heal.

"You're gonna be okay, Sav," I said. She gave me a sad, placating smile, then disappeared into the house. I could hear everyone inside talking, but I didn't want to go back inside—I couldn't. My soul was leading me somewhere else. A pull with the force of a magnet was drawing me to the only place I wanted—no, *needed*—to be.

Taking out my cell, I texted my papa:

I'm going to see my girl.

I slipped my cell back in my pocket and made my way to the blossom grove. As I entered, a sense of instant peace washed through me. It always had, but it had only become more intense after Poppy passed...after she was laid to rest beneath the tree we both loved. My girl rested here, waiting for me—there was no other place on earth where I wanted to be more.

My feet crunched on the cherry blossom petals that had fallen to the ground, the grove an oil painting of various tones of whites and shades of pinks. Like a year ago, when Poppy had left us, the trees' branches were growing bare, the short but beautiful life of the blossom trees coming to another end.

My heart lurched as I saw the white marble headstone up ahead. My steps grew slower as I lowered the emotional shield I kept in place most days. Only for Poppymin did I lay myself bare. Only for her did I expose all of my heart. I stopped when I reached the grave. I lowered to my knees and ran my hands over the grave.

"*Poppymin...*" I whispered, then allowed the dam to break. Allowed the months and months of pain and anguish and missing my baby so much I didn't think I could make it, crash through like a tsunami. I broke so hard that I fell forward, my hands on the earth the only thing keeping me upright, a torrent of tears splashing on the ground beneath me. I let them fall. Tears fell for all that Poppy had missed. Tears fell for all the kisses we should have added to our jar, for the pictures we should have taken, and for the memories we should have made.

For all that had been so cruelly ripped away.

My chest heaved in exertion, my hands shook, and my breathing became labored as I exorcized my grief.

As I allowed myself this moment of complete surrender.

I didn't know how long I cried. But when the tears began to ebb, and my fingers had dug into the top layer of earth, I knew it must have been a while. I took long, deep breaths, my chest and throat raw from the year-long release of sadness.

I was exhausted.

Crawling forward, I rested my back against the headstone and placed my palm onto the grass beneath me. Poppy lay underneath, right here, yet so far away. I inhaled a stuttered breath and whispered, "I miss you, baby." I closed my eyes, feeling tiredness sink into my bones. "I miss you so much…"

It only took a few seconds for a warm breeze to blow past me, threading through my hair. A subtle scent of vanilla filled the air, and, just like that, I could feel Poppymin beside me. I rolled my head to the side, like she was here, right beside me. Sitting next to me. I closed my eyes. My hand tingled, and I saw it in my mind's eye—Poppy's hand wrapping around mine. I left my eyes closed, and met her in a daydream.

A finger ran down my cheek, and when I glanced up, there she was. My heart lurched just seeing her again, feeling her hand clutch mine and her stunning smile spread widely on her pretty face. I reached out and touched her soft skin. Ran my fingertip over the deep-set dimples I loved so much.

"*Hei, Poppymin…*" I whispered, my voice barely making a sound. I held on tighter to her hand, willing this vision, this daydream, to not disappear, to just give me a bit more of this borrowed time with my girl. I needed her with me. I just…I just needed *her*.

"Hello, baby," she said, and I let the sound of her voice wash over me. Like she had always done, she began taking my tiredness away, my pain. I looked down at our clenched hands and brought them up my lips. I pressed a kiss to the back of her hand, to each of her fingers.

She was so warm. So *alive*.

I traced my gaze over her body, healed and no longer failing. Then I studied her face, her beautiful, perfect face… "I've missed you," I said. "I can't even explain how much."

Poppy leaned forward and pressed her forehead to mine. "I've missed you too," she whispered. Then she curled into my side and looked up to the tree branches above. "The cherry blossoms are leaving again," she said, and I wrapped her tightly in my arms. Nothing ever felt like this. Nothing came close to how she fit so perfectly against me, like a higher power had designed us as a matching set. I knew no one would ever replace her.

She would always be it for me.

Poppy glanced up at me, and I made sure I memorized every part of her face. "How is my family?" Poppy asked, like she knew where I had been.

"Good, baby," I said, omitting Savannah from my response. But a flare of concern flashed through Poppy's green eyes.

She knew anyway.

But then Poppy sat up and placed her palm on my cheek. "Rune..." she murmured, as though in awe, "...the lanterns." My heart filled with light. Poppy's eyes shimmered. "They were perfect. So perfect," she said, then melted back against my chest. She lifted our joint hands, kissing my fingers, then pulling them to lay over her heart. I felt it beating. She settled back against me. "Tell me," she said, and I smiled. It was the same every time. Every time I would imagine us together again, every time I would dream of us, she always asked for this. She'd asked this on her final days.

I'd give my baby anything she asked for.

"We'd wake up slowly," I said, and heard the gravel in my voice. I felt Poppy smile. "I'd leave you in bed to doze, warm and sleepy, and go and make us breakfast."

"What would we be having?" she asked, playing along. She loved when we imagined this. When we talked and lived out what should have been.

"Croissants," I said, knowing she loved them. "And eggs."

"And coffee," she said, excitement in her voice. "I'd smell it brewing as I lay in bed, looking out of the bedroom window at the sun shining down on New York." I saw it so clearly in my head. Lived it in my imagination. It felt real. At that moment, I had my girl back and we truly lived this life.

"I'd crawl out of bed, and put on my robe," she said, resting her head back against my chest. I pulled her closer, needing her to stay longer so I could hear about our day. No amount of time was ever long enough. "Then I'd walk through our tiny apartment, and head to where you stood at the stove." The marble of the headstone was hard against the back of my head, but holding Poppy kept any discomfort away. "And I'd wrap my arms around you from behind, pressing my cheek against your back." Poppy paused, and I knew she was as caught up in our dream as I was. "You'd place the cooked food to the side and turn, wrapping me in your arms."

"My favorite thing to do," I said.

Poppy tipped her head up, and smiled, shattering my swelling heart. "And we'd sway to the music you were playing while you cooked."

I nodded my head, because that would have happened.

"You'd kiss me on my lips, one of thousands and thousands that we would have shared."

I nodded, unable to speak.

"Then we'd take our food to our small table by the window and look out at the people below."

I pressed a kiss onto Poppy's head, her hair soft beneath my lips.

"What then, Rune?"

I ran my hand through Poppy's hair, just savoring her being back with me. "I'd take you to Central Park," I said, my voice seeming louder as the breeze around us began to fall away. I pulled her tighter against me, resting my cheek on her head. "The cherry blossoms are in full bloom."

"Yes," she said, happiness lacing her tone.

"And I'd take pictures. So many pictures of you, of *us*, that I would develop later and hang in our apartment." Poppy shifted against me, and I squeezed her harder. Our time couldn't be done. I needed her to stay for just a little while longer.

"We'd have dinner by moonlight," she said, and turned in my arms. She rose to her knees, and I felt the breeze lifting again, smelled the blossom grove more vividly, the dream slowly dispersing.

Poppy placed her palm against my cheek, and I shook my head. "Not yet," I said, grasping to hold onto her.

"Then we'd go to bed," she said, and I shook my head, not ready for her to leave. "And you'd hold me," she said, "and love me, and we'd fall asleep, side by side, safe in each other's arms, and it would've been the most perfect day."

I turned my head, panic setting in, but Poppy guided my face back to hers. "I'm never gone, baby," she said, and her green eyes implored me to understand. She pressed her hand over my heart. "I'm always here." And then she pressed kiss after kiss over my forehead, my cheeks, then finally, my lips. "I'm always in your dreams."

I nodded and turned my face to lay a kiss in the center of her palm.

Poppy gave me a watery smile. "I'm so very proud of you."

I stilled, trying to stay in this moment forever, but as Poppy began to fade, I knew we couldn't.

"I love you," she said, and with her beautiful smile, the love in her eyes and the awe in her voice, the tiredness began to lift from my body, my sadness fading into nothing but pure love for my girl. Poppymin, my soulmate and the forever love of my life.

I cupped Poppy's face. "I love you so much."

"Live for us," Poppy said, and I nodded my head. I kissed her lips, then her cheeks, her nose, her forehead, every part of her that I could as she began to fade away. "I'll see you in your dreams," she said, and I held out my hand as hers slipped from mine, my girl drifting away on the breeze with the falling blossom petals.

I focused on my breathing, inhaling and exhaling five times before I let my eyes roll open. I blinked into the darkness, trying to focus, my daydream broken.

The space beside me was empty, but when I brushed my palm over the place Poppy had just been, I could have sworn it felt warm from where she'd sat beside me. Her scent remained in the air around me, and on my clothes. And when I ran my fingers over my lips, they felt as though they had just been kissed.

I smiled and relaxed back against the headstone. Poppy may have been gone, but she had never left me. I felt her every day. "I love you, *Poppymin*," I said aloud into the silent grove. "I'm gonna make you proud—I promise."

I sat back against the headstone, watching more blossom petals fall, bright stars peeking through the swaying branches. And for just a little while longer, I stayed with my girl.

Read ahead for a sneak peek of
A Thousand Broken Pieces,
which features Poppy's sister Savannah
on a journey of love and healing

Prologue

Savannah
Age Fourteen
Blossom Grove, Georgia

I COULDN'T HEAR ANYTHING BUT THE DEAFENING BEATING OF MY HEART.
Too fast in rhythm, thundering like the destructive summer storms that
ripped through Georgia when the heat became too much.

My breathing grew labored as my lungs began to slowly cease to function.
As the air that was in my chest hardened into granite boulders, pushing down
on me so hard that I was frozen in place. Frozen looking at Poppy fading
away in the bed. Seeing my parents clutching on to each other like they were
dying too. Their baby, their first daughter, losing her fight with cancer before
our very eyes, death hovering beside her like an ominous shadow, waiting to
take her away.

Feeling Ida squeezing my hand so hard she could have broken bones.
Feeling my younger sister's slight body trembling, no doubt with fear or pain
or complete disbelief that this could be real. That this was actually happening.

My face was soaked with the tears that fell like rapids from my eyes.

"Savannah? Ida?" I blinked through the watery haze until I saw my
mama before us. I began to shake my head, my body seeming to jerk back to
life from its numbed catatonic state.

"No…" I whispered, feeling Ida's terrified gaze snap onto me. "Please…"
I added, my near-silent plea drifting into vapor in the stagnant air around us.

Mama bent down and ran her trembling hand down my cheek. "You need to say goodbye, baby." Her voice wobbled—hoarse and tired. She looked over her shoulder to where Rune was sitting on the bed, laying kiss after kiss on my older sister's hands, her fingers, her face, looking at his Poppymin like he always had—like she was made solely for him. A choked cry escaped my lips as I watched them.

It wasn't real. This couldn't be real. She couldn't leave him. She couldn't leave *us*...

"Girls," Mama pushed again, urgency in her tone. My heart fractured when Mama's bottom lip began to tremble. "She..." Mama closed her eyes, trying to gather some kind of composure, cutting off whatever she was going to say. I didn't know how she did it. I couldn't. I couldn't face this. I couldn't *do* this.

"Sav," Ida said from beside me.

I turned to look at my little sister. At her dark hair, green eyes, and deep-set cheek dimples. At her skin red from crying. At her sweet heartbroken face.

"We have to." Her voice was shaking. But she nodded at me in encouragement. Right now, Ida had more strength than I could muster.

Ida stood, never loosening her iron-tight grip on my hand as she guided me up. In this moment, we needed our shared strength. When I was on my feet, I glanced down at our clasped hands. Soon, this is how it would forever be. Just our two hands, no third to hold, to guide us.

Not anymore.

I followed behind Ida, each step feeling like I was wading through molasses as we approached the bed. It was positioned to look out of the window. So Poppy could see outside. Falling pink and white cherry blossom petals drifted by on the breeze, scattering onto the ground as they fell from the trees. Rune looked up as we approached, but I couldn't look into his eyes. I wasn't strong enough to see him at that moment. The moment we had all been dreading. The one, deep down, I never really believed would arrive.

Taking as deep a breath as I could muster, Ida and I rounded the bed. The first thing I heard was her breathing. It had changed. It was deep and rattly, and I could see the exhaustion, the struggle on her pretty face... The effort it was taking her to simply hold on for just a few minutes more. To remain with us for as long as she could. Yet, despite it all, she widened her smile when she saw us. Her sisters. Her best friends.

Our Poppy...the best person I knew.

Lifting her thin, frail hands, Poppy held one out for each of us to hold. I closed my eyes when I felt how cold she was, how light her grip on us was now.

"I love you, Poppy," Ida whispered.

I opened my eyes and fought falling to the floor as Ida laid her head on Poppy's chest and held her tightly. Poppy closed her eyes and pressed the ghost of a kiss on Ida's head.

"I love...you too...Ida," she replied, holding on to our younger sister like she would never let her go. Ida was Poppy's double in every way—her personality, her looks, her outlook on life. Poppy's fingers ran through Ida's dark hair. "Never change," she murmured as Ida lifted her head. Poppy placed her weakening hand on Ida's cheek.

"I won't," Ida said, voice breaking, and stood back, reluctantly letting her hand fall from Poppy's. I focused on that release. I didn't know why, but I wanted Ida to hold on to our sister. Maybe if we just held on to her, together, Poppy wouldn't have to go. Maybe we could keep her here...

"Sav..." Poppy whispered, her eyes shining as I met her gaze.

I crumbled, my face falling as I began to sob. "Poppy..." I said, taking hold of her hand and holding it to me. I was shaking my head, over and over, silently begging God, the universe, *anyone* to stop this, to bless us with a miracle and keep her here with us, even if it was for just a bit longer. We hadn't had enough time with Poppy. We needed her to stay for just a bit longer...*please*...

"I'm...okay..." Poppy said, cutting through my internal pleas.

Her hand was trembling, I brought it to my lips to press a kiss to her cold skin. But when I did, I saw that Poppy's hand was steady, and the trembling was mine. Tears tumbled down my cheeks.

"Savannah," Poppy said, "I am...ready...to go..."

"No," I said, shaking my head. I felt a hand land on my back and an arm thread around my waist. I knew it was Mama and Ida keeping me upright. "I'm not ready...I need you...you're my older sister...I need you, Poppy." My chest ached to the point of pain, and I knew it was my heart breaking into tiny, fragmented pieces.

"I'll...always be...with...you," Poppy said, and I noticed a sallowness to her skin, heard the rattle in her breathing deepen and grow more erratic.

No...no, no, no...

"We will..." Poppy sucked in a faint breath, a *fading* gasp of air. "Meet again..."

"Poppy..." I managed to say before racking sobs took hold of me. I lowered my head to Poppy's chest and felt her weak arms encase me. She may have been losing strength, but that hold felt like a secure blanket around me. I didn't want to let go.

"I...love you...Savannah. So...much," Poppy said, fighting her slowing breath to speak. I squeezed my eyes shut, trying in vain to hold on. Poppy pressed a kiss to my hair. Her sweet scent wrapped around me, and I inhaled it, desperately trying to commit it to memory.

"Savannah." Mama's voice sailed into my ears. "Baby..." she murmured. I lifted my head and met Poppy's weak smile.

"I love you, Pops," I said. "You've been the best big sister I could ever ask for."

Poppy swallowed, and her eyes shimmered with tears. I studied her face, memorized the green of her eyes, the natural streaks of warmth in her dark hair, the peach tone of her soft skin. I didn't want to let go of her hand. I didn't know if I ever would be able to, but as Mama squeezed my shoulders, I did, refusing to disconnect from her gaze until Mama and Papa moved beside the bed and blocked her from my view.

I stumbled back, shock settling in. Ida gripped my hand and curled into my chest. I watched, almost dissociated, as Mama and Papa kissed and held Poppy and said their goodbyes. White noise filled my ears as Mama and Papa moved back, and Rune came to the bed. I stayed, transfixed, Ida breaking against my chest, Mama and Papa falling apart to the side of the room as Rune said something to Poppy, then leaned down and kissed her on her lips...

I held my breath as, seconds later, he slowly reared back. And I watched it. I watched Rune's face and saw in his shattered expression that confirmed she had gone. That Poppy had left us...

Rune's head was shaking as my heart was impossibly cracking even more. Then he ran from the room, and as he did, I slammed back into the here and now with a crash. The sound of agonized crying was the first thing I heard, the devastating noises slicing my soul in half. I looked at Mama, then Papa. Mama had fallen to the floor, Papa trying to keep her in his arms.

"Sav," Ida sobbed, gripping tighter on to my waist.

I held Ida tighter. Held her as I stared at the bed. Stared at Poppy's hand. Her hand that lay unmoving on the bed. Her *empty*, still hand. Everything seemed to be happening in slow motion, like some camera trick used in the movies. But this was real life. This was our house. And that was my sister on the bed. On the bed with no one beside her.

Mama reached for Ida. My little sister fell into our parents' embrace, but I was moving forward like a magnet was drawing me close to Poppy. Like some force was beckoning me to where she lay.

On a stuttered breath, I rounded the bed. And I stilled. I stilled as I stared down at Poppy. No breath came from her mouth. There was no rise of her chest, no flush to her cheeks. Yet she was as beautiful in death as she was in life. Then my gaze dropped to her empty hand again. It was upturned like it wanted to be held just one last time. So, I sat on the edge of the bed and wrapped my hand in hers. And as I sat there, I felt something in me change. In that moment, I lost something in my soul that I knew I would never get back. I brought Poppy's cold fingers to my lips and pressed a kiss to her soft skin. Then I lowered our entwined hands to my lap. And I didn't let go. I wouldn't let go.

I wasn't sure I could.

Rolling Clouds and Stolen Breaths

Savannah
Age Seventeen
Blossom Grove, Georgia

THERE WERE PRECISELY FORTY-TWO CRACKS ON THE LINOLEUM FLOOR. Rob, the therapy leader, was talking, but all I heard was the tinny drone from the heating system above us. My gaze was unfocused, catching only spears of daylight coming from the high windows and the blurred outlines of the others in the circle around me.

"Savannah?"

I blinked my eyes into focus, glancing up at Rob. He was looking at me, body language open and an encouraging smile on his face. I shifted nervously in my seat. I wasn't blessed with the skill of talking out loud. I struggled to put words to the turbulent feelings stirring inside me. I was better on my own. Being around people drained me. Too many of them made me close in on myself. I was nothing like my sister, Ida, whose personality was infectious and gregarious. Just like Poppy...

I swallowed the instant lump that sprouted in my throat. It had been three years. Three long, excruciating years without her, and I still couldn't think of her name or picture her pretty face without feeling my heart collapse on me like a mountain caving in. Without feeling death's unyielding fingers wrap around my lungs and starve them of air.

The knowing pangs of anxiety immediately began clawing their way up from the depths of where they slept. Sinking their teeth into my veins and sending their poison flooding through my body until it had captured me as its unwilling hostage.

My palms grew damp, and my breathing became heavy.

"Savannah."

Rob's voice had changed, even though it echoed in my ears, as everything around me tunneled into a narrow void, I heard its worried inflection. Feeling the weight of everyone's stares on me, I jumped up from my seat and bolted for the door. My footsteps were an arrhythmic drumbeat as I followed the stream of light in the hallway toward the open air. I burst through the door to outside and sucked in the wintery Georgia air.

Dancing spotlights invaded my vision, and I stumbled to the tree that sat on the grounds of the therapy center. I leaned on the heavy trunk, but my legs gave way, and I dropped to the hard ground. I closed my eyes and laid my head against the wood, the rough bark scratching the back of my scalp. I focused on breathing, on trying to remember every lesson I had ever been taught in regard to coping with an anxiety attack. But it never seemed to help. The attacks always held me hostage until they were finally willing to release me...

I was exhausted.

My body trembled for what felt like forever, heart sputtering and lurching until I felt my lungs begin to loosen, my windpipe finally granting my body the oxygen it so badly craved. I inhaled through my nose and out through my mouth until I sagged further into the tree, the smell of grass and earth breaking through anxiety's sensory-blocking fog.

I opened my eyes and looked up at the bright blue sky, watching the white clouds traveling up ahead, trying to find shapes in their structures. I watched them appear, then leave, and wondered what it looked like from up there, at what they saw when they looked down upon us all, loving and losing and falling apart.

A droplet of water landed on the back of my hand. I glanced down, only to catch another drop fall on my ring finger's knuckle—they were coming from my cheeks. Exhaustion rippled over me, consuming all my strength. I couldn't even lift my hands to wipe away the tears. So, I focused on watching the journeying clouds again, wishing I could be like them, constantly moving, never having time to stop and process and think.

Thinking gave me space to break.

I didn't even realize someone had sat down beside me until I felt a subtle change in the air around me. The clouds still held my attention.

"Anxiety attack again?" Rob said.

I nodded, my hair rubbing against the loose bark that was scarcely holding on to its home. Rob was only in his thirties. He was kind and was exceptional at what he did. He helped so many people. Over the past three years, I'd seen a myriad of teenagers come through the therapy center's door and leave, changed, empowered, and able to function once more in the world.

I was just broken.

I didn't know how to heal, how to put myself back together again. The truth was, when Poppy died, all light vanished from my world, and I'd been stumbling around in the dark ever since.

Rob didn't speak for a while but finally said, "We have to change tactics, Savannah."

The edge of my lips lifted as I saw what looked like a daisy form in a cloud. Ida loved daisies. They were her favorite flower. Rob leaned back against the tree beside me, sharing the wide trunk.

"We've received some funding." His words trickled into my ears one syllable at a time as the world, painstakingly slowly, began to fix itself back together. "There's a trip," he said, letting that hang in the air between us.

I blinked, the sun's afterimage dancing in the darkness when I squeezed my eyes shut to banish its blinding glow.

"I want you to go on it," Rob said.

I froze and eventually turned my head to face him. Rob had short red hair, freckles, and piercing green eyes. He was a walking autumnal color palette. He was also a survivor. To say I admired him was an understatement. Punished as a teen for his sexuality by those who were meant to love him, he had fought his way through hell to reach freedom and happiness, now helping others who struggled in their own ways too.

There's a trip... I want you to go on it...

Those delayed words filtered into my brain, and my old friend, anxiety, began to reemerge.

"A small group from all over the US are going on a five-country journey. One of healing." He rolled his head to look up at the clouds that had previously captured my attention. "Teens dealing with grief."

I shook my head, every second making it more pronounced.

"I can't," I whispered, fear wrapping around my voice.

Rob's smile was sympathetic, but he said, "I've already spoken to your parents, Savannah. They've agreed it would be good for you. We've already secured your place."

Playlist

I had a *lot* of songs that helped me write this story. But there were two bands that were basically its *entire* soundtrack. Normally, in my soundtracks, I vary the genres, but I wanted to keep true to the inspiration, and show you the songs that help mold Poppy and Rune's tale.

ONE DIRECTION
"Infinity"
"If I Could Fly"
"Walking in the Wind"
"Don't Forget Where You Belong"
"Strong"
"Fireproof"
"Happily"
"Something Great"
"Better Than Words"
"Last First Kiss"
"I Want to Write You a Song"
"Love You Goodbye"

LITTLE MIX
"Secret Love Song Pt II"
"I Love You"

"Always Be Together"
"Love Me or Leave Me"
"Turn Your Face"

OTHER ARTISTS
"Eyes Shut"—Years & Years
"Heal"—Tom Odell
"Can't Take You With Me"—Bahamas
"Let the River In"—Dotan
"Are You With Me"—Suzan & Freek
"Stay Alive"—José González
"Beautiful World"—Aiden Hawken
"The Swan (from *Carnival of the Animals*)"—Camille Saint-Saëns
"When We Were Young"—Adele
"Footprints"—Sia
"Lonely Enough"—Little Big Town
"Over and Over Again"—Nathan Sykes

To listen to the soundtrack, please go to my page, Author Tillie Cole, on Spotify.

Acknowledgments

Mam and Dad, thank you for supporting me with this book. Your personal battles with cancer have changed not only me but our small family. Your bravery but, most importantly, your positivity and inspirational attitudes in the face of something so difficult made me look at life in a completely different way. Although the past few years have been incredibly rough, it has made me appreciate every single breath of every day. It has made me appreciate you both beyond measure—the best parents in the world. I love you both so much! Thank you for letting me use your experiences in this story. It made it true. It made it real.

Nanna. You were taken from us far too young. You were my very best friend, and I loved you to pieces—still do. You were hilarious, and always such a positive and bright presence. When I thought of Poppy's mamaw, there was no one else I would ever model her on. I was "the apple of your eye" and your best buddy, and even though you're gone, I hope this book has made you proud! I hope you're smiling up there with Granddad, in your own little version of the blossom grove.

Jim, my late father-in-law. You were so very brave until the end, a man to look up to. A man your son and wife were so very proud of. You're very much missed.

To my husband. Thank you for encouraging to write a Young Adult novel. I told you the idea for this novel a long time ago, and you pushed me to write it, despite it being so different from my usual genres. I owe this book to you. Love you always. For infinity.

Sam, Marc, Taylor, Isaac, Archie and Elias. Love you all.

To my fabulous beta readers: Thessa, Kia, Rebecca, Rachel, and Lynn. As always, a *huge* thank you. This one was a toughie, but you stuck with me—even though I made most of you cry! I love you all.

Thessa, my star and mega-assistant. Thank you for manning my Facebook page and keeping me in check. Thank you for all the edits you make for me. But mostly, thank you for encouraging me to keep the epilogue in this novel—we had some stress over that decision, didn't we? Okay, LOTS! But you were my backbone though this. Love you to bits. You never ignore my frantic texts late at night. I couldn't ask for a better friend.

Gitte, my lovely Norwegian Viking! Thank you for jumping into this adventure with me. From the minute I told you I had this idea for a YA weepy—oh, and the guy was Norwegian—you encouraged me to write it. Thank you for the many translations. Thank you for the muse—he's the perfect Rune! But most of all, thank you for being you. You are a true and fabulous friend. You had my back the entire way. Love you, *Pus Pus*!

Kia! What a fabulous team we make! You've been the BEST editor and proofreader ever. This the first of many stories to come! Thank you for all the hard work. It meant the world to me. Oh, and thank you for all the music checks! My fellow Golden Bow(er) (along with Rachel). Who'd have thought that all those years of us playing cello would come in this handy?

Liz, my fabulous agent. I love you. Here's to my first foray into YA!

Gitte and Jenny (both this time!) from *TotallyBooked Book Blog*. Again, I have nothing to say but thank you and I love you. In everything I do, you encourage. Every genre change I make you support. You are two of the very best people I know. I cherish our friendship…it's "as special as special can be."

And a huge thank you to all the many, many more wonderful book blogs that support me and promote my books. Celesha, Tiffany, Stacia, Milasy, Neda, Kinky Girls, Vilma…Gah! I could go on and on.

Tracey-Lee, Thessa, and Kerri, a huge thank you for running my street team: The Hangmen Harem. Love you all!

My @FlameWhores. With me through thick and thin. I adore you girls!

To my street team members—LOVE YOU!!!

Jodi and Alycia, I love you girls. You are my dear friends.

My IG girls!!!! Adore you all!

And lastly, my wonderful readers. I want to thank you for reading this novel. I imagine right now your eyes are swollen and your cheeks are red from all the crying. But I hope you love Poppy and Rune as much as I do. I hope their story will stay in your hearts forever.

I couldn't do this without you.

I love you.

Forever Always.

For Infinity.

About the Author

Tillie Cole hails from a small town in the northeast of England. She grew up on a farm with her English mother, Scottish father, older sister, and a multitude of rescue animals. As soon as she could, Tillie left her rural roots for the bright lights of the big city. After graduating from Newcastle University with a BA Hons in religious studies, Tillie followed her professional rugby player husband around the world for a decade, becoming a teacher in between, and thoroughly enjoyed teaching high school students social studies before putting pen to paper and finishing her first novel.

After several years living in Italy, Canada, and the USA, Tillie has now settled back in her hometown in England with her husband and two children. Tillie is both an independent and traditionally published author and writes many genres, including contemporary romance, dark romance, YA, and NA. When she is not writing, Tillie enjoys nothing more than spending time with her little family, curling up on her couch watching movies, drinking far too much coffee, and convincing herself that she really doesn't need that last square of chocolate.

Follow Tillie Cole
Website: tilliecole.com
Facebook: tilliecoleauthor
Twitter: @tillie_cole
Instagram: @authortilliecole
TikTok: @authortilliecole